SALAMANDER COTTON

ALSO BY RICHARD KUNZMANN

Bloody Harvests

RICHARD KUNZMANN

SALAMANDER COTTON

Thomas Dunne Books
St. Martin's Minotaur
New York

THOMAS DUNNE BOOKS.
An imprint of St. Martin's Press.

SALAMANDER COTTON. Copyright © 2006 by Richard Kunzmann. All rights reserved. Printed in the United States of America. No part of this book may be used or reproduced in any manner whatsoever without written permission except in the case of brief quotations embodied in critical articles or reviews. For information, address St. Martin's Press, 175 Fifth Avenue, New York, N.Y. 10010.

www.thomasdunnebooks.com
www.minotaurbooks.com

Library of Congress Cataloging-in-Publication Data

Kunzmann, Richard.
    Salamander cotton / Richard Kunzmann. — 1st
U.S. ed.
        p. cm.
    ISBN-13: 978-0-312-36034-4
    ISBN-10: 0-312-36034-7
    1. Johannesburg (South Africa)—Fiction. I. Title.
    PR6111.U59S25 2007
    823'.92—dc22

                                        2007026437

First published in Great Britain by Macmillan, an imprint of Pan Macmillan Ltd.

First U.S. Edition: November 2007

10 9 8 7 6 5 4 3 2 1

This book is dedicated to my parents,

Silke and Julius

And to my brother,

Herbert

ACKNOWLEDGEMENTS

The quiet teachers of literature, who patiently guide their students and pupils, and instill in them a love for languages, are often missed on pages like this. Though I had many mentors to whom I am grateful, I would like to especially thank Mr Slabbert, Mr Celliers and Mrs Ackerman for teaching me the joys of literature, and for turning a blind eye when I was reading books in class that weren't a part of the curriculum.

To Sabine and George, I extend my warmest thanks for putting me up during my visit to England. Erica, you helped out when my back was against the wall, and asked questions about the book that needed to be voiced.

Jock McCulloch's fascinating study of the asbestos industry guided much of the writing in this book. Your expertise and straightforward insight proved invaluable. Though we've never met, I must voice my greatest respect for Richard Spoor, a lawyer defending the rights of South Africa's asbestos victims when they needed a champion most. Thanks also to Greg Marinovich for his illuminating book *The Bangbang Club* and our conversations about the violence in Thokoza.

Mary, at Gillon Aitken Associates: thank you for your enduring support, advice and enthusiasm. Peter, the day rabbits stop gallivanting across the pages of my manuscripts is the day you're done with your job as a great mentor and editor. The crew at Pan Macmillan, Stef, Rebecca and Terry, your camaraderie has brought me much pleasure in a profession that can at times be very lonely.

Last but not least, the warmest and most loving of thanks to Monique, whose support helped me finish this book, as her bustling companionship kept me away from it for days. I am also grateful to the Goris family for creating a luxurious space in which I could write to my heart's content.

SALAMANDER COTTON

ONE

Other sins only speak; murder shrieks out
John Webster

1

10.15 p.m., 25 May 2004, Johannesburg

Bernard Klamm sits in the sumptuous study of his Parkview home, deeply engrossed in a book by Sir Laurens van der Post. He is not expecting any visitors, least of all expecting his life to end this night.

The large stuffed armchair he is sitting in is upholstered in polished oxblood leather, secured to its heavy wooden frame with brass studs. On a small table by his left hand stands a snifter of cognac beside a green banker's reading light angled to cast its full glow over Klamm's lap. A quilted blanket, thrown over his seventy-nine-year-old knees, provides some comfort against the cold May wind that blasts autumn leaves over the lawn outside. Blue flames whisper amongst fake coals in the large open fireplace, which is flanked by red-oak shelves filled with books. Two of the other walls are lined with numerous black and white photographs.

The man's brow is furrowed and under bushy white eyebrows his expression is one of either anger or scorn. He inhales regularly in shallow whistles, although he quit pipe smoking more than twenty years ago.

As something in the fireplace crackles loudly, Klamm looks up and glances at the window, noticing how raindrops are collecting on the glass. It is unusual weather for May, indeed.

He does not notice a face staring at him from the darkness beyond, and turns his attention back to the volume he is reading: a detailed study of the Khoisan, who were not only master hunters and survivors but also great historians who documented on cave walls their everyday activities and encounters with other tribes and cultures.

From the kitchen door there is the faint sound of duct tape being torn from a roll. Four strips are neatly applied to one door pane, before an elbow smashes through the glass without any fragments spilling over the floor. This break-in goes unnoticed by the old man in his study. Moments later the door behind Bernard Klamm opens, and soundlessly a figure approaches him over the thick beige carpet.

Reaching for his snifter, the old man suddenly realizes he is not alone. His glass raised halfway to his lips, Klamm fixes his gaze on the mantelpiece. 'I thought I already told you to bugger off. I've nothing more to say to you.'

'Really?' replies a deep voice.

Klamm glances sharply over his shoulder.

'How—?' His eyes widen as his book slips to the floor.

The first heavy blow hits Klamm square in the mouth, breaking teeth and rupturing lips and gums. He slides helplessly out of his chair, sprawling close to the fireguard. Klamm spits out a mouthful of blood on the carpet, then slides an arm under his torso and tries to push himself upright, but the intruder quickly moves around the armchair and sharply boots him twice in the ribs. The old man tumbles back again, his legs caught underneath him at an awkward angle.

Kneeling down beside him, the assailant is panting heavily. 'What goes around comes around, you old son of a bitch.'

The green dressing gown Klamm wears has come loose, exposing his bony chest covered in scraggy tufts of white hairs. Roughly shoving the two armchairs aside to make more space in front of the fireplace, the intruder goes to fetch the petrol can and coil of rope he has left ready outside the study door. On his way back, he picks up a straight-backed chair from in front of the bureau.

Klamm's eyes widen in horror as he tries to get words out of his slack jaw.

'No,' growls his assailant. 'I don't want to hear it.' Pinning his victim to the floor under his knee, the intruder yanks Klamm's arms back and up, and binds them tightly with duct tape. Next, the weakened old man is quickly strapped with cord to the upright chair then doused with petrol all over till the green robe is soaked through. Klamm yelps pitifully as the pink liquid splashes into his eyes.

An ugly smile suddenly spreads over the assailant's face as he detaches the petrol can's funnel. 'Open your mouth,' he orders.

Klamm's eyes bulge as he tries to clamp his injured jaw shut. Tears well up in his eyes as he bobs his head this way and that in an effort to evade the other man's hands.

'Open your *fucking* mouth.' Finally the attacker manages to clamp a hand over Klamm's cheeks. Squeezing them under his fingers and thumb, he forces Klamm to open his mouth. The funnel is rammed deep down his throat, partially blocking a scream. Holding the plastic cone firmly in place, the intruder stoops for the container of petrol and pours the rest of it down his victim's throat. The elderly prisoner bucks violently in the chair, his nose flaring as he gasps for breath. A Lion match is struck and sent tumbling into Bernard Klamm's lap.

The flames blossom like a rare blue rose opening up its petals. Klamm jerks this way and that, till the funnel jammed in his mouth is thrown clear. Screams now escape him and resound in the confines of the study. His green robe steadily turns black; his facial skin blisters and cracks. Grabbing hold of the chair, the intruder heaves it with all his might straight into the fireplace.

Finally, as silently as he arrived, the intruder departs—fading into the cold rainy night like a bad memory.

2

0.04 a.m., 26 May 2004, Soweto

The initial shrill ring of the phone in the living room wakes him. Jacob Tshabalala holds his breath until another ring confirms the call. He wonders who would want to phone him this late at night, then it dawns on him that he is on call this week.

'Are you going to get that?' asks a tired voice next to him, speaking in Zulu.

Jacob grunts as he rises out of bed. Freezing rain and wind are still lashing at the windows. Dressed only in white boxer shorts, he hastens to answer the phone.

'Inspector Tshabalala? Tinus van Schalkwyk here at Parkview. We've got a mess down here, a real big mess. We need you to come take a look.'

Jacob jots down the details on a lined notepad resting next to the phone before disconnecting and then trying his police partner. There is no answer from the man's home, and only a tired voice message on his mobile. Jacob replaces the receiver with a dismissive shake of his head. This is not the first time his partner has made himself unavailable on duty. He returns to the warmth of his bedroom and switches on the light, apologizing to

Nomsa for waking her. Hurriedly he dresses in jeans, a collared shirt and a thick green jacket, then gives Nomsa a goodbye peck on the forehead. As his long-term partner, she is used to such call-outs. After eight years of serving in the Murder and Robbery Unit, Jacob still prefers to live in Soweto, the sprawling township lying west of Johannesburg, as infamous for its violent history as it is renowned for being the birthplace of the country's fledgling democracy. It is a community that gets under the skin, infects people equally with affection and revulsion, binding them to it and rooting them to its dusty roads, its never-ending shacks and bare-brick houses, its nameless streets and thoroughfares lit by spider webs of suspended streetlights.

He grew up in an impoverished district where there were no streetlights, no running water except for a communal tap and where raw sewage trickled along makeshift channels filled with garbage. These days, however, he owns his own house, with its own driveway leading out onto a tarred street reminiscent of any other suburb. The garbage is collected every Wednesday, and thankfully he has yet to suffer a break-in.

It takes Jacob nearly an hour to drive to the address located in an affluent northern suburb. The rain has ceased and the blustering wind dropped by the time he parks his cruiser across the road from two white and blue rapid-response Golf GTIs, still splashing their emergency lights over the high, electrified walls of surrounding properties. The coroner's van is already in evidence, the two men beside it smoking lazily as they wait for the forensic team to wrap up their examination of the crime scene. By the open gate of the victim's house, a uniformed policeman is taking statements from an elderly married couple, obviously neighbours, who stand shivering in slippers and nightwear.

After a quick word with the officer, Jacob heads on down the wet gravel drive towards the house itself, which is set well back from the road. His path is illuminated by lights positioned discreetly among the shrubs that fringe the yellowing lawn. Reaching the front door, Jacob spots a couple of detectives standing over to his right, peering through a window into a well-lit room. One of them is a chubby white man with an upturned nose, the other a tall African with bulbous eyes.

The shorter one notices Jacob first, and raises a hand in greeting. 'Inspector Tshabalala? Come have a look at what we found just now.'

A camera flash from inside the study distracts Jacob momentarily as he crouches to a neatly cultivated flowerbed separating the side of the house from the lawn. Two sunken footprints stand out distinctly.

'Look fairly fresh, don't they?' continues the same officer. 'I'm Tinus van Schalkwyk, and this is Sam Sehlapelo.'

Jacob confirms his own identity, before greeting Sehlapelo in Sotho.

Van Schalkwyk beckons Jacob to follow him further around the side of the house, where they find a team of fingerprint specialists carefully examining the kitchen door. 'Whoever broke in here took the time to first wipe his shoes clean on some wet grass over there. That means no decent footprints on the floor tiles.'

After glancing along a short garden path leading towards some servants' quarters, where a pale light shimmers through frosted windows, Jacob stoops to examine how neatly the pane of glass has been removed, just above the door lock.

'Still the best way of breaking in without waking the neighbours.' Van Schalkwyk looks up at his partner, who nods in response. 'At the time of the incident, the housekeeper was cooking supper in her quarters over there, and says she didn't hear anything until the old man started screaming. She says she was too scared to come out and investigate. When she finally felt brave enough to peer out of her door, she glimpsed a figure hurrying across the lawn toward the gate, but she couldn't make out anything clearly.'

'Nothing?' asks Jacob.

'The lights in the garden weren't switched on then,' explains Sehlapelo.

'Well,' says a lanky technician with messily gelled hair. 'We've found a few fresh fingerprints on the door, but almost none in the study itself. We'll have to compare them with those of anyone who may have had access to the house over these last few days.'

'I see there is an alarm system connected to this door.' Jacob looks up at a blinking sensor positioned above the frame. 'I wonder why it wasn't activated?'

'You know how these rich *okes* get,' says van Schalkwyk, moving aside for the departing technicians. 'They buy themselves the most expensive security toys, use them for a month or two, then forget all about them.'

'When did this murder happen?'

'About two hours ago.'

'And the housekeeper is our only witness of any kind?'

'A few neighbours heard a car revving up loudly in the street round about the time it must've happened. Judging by the way our friend looks, I'm surprised the whole neighbourhood didn't hear him die.'

Jacob goes over to the fridge and opens the door. It is well stocked. The cupboards show no sign of being plundered either. Food rifling usually goes hand in hand with burglary. His nose picks up an unmistakable stench of burnt flesh still hanging in the air. 'Who was he, anyway?'

Sehlapelo refers to his notebook as he follows Jacob towards the study. 'Bernard Klamm, seventy-nine years old. A retired businessman of some sort. Apparently he was originally from the Northern Cape, and moved to Johannesburg to act as a representative of some mining company during the late sixties. More we don't know; it seems he didn't mix much with his neighbours.'

The three detectives cross a wide hallway with natural pine flooring. A large black and white aerial photograph of some desolate town is mounted on the wall to Jacob's left, positioned so it will be instantly visible to guests entering via the front door. He studies the caption beneath it: *Leopold Ridge, 1959.*

In one corner stands an old copper cannon shell upended to serve as a stand for walking sticks and umbrellas, beside which another uniformed police officer is taking a statement from the distressed housekeeper.

Jacob reads the name badge stitched above his shirt pocket. 'Laubscher, will you take the witness into the kitchen, if you don't mind?'

The young constable, sporting a trim black moustache, turns to his superior and nods. He then turns back to the housekeeper. 'Come on, *atta*, you can show me where the tea is, and I'll make us some.'

Jacob pushes open the study door, where a small glass chandelier glitters amidst the last trails of smoke, giving everything a hazy, filtered look, like in an old film. He instantly notices the neat rows of black and white photographs arranged on two of the walls. There is a sudden flash from the far end of the room, where a police photographer is taking some final shots.

'There are several photos missing,' observes Jacob, after a pause.

Van Schalkwyk shoulders his way past his colleague. 'How do you know?'

Jacob approaches the bureau to study the wall behind it. 'Two pictures have been removed recently.' He indicates the empty hooks and the two darker rectangles amid a thin layer of dust. 'Look, three more are missing over there. Do we know what the subjects might have been?'

'I'll ask the housekeeper,' suggests Sehlapelo.

'Better take her from room to room,' Jacob calls after him, 'to check if anything else is missing.'

While waiting for the photographer to finish, he begins examining the contents of the bookcase nearest to him. Van Schalkwyk follows his example by picking out a book from a shelf on the other side of the room. The volumes seem to be arranged more by size and shape than by subject matter, but by and large they deal with hunting and travel photographs, the mining industries and geology.

'Fuck!' cries van Schalkwyk behind him.

Jacob turns, startled, as a book hits the floor. The Parkview man laughs sheepishly and stoops to pick up the large paperback he had been handling. 'Look at this,' he says to the photographer. 'Isn't this the most disgusting thing you've ever seen, hey?'

The photographer looks up from focusing on the charred and partially exposed yellow skull of the murder victim, and peers at the pages van Schalkwyk is holding open for him. The man shrugs his shoulders. 'It's pretty ugly—but it's not real.'

Jacob calls over to van Schalkwyk. 'Let me see that, too.'

The page the detective holds open for him depicts an obscene statuette decorated with countless tumours, horns and phalli that disfigure its body. A long tongue, culminating in a shape like a vulva, lolls out of a mouth split in a wide, leering grin. The entire body is deep ochre in colour, but the eyes are a startling white. Jacob takes the book to study it more closely. For him it is not the image's obscene sexuality that he finds offensive, but the expression so painstakingly carved into its face, the patient care and attention to detail, the *creative* power injected into this idol, almost as if it has been treated with love and reverence.

A yellow Post-it note has been stuck to the opposite page, jotted with numbers and letters that look like abbreviations. Stick-ons mark other pages where whole paragraphs have been underlined. Jacob closes the book and reads the title: *West African Death Cults: A Study in Supernatural Rape.*

'That stuff's sick.' Van Schalkwyk is peering over Jacob's shoulder while wiping his nose with a checked handkerchief. 'What's an old man like him doing with books like this?'

'Could be his hobby.' Jacob hands back the book and begins to examine the rest of the volumes on the shelf. Here they are arranged in alphabetical order, by author. While many are amateurishly published paperbacks, others look academic and well-informed. Many of them have severely creased spines and slips of paper sticking out their tops, again with numbers and letters scrawled in pencil. The books on the shelves along the other wall seem barely touched in comparison.

Van Schalkwyk carefully replaces the book where he found it. 'You think this stuff has anything to do with why he was killed?'

Jacob shakes his head. 'Can't say yet.' He finally turns his attention to what is left of the body, lying sprawled between two expensive-looking armchairs. A banker's lamp lies on the soft beige carpet next to a broken brandy glass, two bloody teeth, and a large wet stain. A Rorschach-like print of blood on the carpet reminds Jacob of a lizard. Even the top of the white-painted mantel has been stained with greasy soot from Klamm's immolation.

'The petrol was brought in this can over here,' explains van Schalkwyk, without even looking to see whether Jacob is paying attention. 'It looks like something you'd buy at any Outdoor Warehouse for a few hundred bucks. The rope binding the victim is standard nylon, also easily available at your nearest hardware store. The victim was surprised at around half past ten, attacked with fists or a blunt instrument, since a couple of his teeth were knocked loose. The killer tipped him into the fireplace while he was still tied up in that chair. Too terrified to investigate, the housekeeper called the Flying Squad from her quarters. Laubscher was first on the scene, just eight minutes after receiving the call. Klamm was already dead by the time he arrived.'

'Let me have a look at that petrol container,' says Jacob.

Van Schalkwyk hands it to him, and Jacob examines it carefully. It has a black metallic sheen and seems somewhat smaller than the ones he is used to seeing. The standard ones for sale also are green, rather than black. He hands it back to van Schalkwyk. 'Please make sure this is catalogued.'

The forensic technician steps aside to let Jacob take a closer look. The dead man's feet lie at grotesque angles, giving the strange impression that the victim has been pushing himself even deeper into the fireplace. A scorched upright chair with a wicker-lattice seat lies on its side, while on the fire-resistant carpet are scorched patches wherever burning petrol landed. The victim's night robe is hiked up above his knees, exposing his bony limbs and pale, hairy flesh. Both hands have contracted into talons, and there are white flecks of paint under his fingernails.

'The pathologist reckons he died of asphyxiation due to smoke and heat inhalation, but only an autopsy will tell for sure. The scratches down low on the mantelpiece indicate he was still alive when he was tipped into the fireplace. We have a feeling this funnel was driven down into the victim's throat.' Van Schalkwyk flaps his handkerchief and laughs. 'Hey, it must really stink going like this at his age—excuse the pun. You float through life without a care, then just before you're due to go, this happens to you. We dealing with a pyromaniac here, or what?'

Jacob shrugs. 'So far, it seems nothing more than some framed photos are missing. That the perp brought along duct tape, a can of petrol and a coil of rope seems to show that he came specifically intending to kill the old man. Those footprints in the flowerbed near the window are so deep that he must've stood watching outside in the rain for some time. A pyromaniac who preys on the elderly? Well, maybe—it happened in Bertrams in 1997. But it may also mean someone wanted to get revenge. This was done by someone much younger and stronger, able to overpower his victim, and topple him into the fireplace.'

Jacob stoops and examines the dead man's left hand more closely. 'We'd better start by talking to his wife if she's still alive.'

'His wife?'

Behind them rises a whimper. They turn around to see Sehlapelo standing near the doorway with the housekeeper, indicating to her the gaps left by the missing pictures.

'Look here.' Jacob beckons van Schalkwyk closer and indicates Klamm's ring finger. The flesh at the base is marginally paler than the rest. 'I don't know where the wedding ring is now, but he definitely wore one up until recently.'

3

2.20 a.m., 26 May 2004, Johannesburg

A comfortable brown lounge suite offers seating for six in the living room, under the angry, glassy-eyed gaze of an African buffalo whose head is mounted high up on one wall. On the large coffee table between them are arranged several books on Southern African game parks. Everyone has now left, apart from the two Parkview detectives, Jacob and the housekeeper. The woman, Paulina—whose eyes droop at the sides, and whose mouth seems strangely snout-like—looks very uncomfortable sitting here on her late employer's living-room sofa.

'Why didn't you tell us earlier that he had a wife?' Van Schalkwyk's mood has deteriorated as they progressed further into the early morning hours, his aggravation now directed at the housekeeper.

'You didn't ask me.' Paulina dabs at her broad, flat nose with a crumpled tissue pulled from her shirtsleeve.

'Does she live here, too?' asks Jacob.

'No.'

'Where, then?'

'I don't know. Mr Klamm, he didn't talk to me much. She's not with him anymore, but she come visit here sometimes.'

'We need to talk to her,' says Sehlapelo. 'Do you have her address?'

'No, I don't have her number. Nothing.'

'Why the hell not?' Van Schalkwyk's sharp tone draws a glance from Jacob.

'It is not my place. I don't know any of his telephone numbers.' Paulina tilts her head back. 'The few times she was here before tonight, they end up shouting almost loud enough for me to hear over there, in my room outside.'

'She was here tonight?' Jacob's high forehead crinkles with surprise.

'Yes, about quarter past six.'

'Quarter past six? Are you sure?' asks van Schalkwyk.

'The news on TV, it just started. I was in my room.'

'Did they argue then, too?' asks Sehlapelo.

'No . . . I don't know. I didn't hear them. I was cooking my supper and the TV, it was on.'

'You didn't see her leave?' Van Schalkwyk sits with one leg crossed over the other, his foot bouncing up and down.

'No, I hear her leave some time around nine o' clock, but I didn't see. I was watching the TV.'

Sehlapelo leans forward. 'Does he have any other family?'

'I don't think so.'

'How long have you worked for him?'

She counts off on her fingers. 'Almost eight years now.'

'Eight *years*?' asks van Schalkwyk. 'And you say you don't know any-thing about him?'

'He employed me to clean, and I cleaned—that is all. He wasn't a friendly man.' The housekeeper keeps her eyes fixed on the table.

Jacob clears his throat. 'Paulina, tell me what you *do* know about your employer?'

She turns her body to face only Jacob, cold-shouldering the Parkview detectives. 'He did not work, because he had the money, and he didn't have many visitors. He stay in his study very much, but I don't know what he did there, because I was never allowed to go in while he was busy. His tele-phone calls, they were few—and always short. He went out often.' She shrugs. 'I didn't speak with him unless he wanted the answers from me, because Mr Klamm, he get angry very easy, you see. I only worked half day, five days a week, and when I finish at one, I got out of his house very quickly. Over weekends I always go home to Ivory Park.'

'Sounds like a regular grumpy old man, *atta*.' Van Schalkwyk interjects as Jacob is about to ask another question. 'Why didn't you like him?'

Paulina ignores him but, when Jacob gestures for her to answer, she answers over her shoulder. 'I'll tell you why. I had really bad flu about a year ago, but do you think he gave me time off? No, not him. His eyes, they go angry, then he shout at me I must stop being such a lazy kaffir, and get back to work. The next day I was cleaning the bathroom—I was feeling worse—and I took a small bit of toilet paper to blow my nose. He was walking past, and he screamed and went red in the face when he saw me. He said no black can take from him without asking, not in his house. He said he was going to take the money for a toilet roll from my salary, at the end of the month. He did it.' Paulina slaps her leg at the memory. 'He *did* it.'

Jacob questions the housekeeper about Klamm's estranged wife, but she cannot recall any specific arguments, just hearing their raised voices. He senses she is not being evasive, she just considered her employment here so unstable that she went out of her way not to antagonize her employer. That included scuttling off to her sleeping quarters behind the garage whenever there was any hint of a quarrel breaking out.

'One last thing,' asks Jacob before dismissing her. 'Was anything other than those photographs missing from the house, or disturbed in any way?'

'No,' she replies bluntly.

When Jacob hears the kitchen door creak with her departure, he turns to van Schalkwyk. 'Is there something on your mind?'

With childlike astonishment erupting on his face, the Parkview detective sits forward and points after the housekeeper with an open hand. '*Yis-like*, did you hear that crap? I never heard anything like it. The bloody maid is telling one *hellsa* lie, man.'

Jacob stifles a yawn and quickly glances at his watch. It is now nearly three in the morning. He rubs his eyes at the thought of the long drive home still ahead of him. 'Why do you say that?' he asks.

Van Schalkwyk glances at his tall partner for reassurance. 'Surely you read the papers? Not a month ago, the discontented housekeeper of some rich family in Bryanston decided enough is enough, and hired some *tsotsis* from Alexandra to come clean out the house; except the burglary turned ugly, and the whole family were executed in their pyjamas.'

'And you think that's what happened here?'

'You heard how he treated her for *eight* years.'

Sehlapelo nods in agreement, although he does not add anything.

'Then why is nothing missing?'

'She obviously just wanted revenge, not his things. Come on, you can't tell me a maid knows so little about her employer. She has to wash his underwear, for Christ's sake. She's hiding something, trying to confuse us with all these vaguenesses. Nothing she's told us about tonight can be substantiated: neither the presence of this guy's wife—if he still has one—nor the fleeing culprit. She was watching TV all night, by herself. That's no alibi—she could've opened the gate for anyone. Two hundred rand is all it costs to have someone killed these days—affordable enough even for a maid, if she hates her boss enough.'

Jacob stares at the table more tiredly than thoughtfully. 'Well, he was also wearing pyjamas, so maybe there *is* a connection with the case you mentioned.'

Sehlapelo cannot help snorting at this sarcasm, and van Schalkwyk's lips grow tight. 'What was that?'

This time Jacob yawns freely, then rises. 'I'm not discounting your theory, Tinus, but I think we should track down the wife first, before jumping to conclusions.'

The two Parkview detectives stand up as well. 'No way.' Van Schalkwyk shakes his head. 'There is no "we" here, as much as we'd like to help you. That's why we called you in the first place. Our little station isn't designed to cope with stuff like this. My job is mostly to keep graffiti off rich people's walls, and sort out drunken domestic fights. That's all, and I have to admit I like it that way. It's easy. No one's going to shoot at me, and I don't have to look at this kind of shit every day.' The smile he gives Jacob exposes small, sharp teeth. 'Enjoy this one, Inspector. I'm going back home to my wife.'

The detectives lock up the victim's house and check on the domestic in her quarters one last time. In the cramped space, she is loudly recounting the night's events to a tired but inquisitive group of neighbourhood housekeepers who are sitting on the floor or crowded on her single bed.

Walking out to the roadway, the police officers go their separate ways. Jacob waits to switch on his car's ignition as the Parkview officers drive off past him. His thoughts abruptly turn to the good times he used to have working on such cases with his previous partner, Harry Mason. At times like this, they would go in search of some coffee, no matter how late it was, then discuss the strategies they would adopt the next day. That does not happen for Jacob any more. The truth is, since Harry quit the service, nothing much about his job has stimulated Jacob. His new partner, a rookie from Springs, is as lazy as he is incompetent. As a team, their performance appraisals have dropped steadily, and so too has the level of interest of the cases assigned to them. With a bitter taste in his mouth, Jacob wonders what Tudhope's excuses will be tomorrow.

4

7.48 a.m., 26 May 2004, Johannesburg

In the Christof van Wyk building in downtown Johannesburg Jacob is sitting at his small desk in a large common room designated for the detectives of the Murder and Robbery Unit. Opposite him, his partner's desk is a precarious mess. This early in the morning the building is still largely empty, the way Jacob likes it because he can then make himself a cup of tea and read the *Sowetan* and *Daily Sun* without interruption. He strolls over to the office he once shared with Harry Mason, pushes the door open and goes inside to stand by the window. From here he can just make out the gleaming new constitutional court. Built on the site of the Old Fort prison, where both Gandhi and Mandela were once held, it provides a stately symbol of a celebration of South African democracy. The irony hardly escapes Jacob: he, a black man, now works in a building once reserved for Apartheid security police, and he is able to stare out at the only prison in the only country to have imprisoned two Nobel Peace Prize winners. He wishes he could still occupy this space, but two administrators who work with computers all day have now inherited that privilege.

Returning to his workstation, he eyes his partner's table with disgust. Amongst the towering heaps of files sit two chewed and flattened Styrofoam cups. Under copies of *Men's Health* and *Magnum* magazines, Jacob spots a number of assignments his partner was supposed to have completed a week ago. When, shortly after the first free elections, Jacob received his transfer to this central bureau from Soweto, he never thought he would find himself working with this kind of slovenly ineptitude again.

The fax machine crouching in one corner of the cramped room suddenly begins to beep and chatter, throwing out two pages. Curious, Jacob walks over for a glance at them. The fax originates from Sam Sehlapelo, with details of the housekeeper Paulina's statement, including what she remembers of the missing photographs. She had dusted the black and whites often enough during her eight years of service to remember the handsome black man featured in all five photos now missing. He had an infectious smile and what looked like a scar near his mouth. One image showed him with an arm draped around Klamm's shoulders, both men grinning widely at the photographer. She remembers frequently wondering how Klamm could have acted so friendly with a black man in his earlier years—for the pictures were obviously very old—when he was always such a blatant racist around her. Even then, the other man had looked considerably younger, taller and heavier than Klamm himself.

Jacob returns to his desk with the fax and smoothes open his morning newspapers. The *Daily Sun* headlines report: *White Farmer Feeds Disobedient Worker to Lions; Sangoma Rapes Girls as Part of 'Treatment'*; and *Rocky Rainfall Plagues Family.*

He sips his tea and reads on. Three pages into the tabloid, he discovers an item concerning a dawn raid on a Sunninghill townhouse complex, which ended in a shoot-out between police and four Nigerian drug dealers. Jacob cuts out the article and places it into a neat file he keeps in the bottom drawer of his desk, one which holds all his clippings about West African criminals. He started this file shortly after the botched arrest of a Nigerian drug baron known only as 'the albino', who doubled as an African witch. It was then that his police partner's wife had been killed, and Harry nearly lost his daughter, too.

Officers begin to arrive for their day's work, though the seat opposite Jacob remains obtrusively empty. Out of the corner of his eye, Jacob sees Senior Superintendent Niehaus approaching, his black moustache greying in gradual synchronicity with the hair at his temples. The fifty-year-old is still relatively new to directing the entire unit, having been the superintendent of the detectives under Chief Molethe. Behind the turtle-shell glasses perched high up on his nose, his eyes look stern but kind.

'Tshabalala, where the hell is Tudhope? I told him to be in early for once this morning.'

Jacob folds away his newspaper and looks Niehaus in the eye. 'You know what, boss? I don't think even Ben knows where he is. I never had this trouble with Joe.'

'Look, Jacob.' Niehaus holds up a hand. 'When Harry quit, you and Joe worked well together, I admit, but I depend on my senior officers to train up the younger guys. Tudhope is inexperienced and just needs a bit of discipline. Anyway, you're not the only one suffering. Harry seems fed up, too, if it's any consolation.'

It is not, thinks Jacob, looking at his watch. Getting up and grabbing his jacket from the back of his chair he says, 'I'm more than happy to train somebody who *wants* to learn. But this guy, he doesn't finish his work, and so constantly puts our cases in jeopardy. Do me a favour, boss, and have a word with Ben. I'm not getting through to Tudhope and I might just end up killing him.'

'That'll be the day.' Niehaus laughs at Jacob's departing back.

5

11.18 a.m., 26 May 2004, Johannesburg

There is not a cloud in the blue sky as he drives towards the northern suburbs, the sun shining brightly but without much warmth. When he arrives at the deceased's residence in daylight, he sees drifts of dry liquidambar leaves have collected against the ornamental wrought-iron gate. The lawn is a vast yellow smear of dry grass. Only two cypresses, one on either side of the driveway, remain a deep green. The house itself looks almost homely in the daylight, half hidden amongst the naked shrubs and trees.

Jacob drives slowly down the gravel driveway, past the front of the residence, till he eventually reaches the twin garages attached to the domestic quarters. To his surprise, he finds an old jalopy parked in front of one of them, all its doors wide open. A young black man in his early twenties is leaning against the vehicle, wearing a floppy yellow hat and casually chewing on a plastic straw.

The detective gets out of his unmarked white Toyota Corolla cruiser and approaches the man. As they confer in Sotho, the reason for his presence becomes clear when the housekeeper appears around the corner, carrying some of her belongings in a box.

'Where are you going?' Jacob asks her.

'Ivory Park—back to my mother,' she replies in Sotho. 'I don't have a job here any more, and it's bad luck to stay here, after the way that man died.'

Jacob jots down the mother's address before turning his attention back to the man helping her move. She has not got too much and soon the car is filled up. Ready to leave, Paulina unwinds her window. 'The old man still owes me my money for the last month. If you find his wife, tell her about that.'

Jacob nods. 'Are you absolutely sure you don't know who that man in the missing photographs is?'

She breaks eye contact with him and plays briefly with her strangely protruding mouth. 'I've never met him here, and Mr Klamm didn't talk to me. There is nothing more I can tell you, detective.'

'That person you saw running away last night, could it have been him?'

Paulina closes her eyes in an attempt to visualize what she witnessed the night before. She shakes her head. 'It was too dark, and I was scared. The figure was just a shadow.'

'And the car that revved so loud out on the street?'

'Look.' She points back over her shoulder towards the gate. From where they are the street is invisible, behind the cypress trees. 'I heard a car, but I didn't see it.'

Once the pair have gone, Jacob lets himself in through the kitchen door and steps into an absolutely silent house. Not even the refrigerator is ticking. Only the smell from last night lingers. The study door opens smoothly, with neither a whisper as it slides over the carpet nor a creak from its hinges. The detective heads straight for the desk set against the wall to his right. His first priority is to make contact with Klamm's widow, and find out more about the man's activities, either in retirement or before.

The desk is neatly kept, with only a phone, a black leather blotter centred on it, and a silver fountain pen mounted on a marble receptacle, while the various pigeonholes are filled with stationery and documents clamped together. A stapled article resting on the blotter draws Jacob's eye: *Satanic Abuse and the Rochdale Affair: What the State is Covering Up.* This document looks like it was printed off the Internet, and he quickly scans it for any recent notes Klamm may have made, but it is unmarked. Testing the four drawers in turn, he discovers that they are all locked. He suspects that the victim may have kept the key on his person, so makes a mental note to phone the morgue and check on the whereabouts of Klamm's personal effects.

Moving over to the corner furthest away from the fireplace, he stands and studies the spacious room in its entirety. What would this seventy-nine-year-old keep locked away in his desk drawers? And why is it only the weirdest stuff in the room that shows signs of having been read?

Each of the tiered bookshelves on either side of the mantelpiece has a broad laminated black strip running across the middle. On closer inspection, Jacob finds that these strips disguise sliding panels. He tries opening them, and is not surprised to find them locked, too.

Returning to the desk, Jacob phones the morgue, and a clerk with a cracked voice puts the detective on hold while he checks the inventory of items found on Klamm's body. Meanwhile, Jacob takes the opportunity of studying more closely the photographs ranged above the desk. They all seem to be from the sixties or even earlier, depicting rural small-town life and mining operations: conveyor belts transporting ore into sheet-metal constructed buildings, workers staring out at the camera over their wheelbarrows, cocopans full of ore being pushed on their railtracks out of mineshafts by gaunt, shirtless Africans, a product being packed into hessian bags and loaded on horse-drawn carts. Finally the morgue clerk comes back on the line: there was indeed a bunch of keys in one of Klamm's robe pockets.

As he replaces the receiver, Jacob finds himself squinting at one particular image, taken somewhere called Pomfret if the sign *Pomfret General Supplies* can be believed, though he has never heard of the place. A young white man in his late twenties, whom he assumes to be Klamm himself, is standing outside the shop, dressed in chinos and a white collared shirt. Hands resting on his hips, with shirtsleeves rolled up to his elbows, he squarely faces the camera with a smile that resembles a sneer.

The phone's sudden loud trill shatters his contemplative silence. Jacob answers it, giving his name.

'Who did you say you were?' presses a suspicious elderly female voice.

'Detective Inspector Tshabalala.'

'A detective?'

'Yes. Can I ask who is calling?'

There is a long silence, then the woman draws a long shuddering breath. 'My name is Miss Henrietta Campbell. Mr Klamm is my estranged husband. What's happened to him?'

'Bernard Klamm was murdered last night, ma'am.'

'That can't be!' the woman replies. 'I saw him only yesterday evening.'

'We are aware that you visited him, so I need to speak with you in order to help reconstruct the last hours he was known to be alive. Shall I come visit you at your home?'

'No,' she retorts, a bit too fast. 'I will come see you at his house, if you don't mind. Will your superior be there, too?'

'My superior?' asks Jacob, confused.

'Yes, whoever's in charge.'

Jacob hesitates, finding the woman's cool and businesslike reaction surprising. It is as if she is arranging a client lunch, rather than talking to a police officer about the death of someone close to her.

'Hello,' comes her impatient voice. 'Are you still there?'

'No, Miss Campbell, it's me you'll be speaking to, or my partner.'

'Well, I suppose that will have to do. I shall be there in about half an hour.'

6

12.02 p.m., 26 May 2004, Johannesburg

A quick search through the other rooms in the house reveals nothing out of the ordinary. Although his house has been richly furnished and well maintained, Klamm himself seems to have owned very little that could be called personal, except perhaps for his numerous books and photographs. In the victim's austere bedroom, Jacob discovers a long safe hidden in the built-in closet, as well as a large annotated King James bible filled with notes scribbled on the same yellow adhesive paper to be found in the eso-teric books in the study below. A grey suit hangs ready on a stand under-neath the window that overlooks the front garden, most likely the outfit Klamm had chosen for today. Jacob finds it difficult to reconcile this old man's conservative orderliness with the obscene way his corpse lay half-naked and charred in his study the night before.

The mobile chirrups on his belt. Checking caller identification, he sighs and answers. 'Yes, Tudhope.'

'Hey, Jakes, where are you, my *boet*? You missed one hell of a session with the boss this morning, let me tell you. He's coming down hard on us these days, eh?'

'Have you finished with the Gordon case yet?' asks Jacob, thinking of the mountain of paperwork lying all but forgotten on his partner's desk.

'Soon, pal, soon. Hey, I hear we've got ourselves a stiff out in Parkview. Sorry I couldn't make it, man . . . I mean last night.' Tudhope suddenly laughs conspiratorially. 'I only got your message this morning. I was out— a new girl, you know.'

'Look, when we are on call, that means we're on call. It doesn't mean we can just switch our phones off whenever . . .' Jacob pinches the bridge of his nose. 'Just finish up with the Gordon case, please.'

'Hey, I told you to relax, man. I've got it covered. The case only goes to court on Thursday.'

'It's Tuesday today, Tudhope. Prosecution needs the rest of the informa-tion *before* they go to court.'

'Right,' his partner replies vacantly. 'So what are we doing about the barbecue?'

'The Gordon case, Ben. *Today.*'

From the window of Klamm's bedroom, Jacob sees a massive seven se-ries BMW with tinted windows turn into the end of the driveway. He hangs up on Tudhope and hurries downstairs to open the gate. With a low growl, the car glides in and comes to a stop at the front of the house just as he is opening the front door. He steps out into the cold, ready to welcome Klamm's widow. The driver's door opens and it takes a few seconds before a leg emerges, dressed in a white stocking and a black, conservative shoe with golden buckles. Next, a set of aged fingers, nails lacquered a bright red, creep round the doorframe. Finally Campbell emerges from the murky depths of her vehicle. She looks to be in her seventies, although the heavy make-up makes it difficult to tell. Only as she starts up the flight of stone steps, with a stiff but confident gait, does she meet Jacob's gaze.

'Are you the young man I spoke to on the telephone?'

'Yes, ma'am.'

'You don't look like a police officer.' Campbell digs in her handbag for a Kleenex. Instead of using it, she crumples it up in her hand with quick, agitated movements.

Jacob smiles. 'I'm a detective; I don't have to wear a uniform.'

She grunts dismissively. Without waiting for him to advise her what to do next, she enters the house. Immediately she sniffs the air, dabs her nose with the tissue and throws Jacob a curious glance. 'What's that smell in the house? What exactly happened here? Someone should open up the windows, let some air into the place.'

'Shall we take a seat in the living room, Miss Campbell?' Jacob indi-cates the direction he would like her to proceed. 'I have some questions for you.'

'I don't want to sit down. I want to get out of here as soon as I can, so please let's attend to only what is absolutely necessary.'

Thinking that she may be reacting so belligerently because of the abrupt loss she has suffered, Jacob offers her his sympathies. Her reply is unexpected. 'Leave it alone. You didn't even know him, so how can you be sorry? Tell me that. Now, what do you need me to sign?'

'I will have to take a statement from you about last night, ma'am. So if we could . . .' Jacob again indicates the door to the living room.

The old woman fiddles with an emerald cat pinned to her left lapel. 'Have you contacted your superior yet?'

Jacob withdraws his hand and rubs his chin. 'Like I've told you, Miss Campbell, I *am* the investigating officer in the matter of your husband's murder.'

'My *estranged* husband,' corrects the woman. 'Only you?'

Wondering whether she is always this abrasive, Jacob grimly replies, 'That's right.'

'But that's outrageous.'

'Why?' He raises an eyebrow, but can guess what she is thinking: Heaven forbid a *black* officer should be investigating this case.

'It just is.'

The detective closes the front door behind him a little too firmly. 'At what time did you arrive here yesterday?'

'I got here around six o' clock.'

Purposefully, and with a hint of menace, Jacob says, 'That probably makes *you* the last person we know of to see Bernard Klamm alive.'

The woman's frosty demeanour suddenly wilts as she finally senses the full gravity of the situation. She clasps her handbag defensively in front of her body, taking an involuntary step backwards, towards the centre of the hall. A strange expression passes over her face, her eyes darting from the uncanny lifelessness of the house all around her back to the police officer's face.

'How did it happen?' she asks.

Jacob describes the incident in brief. 'It's very important for us to establish a chronological order to last night's events,' he continues. 'So when did you leave here, ma'am?'

'I don't know precisely.' Her voice has softened considerably. 'Around nine thirty, I should think. We discussed a few business matters pertaining to our past.'

Jacob nods. 'Was Mr Klamm himself acting strangely in any way, or did you notice anything out of the ordinary when you left him?'

'I saw that maid of his standing in the doorway of her quarters as I arrived. Other than that, I didn't see a soul. Except Bernard, of course, who was his usual gallant self.' She speaks the last words with a degree of bitter sarcasm. 'Which is to say he was trying to convince me of how right he was, and became belligerent when I disagreed.'

'Exactly what did you discuss?'

'Is this really necessary?' She begins to fiddle with her brooch again. 'I came here yesterday to talk with him about private matters, that's all. So what difference does the content of our discussion make? Surely you can't suspect me of killing him?'

'I disagree,' says Jacob. 'The content of your discussion may be relevant. What was it you argued about?'

She tries to glower at him, but she is clearly too unnerved. 'We talked about . . . well, we were trying to finally come to an agreement about the fate of some property of ours in the Northern Cape. It has been a source of contention for years, but each time we came out of our discussion undecided.'

'So what happened in the end?'

'We became irate with each other, as usual. I insisted I was entitled to more than thirty per cent of the proceeds, but he argued that this was all he was prepared to offer me, since the land in question was awarded him as part of a pay package back in 1965, and it had nothing to do with me. I grew indignant then, and told him he could choke on that farm for all I cared.' The woman is clawing at her collar, as if struggling to breathe. 'The reason for all this aimless bickering, I suspect, is that neither of us actually wanted to sell it.'

This time, when Jacob gestures for her to step into the living room, she complies. Once they are seated—Campbell on a large three-seater sofa against one wall, and Jacob in the single armchair directly facing the mounted buffalo head—the detective continues.

'So why did you phone him this morning?'

'You know how it is. One gets in a huff and later regrets it.'

Jacob stretches an arm out over the backrest and nods. 'Remind me when you went home.'

'Nine thirty; I told you that.'

'I'm sorry,' says Jacob, glancing at his notes. 'Nine thirty it is.'

'Yes,' says the woman. 'Once our discussion became pointless, I promptly excused myself. My partner can confirm when I arrived home.'

The policeman flips open a fresh page in his notebook. 'And who is your partner?'

'Detective, how can you possibly suggest either of us had anything to do with Bernard's murder?'

'I'm just closing all the loopholes. I need to make absolutely sure I've got all the information. It's a process of elimination, that's all.'

She opens her handbag and passes Jacob her business card. 'His name is Tobias Rees, and this is our address in Dainfern.'

'How long have you been together, then?'

'Thirty-two years.'

Jacob gives a slight, confused nod. 'Why didn't you divorce Mr Klamm, after all that time?'

Campbell's lips begin to quiver, and she tightens both her fists around her handbag, the white tissue now squeezed through her fingers like soft dough. 'For the same reason that we didn't sell our house in the Northern Cape.'

'And that is?'

She hastily looks away as tears suddenly appear in her eyes. Jacob remains quiet, waiting patiently for her to answer. During the long silence that ensues, he gets the distinct impression that, rather than organizing her thoughts, the woman is willing him to steer away from this topic. Her eyes remain firmly fixed on a display cabinet filled with model cars from the fifties.

'You did not like your husband,' Jacob finally says, 'so why did you never officially leave him for the man you are with now?'

Campbell swallows hard. When she finally speaks, her voice again sounds calm and assured, completely at odds with her body language. 'Does this have to be discussed?'

'Yes,' replies Jacob flatly.

She nods, but still does not look at him.

He redirects his line of questioning somewhat. 'What else did you quarrel about?'

She remains silent.

Jacob sighs impatiently. 'Please, answer me.'

'He wouldn't give it to me,' she replies laconically.

'A divorce?' he guesses.

She nods her head, and gulps down further emotions.

'Exactly how long have you been separated, then?'

'Thirty-eight years.'

'Really? Can I ask how old you are?'

For the first time this haughty woman offers him a smile, and in its brief flicker Jacob sees the beautiful woman hidden deep under bitter, painful layers of life's disappointments. 'Detective, you will allow a lady some secrets, won't you?'

Jacob smiles back at her. 'Of course.'

Campbell heaves a sigh that lifts her shoulders. 'We didn't get a divorce because he refused to allow me one, and maybe some part of me didn't want it, either. You see, there are some things that bound us together tighter than anything most other married couples experience. We went through a very complicated emotional patch, if you will, and this is how we turned out. Tobias always accepted it that way, and Bernard acquiesced because I think he believed, deep down, that he would somehow win me back one day. He got stuck on that idea, you see, like he seemed to get stuck on more and more ideas as he grew older. He was a very stubborn man.'

Jacob regards the woman a few moments, finding this unusual relationship difficult to digest. It seems a strange arrangement, but no stranger than that of a woman he arrested a few years back, who had first left her husband and two children for a Greek lover with a taste for parties, blondes, guns and cocaine, only to move back in when she ran out of the money that funded his debauchery. Three weeks after she returned, the boyfriend moved into the guestroom, the husband consenting to all this for the sake of the children. Three weeks after that, her husband came home to find his own things stored in that same guestroom, and the boyfriend now occupying his side of their marital bed. Both his wife and her lover lay spread-eagled on the mattress, naked and unconscious after an afternoon's drug binge. The kids did not see them this time, which somehow convinced the husband that a dodgy mother was better than no mother at all. Two days later, Jacob and Harry Mason received a call placed by a neighbour who had just heard gunshots. The mother and boyfriend had been free-basing crack all afternoon, and when the husband came home and confronted them, his wife flew into a frenzy, which the boyfriend stoked with wild jeers, urging her to take his .38 and collect on the life insurance. She ended up putting five rounds into her husband's face. But this time the children—a nine-year-old boy and a five-year-old girl—were witnesses. The two escaping addicts were caught halfway to Durban, having abandoned the two kids at home with their dead father stuffed in a closet.

At least, muses Jacob, Klamm's case does not feature kids or drugs, just a strange marital agreement between three older people who have lived with their unusual situation for decades.

'Do you know of anyone who would have wanted to kill him?'

At this she allows a bitter laugh. 'Detective, if you have spoken with the man's housekeeper at all, I'm sure you'll know that Bernard wasn't a pleasant man. If I had to make a list of everyone who disliked the old fool, then it would include just about everyone who ever crossed paths with him in his lifetime. Of course, most of the people we knew together are dead now.'

'Can you think of anyone still alive who might have hated him enough to kill him so near the end of his life?'

Henrietta Campbell's expression clouds as she thinks this question through. 'No, no one. There isn't anyone left from *those* days, I should think. He had a way of bringing out the worst in people, detective, and I suspect that, before your investigation is concluded, he will have affected you that way, too. He was rotten, rotten to the core.' She shakes her head. 'I only wish I had had more courage to dissuade him from some of the things he did.'

Jacob frowns. 'Such as?'

'He was a particularly cruel and ruthless businessman, that's all. He worshipped money and nothing else. Nothing else mattered to him, not even his own family. I can only be thankful that he spared me the details of his dealings, even though gossip regularly had a habit of drifting my way.'

'What was Mr Klamm doing before he retired?'

'He was many things: farmer, miner, businessman—a real entrepreneur.'

Jacob thinks about the eclectic collection of books in Klamm's study. 'Anything else?'

Campbell narrows her eyes as she dabs at her nose with the tissue. 'What do you mean?'

'Did he ever become interested in religious practices, or was he perhaps merely interested in anthropology?'

'No, whatever gave you that idea? He was a practically minded man who couldn't give a hoot about academia, or anything spiritual either. In his spare time he went hunting and also did some amateur photography. He just liked shooting things in more ways than one, I guess.' Campbell's handbag is still perched on her lap, as if she is readying herself to depart at any minute.

Jacob hands over a business card and begs her to call him should anything else come to mind. 'But before you leave, can we take a look around and see if anything is missing—things you remember from when the two of you still lived together?'

She looks at her watch. 'I don't know. I have another appointment.'

'It will only take a minute, and it's quite important.' Jacob rises.

She wets her lips. 'It really will have to be quick, though.'

7

1.22 p.m., 26 May 2004, Johannesburg

Of the house's three bedrooms, the door of only one stands open. Campbell's initial desire to hurry seems to drain from her the moment she goes up the stairs. Her face turning sad and sombre, she hesitantly enters her late estranged husband's austere sleeping quarters, casting unsure eyes over the single bed with its threadbare green throw. A large teak footlocker stands at its base; there are four pairs of shoes resting on a bronze rack, and an old-fashioned alarm clock with ear-like bells stands on the bedside cabinet.

'You know,' she whispers, after a long moment's reflection, 'this is the first time in thirty-eight years that I've been up here. It all looks so different now . . . so soulless.' She steps towards the bed and extends her fingers over the bedspread, as if to probe it for some residual warmth. 'You can say what you want about Bernard, but he was always meticulous in his dress, and he did enjoy his luxuries. But this bed . . . it's like a drifter's, and there are so few items in this room. It's not at all like the man I remember.'

'What did he get rid of?' urges Jacob.

Campbell seems to recover from something deeply personal, her fingers curling up as she retracts her hand from the bed. She smiles sadly. 'Most of our things, things I thought would never leave this house, things that I thought would stay here as they stayed in my memories of this room, of our bedroom, are gone. I left many of my possessions here when I departed. There was a dresser over there. We had a double bed and a portrait of us, painted shortly after our wedding, hung above it. I suppose that when one is the partner that leaves, one somewhat arrogantly assumes the other will keep mementoes of some kind.' She turns and reaches out to touch the annotated bible with one glistening red fingernail. 'I'm surprised to see this here. He wasn't exactly an atheist, but he often scoffed at Christianity. It's one of the reasons why we were separated.' She shakes her head as if at some bitter memory. 'I really don't know what you expect me to find here, or not to find, detective. I don't know exactly what he has sold off in the intervening years, or what else he has subsequently acquired that may now be missing. I don't even remember many of the things we once shared.'

'I noticed there is a safe in the closet,' says Jacob. 'Would you know what it contains?'

'On the farm, he always kept a small arsenal of hunting rifles and pistols. Perhaps they are in there now? He was also a keen photographer and treasured his cameras immensely, so it could be them. I really don't know.' Campbell peeks into the ensuite bathroom, and is about to step back out when she spots something.

Jacob follows her in.

She grabs something lying in the soap dish. 'I'd like to take this, if you don't mind.' She holds up a simple gold wedding band.

Jacob notices that she is not wearing her own ring any more. The flatness in her tone makes him wonder how much this woman is a master at controlling her emotions, moving from one expression to the next at will, or whether her seemingly volatile reactions are just a strange form of shock. It could also be that she really has no feelings left for the dead man, but nevertheless is struggling to rekindle some here in the room they once shared so intimately. The mixed messages she is giving make it difficult for him to gauge her, or to detect what it is she is keeping from him. For, he realizes, she is definitely hiding details from him, judging by her uncompleted sentences and her erratic sidetracks into frivolous details. Though he would love to press her at a later stage for more information about their marital relationship and what exactly drove them apart, for now he is happy to allow her her evasiveness.

Knowing full well he is bending the rules by releasing potential evidence, Jacob says, 'Sure, you can take it.'

'Thank you.' She carefully examines the ring. 'Despite our differences he clung on to me until the bitter end. I don't know if I should see him as some silly lovesick loner, or just an obsessive fool slowly drowning in a sea of his own making.' She slips her dead husband's wedding band onto her thumb, but even then the ring is too large to fit properly.

'People sometimes don't know what they should get rid of in their lives and what they should cherish and remember,' observes Jacob. 'Some people make their decisions and bear the consequences, others make a decision only to revisit everything that led up to that point again and again.'

Reading the house, the room and the treasured ring as an expression of Klamm's state of mind, Jacob sees him as one of the latter—a man who could not let go, for whatever reason. On the one hand he tried to wipe out his past by packing up and removing half his house, but on the other he kept hold of something as small yet powerful as his wedding ring. What was it made him hang on to this woman for thirty-eight years, after she had so obviously rejected him? Was it love? Or something else?

'You're a wise man, detective,' says Campbell, that genuine smile playing over her face for a second time.

Jacob shrugs. 'We all get hurt at some point in our lives, and we have to try to learn from the pain as best we can.'

They move on to the other, closed bedrooms, Jacob's shoes clopping on the pine flooring, Campbell's heels clacking ahead of him. One is an empty chamber which the elderly woman explains was meant to become a guest room but always stood empty, and another, smaller room with its curtains drawn, its furnishings all covered in white sheets that give an impression that even rooms and inanimate objects can possess spirits and secrets. It occurs to Jacob that these unused spaces may have once been destined for children and grandchildren, but now they seem cold and abandoned structures, giving the house a sterile atmosphere. On the threshold of this third bedroom, Campbell abruptly tightens her grip on her handbag and refuses to step over the threshold. 'I apologize, detective. I just can't help you with any of this. I absolutely must go now.'

'Ma'am, did you ever have children with Mr Klamm?'

'No.' She turns on him. 'Why do you ask?' Her eyes appear fearful.

'It just seems this house must have been bought for a larger family.'

'It was bought for prestige, and nothing more.'

'Do you have children now?' asks Jacob, persisting.

'I can't believe how invasive you are.' She brushes past him and heads for the top of the stairs. Over her shoulder, she calls out, 'Honestly, I thought I just had to sign something here; instead, I find myself interrogated as though I might have killed the man with my own hands. That's it. I'm leaving now.'

'Miss Campbell!'

She comes to a stop halfway down the stairs. 'What is it?'

'I'm not accusing you of anything; I was merely attempting to build a picture of Bernard Klamm in my mind. I need to know as much as I can about him if I'm to solve this case, and he seems to have been very secretive. So far, you have been the greatest help to me. Please, will you not at least have a look at the photographs in his study? Several are missing and I'd like to know if you can tell me more about them.'

The old woman rolls her eyes. 'Let's get it over with, then. Quickly.'

In the study she presses the remorselessly crumpled tissue to her nose and winces when she spies the scorched mantelpiece. 'For God's sake, will someone just open the windows in here?'

'Of course.' Jacob hurries to comply. Over his shoulder he says, 'By the bureau two photographs are missing and, from that wall over there, another three.'

She ignores what he is saying and is irresistibly drawn towards the fire-place, towards the lizard print of her husband's blood, the little spray-painted circles left where his teeth fell. The quilt she once made him, and on which they had once upon a time made love, lies carelessly crumpled next to a forgotten latex glove. The chair a neighbour once gave them still lies on its side, useless and ugly now, its backrest scorched and burnt. Jacob finishes opening up the windows and watches her take all this in.

A shudder passes through her, her mouth opens, and a dry whisper gradually escalates into a low wail. 'How? Even to him, *how?*'

The detective hastens over to her, reaches out to lay his hands on her shoulders and redirect her attention, except, at the last second, he remembers her earlier reaction to his skin colour. For her, that had somehow defined his rank and intelligence, so she might consider it inappropriate for him to even touch her. Instead, he steps between her and the crime scene.

'Ms Campbell,' he urges softly, 'that's what I'm here to find out. Come over this way. If we could just have a look at the photographs on the walls . . .'

She peers at the empty spaces for a full minute, her body quivering, her breath coming in short pants. Suddenly her breath catches, her eyes grow wide and she involuntarily claps a hand over her mouth.

'No,' she mumbles, 'it can't be.'

'What is it?' Jacob turns his intent gaze on her.

She slowly takes her hand away and blinks at him. 'I don't remember any of the others, but that one I do. There was a black man in it, with one arm flung over Bernard's shoulder. He had a very bright smile, and a deep scar above one side of his mouth.'

'Why did you say, "It can't be"?'

'He's dead, he *must* be dead.'

'Who is he?'

'José Eduardo Cauto—but he's *dead.*' The woman turns away from him and hastens to get out of the room. 'I'm late, so very late. We'll have to continue this talk at some other time.'

Jacob follows her. 'What relationship did this man have with Mr Klamm?'

'Leave it alone now, please. I must go.'

'Why do you say he's dead?' insists Jacob. 'What happened to him?'

'You'll have to go back to Leopold Ridge for that. I don't want to talk about it now.'

'Please—'

'Not now, not ever again!' She rushes through the hallway and out the front door, fumbling in her handbag for her keys. Jacob comes to a stop on the threshold.

'There is only one person responsible for all this,' calls Campbell as she sinks back into the shadows of her BMW. 'And he's dead. He died in there last night. Goodbye, detective.'

8

2.52 p.m., 26 May 2004, Johannesburg

Back in the study, Jacob approaches the esoteric bookshelf and its locked compartments, feeling that he has somehow been lured into taking a specific direction in this investigation. Of one thing he is certain: the woman is hiding things regarding her true relationship with her estranged husband.

While brooding on these thoughts, he notices that the sliding wooden panels are secured only rudimentarily. He runs a finger along the surface of one, then, fetching a sturdy knife from the kitchen, he slips the tip into a thin gap just above the lock, and levers the knife sharply. There is a resounding crack as the wood splinters and the lock springs loose.

In the space inside are twelve volumes resembling wedding albums, each of them covered in black vinyl with gold patterns embossed on the spine. On the single concealed shelf there is nothing else. He pulls one volume out and notices the front has no title, no lettering whatsoever—just glossy fake black leather. He opens the book, and immediately his skin begins to crawl.

At first he is not sure of what he is looking at exactly, his mind somehow refusing to absorb this meticulous record of horrors. Page after page features a single photograph neatly centred on a matt-black background, and below each image is a caption, annotated in cryptic shorthand, written in blue ballpoint on neat strips of white paper carefully stuck on. Licking his lips, Jacob extends a finger to touch a close-up photograph of a Khoisan adolescent kneeling on a broken concrete floor and staring up at the camera. Her eyes filled with tears, she is clasping her torn dress to her chest. He flips on to the next page, and his breath catches with a sharp hiss. A feral-looking girl with golden-blonde locks and a grime-smeared face bares her teeth at the photographer from her hiding place on the top shelf of a large closet.

In revulsion he throws the album into one of the large brass-studded leather chairs, and yanks out another identical volume. A Griqua girl stands nude on loose floorboards of a corrugated iron shack, her feet looking heavily callused as if she has never been accustomed to wearing shoes. The full-frontal shot shows her sobbing with hands behind her back. One eye is swollen shut, and a deep cut disfigures her lip, while bruises cover her body like sinister dark lichen. A twelve-year-old white girl on the following page does not exhibit any visible wounds, but the outraged scream she levels at the photographer has twisted up her face with an agony that could never be purely physical. Facing her in the album, a pale girl of seventeen who must once have been a gorgeous child stands next to a broken window. The skin of her face and body has been disfigured by surface cuts, and heavy bandages cover the fresh wounds seemingly inflicted by the bloodied shards of glass still lodged in the window frame.

Jacob glances back at the row of books on the open shelf above, of which one title is burnt into his memory: *West African Death Cults: A Study in Supernatural Rape.* An icy shudder slips down his spine and, at the back of his mind, a voice that sounds like his dead grandfather's is screaming for him to get out of this place.

The house phone suddenly shatters the silence, startling Jacob. He slams the volume closed, goes over and picks the receiver up. 'Hello?'

On the desk directly in front of him is the article entitled *Satanic Abuse and the Rochdale Affair: What the State is Covering Up.*

'Detective Tshabalala?' He recognizes the voice as Campbell's.

He feels rather dazed, as if torn from the fabric of reality. 'Yes.'

'What's wrong?' He is about to explain when she continues. 'Never mind, I want to apologize for my abrupt departure. I was just rather badly shaken.'

'That's absolutely fine, but there are still a few things we need to discuss.'

'In due course,' she replies dismissively. From the background noises, he can hear she is on her mobile phone and still driving through traffic. 'I'm calling now to ask whether you know of a reputable detective agency. There is something that I must resolve soon, which Bernard's death has brought into sharper focus. I don't know much about this sort of business and would appreciate some help.'

Struggling to take in this new track, Jacob blurts, 'Excuse me?'

'Do you know any detectives for hire?' she reiterates impatiently.

'What for, exactly? This investigation is already being handled by the police. I must warn you now that a private detective might interfere with the course of the case, and could easily land you in trouble.'

'Nonsense,' she says as her cellular connection fades then bounces back. 'I would want to send him back to Leopold Ridge.'

'I . . .' Jacob fumbles for words. 'Is it protection you need?'

'Are you listening to a word I'm saying? What I need is a detective—a good one.'

Still curious as to what she may want a PI for, Jacob thinks fast and then replies. 'There might be someone, but I'll first have to see if he'll agree to meet you.'

'Please contact the person as soon as possible, then let me know.' She rings off abruptly.

He is still staring blankly at the receiver when he realizes he should have taken this chance to ask her about the hidden black volumes. But what would she know about them? Campbell did not even glance at that bookshelf, nor give any other indication that she was aware of the strange texts Bernard Klamm had been collecting. Separated for thirty-eight years? Again, Jacob wonders exactly what she is not telling him about their marital relationship. Does it have anything to do with this apparent child abuse? he wonders. Briefly he considers that the elderly woman might now want to track down her husband's killer herself; after all, she has admitted that she still possesses some feelings for Bernard Klamm, despite their long separation. Is that not what she meant when she volunteered that perhaps some part of her did not ever want a divorce?

Jacob stoops to test a drawer of the bureau and realizes that this time the kitchen knife will not suffice. Without the keys currently held at the morgue, only a crowbar will do the job. He decides to take all twelve volumes back to the police station and examine the photographs in tandem with their photographic specialists and with people from the Child Protection Unit. He needs to know when and where they were taken, and how genuine the images are.

A part of him wishes for it all to be an artistic stunt, but he knows in his heart that those expressions of terror and hate, anger and despair—so grotesquely frozen by light and chemicals and paper, scream loudly about something else altogether.

9

6.45 a.m., 30 May 2004, Johannesburg

Harry Mason is sitting at the wooden table in their small kitchen, a mug of coffee steaming near at hand, a copy of *The Star* in front of him. Thirty-seven years of age, a widower and father of one, he is looking particularly dishevelled this morning. His blond hair stands up untidily in all directions, his chin resembles a bristle brush, and his eyes have dark bags of sleeplessness underneath them. While he was still in the police service, and before his wife Amy was killed, he kept himself fit and trim in the staff gym, but now a paunch has firmly established itself, and his tracksuit looks as threadbare as he feels.

With a huff of disaffection he tosses the newspaper to the other end of the table. The front page displays a picture of a white armoured cash-car overturned, heavily damaged after a high-speed crash in the Northern Cape. A separate box below shows the president warmly hugging Robert Mugabe during celebrations in honour of South Africa's ten years of democracy, while a news item about a year-old baby raped to death by an assailant trying to cure himself of AIDS fills the ex-detective with contempt for the current state of the world.

He stretches out a hand to stroke the table's wooden surface, a piece of furniture he crafted himself. When he quit the police four years earlier, he took what money he had saved and invested it in equipping himself for the only other skill he knew. It turned out, however, that there was more to the carpentry profession than just fashioning functional household furniture, and his enterprise had not gone too well. Soon he was forced to sell the first house he and his wife had owned, the one into which they had brought their new-born child. Now he and his daughter Jeanie live in a much smaller place in a much less fashionable neighbourhood, and he barely manages to keep her in the best school the neighbourhood has to offer. This morning's news is not the only thing upsetting him, for whichever way he twists and turns to make ends meet, he just keeps falling short every month.

Rubber soles squeak on the kitchen tiles behind him, as a pretty eight-year-old girl with short, curly blonde hair and striking green eyes leans her head against the doorframe. She is dressed in her school uniform: grey skirt, white collared shirt, and a bottle-green pullover. 'Dad,' she begins, in a voice barely more than a whisper.

Staring at his fingers still splayed over the table surface, he does not hear her.

'*Dad,*' Jeanie repeats, louder this time.

Harry turns around to look at his daughter. 'Oh. Yeah?'

'It's almost seven. I need to go to school.'

Harry stands up, scratching at the back of his head. 'Sure, all right.'

'Can Sam come over this afternoon?' she asks.

'No, I don't think today is good. You know how it is.'

She bites her lip, then tries again. 'We'll finish our homework before we go play, promise.'

'Uh-uh.'

Jeanie lowers her gaze. Then her expression brightens some. 'Can I go to her house, then? Will you take me there?'

'Honey, I've got a lot of work to do.'

Her face falls once again.

'Is that OK with you?' Harry tries to smile, but his face feels brittle. 'You understand, don't you?'

Jeanie nods, but nothing in her expression implies that she comprehends him.

'What about your breakfast?' he asks, thinking he can somehow make up for disappointing her by cooking an omelette, though he is not sure there are any eggs left in the fridge.

Jeanie merely shakes her head.

'You want some?' Harry clutches the back of his chair.

She shakes her head fast again, and goes back to her room to fetch her schoolbag. Harry is left staring after her, then sighs. He cannot remember when last they spoke to each other like two regular human beings rather than automata with limited vocabulary.

10

1.36 p.m., 30 May 2004, Johannesburg

The whine of a Black & Decker sander can be heard from the single garage Harry has specially refitted to accommodate his home-based carpentry shop. He has given his two employees, Petrus and Edian, the rest of the afternoon off, preferring to continue by himself—something he has been doing more and more, of late.

Working in faded jeans and a blue checked shirt, Harry has almost finished with a double bed featuring an elaborate headboard. Only its surfaces still need to be sanded smooth, the joints rounded, and a dark brown stain applied to the wood before a touch of varnish. As Harry pushes and pulls the sander evenly along a lengthy stretch of pine, his mind is elsewhere. Below his thick plastic safety goggles his mouth seems to quiver.

He has long since realized that he misses his detective work. For one, it was a lot more stimulating than this, even if frustrating at times. There was always that early-morning buzz of activity, the human interaction he now misses, the ideas, the jokes, the surprises. That look of damning comprehension in the eye of an apprehended suspect.

But most of all he misses Amy. The vacuum her death has left in his life has been almost unbearable.

Suddenly the sander screams angrily in protest. There is a sound of something tearing off and slapping against the wood.

'Fuck.' Harry tears off his goggles and turns the implement over. The sandpaper has got torn through, again.

'Problem, Harry?'

Harry looks up in surprise at the African man standing in the doorway, wrapped up in a colourful fleece jersey.

'Jacob, what the hell are you doing here?'

'Just checking up on my cupboards. They ready yet?' Jacob then grins at Harry, and they shake hands warmly.

Harry wipes sweat off his face. 'I told you they'd be ready on Friday.'

Jacob nods and surveys Harry's workshop. 'Looks a bit bigger in here; what did you do?'

'I sold off a few bits of equipment I didn't need,' Harry lies. He sold off a number of items he *did* need for the finer detail work.

'Where do you park your car now?' asks Jacob.

'In the driveway. Why?'

'You're not scared of it getting stolen?'

Harry shrugs. 'I lock the gate at night, and I'll be putting up some devil's fork fencing soon. What else can I do under the circumstances?' He takes Jacob by the shoulder and leads him out of the garage, across the garden that Jeanie does not play in any more, and into the house itself, feeling embarrassed by his former colleague's roaming eyes. In the kitchen he prepares some rooibos tea for Jacob, coffee for himself. They then move through to the living room, which is furnished with two large modern leather sofas that seem incongruent in their cramped surroundings. It is the same set of green furniture that Amy picked out for their first home.

'What's really brought you here when you should be at work? You're not the type to make casual social calls while you're on the job.'

'Yes, you're right,' Jacob laughs. 'But this time I am on the job.'

'So?' Harry picks up the television remote from the sofa arm and begins to turn it over in his hands. Since he quit smoking four years ago, after his wife died, he finds himself constantly fidgeting with all sorts of loose objects.

Jacob closely studies his friend's unshaven face. 'Harry, what would you say to undertaking some detective work again?'

'What?' Harry blinks a few times, the remote in his hand stopping dead.

'I might have some work for you, *real* work.' As if to emphasize his point, Jacob raises his gaze to a large crack in the living-room ceiling.

'I don't need handouts, Jacob. We're doing OK. I'll just need to keep my belt tight for a little longer.'

'That's not what I meant.' Jacob puts his mug down on the glass coffee table. 'I've—'

Harry holds up the remote. 'Jacob, before you start, I don't need to remind you why I quit the force.'

'You were good at your job.'

He shakes his head. 'That doesn't matter.'

'You're in trouble, Harry. I can see it.'

'Like I said, I don't need your sympathy.'

'You need to do something *constructive*, Harry. There's a lot of unfinished stuff standing out in that garage, stuff I saw in exactly the same state last time I was here. You're not getting anywhere.'

'I am.'

Jacob breaks eye contact with his former partner and resigns himself to a silent nod. Just then they hear the sound of a garden gate opening and closing, feet pattering over the short brick path towards the front door. It opens and Jeanie enters. For a moment she hesitates, then registers Jacob's widening smile, as her father's face crinkles in a sad but somehow grateful expression. Suddenly her eyes light up, then she bolts across the living room, calling out 'Hi, Jacob,' before disappearing down the passage towards her bedroom.

Turning surprised eyes on Harry, Jacob asks, 'And *that?*'

'She's going through a phase.' The remote control has begun to spin around in Harry's hand once more.

'What phase? She's only eight years old.' Jacob has previously been used to the child radiating happiness, always welcoming him with hugs.

'Give it a rest.'

Jacob raises an eyebrow. 'Give it a rest? There was a time when she clung to you so tight, nothing could shake her off your leg.'

'She's just growing up, I'm telling you. Her friends are probably saying it's not cool any more to hug her dad, or something.' Jacob stares down the corridor, towards Jeanie's room with its Avril Lavigne poster fixed to the closed door. *Whatever it is, that is not just a child growing up*, his expression seems to say. 'Trust me,' says Harry, 'the day you and Nomsa decide to have kids, you'll get to know what it's like.'

Deciding to let the matter drop, Jacob returns to the reason for his visit. 'Two days ago an elderly retired man was burnt to death in his home here in Johannesburg.'

'I read about it,' says Harry, setting the remote aside, 'but I'm not interested.'

'Just hear me out, that's all I'm asking. Afterwards you can go back to making cupboards for me, and furniture for your neighbours and relatives. We don't have a suspect yet, although Bernard Klamm was apparently a much-hated man. We've interviewed the housekeeper, her boyfriend, the neighbours, the garden service . . . the lawyer supervising his estate is being just as evasive as his estranged wife. From what I understand, he used to run some mines in the Northern Cape, where he also had a farm, before he was recruited by a large international company called Griqua Geological and Minerals Pty—or GGeM. He moved to Johannesburg in 1965, but went back to visit the farm regularly. It's unclear at this stage whether his death has anything to do with his former businesses, or whether it relates to something he got involved in after his retirement. Five framed photographs were taken from the scene of the crime, and apparently they all show a black man about twenty years younger than the victim. I don't know if they were removed to throw us off the trail, or whether they showed the killer himself and he wants to hide his identity. Miss Campbell—that's Klamm's estranged wife under her maiden name—seems to know this person but swears he's already dead.' Jacob pauses and shakes his head. 'That one, Campbell, is a strange woman. On the one hand I'm convinced she's hiding something from me, but on the other she wants me to find her a good detective.'

'And?' asks Harry.

'I only know one good detective right now who's not doing much in his spare time.' Jacob winks at his friend.

'Jakes, you must be joking. I'm not some seedy downtown private eye, with nothing to do but flirt with dames and slug back cheap whisky that I keep in my top drawer. I'm not a detective any more. I've got a daughter to look after and a business to run. Besides, you need a licence to work independently.'

Jacob finishes his tea and sits back, his face becoming unusually serious. 'Something bizarre is going on here, Harry, and if she gets someone else to do whatever work she wants done, I might miss out on a chance to see the whole picture. A hired hand could make a mess of this investigation before it gets started. According to some people I've talked to, Mr Klamm might as well not exist. I need to find out who he is, and what exactly he did for a living. Both he and his wife moved here from a place called Leopold Ridge. I can't go up there myself because the department hasn't got the money to send me that far without good reason. And I don't want to just hand this over to the Serious Crimes Unit; they've got their own troubles, anyway.' Jacob leans forward in his chair, and Harry echoes the movement. 'Campbell keeps badgering me about finding a detective as if her life depended on it. You've got to meet this woman: one minute she's in tears, the next she's bossing you around. I don't understand her. But she looks like she has a lot of money, and is prepared to spend it. So I can really use someone in Leopold Ridge who is on *my* side, someone I can trust—like yourself.'

Harry sits back and crosses one leg over the other. 'I seem to remember, the last time something really bizarre was going on, I lost my wife.'

'I remember, Harry, and I respect that. It's a difficult decision, I know, but I don't want *you* losing everything, either. This is a chance for you.'

A silence passes between them.

'So what's so weird about this case?' Harry asks.

Jacob sighs, with some relief, and sits back in his chair. 'First of all, I found out that Leopold Ridge is located east of Prieska, south of Upington, in the middle of nowhere. It's dry out there, except right down on the Orange River where it's fertile. There's lots of mining: chrome, diamonds—'

'Asbestos,' chips in Harry.

'Yes, that too. It's one of the poorest places in South Africa, and yet this Klamm guy looks to have been filthy rich. He owned a massive house in Parkview, a nice big BMW in the garage, a live-in housekeeper. He did not do too bad for someone who originated from a wasteland farm all those years ago. According to Campbell he was never a religious man, he even scoffed at religion, yet his bedroom now has a great big bible sitting in it, and his study is packed with books on esoteric religious practices.'

'What's so strange about that, then? Older people often turn to spiritual things as death closes in on them.'

'It may not be about religion.'

'Then what?'

From his notebook Jacob pulls a number of photographs and wordlessly hands them over. After a moment's hesitation, Harry takes them.

'What the hell is *this*?'

'Klamm had hundreds of these, of different girls—all of them, girls. I had them analysed. The range of photos, their quality and condition, suggests he has been taking them, or collecting them, over the last thirty years. He's got volumes of these.'

'How old was this guy?'

'Seventy-nine.'

'Are you asking me, then, to help solve the murder of a paedophile?'

Jacob shrugs. 'I don't know. We need to find out what these are, and what's happened to these girls.'

Harry hands the photos back to Jacob and begins to pace around his living room. 'Where were these pictures taken? Do you know?'

'We don't. There aren't any points of reference in them. All of the photographs are accompanied by shorthand notes, which I'm still trying to decipher. The books in his study mostly dealt with supernatural attacks, or religious cults. I don't really know what to make of it all yet.'

Harry shuffles through the images again. 'Why don't you ask his wife?'

'I've considered that, but I'd prefer to discover what this is all about before I talk to her again. For one, I don't want to badger an old lady with these horrible things if she is unaware of them, and, two, if she *does* know something, I would rather confront her when I'm sufficiently well-informed, because I have a feeling she is pretty good at manipulating people.'

'What does she think she needs a detective for, then?'

'I don't know.'

Harry rubs his mouth, unwilling to make eye contact with Jacob. 'Kids again, uh?' Their final case together had begun with the body of a young girl being found alongside a highway. By the end, many more people were dead, Harry's daughter kidnapped, his wife killed in a car crash. 'You're crazy if you think I'll do this,' he says firmly, despite the sense of exhilaration stirring in his guts, his mind already brimming with theories.

'There's one more thing.' Jacob fishes further photographs from his file. 'I went back to the victim's house again this morning, and searched around some more. I found these in a shoebox under the bed in the victim's bedroom, along with a blue plastic tiara.'

He hands Harry a folded sheaf of paper, inside which are three crumpled black and whites.

'Like a teenager keeping *Hustler* magazines in a secret place?' asks Harry, examining the images. The same girl, just about eight years old, is depicted in all three photographs. In one she is dressed in a tutu and wears a tiara. In another she is standing between two adults, a man and a woman.

'I just don't know for sure, but I reckon the woman in that particular photo looks like a very young Henrietta Campbell.' Jacob leans forward in his chair to point at the photograph now resting in Harry's hand.

'And this is their daughter?' Harry asks.

Jacob nods. 'I think so. But Campbell refused to talk about her to me.'

Harry turns the pictures around. On the back of one is printed, in blue ink, 1958. He hands the photos back to his ex-partner. 'Interesting.'

'So you'll do it?' probes Jacob.

'Now, just hang on. I didn't—'

Jacob raises his eyebrows and folds his hands together as if in prayer. 'Please, Harry?'

'My daughter is in *school*.' Harry now clutches the remote in front of him like a club. 'I can't just ditch her and my business to drive up to the Northern Cape.'

'We both know there is no business to speak of any more, Harry. And you can easily leave Jeanie with her grandparents for a week or so, can't you?'

Harry looks up sharply. 'I see little enough of her as it is.'

Jacob sighs as he pulls out his wallet. Fishing out a business card he places it on the coffee table next to his empty mug. 'Here is her number. I have to go now.'

Harry stares at the contact details, but does not react. Instead, he gets up and leads the way out to the low green gate set in a grey and unpainted concrete wall. Waving his friend goodbye, Harry turns round in time to glimpse Jeanie's bedroom curtain jerking shut.

11

3.13 p.m., 30 May 2004, Johannesburg

Harry drops the business card on the kitchen table and immediately grabs a beer from the fridge, twists off its lid and takes a long draught.

Fuck you, Jacob, he thinks in his friend's absence, though there is more confusion than anger underlying his thoughts. *I don't need this in my life.* Staring at the telephone number typed in green lettering, he takes another swig. The case has already stung him with interest, he knows that, but he can't, he *mustn't*, let it work any deeper into him; he has to pull the sting out. Finishing his first beer, he fetches out another one from the fridge before flopping down in front of the television, the work awaiting his attention in the garage all but forgotten.

Forget—that is all he can do. It would be stupid to decline Jacob's offer; after all, the work sounds interesting and the financial rewards promising. But he cannot accept it, either. He made Amy a promise, the same promise he has been making to his daughter every day for the past four years, and so the only option open to him now is to forget. Somehow, he needs to dismiss the conversation he just had with Jacob.

By the time he crawls into his single bed that night, mildly drunk, the now well-fingered note is lying on his bedside table, weighing heavily on his mind as he waits for sleep to come to him and lighten the burden. Even in the darkness, sleep refuses to take him and, instead, memories of Amy seem to float up from the floor. He remembers her disapproval of his homicide work, how the few police social gatherings they attended together always made her uncomfortable. It was obvious from the outset that she attended these for his sake alone. She hated him endangering his own life this way and socializing with people she thought of as rough thugs. In the end, ironically, it was her life, not his, that was taken. If only he had listened to her, she might still be alive today.

But there's Jeanie, says a voice in his head. *And you're the only one there for her now.*

It has become so difficult of late to remember the mother of his child. What did she smell like? The texture of her hair? He can remember the exact colour of her eyes but not the feel of her skin under his open palm. Some days he seems to remember a particular smile she had, but that may not be a true memory, but a second-hand impression from the photograph kept in his study.

Harry rolls over on his side. The white business card glows faintly but persistently in the darkness of his room. What would Amy say if she saw them now? What would she say if she could see the way her daughter is living? Would she still hate the detective work offered to him? He sits up in bed and switches on the lamp. Rubbing at his nose, he studies Campbell's details. Harry remembers how Amy loved him and Jeanie, both. To put himself in danger now would be a betrayal of that memory, and of the promise he made over her grave.

Scrunching up the card, he throws it into the wastebasket.

12

7.50 a.m., 31 May 2004, Johannesburg

'*Baas* Harry, I cannot work for you any more.' Edian, a man in his fifties with a scraggy greying beard, keeps fumbling with his hat held in front of his chest. Harry has on numerous occasions tried to dissuade the man from calling him *baas*, which comes too close to servility for his liking, but his efforts to get him to call him just plain 'Harry' have resulted in this hybrid.

'Why, what's happened?'

Edian tries on his hat as if to see if it fits properly, then quickly takes it off again. 'It just looks like you need to lay us off soon, so I must make plans now. I *have* made plans.' Harry's other worker, Petrus, is meanwhile standing outside the garage, scuffing at the hardened ground with one boot. His breath exhales a thick fog on this freezing Monday morning.

'What gave you that idea? I'm not going to lay you two off.'

'Then why you keep sending us home early more and more? No, *baas*, this job is not making you money, and when you not making money, you then get rid of staff. That's the way it is. I *know* it—I've been there, *baas*. I know you a good man, and maybe you struggling to say it. That's why I'm making it easy for you, *baas* Harry.'

That was indeed how Harry had picked up Edian to begin with. Before he began working here he had been a skilled worker for a Timber City branch out in Randburg, but retrenchments there had put him out on the street. He had then been forced to advertise his carpenting skills by holding up a handful of woodwork tools to drivers passing by on Main Street every morning.

'Jesus, Edian, don't do this to me. I wasn't planning to lay either of you off. I just needed some time on my own occasionally. You're still getting your salary, aren't you?'

'I'm sorry, *baas* Harry, but I already get a better job.' Edian nervously looks over his shoulder for support from Petrus. 'They pay me more; they give me the medical aid. It's a good one.'

Harry turns his gaze to the other man with his back turned to the conversation as though he has no part in it. 'Petrus too?'

'*Ja*, we both get the same job.'

Harry nods reluctantly. 'Where are you going?'

Edian puts his hat on again, adjusting it for a second time, as if buying himself a few seconds before he answers. 'The Timber City.'

'In Randburg?' Harry smiles wryly. 'After they fired you the last time?'

Edian shrugs. 'New management and everything.'

Petrus glances back at them furtively before returning to his contemplation of the frost on Harry's lawn.

'When do you want to leave? Are you giving me any notice, or is this it?'

Edian kicks at some sawdust piled at his feet. 'They said we could have today to sort things out. If we are not there tomorrow, the work will go to someone else.'

Harry shakes his head. 'Wait here, and I'll fetch the money I owe you. I'm sorry to see the two of you go.'

Edian does not reply to that, though Petrus mumbles noncommittally as Harry passes him on his way out of the garage.

He makes it as far as the study before throwing a wild punch that smashes into the closed paper-thin door, denting it. Swearing loudly, he boots it open. He barely resists sweeping everything off his desk, and forces himself to take a few calming breaths.

Amy smiles at him from a golden frame standing next to an outdated computer. There, she is dressed in a simple flowing white summer dress, a diamond glittering from the necklace encircling her throat. He remembers the day that photograph was taken—just a year after they were married. To celebrate their anniversary, they drove out to a bird park in Krugersdorp. There they stopped to watch the birdman who would whistle bars of Strauss's 'Blue Danube' to the pair of endangered blue cranes under his care. The elegant birds, with feathers ranging from white through silver and grey-blue in colour, would synchronously flap their wings and leap into the air, while their keeper danced around their enclosure pretending to conduct the music with his rugged hands, as if he were the famous composer himself.

Harry unlocks the right-hand bottom drawer and counts out the money he owes his two workers from a small green cash box. Replacing this in its hiding place, he spontaneously reaches out to touch the framed photograph of his wife. With a sudden burst of energy he hurries from the room, a weighty decision having been made in this fleeting moment.

13

10.53 a.m., 2 June 2004, Johannesburg

Dainfern, Stapleford Avenue, number fifteen. 11.30 a.m., sharp. That is what the man had said when they spoke on the phone. He has never been here before—Dainfern, a reserve for the filthily rich, a veritable playground for racehorse owners, polo players and weekend yachting captains of the Hartebeespoort dam. Driving along William Nichol Drive and swinging down Fourways Boulevard, he eventually approaches the expansive security estate from the south. The place, when he reaches it, is a doll house built in crude imitation of a Tuscan village. It has always surprised him that the richer the rich become, the more homogeneous they become. He may as well now be heading for Siena, the only difference being that the residential estate sprung up in the twenty-first century, in a valley, not on a postcard hilltop—while, in the distance, a huge glittering sewer pipe bisects a horizon that features not abandoned castles and olive groves but dry veldt and squatters' camps.

At the boom gate Harry Mason is interrogated by a man in a crisp green security uniform while cameras fixed on stalks of metal eye him like he is a snake entering the Garden of Eden. A call needs to be put through to number fifteen before he is allowed to pass with precise directions of which way to go. Driving along the manicured avenues, Harry wonders if Henrietta Campbell will have expected him to dress up for their coming appointment. Though number fifteen is built of terracotta-coloured brick, in design it veers considerably from the standard nouveau-Tuscan look. Its double-storey structure is more reminiscent of Spanish architecture, with its patios and black decorative ironwork, portcullises separating living spaces.

Harry feels apprehensive as he approaches the front door, doubting whether he wants to go through with this after all. He badly needs a cigarette to calm his nerves, a craving he has not experienced in ages. A brass plaque above the doorbell reads: TOBIAS REES ARCHITECT. Harry presses the button but hears no corresponding ring from within the house. Scuffing his shoes on the welcome mat, he makes sure his soles are clean enough before he enters this luxurious residence.

Abruptly, the intercom comes alive with static, and a man's voice speaks up, 'Mr Mason, I'll be with you shortly.'

Harry is just about to reply when he hears a loud click and the microphone falls silent again. He is forced to wait a full five minutes before the door finally swings open. The man blocking the entrance seems to register great surprise at finding him there on the doorstep, as if he is a prodigal son returned. Tobias Rees then stretches his hand out in a gesture, not of friendliness, Harry thinks, but well-practised and businesslike affability. His age hovers somewhere in the seventies, with a mane of frosted hair combed back, and blue eyes that glint like a raptor's. The man is stereotypically dressed in a range of Lacoste: loafers, chinos and a blue and cream striped polo shirt. He folds his other hand over Harry's as they still shake hands, a gesture the ex-detective has always found distasteful because he has never met an honest man who confirms a handshake that way.

'Good to meet you, Detective Mason. Is that the right term?' Rees continues to hold on to Harry's hand, even though they have stopped shaking.

'Harry will do fine,' he replies, as his eyes wander over Rees's shoulder and take in the house's interior.

'Fine, fine, won't you come in?' Rees steps aside and holds out his arm welcomingly until Harry is past him, then brings the same hand down on Harry's shoulder. 'Henrietta will be with us in a moment. She is not feeling too well after this news about Bernard.'

'Oh?' Harry takes his jacket off and drapes it over his arm. 'You knew him on a first-name basis?'

'Of course.' Rees laughs dismissively. 'When one reaches a certain age one can put aside childish things, as they say, and in our case the boisterous jealousy of our youth receded. Over the years we continued to move in the same circles, though never quite on the friendliest of terms—I won't lie to you. Can I take that from you?'

Harry holds up his jacket. 'No, thanks, it's fine where it is.'

'Suit yourself. Follow me.' Rees again holds out his hands like a traffic warden. The way the man pronounces his s's reminds Harry of a bee trapped in a bottle.

The guest trails after him across the hallway and down three steps leading into the skylight-lit living room. A large television is tuned to a rugby match between France and Australia and, beyond, a sliding door stands open, overlooking a small patch of garden. Two coffee mugs sit on the table, and a Margaret Atwood novel rests on one of the empty cream-coloured couches. The room smells like a mixture of baby powder and lavender.

They continue to the den, which is up another three steps and separated from the living room by a sliding glass door. Rees is clearly a fisherman, for a stuffed trout is mounted on the wall above a display of lures and a drinks cabinet filled with various whiskies. A number of tomes on architecture adorn a wide shelf next to a draughtsman's sketching table. Rees begins firing questions at Harry about his years in the police service, while proceeding to fix them each a single malt, straight up, without asking if his visitor even wants one.

'Cheers.' Rees hands Harry his drink and seats himself in a plush brown chair, indicating for Harry to do likewise. 'I suppose you know why you are here?'

'Actually, I don't.' Harry sits down, too, but does not make himself comfortable, the drink remaining untouched in his hand. 'I know that Miss Campbell wants me to take a drive up to the farm Mr Klamm owned, and take a look around.'

'That's all?' Rees raises his eyes. 'I assumed that police officer Henrietta has been in contact with would have spelled things out to you more clearly by now.'

'No one has yet, and frankly I like it that way. I'm a bit old-fashioned in preferring to hear it straight from the horse's mouth.'

A smile twitches at the corner of Rees's mouth, as if the suggestion of his life partner as a horse amuses him. Though Rees's skin is heavily dappled with liver spots, Harry figures the architect is still handsome, with a sharp, noble nose, dark eyebrows, and gentle crowsfeet around the eyes. The sly alertness in his gaze, however, makes him seem rather shifty and unappealing.

'I want you to find my missing daughter.' The voice Harry hears is unsteady but nevertheless forceful. At the sliding glass door stands a woman, dressed formally in a navy-blue jacket and trousers, white silk blouse, her hair styled roughly like an onion—bulbous around the ears and tapering up to a point above the crown.

Harry jumps up and sticks out his hand. 'Ma'am.'

'Aah,' says Rees, remaining seated. 'The lady of the house. I was under the impression you two had already spoken, Henrietta.'

Campbell allows Harry to shake her hand, while shooting Rees a look that is difficult to gauge. 'No, we haven't met.' Seeing that no other chair is in the room, and realizing that Rees is not about to give up his own seat, Harry gestures for her to sit down in his place. He sets the untouched glass of whisky down next to a cartographer's globe. 'Thank you,' mutters the elderly woman as she settles into the chair he vacated. 'I wanted to talk with you in person, see what kind of a man you are.'

'Your daughter is missing?'

She nods, staring fixedly at the floor. 'Has been for thirty-nine years, detective. Her name was Claudette. She was only nineteen when she disappeared, in the autumn of sixty-five.'

Harry's heart sinks at the news. He had hoped this would be something routine that he could wrap up in a week before Jeanie missed him too much. But a cold case? From thirty-nine years ago? Out of the corner of his eye he notices Rees steeple his fingers and observe them both intently.

'Did the police not come up with anything at the time?'

'They are the very reason why she is still missing,' says Campbell.

'If she hasn't surfaced after thirty-nine years, I fear it's almost certain that she is long dead.'

Her eyes flash with abrupt anger. 'Of course I've *considered* it,' she says irritably. 'In fact I agree that is most likely the case. What I want you to do is find out what happened to her—and, if possible, find her remains.'

'There's a good chance I won't find anything.'

'You come highly recommended, Harry,' interjects Rees. 'Surely you're not giving up so easily?'

'There are other private investigators with more experience of dealing with cold cases, as we call them.'

'Are you turning down our offer, then?' A smile of victory seems to creep over Rees's lips.

'No, I'm not,' Harry replies, bridling. 'I'll look into it, but I want you to be aware that picking up a trail this old is very difficult work, and it can also get quite expensive.'

'Cost isn't a concern,' says Campbell. 'I'm nearing the end of my life, and my only child is still missing.'

Rees interjects. 'Yes, well, cost may—'

'For *years*,' Campbell raises her voice to re-establish dominance, 'I let the matter lie, pretending I could move on, hoping that the pain would subside—but it still hasn't gone away. Tobias has been wonderful in that way, but no amount of his affection can erase the loss of my daughter.' She glances at her partner, but the smile that should accompany such warm sentiments does not appear. 'And now, with Bernard dead—murdered, it seems—those events of sixty-five are coming back to haunt me all over again. This can't go on; it just can't.'

'When exactly was the last time you saw your daughter?'

'It was the third of August, nineteen sixty-five,' says Campbell. 'I'd better fetch something for you; it should make things clearer.' Groaning slightly as she gets up from her chair, the woman totters from the room, leaving Harry alone with the hawkish Rees once more.

'I'd appreciate it if you could deal with this matter as quickly as possible,' says Rees. 'The sale of that farm will earn us a bit of money, and would close a difficult chapter in her life, but she won't go through with it until she knows what happened out there. I suspect she'll exhaust every avenue, and I suppose every cent to her name, finding her daughter or discovering what happened to her. If you're any sort of decent man, you'll not take advantage of her desperation.'

'You don't necessarily need a detective for this,' replies Harry. 'Some good counselling can be very beneficial for those who've lost a loved one, or so I'm told.'

Rees leans forward. 'I want to see that place sold and out of our lives. This is the only way that Henrietta will do it.'

Campbell steps back into the room, an A4 scrapbook clutched to her chest. She sits down, opens it on her lap, and turns it round to face Harry. On the left page is a large black and white photograph of a young woman resembling the girl in the photographs Jacob showed him three days before. Her hair is straight and black, her eyes dark pools of mystery. A bitter, disinterested smile is frozen on her face. On the right is a newspaper clipping from the *Prieska Herald* that screams,

CAUTO FOUND GUILTY OF RAPE AND MURDER

There is a blurry photo of a young African staring defiantly at the camera. His face is badly bruised. A caption reads:

Judge Visagie rules not enough evidence for death penalty

'José Cauto was one of Bernard's more trusted labourers,' says Campbell. 'Until he seduced our daughter.'

Taking the scrapbook from the older woman, Harry scans the article. 'If this man was found guilty of the rape and murder of your daughter, why are you now talking to me? Isn't the case closed?'

'I don't know what passed between my child and that man, but I don't believe it was rape . . . not any more. The night Bernard found out about them, he went after Cauto. My daughter tried to warn the man. It ended with Bernard torching that black's shed and beating him within an inch of his life for interfering with our Claudette. I find it hard to believe that the pig would have had strength enough to stand up after that, much less kill my daughter.'

Shocked by the callous indifference in her voice, Harry concentrates on the article in front of him as Campbell relates to him her version of the story. Cauto was given a life sentence despite the lack of a body and any eyewitnesses. 'How exactly was it proven that he raped and killed your daughter?' he asks when the woman finishes.

'My husband was a powerful man in the area, Mr Mason. The mayor of Prieska would invite us to dinner every Tuesday, the magistrate and the state prosecutor were our frequent houseguests, and I even knew the defence lawyer from Kimberley—he'd been in our social set, too. Bernard was well respected in those days, despite his ruthlessness in business dealings. For years we owned the only American-made sedan in the area, and Bernard was the only man in the whole district to regularly fly on trips overseas. In short, he was considered a figure of the highest status and everyone wanted to associate with him. If he really wanted to get rid of someone, he could have managed it; and if it was merely a black who was both arrogant enough to touch a white girl in those days, much less *his* daughter, people were even happier to help him bend the law. That Cauto was lucky to even make it to trial.'

'Why haven't you shown this to detective Tshabalala?'

'I . . . I was afraid . . .'

Harry tilts his head. 'Afraid of what?'

'I was standing there in the room where the father of my child was killed! And I couldn't very well describe to a *black* detective what my husband had done. Whether Cauto was innocent or not was not my concern. I myself was *disgusted* by what that black did to my daughter. Even if there weren't segregation laws, it wasn't right. God did not mean for us to cross racial boundaries. That Cauto nearly destroyed our family name, and we would've been ruined if something drastic hadn't been done. I know I should feel remorse for what Bernard did to the Mozambiquean, but I don't. He defiled an innocent girl we raised to become a debutante. She was lost the moment he laid his paws on her.'

'Have you considered that she might've committed suicide?'

'Yes, of course.' Campbell sighs irately. 'But a body was never found. I must admit, though, that the farm was never properly searched, either, and it was large, by all accounts. She might also have run away, of course, but where to, without taking a car? All I know is that Claudette disappeared without a trace.'

'If Cauto didn't kill her, then who else do you think might have done it?'

Campbell stares at Harry, her head shaking from long-pent-up emotions. Abruptly, her controlled posture deflates. 'Bernard. I can only think of Bernard.'

'Your husband?'

'Oh, I don't know!' Campbell suddenly slaps her thighs, jumps up. 'He was so angry that night he could've done anything. It's the reason we broke up; I just couldn't trust him any more, not after witnessing what he was capable of. He kept trying to convince me that it *was* Cauto who did it, and that he himself had just hurried justice along a bit. But I couldn't quite believe him even then, and we've been arguing about it for thirty-nine years. What did happen to her? Where is she now? In all that time I would sometimes believe him when he declared his innocence; other times I'd be convinced he was just lying to me, as he did on so many other occasions. The loss of one's child, without closure—it wrecks your entire life, Mr Mason. Last Tuesday, he and I were talking about the sale of that bloody farm. Once we again began talking about what had happened that terrible night, I lost my temper *again*. I couldn't . . . I can't let it go. Not then, not this time.'

Rees holds out a hand. 'Calm down, Henrietta.'

'Don't you tell me to calm down, Tobias. Claudette deserved better in life, better than that damned kaffir, better than her father—and, yes, maybe better than me!'

'She wasn't the most sta—'

'Don't you say it!'

'Henrietta—'

'You never knew her! Don't you *dare* say anything about her.' Rees is about to continue saying something, when she cries. '*Don't!*'

A stand-off silence ensues, the two glowering at each other.

The floorboard creaks as Harry shifts uncomfortably on it. 'Is this José Cauto still alive?'

Still glaring at Rees, Campbell answers. 'He went to prison very soon after Claudette disappeared. I didn't care to hear about him after that.'

'Is he the man you remembered from one of those missing photographs?' asks Harry.

'Yes.' She turns to face Harry. Once she takes her angry gaze off him, Rees springs up to pour himself another whisky. The bottle neck clanks hard against the crystal. 'It's him all right; he had a scar on his cheek. He always used to smile like he didn't have a care in the world.'

'How old would he be now?' Harry asks.

'In his sixties, I should think.'

'Do you know to which prison they sent him?'

'I really didn't care at the time, and I never tried to find out later. I just wanted to stay as far away from that man, or any thought of him, as possible.'

Harry nods. 'Can I borrow this?' He holds up the scrapbook.

Campbell sighs with relief. 'Does that mean you'll accept the case?'

'I'll take it, ma'am, but only if you're prepared to fully cooperate with me. And I'll tell you this straight up: Detective Tshabalala is a good friend of mine, so what I know, he knows. That's going to be the way I work. If you've got a problem with that, we call it quits now.'

'Can you solve this business by the end of the month?' asks Rees after gulping down a mouthful of liquor. 'I only ask because Henrietta here is under a lot of strain.'

The woman glances sharply at him, her expression filled with contempt.

'I can't make you any promises,' replies Harry.

Outside, he is unlocking his car door when Rees appears uncomfortably close behind him. The architect has already given him directions to the farm in the Northern Cape as well as details of its current occupants. 'Wish I knew what the place looks like these days, but I've only ever seen the photos Henrietta has shown me. I'd appreciate it if you could tell me a bit more about what's up there. Henrietta is holding off estate agents and surveyors until you've wrapped up your investigation, but it would be nice to get an idea of what kind of property we're dealing with.'

He pauses, then continues in a quieter voice. 'We're offering you seven thousand rand for the week. I'll arrange in advance that you stay at the farmhouse itself because that's where your investigations will surely start. The hicks looking after the place will just have to make do with you, and if they complain, I'll just toss them off the property. I certainly won't be as easy on them as Klamm was. That man went soft in his old age—don't know why. Used to be one hell of a businessman, even if he was an arse-hole.'

Harry slams the car door shut and winds down his window to study care-fully this man who is all of a sudden trying to pass himself off as everyone's favourite uncle. He cannot yet decide whether it is Rees's arrogance or his oily manner that determines Harry not to be manipulated by this architect.

'Ten thousand and I'll do it.'

'Don't you think that's a bit steep?' Rees's shark-like smile freezes on his face.

'I don't know what it is, Rees, but you're up to something. I can smell it on you like the sulphur on Lucifer's breath. Don't play nice guy with me; I don't take to it well. If I find out you're setting me up, there'll be hell to pay.'

Rees's politeness evaporates. 'No need to get cross with me, Mason. I'm not a gangster, nor am I a murderer. I'm merely looking out for the woman I love, who just happened to marry the worst cunt I've ever met, and likely will ever meet. Ten thousand is fine, but you better find something useful for that kind of money.'

'That entirely depends on what kind of a chase you're sending me on,' replies Harry.

14

1.12 p.m., 2 June 2004, Johannesburg

'Harold, are you sure you want to do this?' Only Harry's mother calls him by his baptismal name. Joan Mason's British accent is still strong, despite twenty-five years of living here in South Africa. She is still attractive at sixty-one: skin still glowing with health, fair and silken hair, blue eyes glittering with occasional defiance.

The afternoon sun is hot enough to keep mother and son sitting on the shaded porch of her cottage rather than out in the garden where water from the sprinklers rustles amid the well-kept foliage. Large coffee mugs stand on a small square table between them. Harry's father passed away nearly a decade ago, but his retired mother keeps going strong, maintain-ing the house with the help of a housekeeper and gardener. Harry has stopped by his mother's place on his way back from his encounter with Campbell and Rees, to see whether she would mind looking after Jeanie for a week. It would either have to be her or Amy's parents taking his daughter in for a week.

'The money is good,' replies Harry, 'and the job sounds straightforward.'

'But?'

'I'm not quite sure what it is, Mum. It's difficult to place.' His British accent is amplified whenever he is in his mother's presence, as if he is still scared of her correcting his language the way she did throughout his schooling. 'The wife wants me to drive up there and find out what happened to her daughter; her partner, however, seems to have something else up his sleeve. In my opinion, he seems overly interested in the property itself.'

'And?' Joan Mason's arms are crossed stiffly in an intimidating posture that fits naturally with her wiry frame.

'I don't like walking into something I don't have some control over. Besides, a week is a long enough time to leave Jeanie here with you.'

'*Rubbish.*' His mother frowns. 'I'm up for it, and the girl surely is too. It's about time you took on a decent job again. I've been worrying about you constantly lurking in that garage of yours, hiding behind all that unfinished wood like a lost termite. Don't you worry about Jeanie. It'll do the girl good to get out of that house of yours.'

'Jesus, mother,' says Harry. 'Any particular reason why you're gunning for me like this?'

'No need for that talk. You've been sulking long enough, and for no reason at all. We all loved Amy very much, but to suddenly drop off the deep end again is unacceptable when you have a daughter dependent on you. It's been four years now—four years in which your daughter's needed you more than Amy has.'

'Don't talk like that,' growls Harry. 'I've been taking care of Jeanie as best I can. It's just . . . I get these days when I miss Amy badly. Some days it's worse than others. It's just been a string of the worse ones, lately.'

His mother sighs and looks away. 'Have you asked Jeanie what she thinks of all this business?'

'I didn't want to talk to her about it until I decided whether to take the job or not.'

Joan takes a biscuit from the plate, taps it on the rim of her mug and bites into it. 'Of course you're taking this job,' she says. 'I can see it in your eyes. But it sounds to me like you want to inform her of your decision without discussing it with her first. She is old enough to have a say, you know. Why don't you take her along with you?'

'What?' Harry looks up from a paradise flower he has been contemplating through the *stoep*'s balustrade. 'Mum, this woman's husband was just killed by some pyromaniac who may or may not come from Leopold Ridge. How can you even ask me that? I'm about to start looking for a girl that's gone missing thirty-nine years ago, so when am I going to have the time to mind Jeanie?' He does not mention the unnerving photographs Jacob showed him three days before.

His mother shrugs with a lopsided smile. 'Oh, Harry, I'm just testing you! You *could* spend some more time with her, though. She needs it.'

'She's growing up, that's all.' Harry's attention now darts towards a hoopoe landing on the yellowing lawn. 'I told you that before.'

'Harold . . .' Joan reaches across the table and takes hold of her son's chin. She softens her tone. 'Look at me. I know when a child is hurting, perhaps better than most mothers do. And Jeanie *is* hurting. It's unnatural for a girl her age to stop smiling and talking to people. She's only eight, not eighteen.'

Unbidden anger rises from deep inside him. He turns his head so that his chin slips free from his mother's grasp. 'What happened to me has nothing to do with Jeanie.'

'You don't need me to draw parallels for you.' Her voice grows sterner in reaction to his rejection of her touch. 'And you also don't need me to warn you that her father's sudden disappearance for a week isn't going to make things any better between the two of you.'

'She'll understand.'

'Will she?' Joan's face darkens. 'Someone of her age just doesn't understand the complexities of securing a good income, and therefore the necessity of work. All she understands is that her father has cut her loose without telling her why, and is now going to go off and leave her when she needs him most. Jeanie was as affected as you by Amy's death, perhaps even more than we are aware of. You had better keep that in mind.'

Harry pushes his chair back and gets up to lean against the railing, staring out into the garden. 'What exactly do you expect me to do? I've been working around the clock to make ends meet, and now that an opportunity has cropped up to earn in one week what I previously earned in two months, you decide to lecture me about my obligations. I *know* what they are; I just haven't had the time.'

His mother begins to collect the used dishes from the table. 'Harry, I never said you are a bad father. I know the opposite is true, but it's easy to lose track of friends and family when you're preoccupied. You've got a habit of shutting up under stress. Amy let you get away with that, but don't do it now with Jeanie.'

Harry maintains a long silence. 'I'll take her to Zoo Lake, speak with her. It's all right, then, if you look after her for a week?'

A hand touches his shoulder. 'Of course it is, my boy. Of course it is. Just make sure she *understands* what you're doing, and why.'

15

9.16 a.m., 3 June 2004, Johannesburg

Detective Sergeant Ben Tudhope is a stocky man in his late twenties with mouse-brown hair and bright brown eyes. His physique, like an up-ended triangle perched atop two stilts, suggests that he works his upper body daily at the gym. He might have been considered attractive, if the slant of his eyes did not make him look perpetually tired and bored.

'Look, Tshabalala, I fucked up. I'll say it so you can hear it clearly, all right?'

Tudhope is casually leaning against one of the stuffed armchairs in Klamm's study, letting uninterested eyes wander aimlessly around the room. Barely listening to his partner's excuses, Jacob pulls out the set of Klamm's keys retrieved from the morgue, and sets to work on the locked drawers.

'The court date was set several months in advance,' replies Jacob over his shoulder, 'and the prosecutors badly needed that paperwork. There's no point collecting the evidence if you can't get it ready for court.'

'For the millionth time, I'm sorry the fucking docket was late to court— and it won't happen again. My point, though, still is what the hell do these lawyers know about *our* lives? They're not half as overworked as we are, right? So where's their gratitude? Fuck that, man; have they ever been shot at? Have they ever climbed in and out of the wreckage of minibus taxis, collecting pieces of bodies? Sometimes I think those types don't even know what police work is. Charlton seems rooted to his office, like he hasn't budged from that chair in a million years, yet he's always complaining and moaning, pushing us for this or that. It's fucking tiring, man. That's all I'm saying.'

He pauses, as if in hope of Jacob throwing in his own complaints. When he sees that nothing is forthcoming, he continues. 'Jesus, I feel tired— didn't get to bed till four this morning. How 'bout you?'

As one of the drawers opens up, Jacob begins to flick through a neatly labelled row of red suspension files. 'Hmm?'

'You listening to me at all? I said I only got to bed at four last night. Met this blonde with titties like this.' He spreads his hands in front of his chest. 'How 'bout you? What did you do?'

'That's usually when I get up.'

'At four in the morning?'

'Quite often, yes.' Jacob is not inclined to tell Tudhope this is how he raises a little extra money to make ends meet. Every day, after breakfast, he and Nomsa collect a few neighbours and other acquaintances in the little Nissan *bakkie* he drives, before leaving Soweto to head into Johannesburg. On their way he drops off people at their respective workplaces, until he finally kisses Nomsa goodbye outside Hyde Park shopping mall, and begins the final leg of the journey to the office in Braamfontein. In the evening he does the same in reverse order, often not getting home till eight. If he is kept working late, he has to warn everyone to catch one of the irregular bus services or a crowded taxi.

'Please do me a favour later, will you, Ben?'

'*Ja*, sure, partner.'

'Can you please track down where that petrol container the killer used came from. I have a feeling it's not a standard make.'

'I'm on it.' Tudhope actually takes a notebook from his back pocket and makes a note.

To his relief, Jacob finds only old bills and invoices in the bureau drawers. He has been half expecting something similar to, if not worse than, the photographs he found in the locked bookcase compartment. He scans through the remainder of the files as he lifts them out of the drawers. Though these documents may later yield valuable clues, there is nothing that stands out as significant—except in one drawer he finds a long silver safe key.

'So, who's this guy Harry Mason thinks might be a suspect?' asks Tudhope.

'José Eduardo Cauto.' Jacob heads for the stairs, key in hand. 'According to Campbell, he was about seventeen when Klamm first took him in. He'd already worked on the gold fields, and Klamm became quickly impressed by him.'

'Seventeen? Then we're looking for someone, like, sixty years old?'

'Could be even older. They'd been working together for a number of years before the disappearance of the victim's daughter.'

'Fuck.' Tudhope laughs. 'We're tracking down some grumpy old man. Hey, listen, you coming tomorrow?'

'Tomorrow?'

'Yeah, the guys have decided to have a *braai* at Top Star.'

'The drive-in?' Jacob cannot stifle a laugh. 'It'll be freezing there.'

Near the city centre, atop an old mine tailing now covered in grass and paved with tar, the bleak and windy drive-in affords a spectacular view of the natural bowl in which the city lies.

Thinking that he has hooked his partner with this madcap idea, Tudhope bounds up the stairs after him. 'Yeah, like, it's mad, I know, but it'll be cool, man. I'm going, and I'll bring my new bird so you can meet her.'

'Not me,' says Jacob over his shoulder. 'It's definitely not for me. I've got better things to do than catch a cold while waiting for a burnt *wors* in a dry roll. Winter is just not the time to do these things.'

Jacob was quite surprised when Harry Mason called to say he had accepted the assignment, and even more so when his friend later passed him the scrapbook containing aged articles on José Cauto and his conviction. 'She couldn't talk to you about it,' was all Harry would say in response to Jacob's queries. 'Bit of a bitch, really. But here is your prime suspect, if he's still alive.'

Jacob has already requested the docket on Claudette Klamm's supposed murderer, but the internal mail system is notoriously slow, if such an old case file can still be located at all. When Jacob pulls open the closet, a smell of naphthalene almost punches him in the face. Brushing aside the covered suits hanging in front of the safe, Jacob inserts the long key.

'Whoa, look at that!' Tudhope steps up close behind Jacob's shoulder. 'What do you think he kept in there?'

'His wife thinks his rifle and pistols may be in here, perhaps his cameras. Let's have a look.' There is a resonant thud as steel bars slot back with the lever's twist. Jacob pulls the safe door open.

There is no rifle evident, but two pistols lie on the top steel shelf, above a collection of cameras and lenses. The third shelf down contains two bundles of fifty-pound bills, easily totalling more than ten thousand rand in cash. A passport lies next to the money. A single red album occupies the fourth and lowest shelf, drawing Jacob's attention. He slides it out and sees a childlike paper heart, coloured in rusty red crayon, has been stuck to the front of the book with words scrawled across it:

TO PAPA
with love,
CLAUDETTE

Tacked to the album is a slip of paper with the name Freddy Meyer and a phone number written on it. Behind the album, deep inside the safe, lies something else, and Jacob reaches in for it.

'What you got there, bru?' Tudhope presses closer to look over Jacob's shoulder.

The detective pulls out a furry white pullover, caked with soil and what looks like dried blood.

TWO

An Ambush on the Open Road

1

6.37 a.m., 7 February 2004, Groblershoop

The road was like a long black tongue rolled out over an endlessly flat landscape of dust and grass and dry foliage. The horizon was merely a haze, the sky the blue of dreams, light white clouds like a film of sleep in tired eyes. The only sound was of the sea trapped in a conch shell, and the drone of one distant engine.

The bottle green cash-car that eventually appeared bore the motif SE-CURITAS printed on its side in large white letters. This was not a heavily armoured vehicle, but a standard Hiace Toyota fitted with reinforced door panels, bulletproof windshield, and a steel cage secured inside its window-less rear. The scream of the vehicle's overtaxed engine reverberated against the walls of a pass, cut through the rock of a slight hill.

'Henk, you think they'll let us go early today, like they did last week?' asked the Griqua driver with yellowish skin and a lean face.

His partner, a man with red hair and a thick moustache took a sip of his Coke. '*Weet 'ie*, Dirkie, *weet 'ie.*' There was an R4 automatic rifle resting between his legs.

The driver reached out, fumbled with the air vents on the dashboard. '*Vokken* winter's coming and it's still so bloody hot. They could give us one of them cars with decent air-conditioning, you know, like they have in the cities.'

'*Ja.*' Henk's eyes were fixed on the road flying past under their wheels. 'You think you could slow down a bit?'

'You kidding me? I just told you it's too fucking hot in here, man. You not the *poephol* who sits in here baking his balls off all day, while you *blik-sems* jump in and out.'

'Fuck's that!' Henk grabbed the steering wheel and yanked it a hard left, as something large, beige and upright ran across the road, trailing a line of . . .

Four explosions shook the car a split second before it tipped. Dirkie bellowed in surprise, and from the rear of the vehicle there was a shrill, 'Wha—?'

Travelling at a hundred and sixty kilometres an hour, with all four of its tyres blown out, the car cleared the road surface as it flipped over. The three astonished security guards experienced suspension as time slowed for them and the world tilted. Then they hit the tarmac, broadside.

The impact smashed Henk's head against the passenger window, dislocating his left shoulder and snapping three vertebrae in his neck. He was dead in an instant. Chunks of metal were torn from the side of the vehicle and turned into shrapnel. The roof was ripped open, roll bars imploding, till the vehicle finally slid over into a ditch, a cloud of dust rising from the spot where it came to rest.

Forty-five minutes later, a farmer pulled up in his truck, to shoo away the vultures already picking at a mutilated body which had been dragged clear of the breeched cage in the cash-car's rear.

THREE

La raison du plus fort est toujours la meilleure
The reason of the strongest is always the best
Jean de la Fontaine

1

10.05 p.m., 26 October 1992, Thokoza

Outside, the night was listening. He could hear it holding its breath: no dogs barking, no one strolling along the street, nothing stirring but the crickets sawing their legs together and vermin scratching around in the bullet-pocked dustbins of Khumalo Street. The night's carefully held breath was like the moment of expectancy before the next lash falls across a naked back.

Then Sheik Kheswa could hear Bongile pissing in the neglected garden outside. He glanced out through the broken window to see the vague silhouette of his comrade, the shadowy grey beanie perched high up on his head his most recognizable feature. Beyond the garden wall a streetlight glowed, as yet undamaged by the violence, a lonely orange halo in the dead of night. The bare-brick house itself was completely dark and cold, even though it was already late October and summer well on its way. Embers were dying in a five-litre paint can they used for cooking and the living room had a strong chemical smell to it that gave him a headache. Having grown up in Thokoza, Sheik never thought he would ever hear a township this quiet.

A match flared in the darkness behind him, briefly illuminating the trashed living room. The cloying smell of *dagga* assaulted his nose momentarily, as Matthews took a deep drag from the fifth joint they had skinned that night. Holding his breath, he held it out to Sheik.

'You think they'll come out tonight?' asks Matthews in Tswana. His voice sounded young, that of a fifteen-year-old, floating nonchalantly somewhere between bored and stoned.

Sheik took a deep drag, retained the smoke in his lungs as he stared at the cherry tip. After twenty seconds he exhaled, took another hit, and handed the rest to Kgabo, who was sitting on the fake leather sofa in front of a blank TV.

'If they don't come out tonight we go to them, easy.' Sheik sucked on his dried-out tongue with a loud smacking sound. 'They have to be driven back into their pens, those Zulus.' He was large for his twenty years, tall, strong and overweight. His eyes sat too close together, and fuzz sprouted from his chin. Sheik's ears were abnormally small for such a large head, but he could hear better than most.

Matthews snapped his fingers twice. 'Tonight, man—tonight I'm going to hit my first *mdlwembe*, right fucking here.' He indicated a point between his eyes. A month ago, some of the hostel-dwelling gold miners had snatched his brother off the street and accused him of lynching one of their own. He had disappeared into the fortified hostel called Mshaya'zafe, meaning 'beat him to death' in Zulu. His mutilated corpse turned up a few days later in an open stretch of veldt south of Ulundi—the area of Thokoza now controlled by migrant Zulu workers, and named after their people's capital in Kwazulu-Natal.

Kgabo, who still tried to go to school once in a while, and was good with a pennywhistle flute, took a noisy swig from a bottle of Mainstay cane they had confiscated from Tannie Tamasane in return for protection. That Shona bitch seemed to have momentarily forgotten who they were, and had at first refused to pay tribute to the members of the Bad Boys gang. What did she know of being a young warrior, of being a comrade, a brother in arms? People like her, living safely to the west of the no-man's-lands, did not always fully understand the services Sheik's comrades rendered the community in these difficult times. The police certainly did not manage to contain the marauding migrant workers, so when tributes were not readily forthcoming from people like Tannie Tamasane, supplies for maintaining the defence of the community sometimes had to be taken by force. She had argued they had no right to anything, since they had nothing to do officially with any of the community self-defence units that had sprung up when the trouble first began; she had even dared to tell them they were nothing but *tsotsis*, and that their mothers should be ashamed of them. But after the details had been explained to her in a way that anyone could understand, she had readily agreed she was wrong and they were right.

Bad boys, bad boys . . . Sheik hummed this refrain as he ruminated over the incident. Yes, Tannie finally saw it their way. With a wipe of her broken lip and a tooth lying in the dust, she had got up and fetched Sheik and his coms a good supply of booze, enough to last them a day or two. She had always been the brightest of the *shebeen* queens.

Bongile scuffed the kitchen doorstep coming in. If the *zol* had not taken some of the edge off their nerves, his comrades inside the room might have been startled, and even shot him by mistake. As it was, he smiled and told them they were fucking selfish bastards. 'Look how you wait till I'm outside, admiring the view, before you light up. I could kill the whole lot of you bastards.' He drunkenly waved his *kwash* at them in the darkness. The zip gun—a steel pipe, with tightly bound rubber strips and nail doubling as a firing pin—could fire only one bullet at a time. It was a crude weapon, liable to misfire, even explode, but many of the youths fighting the present 'war' used them.

A string of sounds like firecrackers going off erupted in the distance. It was an exchange of gunfire. The coms looked at each other, their expressions all saying the same thing: the Zulu dogs were coming out.

The TV explained it was black-on-black violence, black parties jostling for political power in the build-up to South Africa's first democratic elections. Sheik knew differently. He had seen the *umlungus*, their faces painted black like Africans, stalking through Thokoza: white instigators shooting community members and supplying the Inkatha Zulus with weapons in their hostels. He had seen women screaming for help and pleading before the advance of the Casspirs—those huge armoured personnel carriers of the South African Police Force—as their men and children lay dead or bleeding in the streets amongst the burning tyres, the bricks and rocks used as missiles, the shattered remains of Molotov cocktails. Over the past few months he had witnessed what happened if they allowed Zulus to live. Sheik and his coms had joined the Bad Boys to help maintain order here, waging a necessary war so others could go to work to earn money and bring home food. He knew his place, and his place was here, on the edge of the dead zones.

Four faces now peered at him in the darkness, and Sheik knew anticipation nested in their expressions. 'Let's go, then.'

He hefted the AK-47 lying on the abandoned dinner table. There were only five bullets left for it, but it scared the shit out of anyone on the street. He also had a 9 mm Beretta stuffed into the pocket of his blue overall trousers, taken from the body of a lone policeman shot dead two weeks ago. Sheik's coms were armed with an assortment of small calibres and two *kwashes*.

'*Uhh-su-thu! Uhh-suhh-thu!*' It was a Zulu battle cry, in a deep, angry rumble. Whistles began slicing through the night; a chorus of *Eh-jah! Eh-jah!* resounded, taunting and confident. The Zulu miners were coming out to reclaim territory lost the night before, to raid the houses surrounding Ulundi for food and supplies—and, Yo-Yo the chicken-seller claimed, women too. A group of young men hurried past heading towards the no-man's-lands. Sheik began humming the 'Bad Boys' refrain again as, with a satisfied smile, he gestured for his coms to follow him out into the night.

The silent darkness finally exhaled, its breath quickening as all hell broke loose. Heavy gunfire echoed up and down the streets as the coms ducked and weaved behind walls; cries of alarm punctured the air that was murky with the smoke from countless coal fires. The streets had come alive. Families still living in the houses stranded here in the dead zones began hastily bolting doors, drawing curtains, extinguishing all their lights. One of the last daredevil minibus taxis arriving to drop people off on the main drag of Khumalo Street u-turned, careening wildly across the street, before speeding south again. A large African woman in bright clothes, clutching her weekly shopping to her chest, staggered blindly across the street, while wailing in fear. A man called out to her that she was heading in the wrong direction—'Come, Mama; *this* way! *This* way!'—before a rock landed on the tar near him, exploding in a spray of brown dust, and he turned to hightail out of danger's way.

All around were the warriors and thugs, the self-defence units and button-smokers with nothing else to do, the white lions and *tsotsis*, the brave and the cowardly, predators and parasites, vigilantes and criminals, the misinformed and genuinely concerned—whoever and whatever they were, they carried weapons. This was a war on the eve of peace.

Dark faces with glistening white eyes peered out at the encroaching chaos over walls, from around corners and behind stationary cars. Very few faces were hidden by balaclavas or handkerchiefs—this was not the Wild West; this was Thokoza, where your enemy might know your face and the police did not care what you looked like as long as you were black. In the mob's hands, sharpened bicycle spokes, long tempered-steel rods with their ends filed down into glinting tips, axes, hunting knives and switch blades, *knopkierries, pangas, sjamboks* and *assegais*, broken-glass bottlenecks . . . and guns, guns, guns. If mothers and sisters were lucky, a Casspir would speed down Khumalo Street, spraying bullets in all directions from apertures in its armour covering, not a care in the world as to who got hit, or whose fault it was, but at least momentarily breaking up the conflict. The same bullshit-covered arm of the law would extend a hypocritical helping hand in the morning, when Black Marias and more of those same Casspirs would arrive, and white cops would pick up black corpses in the fields, the streets, the gardens, and toss them into open trailers to be carted off to the nearby Natalspruit hospital morgue, or to Hillbrow morgue where the body count had not yet filled up the fridges faster than the dead could be processed and buried.

Sheik ground his teeth anxiously as he carefully peered through the bars of the wrought-iron gate, located a few houses down from the house his pack had appropriated. Fire lit up and died in his eyes, reflecting shattering Molotovs. From their present position they could hear bullets cutting through the air. Jabu, his face strangely concave with an elongated chin, dressed in a green Kappa tracksuit top, was huddled next to Sheik, craning his neck to see something. Another bottle of cane appeared from nowhere and was passed to Sheik, who declined the offer.

'Matthews,' Sheik whispered.

He did not get a response. Hating nothing more than being disobeyed or ignored, he glared back at his comrades. *'Matthews!'*

The teenager sat apart from the rest, fiddling with his shoelaces. He kept rocking back and forth, seemingly oblivious to the occasional crack of a bullet striking the bricks above his head. Sheik stood up suddenly, heedless that the rival combatants would now see his head and chest loom over the garden wall. In three quick paces he reached Matthews, and seizing him by his windbreaker, he pulled the teenager towards him so that his warm breath washed over the other's face.

'You turning chicken on me?' he growled.

Matthews' eyes widened and he gripped the wrists holding him. 'Jesus, no boss, I was just thinking about shit.'

'Thinking of what exactly?' Sheik shook him. 'Running away?'

A lull in the shouting and gunfire gave the impression that the night had stopped to listen once more, as if it had heard the coms arguing somewhere in the darkness and was searching for them.

'Who are you?' demanded Sheik, far too loudly, so that Bongile hissed a warning. Jabu threw the bottle of cane aside and checked his gun, sure they would momentarily have unwanted company.

'Matthews,' cried the youth. 'I'm Matthews, your friend.'

'Rubbish!'

'Your *friend*!' Matthews shrieked again as Sheik crushed him up against the wall.

Just then a volley of large-calibre bullets raked across the brickwork nearby, puncturing it, erupting puffs of sandy dust. Sheik instantly dropped Matthews and threw himself sideways out of harm's way. Bongile crawled forward, jammed his 9 mm through the bars of the garden gate, and blindly returned fire. *Crack-crack, pat-tah, pat-tah*—shots erupted from dozens of hideouts lining both sides of the street.

Sheik shook a finger in Matthews' face. 'You're a Bad Boy, *mjita*, before anything else—and don't you forget it.'

Matthews was about to reply when Sheik clamped a hand over his com's mouth. He had heard something else over the cacophony. Without a word to his comrades Sheik threw himself on his stomach, while drawing his pistol. Kgabo fumbled in the darkness behind him till he found the cane bottle, then took a massive gulp of spirits that brought a grimace to his mouth. The last time Sheik had responded like this, they had lost one of their men in an ambush.

On the other side of the garden wall, the hostel-dwellers were now beating a hasty retreat. The night's raids had gone badly for them and, like rivulets of mercury, small groups and individuals were trickling back towards the migrant Zulu miners' stronghold, the hostels, where twenty men were packed into rooms meant for eight.

Sheik, like an obese worm, wriggled carefully over the dirt towards one corner of the gutted cottage. He then peered along one side of the building and in the near darkness he could make out the figure of a man slumped against the side garden wall, staring up as if to see whether someone else would follow him over it. He was breathing loudly. Every now and again the man let out a soft whimper.

When a group of four gunmen went running past, Sheik realized from their urgent exchanges that they were hunting a wounded Zulu. He smiled inwardly as he saw the injured man relax and turn his gaze down towards the front garden. Moments later, he began slowly crawling towards the front garden gate—towards Sheik, towards the Bad Boys.

Sheik retreated slightly, silently signalling for his comrades to move further along. He did not want this injured hostel-dweller spotting his coms the moment he neared the corner. Sheik stood up, careful not to give away his position. Seconds ticked by as the wounded man struggled closer. Finally, a tentative elbow emerged past the corner of the house, the injured man failing to notice Sheik's foot close by, so intent was he on reaching the wrought-iron front gate, and the safety of Ulundi beyond. An unbridled joy swept over Sheik as this Zulu passed close by him, unaware of his presence.

His excitement turned into something akin to a sense of omnipotence, and he almost laughed out loud. This man's future was his, all his own, and the moment was too good to miss, or to end too quickly. What point was there in just shooting this creature as it crawled in the dirt? The Zulu are an arrogant race, he thought, so why allow him the dignity of a bullet in the back of the head? He had the whole night ahead of him to relish this new experience of power. None of the Zulu's cohorts where near enough to come to his rescue. Sheik held his breath and watched as the man's fingers clutched the loose soil as he kept dragging himself forward.

Noiselessly, Sheik stepped forward from the wall, a malicious smile breaking over his face. He raised his gun and took careful aim. At point-blank range, the bullet entered the back of the man's knee and exited through the front of it, blowing out with it large chunks of bone and cartilage. The Zulu screamed into the silent night—a night that was once again listening attentively.

2

6.15 a.m., 15 January 1998, Tembisa

Sheik Kheswa stood on the coupling that attached two rail carriages, listening to the *clacki-di-clack, clacki-di-clack* of the locomotive running over rails. Dusty fields of grass and blooming pink and white cosmos flowers flitted past. The sky was so hazy it looked like it had icing sugar spilt over it.

Something thumped against one inter-connecting door; then, seconds later, there followed three more thumps. Sheik looked up to see someone's head being smashed into the Plexiglas, flattening his hair against the window. He could hear indistinctly Jabu's voice demanding money.

Turning back to view the scenery, Sheik remembered that night in Thokoza, five years ago, which taught him the world did not depend on moral or political positions, but on the strength of opportunists. Kgabo had left them halfway through the night, grunting in disgust, while Bongile had thrown his *kwash* aside, protesting. *Aieh wena*, Sheik could still hear him say, *this is not right, Shakes. He may be a* vokken *Zulu, but this isn't right.*

When the votes were finally cast and the violent tides in Thokoza had turned, Sheik had simply left the area. Pongo, Gugulethu, Tembisa—he drifted from one shantytown to another with Jabu and Matthews in tow, picking up new members here and there, losing them again as readily later on. It did not bother him, this aimlessness.

The connecting door was yanked open, and Jabu stepped out, grinning widely. He was holding up some victim's orange post-office bankbook. Inside was a fifty rand banknote, whose wrinkles had been carefully smoothed out by someone who appreciated the value of the little money she earned. There used to be a police presence on the trains, but they were withdrawn after the government realized officers were being targeted by gangs out to seize their weapons. The way Sheik reasoned it, it was simple: the whites had never used the trains, so they never saw the need to pump money into this transport system's security. Therefore the locomotives were rich for his picking. In the townships, there were hardly any formal commercial enterprises, let alone banks or post offices where Africans could safely keep their money. The apartheid government had seen to that, and the current government had so far done little, if nothing, about solving the absence of business in the townships. This all meant that the hundreds of commuters travelling daily between the townships, the mines, business districts and white suburbs often carried a surprisingly large amount of cash on them, especially at month end.

There was an art to robbing passengers, which Sheik and his team had mastered early on. You had to wait for the right time to board: too early and the trains would be choked with people—risky, even though it guaranteed high yields. If you got on too late, the potential pickings were not that plentiful, but you were less likely to meet resistance from the commuters. You also needed to get off at a station from which you could easily make your getaway, not some *pondok* out in the veldt where you might have to wait much of the day for another passing train to take you home.

'Next carriage?' suggested Jabu.

The door behind him opened, and Matthews joined them on the cramped gangway outside. He scratched his scarred cheek where, the week before, a burly woman had lacerated it as he groped under her T-shirt for the money hidden in her bra.

'*Ja.*' Sheik drew his pistol and tore open the next carriage door along. He strode down the central corridor, his face transformed into a violent sneer, though he felt deadly calm inside. His eyes flicked from person to person, gauging who might cause them trouble, who was the likeliest victim. He headed straight towards the far-end exit, for which people were already scrambling.

'Back away from the door!' He barked in Tswana, levelling the gun at them. 'Sit down!'

People fell to the floor or tumbled aside to evade the expected gunshot. Only one man in his early thirties stood frozen in time like a photograph image. Sheik did not break his stride, and the butt of his pistol swung in a backhand arc. The man dropped like a felled sapling into the lap of a thin woman dressed in a pink domestic's uniform. Sheik turned back to survey the carriage, now that he blocked their only escape route.

Fearful men and women stood clutching silver steel poles, or sat motionless on fake green leather seats which had split to reveal the yellow sponge underneath. Most of the passengers averted their eyes so as not to draw attention to themselves.

Jabu was already collecting coins from a trembling man in his sixties. Matthews began shouting at a woman and, without warning, flicked open the car antenna he carried and lashed out at her. Sheik saw no need to rein him in, simply closed his eyes and arched his back under the familiar rush of excitement pulsing through his body.

Matthews and Jabu gradually worked their way towards him, in the process roughing up passengers who had grown accustomed to hiding their pittances of cash in various concealed places on their persons. The women typically kept their cash concealed in their bras or even knickers, but some had cleverly sewn pouches inside their clothes.

'Bullshit!' yelled Matthews as he raised his weapon threateningly, and Sheik could hear a young woman's voice beg him not to hit her. He could not see her, as he was lying on the floor behind a row of seats. The tone of her voice was high-pitched to the point of hysteria, and Jabu exchanged a glance with his leader.

'Then give me your money!' Matthews yelled at her in Sotho.

'I don't have any. Look. Take my bag—take everything, I haven't got any.'

Sheik moved closer, attracted by the sweet tone of her voice. Her face was in harmony: beautiful and young. About twenty years old, she was smartly dressed in a black skirt ending just above the knee, a white cotton blouse that billowed around her full breasts, while her hair was cut short and neatly combed, neither straightened nor braided. The handbag she held up to Matthews looked elegant and new.

Matthews turned to Sheik. 'Can you believe this bitch?'

Wordlessly Sheik handed Jabu his 9 mm, then squatted down in front of the frightened girl, who was breathing rapidly. Sheik calmly held her wild-eyed gaze as he took the handbag and upended it. A lipstick, a comb,

two tampons, Tic-Tacs, various receipts and a mobile phone spilled out—
but no purse, no money. Not a cent.

Sheik delved quickly through her belongings strewn over the steel floor,
then picked up the Nokia and handed it to Matthews. The carriage had
gone deathly quiet; only the train's rhythmic *clacki-di-clack clacki-di-clack*
could be heard over the girl's stifled sobs.

'You're a student?' asked Sheik.

She gulped. 'What?'

'Are you a *student*?' repeated Sheik, shuffling closer. She smelt of In-
gram's Camphor Cream. Her foot jerked violently when it came into contact with his.

'No, I'm not.'

'So you work, then?'

She drew herself back up against the wall. 'Yes.'

'You like buying pretty things in the big city?'

The young woman did not answer.

He knelt and rubbed the hem of her skirt between two fingers. 'Where
is all the money you buy such nice skirts with?' He tossed her empty
handbag over his shoulder. She convulsed as if some charge had emanated
from his body.

'Leave her alone.' This came from an elderly woman wearing a blue bandanna wrapped around her head, who glared at Sheik.

Matthews reacted instantly: raising the radio antenna, he lashed out at
her. She cried out, though the blow stopped millimetres before touching
her cheek. 'Go on and watch the scenery, *magogo*,' he snarled. 'This doesn't
concern you.'

'Sista, please, if you have the money, give it to them.' The man who
spoke was clinging onto a nearby pole. He wore a yellow hardhat, and a
kindly expression. 'It's not worth what those people might do to you.'

'Listen to him. That's good advice.' Sheik gestured at the miner with
his thumb.

'I haven't even got a bank card,' whimpered the young woman. 'That
was all stolen from me *last* week.' At this she began to sob. 'What must I
do? I have a babe at home, and my mother to look after, too.'

Sheik glanced back down at the contents of her handbag. As the train
rocked violently, a tampon rolled up against his shoe. He picked it up and
stared at it as if he had never seen one before, his eyes seeming to glaze. 'You
know,' he said, 'when I first got into this business, people were more honest.
They either had the money or they didn't. But these days it's more difficult

getting it out of you, especially you women. I know you sometimes hide it in your underwear—and it's fun for us looking for it.' Sheik shuffled closer to her and placed one hand firmly on her ankle. The smell of sweat in the confined space of the carriage reminded him of sex. She flinched, but decided not to antagonize him further by trying to break free. 'But now I hear you even stick it up your cunts, too. I wonder if that's true?'

'No!' she shrilled.

'*Sista*, give him the money,' implored the miner.

Smiling shark-like, Jabu aimed his pistol at the young man's face. 'One more fucking word out of you and I'll pop a few in your mouth, I swear.'

The woman grabbed the hem of her skirt and pulled it down protectively between her knees. A silvery tear streaked down her lovely face.

'You can't do this in front of us. We're not animals.' The woman with the blue bandanna struggled to her feet. 'Leave her *be*!'

This time Matthews struck with his antennae the arm she brought up to defend her face and instantly a dark welt appeared. His second blow fell across her head as she dropped back into her seat, screaming. The passenger sitting next to her pulled the older woman down on to her lap, out of his reach.

Sheik's hand was slowly running up and down the girl's leg, fingers tiptoeing over the toffee-coloured skin. His voice had grown deeper than usual, and hot breath escaped his parted lips. 'You haven't answered me.'

'It was stolen last week,' she whispered in a voice that slipped from fear into resignation. 'It's all gone, I swear.'

'Then how do you expect to pay us our due?'

She remained silent, sensing how futile her input would be. Instead, her head bobbed from side to side with the movement of the train, tears accumulating on her upper lip. Sheik shuffled closer, between her outstretched legs. He could sense almost every pair of eyes in the carriage straining to look elsewhere, and every pair of ears fighting against their owner's macabre curiosity to hear what would happen next.

'Jabu,' he ordered, 'no one leaves the carriage.' He would have every passenger here bear witness to his power.

'Sure,' came the reply. 'Anybody fucking move, I blow your head off.'

Though the young woman's shoulders were shaking convulsively, the rest of her body had gone limp, resigned to her fate.

'Matthews, your knife.'

His comrade reached into a pocket and pulled out a short blade, its well-worn handle duct-taped. Sheik took the weapon offered to him and seized the front of her blouse. She grabbed his wrist: 'No. I swear I don't have any money. Don't do this, *please!*'

Sheik merely smiled as the blunt knife tore through the fabric. She wore a white bra—cheap nylon, nothing fancy—and this mildly disappointed him. Seeing no bulge to suggest concealed cash, he nevertheless clamped ugly hands over her breasts. Her eyes pinched closed, a warm tear falling on his arm as he let one hand slip around her waist, probing for any pockets sewn into the lining of her skirt. He found nothing there, but his hands lingered on the warmth of her belly and back. Her expression of helplessness was arousing him no end, and Sheik closed his eyes for a moment to savour his power over not just this girl but the other passengers, too. A familiar burning heat was fast building up in his crotch.

The moment one hand travelled up the further side of her naked thigh, she tried to kick him away without letting go of her skirt. Sheik merely laughed. 'Matthews, come hold her for me. The bitch has got something, I fucking bet you.'

'I have nothing!' she wailed.

Sheik shook his head with a grin. 'I still have to check, don't you understand? We need our payment.'

Matthews pinned her arms behind her as Sheik set the knife down. A plea from some woman further down the carriage went unheard. Sheik then got a firm grip on her underwear and pulled it free, despite her kicking and screaming. The word GIRL was printed in black on the delicate white fabric.

3

3.41 p.m., 3 June 2004, Leopold Ridge

Dressed in his khaki uniform with shiny brown shoes and a badge on his left chest, Sheik Kheswa stood in front of the *Ridge Superette.* He held a cruel-looking flick knife in one hand, a chunk of *kudu biltong* in the other. Chewing on a strip of the cured meat, he contemplated the town's only thoroughfare, the tiny police compound behind a high barbed-wire fence, and the paint flaking from the two prefab buildings that comprised it. Leopold Ridge was a settlement small enough not to exist on most national roadmaps, and the nearest police stations equipped with more than just stationery were to be found in Prieska, Niekerkshoop or Marydale, towns lying several miles distant in different directions. On the crumbling roadway, near where the railway tracks cut across it, a crowd of African children were playing with a pair of toy cars made from twisted wire, with wheels fashioned from compacted black plastic bags. A cluster of old-style frontier buildings sagged together like tired old men behind the sturdy trunks of giant blue gum trees. This place was expiring, under constant exposure to the burning sun and the wind's dry breath. In this place, life had never been cosseted or nurtured, and that suited him fine for now.

Emerging from the supermarket, a gaunt and pale man stumbled past him, started fumbling for something in his pocket while trying to balance his shopping on one knee at the same time. Casually lifting another piece of *biltong* to his lips, Sheik watched him, unnoticed. Finally the man retrieved the keys he was searching for and started towards a battered old Land Rover parked opposite the portico.

'Willie,' said Sheik.

The man froze, and it took a few moments before he turned around with a sheepish smile. The white man looked an unhealthy fifty, with curly black hair dropping to his shoulders and an unkempt moustache. He was dressed in beige shorts and a short-sleeved shirt, long woollen socks and well-worn hiking boots.

'Sergeant Kheswa, hello.'

Sheik smiled and offered Willie Erasmus some *biltong*. 'Doing some shopping?'

'*Ja*, our monthly groceries. You know how it is: my wife doesn't drive, so it's me going backwards and forwards all the time.' Willie set his assorted shopping down by his feet.

'You still spitting the blood?'

A mortified expression crossed Willie's drawn face.

Sheik burst out laughing. 'I'm just joking, man. But, you know, I always say it's better to look death in his face—that's if you're a man.'

Willie responded with a wan smile half hidden under his moustache. His eyes crept towards the Land Rover, looking for an escape route.

Sheik stuffed the remaining side of *biltong* into a chest pocket, and cleaned off the blade before closing his flick knife with an exaggerated gesture. 'How're your chickens? And the farm, it's doing all right?'

'*Ja*, we *ma* go on as always.' Willie struggled to pick up his shopping again.

'Hey,' Sheik started forward. 'Let me give you a hand with those.'

Willie almost took a step backward. 'I'm fine; this one's mine.' He nodded at the nearby Land Rover.

'I know the fucking Landie's yours.' Sheik grabbed hold of two of the bags. 'What you acting like I'm gonna kill you for, hey?' His English was thick and guttural, quite difficult to understand. 'Just get the door; I'll carry these over for you.'

Willie unlocked the rear door and let Sheik place the bags on top of a sack of chicken feed. Before Willie could shut the door, the police sergeant yanked it free from his hands and slammed it shut with unnecessary force. 'Let's go for a drive.'

'But—'

'*But* nothing. Get in the car.'

Willie obeyed, leaning over to unlock the passenger door. 'Where to?'

Sheik glanced over at the police station before pulling down the visor. 'To the club. I want to show you something.'

Willie's anxiety rose a notch. 'But there is nothing out that way. What do you want to go there for?' Whenever he spoke, his words were accompanied by unpleasant wheezing.

'You don't trust me, Willie?'

'No, I do,' Willie countered, 'but I need to get back home. Martha's cooking right now and she nee—'

'Start the fucking car then, and get going.'

Willie fell quiet and turned the engine. At the bullet-ridden stop sign he took a left into De Beer Road and headed north, towards the old Henning Visagie Club on the outskirts of town. Green water tanks mounted on steel stilts loomed higher than the single-storey matchbox houses lining the road. Their few gardens featured only small patches of scraggly grass.

Abruptly, the driver began coughing in loud, dry whoops. Sheik glanced at the man in disgust as he then wiped his mouth with a stained handkerchief, kept permanently at hand on the dashboard. 'What's this about?' Willie finally asked.

'This is for you.' Sheik pulled a neat roll of one hundred rand notes from his pocket and tossed it into Willie's lap. 'You can count it, if you like, but it's all there as agreed.'

As the driver held up the fat roll of cash, his face broke into the kind of brave smile people wear when accepting condolences. 'Thanks.'

'What? You not happy with it?'

'*No*, that's not it.' Willie stuffed the money into a pocket. 'I'm happy, really. Thanks, sergeant.'

'The man whose farm you live on, Klamm—he was killed a few days ago,' said Sheik. 'You hear about that?'

'Yes. How did you know?'

'I just know,' replied Sheik, turning his close-set eyes on Willie. 'I know about a lot of things.'

The man did not register this meaningful glance as he opened the Land Rover's window, before clearing his throat and spitting out a gob of opaque phlegm. 'Nobody told me yet what happened.'

'Someone break into his house,' replied Sheik. 'Burnt him alive.'

'*God's weet*, you don't say? He was a nasty bastard, deserved something bad—but to be burnt alive? Who would do a thing like that?'

'Doesn't matter; he's dead now.' Sheik waved a hand dismissively. 'The thing that's important now is that you hang on to that farm a bit longer.'

'How'm I supposed to do that? It's already being put up for sale. Some *stadsjapie* called Tobias Rees phoned yesterday to tell me that.' Willie closed the window again.

Sheik nodded, as if expecting that news.

The driver looked at him, confused. 'But all that's got nothing to do with me—you know that, don't you? I can't do anything about it, if they want to sell, and . . . how much is "a bit longer"?'

Sheik shrugged. 'We'll see. There are a few things I still want to take care of.'

Willie rubbed his nose with a single finger. 'Well, ah . . . you see, sergeant, I'm not sure what's going to happen to me, and . . . well, it's something I've been meaning to talk to you about.'

'I don't want to hear your excuses,' said Sheik. 'We've got a deal.'

'*Ja*, but I might have to go to hospital soon, for longer this time. I mean, you know about my lungs.'

The last of the residential lots flashed past, this one containing nothing more than an abandoned caravan, its wheels rotten and windows long broken. The landscape beyond now consisted of blackened rock, quartz glittering in the sunlight, and determined scrub gripping the earth with desperate roots.

'Sergeant?'

'You hang on until I say I'm finished with you.'

'I'm fucking *dying*, sergeant!'

Sheik threw the man a warning glance.

Willie quickly turned his gaze back to the road. 'Shit,' he said. 'I didn't mean to yell. Sorry.'

'You don't want to be leaving your daughter and wife alone, do you, with me around?'

Willie glanced uncomfortably at Sheik, not sure how he should answer that.

The sergeant smiled. 'I thought not.' Then he pointed. 'Over there.'

Between two low, crumbling perimeter walls the entrance consisted of a rusting wrought-iron arch spanning the driveway, embellished above with a faded plaque bearing the club's name. The buildings beyond were in various states of ruin, since enterprising homebuilders had long ago stripped the place of anything that could be carried away on backs, shoulders or in wheelbarrows. Wilted weeds and wild grasses flourished where the concrete forecourt had cracked under the sun's unrelenting blaze. Dead trees, their bark burnt white, pointed to the cloudless heavens in silent accusation.

Willie brought his Land Rover to a stop in front of the large gutted clubhouse. An emblem above the entrance had been riddled with buckshot, spent red shotgun shells trampled into the glittering white dust beneath.

'Follow me.' The passenger door squeaked open.

There had formerly been a small reception office just beyond the entrance, where slatted windows had once occupied a now gaping hole in the wall. They passed a large void where double doors once hung. Sheik peered inside and imagined the exclusively white social scene that must have played out there every night for decades: wives in summer dresses seated at tables, gossiping about their men; children chasing each other round and around on the few occasions they were allowed into the same room as the adults; the massive bar at the opposite end, manned by exclusively black servants polishing glasses and serving state-sponsored booze in this little oasis of prosperity; while over to one side the men were playing snooker or darts, building up courage to ask some woman other than their own wife for a drunken dance. A square of sunlight now illuminated the dance floor where a large section of the roof was missing.

'Tell me,' Sheik asked over his shoulder, 'why do you have all those Angolans working on the farm?'

'No one else will work there.' Willie looked over his shoulder through the main entrance to where his car was parked. 'The other blacks are too scared of setting foot on the property, and no white man is prepared to work for me.'

'Why not?'

Willie shrugged. 'Your people are a superstitious lot, and the whites, I guess, are too proud to work for a poor farmer.'

'Ah, pride. They think they're better than you?'

'I used to be a miner, and now I'm a dying man with no land of his own. I couldn't pay them what they're looking for, even if they're currently unemployed. In that respect, you can always find a black man willing to do the farm work.'

'And a black man does *not* have pride? He'll do whatever you ask him to do?'

'No, that's not what I said. It's been like this since before I took over the farm—I mean that no one wants to work on that land. Klamm warned me it would be like this.'

Sheik stopped walking and turned around. 'You want to know what people tell me about that place?'

They were now in a long, dark corridor, like a tunnel with white light glowing at each end. The walls smelled of raw concrete. There was not a breath of air, another soul, a sound.

Willie stretched out an arm and rested it against the wall. 'They say a devil lives there. They say it walks upright, like a man, but is covered in spines the way a porcupine is. Some say it's half-burnt and the size of a child; others that it's tall like you, and tan-coloured with long talons and sharp teeth. They say this *kak* with the children started there, even that Klamm's daughter was the first girl taken by it. *Ja*, I know all about that. Even people like my wife believe it, too. It's not just the blacks.'

'But you don't believe what these people say?' asked Sheik.

'Klamm's rent was dirt cheap, and it was all I could afford at the time. I don't have the luxury to believe in old wive's tales—I have two other mouths to feed.'

'I hear your daughter is—'

'Look, what's this about, sergeant?' Willie was blinking rapidly. 'What the fuck are we doing out here?'

Sheik regarded him a moment, then smiled. 'Out back. Come.' He proceeded the rest of the way through the building, and at the back exit they stepped out into a dilapidated yard which once had been a parking area for the staff.

Willie gasped, stopped dead.

Sheik gestured for him to follow him. 'Come on, man. You wanted to know.'

In the middle of the yard was a chair, and in it, facing the opposite direction, sat a uniformed man. A dead man. Willie could see this by the way the hands tied around the back of the chair had discoloured. Flies were swarming around the corpse's head, eager for the moisture, so rare in this arid landscape.

'*Jee-sus*, sergeant!' Willie's eyes bulged, as they flicked from one police officer to the other. 'Someone killed a cop? You kill him? You kill him? Why the fuck did you kill a cop?'

Sheik grabbed Willie by the shoulder, amused. 'You're in real trouble, Willie. You know that, don't you?'

'What?' Willie licked his lips, eyes returning to the corpse. Why? I didn't do it.'

'He was found on your farm.'

'*My* farm? Like that? Who found him like that?' The panic in his voice threatened to get beyond control.

Sheik chuckled. 'No. He was caught snooping around. Come closer, take a good look.'

'I'd rather not, sergeant.'

'Oh, you'd better.' Sheik dug his fingers deeper into Willie's shoulder, enough to make the farmer wince, and guided him closer to the corpse. Willie started coughing violently at the smell. He wiped his mouth desperately as they moved around to contemplate the dead policeman's face. It now looked like bloody papier maché, and not much about it was recognizable.

Sheik laughed. 'Hey, don't he look good?'

Willie's already pale face blanched even further.

'Did you invite him onto your property?' The hand on Willie's shoulder tightened.

His terrified eyes met Sheik's. 'No, I swear I didn't.'

The sergeant allowed the following silence to stretch on for seconds, savouring a familiar growing excitement. 'Because, you know, I wouldn't want to have to arrest you for this.'

'*What!*' Willie's eyes were now blinking uncontrollably. 'But you can't. I didn't do it.'

'There's evidence.'

'No!'

'Yes, there is, and if you're not careful I'll have to take you in. Then what about that fat wife of yours? Uh? That stupid daughter. Then what?'

'Jesus, sergeant, don't. I'm begging you. I had nothing to do with this *oke*.'

'That's good, Willie. Because if you're trying to double-cross me, I'll find out. If you're messing with me, I'll kill you, but not before I fuck that bitch of yours over the back of a chair and skin your daughter alive. You fucking hear me? Do you believe me when I tell you this?'

'I hear you. Jesus! I *hear* you!' The man was jumping from foot to foot as Sheik's fingers dug deeper into the flesh of his shoulder. Suddenly his eyes widened at some recollection. 'I had nothing to do with this other guy that's coming here now, either. I swear.'

Sheik grabbed him by the neck and yanked him forward, close enough to the blond policeman's corpse for Erasmus to see the fillings in his wide open mouth. 'What are you talking about, man?'

'That Tobias Rees, he said he's sending someone up here to take a look around. Said he'll be around for a week or so.'

'A *week?*'

'*Ja.*' Willie gagged as he tried not to inhale this close to the corpse. 'The guy's name is Harry Mason.'

'Who is he?'

'I don't know. Jesus, let go, please!'

Sheik released Willie's neck and swore aloud in Tswana. The farmer coughed raggedly as he stumbled away. For a few moments they were both lost in their own worlds, Sheik staring out at the distant hills, trying to calm his turbulent thoughts, while Willie massaged his shoulder, gulping mouthfuls of fresh air.

'There's one other thing,' mumbled Willie, eventually.

Sergeant Kheswa turned on him. 'What now?'

Willie plucked nervously at his moustache, as if about to confess some shameful secret.

'*What!*' bellowed Sheik. 'You think I'm going to stand here all day, and wait for you to speak? Spit it out.'

'Something killed my two dogs last week,' Willie finally said.

'What you talking about, "some*thing*"? Did someone shoot them? Or poison them? My people didn't do that.'

The farmer wiped his forehead with a forearm, shook his head. 'Found them dead, two weeks ago. They were cut up real bad. Zelda says she woke up and heard something outside, and let the dogs out. The bull and lab both went after a shadow, like lightning. They got hold of something beyond the security light. There was a fight which woke me up, but by the time I got out there, not much was left of them.'

'You think it was a leopard?' asked Sheik, with growing interest. 'They still found around here, aren't they?'

Again Willie shook his head. 'The wounds, they weren't claw or bite marks. Those cuts were made by something very sharp. Besides, my dogs were never stupid enough to go after a leopard.'

Sheik held the man's gaze a few seconds longer, as if weighing up his story. 'So what the fuck are you telling me this for? It's not my problem.'

'Something's been creeping around our cellar ever since.'

'What you mean?'

'I first thought my wife's talking shit again, and my daughter . . . well, my daughter's my daughter. But this time there really *is* something scratching around down there. Whenever I open up that door, though, it's already gone. It keeps breaking open the coal hatch, but so far I haven't caught anyone doing it. That's why I think it must be some*thing*, not some*one*.'

Sheik suddenly roared with laughter. 'Not you too!'

'I swear! I *know* something's down there . . . 'cause it's slowly digging up the basement.'

'Come on, Willie.' Sheik wiped at his eyes. 'Your wife finally get to you?'

'I don't go down there often, as it sets my daughter off. But last night, I did. Bricks have been tossed around, and soil is piled high in places.'

'You as crazy as that child of yours,' huffed Sheik. 'Next you going to tell me it's her that's come back—that Klamm's daughter.'

'No, listen—'

'Shut the fuck up, Willie.' Sheik's voice grew serious again, as if tired of the sport. 'I'm having enough here. You're bullshitting the wrong person. All I want to know is that you're making sure we don't see anyone else driving into that range. Keep your fucking workers down in the valley too, OK?'

Willie nodded hesitantly, his expression resigned. 'What about this guy Mason?'

Sheik turned to stare for a long minute at the corpse of the uniformed Marydale policeman. The name stitched onto the stained shirt pocket read GALLOWS. Willie waited submissively, his hands clasped in front of his crotch like a child expecting to hear what his punishment would be. Finally Sheik smiled and thumped him on the back. 'Here's what you gonna do.'

They walked back to the four-by-four, Sheik carefully explaining his plan. It was not complicated, but he ran through it three or four times, making sure Willie understood. Then he let the chicken farmer get into the Land Rover, and actually waved him goodbye.

Half an hour later a beat-up, chrome-green Jetta pulled into the abandoned recreation complex, Kheswa's old-time comrade Jabulani Mahlangu sitting at the wheel. Stuffing the policeman's putrid body into a ruined shower stall, they cracked open two ice-cold Black Labels for the drive back to Leopold Ridge, confident that they had made their point to Willie Erasmus as strongly as possible.

FOUR

Fear of the Dark

1

9.08 p.m., 3 June 2004, *Oranje Genot* **Farm**

He had lived there nine years, but not once did it ever feel like a home; it never felt like a place where an ordinary family could have been raised, either.

It was completely dark in the house. In one hand he held a paraffin lamp, throwing flickering light in an orange circle around him, in the other was the bundle of money the dirty cop had given him. The roll of banknotes felt heavy, like lead.

The dark corridor beyond the living-room door was short, with stairs immediately to the left of it, leading up to four bedrooms, two of them currently unoccupied. In the paraffin light, the large strips of paint peeling from the high walls seemed like grey lolling tongues, the accumulated spider webs beyond the range of his wife's broom looking even thicker than they did by daylight. A little on from the staircase was a heavily bolted door, which Willie Erasmus preferred not to look at, though he listened intently for any unwanted sounds originating from behind it. At the far end of the corridor, barely within range of the lamplight, were another three doors, two facing each other, the third directly ahead. The corridor with its three doorways at the far end always reminded Willie of a crucifix, and when that leading to his daughter's playroom at the far end stood open, the wooden image of Jesus hanging dead centre on the white wall beyond completed the image.

Normally, he would not have been so hesitant standing here on the threshold, but he had seen a lot that day. The image of the dead cop Gallows still festered in his mind, unwilling to leave him alone, and his eyes darted to the sealed cellar door as he quickly stepped past it, his heavy shoes clopping on the wooden floor despite his effort to move quietly. Every bolt was still in place.

What was that? He halted, his breath catching. Had he heard a sound like grating gravel? He listened. Nothing. Willie closed his eyes and licked his lips. *Get a grip*, he thought. *You're starting to behave like your wife.*

He moved on and opened the door at the far left to reveal a study containing little more than the desk and chair that faced the window. A few files were stacked on otherwise empty and dusty shelves. Setting his paraffin light down on the desk, the farmer closed the door behind him, again as quietly as possible. Briefly he peered out the window before drawing closed the check curtains. Willie then looked down at the roll of money in his hand, and beyond it to the dirty-brown carpet he stood on.

Pulling it aside, he carefully prised loose the two floorboards to reveal a small hollow space beneath. He stuck his hand in and fished out a Dairymaid plastic ice-cream container. Just then, a sudden creak in the corridor stopped him dead. He waited, listened. Another creak. His heart hit his throat, eyes widening.

There was an audible tap against the door, just before its handle began to slowly turn.

He was suddenly very aware of what happened to his two dogs. He had found Marcy, the black labrador, with most of the left side of her snout sheared off, exposing teeth and gums, the long laceration turning downward to open up her throat, while the Boer bull had suffered two deep stabbing wounds, one in the middle of his chest, one right behind a foreleg.

Realizing all his weapons were upstairs with his wife, Willie turned around fearfully. As the door creaked open, the first thing he saw advance through it was the sharp tip of a large carving knife. Back-peddling fast against the desk, the farmer inadvertently kicked the carpet so that it partially dropped into the gaping hole in the floor.

'Jesus, Zelda!' he hissed in Afrikaans as he saw his eleven-year-old daughter's frightened face appear, 'what the fuck are you doing?'

The fear in the girl's eyes turned to obvious relief when she realized it was only her father. Her expression, however, turned to surprise when she noticed the hole in the floor.

'Zelda!' He spat when she did not answer. 'I'm talking to you.' His eyes flicked up towards the ceiling, as he listened for further signs of movement. 'Wait for me out in the passage, *now.*'

She nodded wordlessly and retreated, eyes sill fixed on the mysterious gap in the floor. Another warning hiss from her father distracted her, and the door clicked behind her as she swung it closed.

Hastily, he retrieved the ice-cream box from beneath the floorboards, dropped the roll of money into it, and concealed his hiding place once more. He opened the door to find Zelda huddled against the door opposite, the paraffin light he held casting an eerie light over her face, and tattooing her skin with subtle shadows. Her cheeks, he noticed, were glazed with tears.

'Give me that knife,' Willie whispered, holding out his hand. 'What the hell are you creeping around the house for, at this time of night?'

'I thought it was that thing which killed Marcy,' said his daughter courageously.

'If you think someone broke into the house, you go to *our* room, understand? You wake me up or, if I'm not there, it's your mother you wake up. But don't ever come down here yourself. Wait a minute, what's this?'

Willie grabbed hold of the girl's left wrist and brought it closer to the light. Her palm was swollen and exhibited a fresh cut. She winced as he tried to uncurl her fingers further.

'How did you get this?' The paraffin flame was hot against his cheek, and his daughter had to close one eye against the glare.

'She did it,' Zelda whispered. 'The little girl.'

The wooden banister above them creaked loudly. Willie spun around, holding the lamp up higher. 'What's going on down here?' a female voice inquired in Afrikaans from the darkness above.

'Mama let her do it,' blurted the girl.

'I did no such thing.' Willie could make out the light-blue haze of his wife's billowing nightgown, the square lenses of her glasses glittering in the half-light as she came down the stairs.

'*She* did. Papa, look at it. It hurts.'

'I didn't let anything in.' His wife's expression was distraught as she stepped further into the sphere of light. 'It's begun again, Willie, and I don't know what to do any more.'

Her husband turned back to look at his daughter, now staring at him defiantly from underneath the wild hair falling across her face. Suddenly he felt more tired than he had done in years, as the shadows around them seem to press in on him. *Not again*, he thought as the world began to spin. *Not now.*

'You feeling OK, honey?'

He blinked. His wife was now standing next to him, her cool hand resting on his hot neck. Fighting the dizziness that overwhelmed him, Willie discovered he was leaning for support against the wall with the same hand that still held the knife. As he looked from daughter to wife, suddenly a hot, embarrassed anger filled him. 'I'd be OK if it wasn't for you two women! If those cuts weren't done by *you*, or *you*, then who the hell caused them?'

The moment he asked this, he regretted it. He should have known better.

It was his wife that began. 'You *know* what—'

'*Ag kak, man!*' he bellowed, a violent coughing fit interrupting. 'I warned you. I don't ever want to hear any of that shit again. Not from you . . . or you, either.' He glared at his small family. 'Is that understood?'

Suddenly all three of them heard a noise issue up from below. It was indistinct but definite, before there was quiet once more—as if it, too, was now listening intently.

'It's here!' His wife grabbed his shoulder, just as Zelda's arms went around his waist. 'God have mercy, it's come for—'

'Hush, woman.'

'If you think you know better, then why don't you call the police?'

'No! I mean *no*. No one's calling the police.'

'Then go outside, Willie, and find out what keeps getting back into our house. If it's some animal you'd better shoot it. Our two dogs are dead, for heaven's sake. Go on, get out there. I can't bear this any more, Willie, I swear.'

His eyes blinked uncontrollably, as always when under stress. His wife kept shaking his shoulder, but he did not immediately respond.

'Willie?'

'No.' He tightened his grip on the knife. 'I'm not going outside. I'm done with this nonsense. There's nothing out there. We're going upstairs, and that's that.'

'What? No, you—'

'That's *that*!'

Despite his definitive command, not one of the three moved for a long moment. Instead they listened outside the locked door, each for reasons of their own, as if unwilling to break up their fearful communion and leave the pool of faltering yellow light.

FIVE

In the Place of the Lost Goat

1

9.10 a.m., 5 June 2004, Johannesburg

Eleven days after Klamm's murder, Harry and Jeanie Mason drive into West Park cemetery with a fresh bouquet of flowers made up of blood red roses and soft pink and white carnations. A number of cars are already parked along the broad avenues under naked trees, families strolling along the pathways and cleaning out wilted flowers from the iron vases. The sky is a light blue, and an icy wind sends brown leaves skittering over short, yellowed grass.

Feeling sombre and alone as they walk towards his wife's grave, Harry reaches out to take Jeanie's hand and squeezes it hard. 'So, it's fine if I go away for a week? You'll be OK with nan Joan?'

His daughter has been pouting all morning and takes some time to answer. 'No, I don't want you to go, Daddy.'

'Jeanie, I know it doesn't sound good, but it's got to be this way.'

Jeanie looks up at him, her eyebrows twitching. 'You're going away and you're leaving me here alone. Mommy says you shouldn't do that. Mommy thinks you shouldn't do police work either. She says it's dangerous, and you mustn't ever do it again.'

'Mommy says all that?' he asks.

Jeanie nods.

'How come you can speak with her?'

Jeanie shrugs. 'Uncle Jacob says she's always around, even if I can't see her.'

'Well, he's right; but did he say she can talk to you?'

'No, but she doesn't need him to give her permission.'

Harry smiles. 'Sounds like Mommy chats with you often, then.'

Jeanie nods vigorously. 'Doesn't she speak with you?'

Harry thinks of the lonely nights when his bed feels like a cold black sea, the flotsam of their previous life together floating past. On occasion he sees her face floating above it all, and smiling down at him. 'Yeah,' he replies. 'Sometimes.'

'So are you going to listen to her?'

'What do you mean?'

Jeanie scowls at her father. 'The *police* work. You're not allowed to do police stuff.'

'Honey, it's not really police stuff.'

'Then what are you going to do in Leo . . .'

'Leopold Ridge,' finishes Harry. 'I'm going to look for someone who's been missing a very long time. I have to find her for her mommy, but it's nothing like chasing robbers.'

Jeanie comes to a standstill and stares resolutely at her father with stern green eyes. 'So why did you pack your gun, Daddy?'

'How did you . . . ?'

'I saw you cleaning it. You promised. You *promised*, no more police stuff.'

Harry kneels beside his daughter and gently grasps her by both shoulders. 'Jeanie, what happened to you and Mommy, that was very bad. I don't know . . . I wish I could make all that go away, so you don't have to live with it, and Mommy could be back with us again, but I can't. I can promise you this, though: I won't ever let something like that happen to you again, OK?'

'But what about you? Why are you leaving me like this? What if you die, like Mommy?' Jeanie's expression darkens.

'It won't happen.'

'But how do you know?'

Taking his daughter's small hands, Harry shuffles off the concrete path to make way for an approaching couple and their three cavorting children. He inhales deeply, but Jeanie beats him to speaking first.

'Mommy is angry with you—very, very angry. And she doesn't want you talking to me about what happened, and she doesn't want you to take your *gun*.' She jerks free from her father's hands, and turns away from him to stare after the family that has just passed.

'Jeanie.' Harry reaches over to touch her shoulder. She ignores him. 'Come on, Jeanie.' All his daughter does is fold her arms across her chest and shake her head, much the same way her mother used to do when she got angry with her husband.

'Listen, babe, this really *is* different. It's almost like police work, but it's not as dangerous. I'm taking the gun for just in case. Please don't worry about it.' Harry waits for a response. 'Could you turn around for me? Jeanie?'

Slowly his daughter turns around, to stare at his knee.

'It'll be all right, I promise. And when all this is finished, Daddy will have some money to take us on holiday somewhere—just you and me.'

Jeanie huffs at the futility of her earlier pleas. 'I don't want you to go.'

'I *have* to go. Please understand that, my angel. Now, take these and bring them to your mother.' Harry hands his daughter the bouquet.

'I miss her, Daddy.'

'I miss her too, honey.'

Hoping she will reach up for a hug, Harry is taken aback when Jeanie merely bolts away from him to head for her mother's grave.

An hour later, Harry's Nissan pulls into his mother's driveway in Waverly. With hardly a greeting to her grandmother, Jeanie clambers out of the car, collects her small suitcase from the back seat, and lugs it off to the guest-room which has been prepared for her stay. The bed is piled high with many of her older, unwanted toys.

'Not happy about you leaving, is she?' Joan accompanies Harry inside.

'I knew she wouldn't be.'

'Wait here, I'll make us some coffee.'

'I need to get going.'

'Nonsense!' Joan holds up a hand. 'It's a long drive, and you'd better have something to keep you awake.'

His mother disappears into the kitchen, leaving him to drift around a living room filled with porcelain figures of European royals and hundreds of framed family photographs. Harry is holding a picture of Amy taken in Dullstroom, two weeks after their engagement, as Joan returns with a plunger of aromatic filter coffee.

She sidles up to her son with the tray and looks at the photograph. 'She was a beautiful woman, wasn't she?'

Harry chuckles, lost in recollection. 'I took this photo the day we fell in the water. I was trying to show her how to fly-fish.'

His mother smiles as she puts the tray down on a table. 'What did you tell Jeanie that's made her so upset?'

Harry replaces the photograph in its allotted place amongst the ranks of others. 'Just what she needed to know.' He shrugs. 'It doesn't matter how I said it, it would still have upset her.'

'No, Harold, that's not true. You still need to learn what tact is, and how it applies to children. Some things you keep to yourself because they confuse them, and with other things you have to be more open and honest with kids than you'd ever be with adults. You could share a bit more of yourself with your daughter, you know.'

Harry flops down on the long white couch. 'Thanks for the advice, Mother. Next time you leave an eight-year-old kid behind to go find a dead one out in a desert somewhere, I'll be sure to offer you the same.'

'I didn't mean to insult you, Harold. You know she's always welcome here.'

Feeling ashamed, Harry lowers his voice. 'I know. Thank you.'

Later he gently knocks at Jeanie's door. With no answer forthcoming, he pushes it open to find her sitting on the edge of her bed, her packed suit-case still standing in the middle of the room. When she glances up at him, her forlornly angry expression surprises him.

'I'll be going now,' he murmurs. 'You look after yourself and be nice to your nan.'

She does not reply, though he can see her lips begin to curl downward.

'Don't make it this hard, angel,' says Harry as tenderly as he can. 'Before you know it I'll be back.'

Jeanie sobs. 'It already is hard.'

Harry touches her head and is glad when she does not draw away from him. He traces his hand down one side of her face.

'It won't always be like this, I promise.' He bends down to kiss her on the top of her head.

Abruptly, she reaches up and hugs him as tight as she can. Harry closes his eyes as he hugs her back, and breathes in the apple scent of her hair. Somehow, he thinks, he will find a way to give her back the life he always wanted for her. *Somehow.*

2

10.28 a.m., 5 June 2004, Johannesburg

Accelerating westward on the N12, Harry speeds past stretches of ram-shackle shantytowns existing on the edges of the City of Gold. These gradu-ally give way to flat, ever-expanding, golden fields of highveld grass shimmering in the sun's yellow glow. Large gold-mining operations, with their own shack-sprawls, dot every horizon, reminding Harry that Gauteng, despite its stains of glitz, is nothing more than a province of fool's gold painted with a cheap veneer of first-world prosperity.

In the North-West, veldt fires and firebreaks have rendered the countryside black and bare in places, but the white-painted farmhouses built amongst clusters of evergreen trees, near rivers and on ridges, are a return to the quietude expressed in still-life masterpieces.

Stopping at an Engen garage in Kimberley to refill, to stretch his aching limbs, and to drink some coffee in the BJs diner, he realizes he once sat in one of these same red booths with Amy back in 1995, when they drove to visit Cape Town for a week. He had been staring at her sucking on a strawberry milkshake, when she caught him smiling.

'What the hell you grinning for, bear?' she had asked.

He shook his head. 'I just think you're beautiful, that's all.'

'*Sure* that's all?' Abruptly Harry felt her bare foot slide up the inside of his leg until it came to a rest in his crotch. She had raised one eyebrow and smiled wickedly at him. 'Because I can make you think of a whole lot of other things.'

He laughed and grabbed hold of her foot. Kneading it, he replied, 'What's it with you and driving long distances?'

'Oh God,' she moaned softly, 'don't you *ever* stop that. Jesus, are you trying to make me pull a Meg Ryan? I don't know, maybe this feeling has something to do with sitting still next to my gorgeous beau for hours on end. I'm not allowed to touch him while he's driving, and so I let my mind roam, and boy, does it go places.'

Harry is up and out the door before the sudden lump in his throat can get any thicker, the money for his bill carelessly spilled over the table. The echo of her voice trails after him like the scent of jasmine flowers lingering in the air.

Memories of his dead wife are still whispering to him when he turns his vehicle onto the R357 and sees a woman standing by the side of the road, wearing nothing but a faded light-blue summer dress that billows in the freezing wind. One hand is raised to flag for a lift. Sitting in the dust next to her is a young boy, scratching in the sand with a stick. Harry's eyes catch hers as he applies his brakes. In the moment of passing her, he sees her expression turn sour, when she registers that he is a man alone in a pickup. Halting, then racking the engine into reverse, he watches her drop her arm and look back along the road as if hoping that another car will head this way before he has a chance to pull up next to her. The woman's long light-brown hair is tied back in a ponytail, her blue dress stained, and one of her thong sandals has a broken strap.

Leaning over to wind down the passenger window, Harry calls, 'Hi, where you going?'

She looks to be in her late twenties. Tears have recently streaked through the grime on her face, but her eyes are like unstained empyrean drops.

'*Dag, meneer.*' Her husky voice starts to crack and she clears her throat to try again. 'We're going to Prieska, if you'll take us along.'

Harry scratches the back of his head as he fumbles to reply in Afrikaans. 'No problem; I'm heading that way myself.'

She smiles a strained smile and thanks him. Harry jumps out the car and comes around the back to help the woman with her luggage, only to remember that he had not seen any. 'Your things?' He asks, accidentally in English.

She drops her gaze and shakes her head. 'I didn't bring anything along.'

From the way she says this, Harry surmises that she has no possessions at all.

'Hello, *oom*,' says a young voice at his knee.

He looks down to see the little boy has stood up, and is determinedly holding out one paw for a handshake. Like the woman, he is smeared with grime.

'Hello, little man,' says Harry in Afrikaans, as he takes the boy's hand. 'What's your name?'

'Gabriel.'

'Hello, Gabriel. How can I help you and your mom?'

The little boy nods his head vigorously. 'We want to go home.' His hair and eyes are both a sandy brown, his clothes seem paper-thin.

'We . . .' the woman shifts from one foot to the other, very uncomfortable with what she has to say. 'We don't have any money, and I can't pay you any other way.'

Harry shrugs. 'Doesn't matter. I wouldn't take your money anyway.'

'You sure?' Her eyes narrow at his casual response, as if she wants to make certain nothing else will be demanded from her during the journey.

'I couldn't live with myself, leaving you out here in the cold.' He smiles reassuringly. 'So it's Prieska for the two of you?'

'*Ja.* Thanks, mister. It's really good of you to take us along.'

'You can call me Harry.' He waits for her to introduce herself, but when she only nods, he continues. 'Well, let's not stand out here in the cold any longer. All aboard.'

On the road again, with Gabriel safely installed in the back and the woman in the passenger seat next to him, Harry asks her a few questions about where they have come from, and where they are going, but her curt replies and stony expression bring his attempts at conversation to a quick end. He turns his attention back to the road, and cranks up the heat for them. After a moment's consideration he turns the music up a notch as well, uncomfortable with the awkward silence emanating from the woman. He tries to ignore, as best he can, a smell of sweat and stale unwashed bodies steadily permeating the car.

As it inches down toward the horizon, the reddening sun increasingly turns the harsh landscape into shades of grey and ochre. In places the plant life is reduced to nothing more than bristles of vegetation clustered around large blackened boulders that are covered in tenacious lichens. There are no vehicles visible in front of them and only a distant light far behind. They pass what Harry assumes to be a survey station, although it adds to the surreal impression that they are travelling through a lunar landscape. The station consists of five green igloo-like buildings grouped around a square caravan raised on blocks, while the road in front is straight as an arrow. Harry continuously finds himself glancing at the woman by his side. She seems to be sleeping now, her left hand cushioning a tired face against the seatbelt strap. Without all that grime, and wearing some clean clothes, she might look beautiful—judging from the sharp lines of her cheekbones, her strong chin and long eyelashes, which give her a naturally proud and sophisticated air.

Abruptly she starts awake, her eyes immediately catching him looking at her. Harry jerks his gaze back to the endless stretch of road ahead. Yawning, the young woman sits up straighter in her seat.

'Thank you,' she says unexpectedly in English, 'you've been very kind.'

'No problem,' replies Harry. 'Are you two going to be all right when you get there? I mean, it looks like you've been on the road for quite a while, and it's going to be night soon—a cold one at that.'

Her gaze wanders out the window and in a deep, sonorous voice, she replies, 'I don't know. I honestly don't know.'

'If you don't mind me asking: why are you both all the way out here, in the middle of winter and wearing only summer clothes?'

The woman closes her eyes and shakes her head. 'I don't want to talk about it, please.'

'Sorry.' Harry tightens his grip on the steering wheel. 'None of my business.'

A sigh of relief escapes the woman's mouth as a halo of light finally appears on the horizon. It is Prieska—meaning the Place of the Lost Goat in the Khoisan language—and it is the closest to the edge of the world as Harry has ever driven. Crossing a large bridge over the broad muddy Orange River, they stop at a petrol station on one side of the town's main drag. Harry is the first to get out, stretching painfully cramped limbs. The temperature has already fallen to near freezing, and he can see large goosebumps break out all over the woman's exposed skin as she opens the rear door for her son.

The boy immediately begins to complain both at the cold and being woken, but his mother quickly silences him with a stern reprimand. She offers Harry a surprisingly warm smile. '*Dankie.* I thought we'd never get here.'

'You want to get out right here, in this cold? Isn't there somewhere better I can drop you off, someplace warmer, at least?'

'We'll be all right,' she says. '*Kom*, Gabriel.' She makes to leave.

'Jesus, ma'am, it's *freezing* out here. Both of you'll drop dead before long.'

An approaching petrol-pump attendant interrupts Harry by offering to fill up his car. The mother hangs around, swivelling rapidly at the waist to keep warm, the boy locked in her arms as she waits for Harry to finish the negotiation.

'Look.' He turns and puts his hands on his hips, regarding the woman squarely. 'If you won't let me drop you off somewhere else, then let me at least give you something warmer to wear. I've brought along enough clothes to go around.'

Digging into his duffle bag on the back seat, Harry comes up with two jerseys. The boy immediately reaches for the fleece number but, looking perturbed, his mother tries to restrain him.

'No, we can't take—'

'It's all right, really.'

Her face is confused, surprised. 'But they look so new.'

'Just put them on before you keel over dead.'

Harry smiles as the little boy starts struggling with the impossibly long adult sleeves. 'Can I get us all some food now? You two must be hungry.'

An incomprehensible look resembling hurt crosses the woman's face. 'You've done enough already.' Tears well up in her eyes. 'We have to go, now.'

'But—'

She is already walking away, settling her son back on her hip. Over her shoulder she calls, 'God bless you, mister.'

3

He is lost now; he is sure of it. Besides that, a car has been trailing him ever since he left that garage in Prieska, hanging back deliberately, despite his slackening off from a speed of one-forty to ninety. Harry decides to pull over and wait for the vehicle to pass.

When, the day before, he spoke to Willie Erasmus on the phone he was told he would find a narrow track leading off the scraped R384 dirt road towards Leopold Ridge, twenty-three kilometres beyond Prieska. Harry wipes at his tired eyes, wondering how he could have missed this access road. He checks his mobile but the signal is as dead as roadkill.

Suddenly his pickup is enveloped in a dusty blaze, as brights are flicked on. Hearing the approaching vehicle decelerate, he reaches for the pistol he has tucked in the door compartment. He decides this is neither the time nor place to take chances.

A green Jetta pulls abreast of him. Cocking the 9 mm, he keeps it carefully out of sight.

A podgy African wearing a black windbreaker, pokes his face all the way out the other car's passenger window. '*Heta*,' he shouts, 'you lost, my friend?'

Harry winds down his own window. In the glow of the other car's dashboard, he notices that the driver's expression seems unnecessarily strained, like a getaway man who is waiting for his cue to take off. 'No,' says Harry. 'Just checking my map, that's all.'

'You from Johannesburg, friend?' The passenger's eyes are set rather close together, and the smile plastered over his face seems insincere.

'Yes.' Harry's thumb runs over the hammer of his pistol. 'How'd you know?'

The passenger laughs and points a finger back towards the rear of Harry's car. 'Your licence plates, man. Listen, where you going at this time of the night? Maybe we can help.' The man's accent is thick and sluggish, and Harry has to concentrate hard on what he is saying.

'I'm looking for the farm called *Oranje Genot*.'

'Ah, the Erasmus place.' The African turns to the driver, nodding his head vigorously, as if they had a bet going earlier. 'You looking for Willie, then?'

Relaxing his grip on the still hidden gun, Harry says, 'That's right. Willie Erasmus. Do you know him?'

'*Ja*, sure. It's a difficult entrance at night,' says the man. 'We'll take you back a few kilometres. You just follow us.'

As the driver finally turns his eyes on Harry, the open hostility in them surprises and unnerves the ex-cop. Despite the passenger's apparent jovialness, Harry has seen enough in his career to know that hell's kitchen is burning in the other man's gaze. He again tightens his grip on the gun.

The passenger thumps the side of the Jetta impatiently. 'Come on, man! You want to stay out here all night, looking at a map?'

As the two cars sit idling, the heater roaring steadily in his ears, Harry weighs up his options. The man is probably right about having to head back some way; he had started to guess as much himself.

'Yeah,' he says in a voice calmer than he feels inside. 'OK, lead on and I'll follow you.'

The passenger whoops triumphantly as if his favourite team has just scored a goal, and sits back again in his seat. The Jetta throws a sharp u-turn and shoots back into the darkness, hardly waiting for Harry to turn too. Uncocking the weapon, he replaces it in its holster, and shifts into first to follow the rapidly departing vehicle.

Ten minutes later, the car in front slows to a trundle in a gentle curve in the road. The driver flashes his lights before suddenly speeding off again, one hand waving from the passenger's window. Harry flicks on his brights once in return, then points his car towards the white wooden pole marking an entrance. True to the man's word, the tiny rust-flecked white sign has *Oranje Genot* painted on it.

Casting a confused glance after the departing Jetta's tail lights, Harry continues up the rough side track.

SIX

A Hijacking on the N10

1

11.52 p.m., 22 May 2004, Marydale

It was night. There was no light and the world was quiet, except for a faint bass escaping the rowdy bar to one side of the enclosed truck stop. Three figures slipped over the property's low concrete wall, and immediately headed towards an isolated sixteen-wheeler truck parked near the back wall of a massive mud-churned courtyard. Its purple tarpaulin read McGuire Steel and Cabling.

The truck stop lying on the outskirts of Marydale had only one poorly lit security gate, facing the N10, the main route to the Namibian border. It possessed the bare essentials, nothing else: two rusty diesel pumps, a small supermarket that was only open by day, ablution blocks with filthy showers and even worse toilets, a rowdy shebeen regularly filled with prostitutes, gamblers, cheap alcohol and plenty of *dagga*. Truckers slept in their cabs while the one security guard, who got paid three bucks fifty an hour—not even enough to buy a loaf of bread—stood freezing in the doorway of his wooden hut by the gate. At least two whores in skimpy dresses were currently keeping him company at his post, waiting to pick up the next driver who might arrive for the night.

Crouching low, and their faces concealed under balaclavas, the three intruders approached the McGuire truck's cab from the rear of the vehicle. One kept a constant eye on the bar and the entrance gate, while the other two drew pistols.

As silently as possible, each mounted the two steps to a cab door on either side. The front of the truck barely rocked. They discovered no one on the front seat, though the curtains to the bed area in back were closed. Both cab doors were securely locked. One of the intruders shook his head in disappointment and dismounted. It was Sheik Kheswa who first pulled his hood off and tucked his pistol into his pants. Jabulani Mahlangu stayed on the driver's side of the cab, deftly keeping down and out of sight of the window or side-mirror.

'*Heta!*' yelled Kheswa. When no one answered, he picked up some loose gravel and flicked it at the cab window nearest to him. '*Hetada.* Friend! Open up.'

The curtains inside the cab moved apart and a tired African face in its late twenties appeared. 'What is it?' shouted the middle-aged man. 'I'm sleeping.'

From the corner of one eye, Kheswa could see his other accomplice keeping watch, hidden under the truck behind one huge wheel. 'Can you help me? I need a spanner, size eighteen. It's for my truck.'

The driver wiped sleep from his eyes and stared at his dashboard clock. 'It's almost twelve o'clock—what do you want to work on your truck for? There isn't even any decent light.' His breath was already fogging up the cab windows.

'I know, I know. But I need to be at the border post close to six, and I've got some shit in the refrigeration unit that's coming loose.'

The man grunted in annoyance. 'Wait there,' he yelled.

Kheswa cast an eye over his shoulder at the guard still conversing with the prostitutes, and then at the illuminated bar, from which steam was escaping into the freezing night air.

'What's happening?' came an urgent whisper from underneath the truck.

'He's getting dressed. Stay cool.'

The driver shifted out of his bed onto the front seat, still buttoning his jeans. 'Which one's your truck?' He instinctively checked his mirrors.

'What?' Kheswa cupped his ear.

'Which one?' The driver pointed around at the other trucks.

'Can't understand you. Open the door.'

The driver frowned. 'First tell me which one's yours.'

Kheswa gestured over at a large green truck with TZANEEN ABATTOIRS scrawled along the side of its trailer. He turned back. 'Come on, I can't head into Namibia tomorrow with a truckload of rotting meat. Just give me a hand, friend.'

The driver's eyes widened. 'What you talking about? That's Doc Mabandla's hauler.'

'Open the fucking door!'

The man reached for the horn.

Jabu swung into view, levelled his pistol at the back of the driver's head, and pulled the trigger twice. Blood and glass sprayed out over Kheswa as he ducked, the sound of gunshots reverberating over the silent parking lot.

'*Shit!*' screamed the third man as he bounded out from underneath the truck. 'What happened?'

With a shout, the guard at the gate took two uncertain steps in their direction, the prostitutes staring open-mouthed after him.

Kheswa hauled himself up to the passenger door and smashed in the rest of the bloody shattered glass. He reached in and opened the door from the inside.

'Move it!' yelled Jabu.

Yanking the dead driver's body free of the cab, he then slid over to the driver's door and threw it open for Jabu. 'Where the fucking keys? You see the keys?'

As they fumbled around on the dashboard, in the glove compartment, the third shadowy figure shouted, '*Wena*, they're coming this way.'

The alarm having been raised, truckers were now spilling out of the shebeen like army ants.

'Where are the fucking *keys?*' yelled Kheswa.

'Hey, kid,' Jabu leaned out and hissed. 'Check him—check the driver's pockets.'

The security guard was running back into his wooden hut.

'Found them,' yelled the third intruder. The set of keys glittered in the light as he held them up.

'What you standing there for, man? Throw them to me,' Jabu shouted. 'Now, get up here! No, not this side, you cunt. Shakes', Shakes'.'

The truck roared to life as the kid scrambled round the front of it.

The panicking guard's first shotgun blast was nothing more than a distant flash of light and a puff of cordite. Two annoyed truckers from the bar stormed across the courtyard, bellowing for the use of his weapon. Soon the three-way argument between them was attracting its own attention, while Jabu brought the truck around in a wide sweep, aiming its nose directly at the gate. Then he floored it properly and the engine's enraged growl drew every face back in their direction.

'Let's move!' Despite feeling in control, Kheswa was gritting his teeth.

The truck vibrated as Jabu shifted into second. 'It's too slow.'

'We'll make it, com.'

The guard and would-be heroes were still yanking at the shotgun between them like dogs fighting over a bone. The rest of the onlookers were meanwhile scrambling for cover.

'Quick! Give me your gun.'

Jabu flipped it over to him.

Kheswa stuck out both arms, firing at the three bickering men with his two pistols.

The guard screamed and bolted for his hut, while the man who had gained possession of the shotgun pumped it once, then turned to face the oncoming truck.

'What's he doing?' shouted the kid. He pressed his hands to his ears.

Kheswa fired again, but missed.

The shotgun flashed a second time. This time the cab erupted with sound as glass splintered. Jabu flinched back, the kid screamed and ducked, but the windshield held.

'Motherfucker!' yelled Kheswa. He dropped one gun and, using both hands, took careful aim with the other.

'Got him now.' Jabu bore down on the man, flicking on the truck's powerful brights. A blinding halo of light forced the man to throw up a hand to shield his eyes. Not losing a second, Kheswa put three rounds into the solitary figure: neck, chest, stomach. He dropped dead where he stood, a second before Jabu roared over the corpse and smashed through the flimsy gate.

SEVEN

In the little world in which children have their existence . . .
there is nothing so finely perceived and so finely felt
as injustice.

Charles Dickens

1

9.13 p.m., 5 June 2004, *Oranje Genot* Farm

The two-storey Cape Dutch farmhouse stands on a slight rise at the end of a winding dirt track, deep in the bush. An unkempt lawn, flowing up from near the crude cattle gate, is the only refinement that separates this residence from the wild. Harry halts his pickup behind a battered old Land Rover parked in an open garage. A solitary security light mounted on a lofty pole casts a dreary light over the gutted remains of rusty farm machinery, which lie scattered in the unkempt grass.

Running over the lawn, a sleeper-block trail leads up from the garage to the front door. Harry stretches and yawns as he approaches the house, a feeling of trepidation settling in his heart. This domestic arrangement is not at all what he expected after the opulence of the Rees residence; he had at the very least expected there would be dogs leaping up at his car, but there is not a sound other than crickets sawing in the grass.

Before he can knock at the heavy front door, it creaks inward. His exhausted spirits drop further when he views the interior.

The only electrical illumination in the dark room is produced by radiant kaleidoscopic images from an ancient TV to one side of the recessed fireplace, which holds a low-burning fire and provides this living space's only warmth. A paraffin lamp burns on a table in one far corner. The floor has been stripped of any original carpeting, and now tattered zebra and impala skins make do to ward off the cold chill seeping up from the earth.

'*Kom in.*' The voice makes Harry drop his gaze to where a feral-looking girl about ten years old is holding open the door. Her eyes are jet-black, mouth set in a serious line, her feet bare, and in the murky light he cannot make out whether her skin is naturally deep brown or whether she is as grubby as the two hitchhikers earlier.

'Hi.' He does his best to smile at her.

'My name's Zelda, *Oom*,' she replies in Afrikaans.

A sound from the sagging brown couch draws Harry's gaze to the sickly looking man who sits there, his one arm hanging over the backrest and haunted eyes carefully studying the new arrival. Translucent plastic pipes feed into his nose from some contraption behind the couch which has a tablecloth draped over it. A number of blankets cover the man's ailing body, but the pump-action twelve-gauge shotgun propped up within easy reach against the armrest looks suitably menacing.

'You must be Harry Mason,' he wheezes.

Harry steps past the girl and crosses the floor, his hand held out. 'Willie Erasmus?'

The farmer grabs Harry's hand with obvious relief at not having to get up to greet the newcomer. 'That's right. Welcome.'

'Sorry I'm so late. The trip took longer than expected.'

'That's fine. Sit yourself down. My wife will get you something, but just now—she's fixing herself up. You *mos* know how it is with women when guests arrive.'

The sound of someone clopping heavily down wooden stairs reaches them from beyond a closed door, which opens revealing an overweight woman in a warm pink dressing-gown and puffy woollen moccasins. She is carrying a paraffin lamp and thick-lensed glasses are perched on her nose. Smiling to reveal several crooked teeth, the woman introduces herself in Afrikaans as Martha. As she speaks she shyly fiddles with a golden cross suspended from a chain around her neck. It seems that the badly plated jewellery has produced a rash of ugly red welts where the necklace has made contact with her skin.

Willie struggles free from his respirator. 'I still manage without it, much of the time,' he explains. 'But I find when I use it I don't get tired so easily. Hope you don't mind it—some people do. Come, Zelda here will help you unpack.'

Once he is handed a cup of tea and everyone is settled in the chairs ranged in front of the television, a few rudimentary inquiries float Harry's way, the parents clearly more concerned with watching the programme than discovering anything more about their visitor. Strangely, the wife keeps getting up to peer out the front window, as if she is expecting some-one. Her husband finally tells her sharply to sit still and watch the show.

All this while, their daughter is sitting beneath Willie on the floor, wrapped in the folds of one of his blankets. Every so often, she wordlessly pulls his hand down towards her head, but he quickly withdraws it, time and again.

'Zelda!' He eventually loses patience. 'Stop it.'

Throwing herself over on her side, Zelda first stares up at Harry, as if he is somehow guilty of this rebuke, then turns her angry gaze back towards the television.

He finds its bright colours straining his tired eyes here in the darkness, till the lids steadily become heavier. His eyes finally begin to droop closed; instantly his head feels warmer, the room intangible.

Where are you, Harry? Her voice is soft, comforting.

I'm here, he replies.

What are you doing there?

The memory of a grime-streaked face with strong cheekbones and sky-blue eyes floats into mental view. Her face, however, has now some older, more familiar sadness in it.

I'm working, he explains.

That feeling of tilting increases, as though the world is slowly swallowing him up. He is falling, falling . . . then there she is, Amy, but she is not happy to see him. Her hands are pressed up against glass; she is screaming, terrified. Inexplicably they are rushing towards each other at a frightening speed. She is trapped behind a window pane—no, that's not quite right. It is a windshield.

What are you saying? I can't hear you.

Get Jeanie!

He jerks awake, spilling cold tea over his lap.

'You all right, man?' The farmer and his wife are both staring at him.

Harry glances at the television. The same show is still on, but Zelda has left the room.

'Yeah.' Harry scratches his head and laughs. 'Just really tired. Ten hours on the road does that to you, I guess.' He quickly drains his cup of tea and announces he will be retiring.

Martha uncurls herself from the sofa, which creaks in loud protest. 'Let me show you to your room.' She fetches Harry a paraffin lamp of his own and they pass into a narrow hallway. Martha gets halfway up the stairs before she apologizes and heads back down to check the locks on one of the doors. Then they proceed upstairs again, and she takes him to his room.

The stout double bed looks comfortable, layered in thick blankets. A giant footlocker stands in front of it and a large pine wardrobe faces the small window opening on to the rear of the farmhouse. He is relieved that this room, at least, is what he might have expected.

'I'm afraid we don't have heaters, so I've left you a pile of extra blankets in the wardrobe.' Lit by the orange glow from her lamp, the woman's face is touched with concern.

He gives Martha an exhausted but reassuring smile. 'It's perfect, thanks.'

She bids him goodnight and heads off to her own bedroom at the far end of the passage. Harry closes the door behind her and tries the light switch. A bulb flares brightly, and he switches it off again, too tired to wonder why they use no electricity except for watching Saturday night television. He removes his shoes and collapses on the bed without undressing further. Once he extinguishes the paraffin lamp, a velvety darkness engulfs him.

Some time later, he is startled awake again, instantly alert. He listens hard, but hears nothing, sees only the silvery glow of moonlight through the curtains. As he begins to think that he must have been dreaming, he again hears a wooden stair tread creak loudly. Harry turns his head towards the door and wonders who might be creeping upstairs this late at night. A series of dry coughs identifies Willie Erasmus's approach, but before Harry can start to relax, the man stops abruptly outside his bedroom door. A hand falls gently on the door handle, and for one panicked moment he has visions of Erasmus bursting in on him with a shotgun.

Harry gets ready to roll himself off the other side of the bed, should the door start to open.

For two long minutes, both men listen carefully for telltale signs of life on either side of the door. Time seems to stretch into eternity, each passing second cooling the sweat of fear that broke out on Harry's brow. Eventually, Erasmus lets go of the door handle and shuffles off towards his own room. As he hears mattress springs creak faintly along the corridor, Harry sits up shuddering with alarm.

Get a grip, he reproaches himself. He gropes around on the bedside table, only to remember that he has given up smoking.

When last did he feel this spooked? He does not remember. Harry gets up from the bed and pushes back the curtains. The landscape is beautiful, even at night, with the haunting silver glow of a clear moon and the Milky Way illuminating the expanse of bush. In the distance he can distinguish the course of a river by the dark silhouettes of trees growing densely along its banks. He guesses that it must be the mighty Orange River snaking out from the shadow of gentle black hills beyond.

What the hell are you doing here, mate? You gave up this cops 'n' robbers game a while ago.

The faint disquiet he felt on first arriving at *Oranje Genot* resurfaces now in full force. Before he took on this job for Campbell, he never stopped to consider whether he was still up for this kind of work. He was too busy justifying the undertaking to himself, to Amy's memory, and even to Jeanie. Now he is already deep into it, perhaps too far to pull out.

Something happening below the window catches his eye. Harry frowns, leaning forward to get a better view. At first he cannot be sure, but then it happens again. A tiny red dot flares in the darkness, before tracing down into deeper shadows and fading away. He then realizes someone is standing smoking a cigarette out there, and probably watching the house.

Wondering if it is a security guard, Harry continues staring, but the more he stares, the more the darkness becomes amorphous, and soon he is seeing all sorts of various shapes roiling in the blackness, the way monstrous figures appear and vanish in the clouds. Blinking to ease his eyes he returns to bed and eventually falls asleep, dreaming of a man with smoking red eyes, who lurks in the shadows somewhere below his window.

2

8.21 a.m., 6 June 2004, *Oranje Genot* Farm

When Harry finally comes down for breakfast the next morning, he finds Martha Erasmus bustling about dressed in dungarees and a white T-shirt. There is the savoury aroma of bacon in the air, and the steel lid of a kettle is clattering loudly. The woman's greeting is, however, not as welcoming as her kitchen, and her expression is strained, almost grim.

A few minutes later Willie Erasmus enters through the back door from outside, and takes the chair at the head of the table. A lukewarm greeting to Harry escapes his lips, then the meal proceeds with the same uncomfortable paucity of conversation as the night before.

'So you're staying a week, huh?' says Willie, eventually.

'That's right.' Harry then thanks his hostess for the meal, but she hardly seems to notice, her eyes pinned on her husband.

'And who's paying for your stay here? I mean, I can barely feed my own family, and now there's you, too.'

Convinced that Rees must have sorted out this part of the deal beforehand, Harry stumbles over his explanation that their additional expenses will be settled by Henrietta Campbell's account. This promise apparently does nothing to cheer the farmer and his wife.

'What are you supposed to be doing here, exactly?' Willie continues, trying to sound firm despite his shortness of breath and wheezy voice. Harry can sense the farmer's leg jumping nervously under the table. 'You with a bank, or something?'

'Ms Campbell just wanted me to take a look around.' Harry is not quite sure whether he wants to disclose details of his case.

'A look around—what does that mean? She planning on selling the place out from under my feet? Was she ever going to tell me?' Erasmus has begun to blink frantically, as if he has sweat running into his eyes. 'Because if they want to run me off the land without telling me first, I'll hold my ground by force if I have to, I swear.'

'I don't know whether they intend to sell.' Harry holds up one hand. 'But I know my stay here has nothing to do with any of that. She wants me to look into something that happened here a long time ago.'

'And what's that?' interjects Martha. 'Is it about her daughter—the one that went missing?'

'You know,' Willie ignores his wife's question, 'this is all I need. If that woman's gonna run me off . . . if she thinks . . . I never got a bloody cent from them to cover the maintenance of this place. Never, in the nine years I've looked after the place.'

'I'm just investigating—'

'*Investigating!*' Poorly concealed alarm crosses Erasmus's face. 'What do you mean, "investigating"?'

Martha slaps a plump hand on the table. 'I *told* you; it's about that girl who won't stay dead.'

'Wait a minute.' Erasmus holds up a hand to silence his wife. 'Let him talk.'

'You know something about Claudette Klamm's disappearance, Martha?' Harry asks her.

A sudden quick movement from Zelda, sitting opposite Harry, attracts his attention to the abundant scars on her arms, before she pulls them off the table. He had not noticed them the night before, but then it was dark and he was exhausted.

'Martha, I told you to shut up about that *kak*.'

Zelda's eyes are fixed on Harry's as she begins to slowly slide off her chair.

'Tell him,' Martha urges her husband.

'Now wait—'

'*Tell* him.'

Harry glances questioningly at the other two adults. 'Tell me what?'

Abruptly, Zelda gives a squeal and bolts out the back door to the farmyard, the clamour of her retreat sounding a mixture of fun and hysteria.

'*My magtig, meisie!*' yells her mother after her. 'Not now!' She turns to Harry and, by way of apology, says, 'Sorry about that; she gets like that when . . . well, when . . . she's just a very sensitive girl.' Harry can see how areas of the woman's throat and face have splotched bright red with emotion.

'You can tell that woman, and that Rees guy too, that I'm not budging, not now. I don't have long to go, so they can bloody well sit tight. When I'm gone, they can take the place back. You tell them that.'

Martha has begun to busy herself with cleaning up. Her head is bowed but her spine tense as she plunges both her hands into steaming hot dishwater. After a moment she withdraws them and shakes her hands violently, foam flying everywhere. 'Excuse me,' she mumbles, scuttling from the kitchen.

Erasmus fidgets with his coffee cup, pretending to be unconcerned by his wife's sudden departure from the room, which leaves him alone with the stranger.

'Look, Willie,' says Harry in a soothing tone. 'I very much appreciate your having me here, and I'll try to get underfoot as little as possible.' When the man does not reply, Harry pushes back his chair and stands up. 'Is there somewhere I can make a few phone calls? My mobile doesn't get reception out here.'

Willie gives a smile that to Harry seems totally work-weary. 'You'll have to drive to Prieska or Leopold Ridge for that. Prieska may be better, though. They've stolen the lines again, since we spoke.'

'You don't have a phone in the house?'

'I have a phone but not much else. It's going to be months before they replace those lines again. Hell, last time they even hijacked the Telkom trucks that were bringing in the new cables.'

'So you're stuck out here with just a TV to keep you in touch with the rest of the world?'

'We've got a CB radio in the study.'

'Right.'

'You a journalist, then?' asks Erasmus.

'No. Why?'

'I'd appreciate it if you don't talk about ghosts and haunted houses in front of my daughter.'

'Ghosts?'

'Yes, fucking ghosts. I don't want you encouraging them, you hear me?'

'Sure. No ghosts, no haunted houses, I promise.' Harry starts for the door, but stops. 'What exactly did Bernard Klamm do for a living?'

'He owned a few of the mines in the area, but made most of his money by ripping off the people who depended on his general stores, which were the only ones near some of the remotest mines and communities. He was a greedy Jew in my book, charging ridiculous prices for equipment, and cheating miners over the weight of their ore. Not an honest man, but fine by me, as he gave me this place for next to nothing. Never been able to figure out why.'

'Did you work for him, back in the day?'

'No, I moved to the area after he was already living in Jo'burg.'

'What did he mine here?'

'Asbestos.'

3

10.09 a.m., 6 June 2004, Leopold Ridge

The sun is already sitting high in the sky as Harry pulls into Leopold Ridge. It seems to be little more than a junction of two scraped dirt roads and a railway line; the handful of houses would have looked derelict but for some curtains in the windows and the odd beat-up jalopy parked in the roadway. Harry stops outside a small central prefab complex, protected by a high wire fence and with security lights mounted on four corners. A little way on stands an old church built from sandstone blocks. People in their Sunday best are spilling down the front steps, a service having just finished.

Harry walks across the road towards the closed-up supermarket, where two public telephones are anchored to the wall. He is relieved to find that the telephone lines in the village are functional, and puts a call through to Jacob.

'How's it going out there?'

'What, besides being stranded with the Addams family? Fine, I guess. I have some information on Klamm: he was apparently in the asbestos industry, and otherwise ripped people off on a regular basis.'

'I found that out in the meantime, my friend. It seems GGeM gave him the title to *Oranje Genot* in 1965. It was some sort of incentive to join as an executive in their company, which mined asbestos extensively in South Africa. It meant Klamm and his family moving to Johannesburg that same year, keeping hold of the farm as an asset and holiday retreat. He retired from the company's board in 1983 with a very healthy financial package. After that he became some sort of special adviser on the asbestos industry to lobby groups.'

'What else you got?'

Jacob tells him about the red photo album discovered in Klamm's safe, the telephone number written on a slip of paper, and the blood-caked white jersey.

'Wait a minute. A white jersey?' Harry recollects reading about such a pullover in the file Campbell gave him. Claudette had been wearing it the night she disappeared. 'Christ, Jacob, it must belong to their missing daughter. Has the blood been tested?'

'Haven't heard back from the lab yet.'

'And you found it at Klamm's place?'

'Yes.'

'Then she was probably killed by her father, like Campbell suspects. In that case, what am I doing all the way out here?'

'You're going to do something for me, that's what.'

'Uh-huh?'

'This phone number has a Prieska extension. Find this Freddy Meyer for me. I phoned it, but it's been disconnected.'

'Give it to me.' Harry writes down the number.

'I find it strange that the red photograph album contains numerous pictures of Claudette up to around the age of adolescence, but nothing afterwards. It's as if she stopped existing for Klamm when she turned fourteen.'

'Fourteen?' mumbles Harry. 'That's about the same age as most of the girls appearing in the other pictures.'

'I was thinking the same thing,' replies Jacob. 'But I don't have a clue what that means, unless he had some fixation on fourteen-year-olds.'

'Have you checked if Klamm had a criminal record for sexual offences?'

'Of course, yes. And, no, he didn't.'

'Hmm, doesn't necessarily mean he wasn't up to something. Could've been getting away with molestation all these years. Have you spoken to the Campbell woman about any of this?'

'No.'

'You should, now. Find out more about their marital relationship—paedophiles tend not to relate well to other adults. That might be the true reason he and Campbell broke up.'

Jacob sighs. 'My priority is to find out who killed Klamm, so his daughter is your deal. I've got a few things here I need to check out—especially the angle on Cauto, this guy who was meant to have murdered her.'

'Sure, Cauto is a strong lead, I'll give you. But if Klamm was molesting kids and someone found out about him, found out where he *lives*—some relative, even an older previous victim—you got yourself another suspect. Listen, while we're at it, I've got a feeling about this Rees character, too. Look into his history, will you? He's pushing Campbell real hard where the sale of that property in the Northern Cape is concerned. Maybe he's just a greedy old bastard, maybe it's something else, I don't know.'

Harry rings off. Without actually registering them, his eyes track a family of four crossing the street. Behind his blank stare, puzzle pieces are shifting, flipping around, finding ways to fit the picture of Klamm forming at the back of his mind. The big issue is whether the disappearance of Klamm's daughter, those pictures of the other girls, and then the man's murder have anything to do with each other. Wherever the case may lead, the white pullover is the most important clue so far. He looks at the telephone number in his hand.

'Ah, Mr Gauteng!' Harry turns around to see a rotund African, a year or two younger than himself, step onto the raised concrete platform fronting the Ridge Superette. He is dressed in a beige police uniform. 'Find the place you were going OK?'

It takes Harry a few seconds to recognize the man's face from the night before. 'Oh, hi. Yes, I did, thank you.'

'OK, no problem, no problem. So you living out there with Willie?'

'For now. I didn't realize you were a police officer.'

'Yes.' Sheik laughs and points at the badge sewn to his shirt, just above the breast pocket. 'That's me, Sergeant Kheswa.'

'Harry.'

Despite his jovial performance, the man's eyes appear cold, his face not as animated as his laughter. He also stands very close to Harry in a way that's aggressive, not familiar.

'Are they selling that farm now, or what?' the police officer asks.

'I don't know.'

'You don't know? Then what you here for?'

'Just to take a look around,' says Harry evasively.

Kheswa laughs again, clapping one hand on Harry's shoulder. 'Look around, there's nothing but sheep, sick and tired people, and dry bush. It's boring out here, man.'

Harry shrugs, resenting the hand lingering on his body.

'You know, Harry,' Kheswa directs him so that they are facing his car across the road, 'I saw you coming into Prieska last night with that woman.'

'Oh? Were you watching out for me?'

'No!' Kheswa puts on an offended face. 'No, of course not. We were just in town and along comes this Gauteng bakkie—what a nice, nice car— and I say to myself, "This must be the guy that Willie told me is coming," because up here we have no secrets, none at all. It's so small and dry, we just gossip all day around here, you know? And I say to myself, "This man, he's going to get lost here at night, let's go help him out." And you did, you did get lost.' Kheswa laughs again, thumping Harry on the back for emphasis.

Harry forces a smile. 'Yes, I got lost.'

Sheik looks at his watch. 'Look, I must get back to work now, but I see you again. You need anything, you get hold of me first, all right? You come speak to Sheik. Just ask for Shakes, né?'

'Sure.'

Harry watches Kheswa cross the road and step over a heavy nail-spiked chain, which seals the access to the police station. He meanwhile cannot shake the feeling of watching a cobra retreating into the grass.

Turning back to the public telephone, he fishes out the last of his coins and dials his mother's house. Harry secretly hopes to hear his daughter pick up first, all excited and flushed to be hearing from him, but the house phone just rings and rings. There is no answer, and no chance to leave a message.

4

1.21 p.m., 6 June 2004, *Oranje Genot* Farm

Sunday lunch in the eating area of the living room is a hardy meal of *bobotie*, potatoes, rice, beef, lamb, and a variety of vegetables—a spread Harry thought impossible since the family seem unable to even foot a normal electricity bill. Though Willie eats little of the feast his wife has prepared, Harry is amused by the way he attacks his food: one arm wrapped around his plate, his fork skewering everything with the speed and force of a piston-driven harpoon. It reminds Harry of the way prisoners eat, impatient and defensive, as though constantly on the lookout for someone who might steal their food ration. He also has a chance to observe Zelda more closely, and sure enough, there are older scars among fresher wounds on her forearms. If she was any older, he might have assumed she had attempted suicide more than once. It occurs to him that the photographs Jacob showed him depicted girls with similar injuries on various parts of their bodies, but mostly on their forearms. A few of those girls looked like they had been knocked around a few times: ugly bruises around their eyes, swollen lips, torn clothes.

Zelda catches him staring at her, and abruptly sticks her tongue out at him.

'*Sies, meisie!*' reprimands her mother. 'Since when do we do that to guests?'

Harry laughs out loud. 'It's all right. She caught me staring and I shouldn't have. Mind if I ask what happened? Those scars look nasty.'

Willie ends his violent assault on his meal, one cheek still stuffed with food. He glares around at the others. 'She had an accident.'

Both wife and daughter deny this loudly.

'Bloody hell, woman!' Willie fixes his attention on Martha. 'This is a decent family at table; we'll not discuss this nonsense further. Is that clear?'

Not wanting to cause more conflict, Harry tries to redirect the discussion. 'You have security on this farm, Willie?' He has been wondering about the cigarette-smoking figure he thought he saw in the darkness last night. 'I'm so used to high-voltage fences and lasers where I come from, it's a miracle to see you living so carefree.'

'*Ja*, I brought in some Angolan refugees and trackers from Schmidtsdrift and Pomfret a few years ago—they're the only ones you can trust around here. They look after the place. I've told them all to stay far away from the house, though, 'cause after dark I'll shoot anything that moves, easy.'

'You have a lot of farm killings here in the Northern Cape?' asks Harry, surprised. The massacres of entire farming families are more typical of Mpumalanga and Natal than the other provinces.

'Not that I know of,' replies Willie. 'But you can never be too careful.'

'It killed Marcy, Papa,' whimpers Zelda. 'Mr Harry, it was the same thing that did this to me.' She holds up the arms Harry had been eyeing earlier. Instantly, her mother hisses a warning, and tries to cover up the wounds with her serviette.

'Zelda! What did I just say?'

'Willie—' begins Martha.

'Not *now*.' The farmer immediately begins to cough. After a few drawn out moments he finally catches his breath again, and turns on his daughter. 'You—go to your room.'

'She's not finished eating. At least let her finish her meal.' Martha is nervously toying with her gold necklace again.

'I don't care. When I say she goes, she goes. I won't have disobedience, you hear me?' He turns to his daughter. 'I *won't* have it.'

The girl slides off her chair, tears welling up in her eyes. There is something about her defeated manner, the droop of her shoulders, which Harry will remember with pity later in the day when he starts worrying about his own daughter, and wondering how she is adjusting at her grandmother's.

'Marcy?' he questions the farmer.

Willie is still watching his departing child. 'We had two dogs here, but something killed them a week or so ago. For a few days, I had two of my guys keep an eye out for a predator after dark, but they saw nothing.'

'What could it have been?' asks Harry, curious.

'I don't know. The animals are both dead and that's that. It's not the first time dogs have been killed on a farm. It was something—or some*one*. Does it fucking matter? Point is, I'll now shoot anything that moves out there, I swear.'

Wordlessly, Martha rises to clear away her own unfinished food and the rest of the dishes, her face drawn and sour, the way it was that morning.

'Don't you look at me like that, Martha. Don't you *dare*. It's not what you think it is. For heaven's sake, all a man wants is a bit of peace, just a bit of peace when he's eating his lunch. I can't even have that. There never is any god-damned *peace* in this house!'

For a second it looks like the farmer is about to sweep the remaining crockery from the table, but instead he storms from the dining area.

5

An hour later, Harry is sitting beside Willie Erasmus in the old Land Rover, heading down a relatively well-scraped farm track towards the R384, a route connecting Prieska and Niekerkshoop with Leopold Ridge.

'I'm sorry you had to see that back there. Things haven't exactly been looking up for us, and the wife and daughter aren't cutting me much slack either. I'm none too well, Martha doesn't know the first thing about finding herself work, Zelda has had to leave school, and now it looks like I'm about to lose the farm, if it's sold. I tell you, difficult times these. You married, got kids?'

'My wife died four years ago—got a girl a bit younger than Zelda.'

'Shit. Sorry to hear that, man. Me, I don't know what I'd do without those two, even if they're a bit crazy most of the time.'

'There's one thing I did learn from the way things turned out, Willie. We were a happy couple, even if we fought a lot. The time we spent arguing, however, we could have spent so much better—we *would* have used better—had we known how little of it we had left. I gave my wife a lot of crap over nothing, things I thought at the time were important, but which I now realize were stupid and selfish.'

Willie turns to regard him. 'So what are you saying?'

'Not much, I guess,' says Harry. 'Just make what you have now work for you, because no man ever knows how much time he has left with his family.'

'I know that. I don't need you to tell me that.'

'Good.'

'I *know* that,' reiterates Willie. He turns his attention back to negotiating the dirt track.

Before reaching the 384, they swing up a rutted and overgrown path north-east. Within minutes, all signs of humanity disappear as they head into more hilly country, a dry tributary of the Orange River ever-present on their right.

'How big's this farm anyhow?' asks Harry.

'About three thousand hectares.'

'That big?' says Harry in surprise. 'And you look after all of it?'

At this Willie laughs. 'Most of it is unusable land. A big drought a few years ago turned grazing into nothing more than glittering sand. Soon those red dunes from up north will be invading us, too. I have karakul and cattle, and we try to go grow some lucerne closer to the river. Poultry is my main business, though. My father kept a whole lot of chickens, and that's where I learnt.'

'You keep your chickens all the way out here?' says Harry, clutching onto the door handle for stability. The track has turned much rougher, the SUV alternately bouncing over loose boulders and skidding through soft sand.

'I keep them close to a good water supply, near where some of my workers live. Besides, the chicken pens are built on some old foundations, which saved me a lot of money. Then there's always the smell of the birds, which Martha hates.'

'But all the way out here? Aren't you scared of stock theft?'

'It's happened before, but I moved some of my guys closer to the enclosures, and there hasn't been any trouble since.' Willie chuckles again. 'Man, I'm glad I thought to get hold of them lot. Most were native Angolan trackers and scouts, brought back by the army when the border war ended. They couldn't return home because they'd get lynched for working with the South African forces.

'I was there myself, you know. Four years I spent looking after a radar tower on the border of who-knows-where. All you could see was grass; nothing but grass and weak little trees you couldn't even climb. The only thing I learnt for my own good in that time was a bit of Portuguese from an old pal stationed there. That guy! He'd get us all drunk on stolen officers' stock, then fire us up for a game of rugby with a live mortar for a ball. Man, were we *bored*. Anyway, I learnt a bit of porra, and these days that's what I can talk to the people on my farm. No one else wants to work here, which suits me fine. These guys, they keep to themselves, do their job and they don't drink. The local blacks don't like them, and I think the feeling's mutual. The only time they ask to be run into town is when they need supplies, or want to spend what little Christmas bonus I can afford.'

Harry again thinks of the shadowy figure watching the house the night before, and wonders whether Willie's workers are as predictable as he thinks they are.

Ten minutes later the terrain becomes even rougher. A dried-up creek runs parallel to the track, thickets of trees and scrub growing in the sandy riverbed. Two lines of twenty-foot, white-domed chicken huts come into view, contrasting starkly with the veldt surrounding them. A rusty fence surrounds the entire compound: a sorry attempt to keep jackals and other predators at bay. Climbing out of the vehicle, Harry sees pipelines leading from this rundown complex into the riverbed, and guesses a borehole must have been specially drilled to supply the poultry enterprise with water. Someone whistles at them from a thick copse of thorn trees, as an ebony-black seated figure raises his hand in greeting from the cool shadows.

'There they are.' Willie waves back. 'It helps to have them not speaking any of the local languages, otherwise they'd probably end up not wanting to work for me, either.'

'Why do you say that?'

'People talk a lot of crap in these parts, and it spreads real quick, too.'

'What do they say?'

'You listening to me, Harry? I said it spreads real quick, which means I don't like it spreading further, which means I don't want to be talking about it.'

'Has it got anything to do with Klamm's daughter?'

'His daughter disappeared before my time, so I can't tell you much about that. Now, let me show you around.'

The huddle of trees the two Angolans have chosen for their camp is cool and well-utilized. A barbecue grille sits atop bricks, with dead black coals underneath it. Two-litre Coke bottles contain some water for them to drink in the hours of heat and tedium. Both men are armed with 9 mm pistols, and the shotgun they must share while on patrol leans against a nearby tree. The two guards grin up at Harry from where they are sitting, one nodding at their swift introduction. They are both short and scrawny men with beards and unkempt hair, so neither of them looks similar to the broad-shouldered and heavy-set figure Harry thinks he saw the night before.

Willie spends the next half hour describing to Harry the excruciating details of his chicken-farming operation. Rusty water feeds, connected to low-hanging pipes, drip-drip into plastic saucers, dusty spray cans filled with murky liquids stand discarded in corners, and sacks of feed and old boxes of medication have been carelessly spilled in places. His fowl are a sorry-looking bunch, clearly stressed and diseased: some are pink with hardly a feather left on their bodies, others scrawny with knobbly growths on their legs. As inexperienced as Harry is with livestock, it is obvious to him that the number of birds here is far less than the compounds were originally designed for, and if it is true that this is Willie Erasmus's main business, profits must surely be too slim to support a family, much less his workers. Despite his best intentions to go on appearing interested, the humid heat and foul stench soon drive Harry away from the enclosure.

Outside, Harry surveys his surroundings. Some other, larger complex must once have stood on this same site. Cement foundations, cracked and split from years of exposure, dot the surrounding landscape at irregular intervals, while a newer hut and outhouse have been built off to one side.

'Come,' says a heavily perspiring Willie. 'Look at this.'

They cross the sandy riverbed and head up a low hill densely overgrown with knobbly trees. The farmer stops frequently, struggling for breath, but is unwilling to turn back even at his guest's urging. At the top of the rise, Harry is surprised by their elevation; the land is spread out before them in a breathtaking panoramic view in three directions. To the north the foothills rise to eventually form part of a craggy belt of low mountains; to his right, he can see the muddy Orange River snaking past in the distance. White storks sun themselves in the branches of weeping willows that grow all along the riverbanks. Closer to the chicken pens, he can see a series of overgrown tracks criss-crossing the entire area, while to the south-west the house is partially hidden both by the distance and foliage. Further still lies a cluster of huts, where most of the farmhands must live.

'Beautiful, isn't it?' Willie is now clutching at his chest, clearly in some pain.

'Yeah,' says Harry, 'that it is.' He closes his eyes and concentrates on the fresh breeze soothing his hot face.

'I wouldn't mind being buried up here,' says Willie. 'It's so peaceful: no one to rush you, and you're raised above the troubles of the world. You can see so far; it's as if up here you have a chance to appreciate God's grand plan.'

Harry opens his eyes and quietly studies this man who is contemplating the world with the wonder of a child.

The farmer turns reddened eyes towards him. 'You haven't asked me.'

'Asked you what?'

'What's wrong with me.'

'I figured you'd tell me at some point.'

'Mesothelioma, that's what I have. The doctors say I only have a few more months to live, if I take it easy. But I can't just sit around at home. The place needs running, and though some of these guys will go on working for me after I'm bedridden, most of them would rather stay home and tend their own crops.'

Harry nods, not particularly surprised. Since the nearby mining communities of Prieska, Koegas and Kuruman started dragging British mining companies to court, the epidemic has been all over the media in flashes of sensationalism. 'Sorry to hear that. Is there nothing they can do?'

A huff that may be a laugh escapes the man. 'Sure. If I had the money they could put me on more medication, drips and feeds that numb my arms, and tap some of the juice building up in my chest, but that would just be wasting the cash I don't have in the first place. It's fucking incurable; this disease is a bottomless hole that sucks up everything I am, everything I had. I never even received medical aid.'

'Can't you seek compensation from the company you worked for?'

This time Willie does begin to laugh. After their climb it comes out as a loud, staggered wheeze. He suddenly grabs hold of Harry's shoulder for support.

'The *big* companies—the owners of the mills and larger mining sites—they're getting nailed now, yes. But they played it smart long before everyone cottoned on. You see, they bought a lot of their raw asbestos from smaller, independent producers. These tributers, they went bankrupt way before the big companies. They're long gone now, and so are their owners. They had nothing formal to do with the big guys, and they hardly kept any sort of records. No, those of us that worked on the smaller sites have been left out here to rot.'

'But surely you could go to the hospital in Prieska for treatment? Don't they run a special unit these days?'

'*Ja, my boet*,' Willie sighs wearily. 'And maybe we'll have a white president again. I don't know how it is in the big city, but our hospital is nothing more than an oversized clinic, where you can sit for days if you don't have an emergency to be seen to, 'cause everyone else is either rotting from AIDS or *vrot* lungs. The queues sometimes look like they wrap right around the hospital building. No, I don't have the time for that. I'd rather die out here, and be buried up on this hill.'

A silence falls between them as Willie struggles with his emotions and also for breath. 'There's a reason I brought you up here,' he finally continues. 'I'm fine with you staying at the farmhouse, but I don't want you heading over towards that range. Those tracks over there lead down this way from hills where good veins of asbestos were once exploited. They were close to the surface, easy to reach. The mountains behind them are called the Asbestos Range, and were rich in blue asbestos. That's one corner of the farm, by the way. There's an entrance in the fence there, but no one uses it any more.'

Willie points out various other distant locations, describing landmarks that evidently must be seen up close before they might be recognized. Finally, he gestures to the cement foundations underlying the area of the chicken enclosure. 'This here used to be an asbestos mill, of sorts. I worked at places similar to this: first outside Koegas, then at Pomfret. I was a foreman then, well respected. Now I'm just a scruffy farmer waiting to die.'

'I'm sure it's not all that bad, Willie.'

'Ah, fuck, what do *you* know, hey? Don't worry about it. None of your concern.' Erasmus's tone is difficult to place: it sounds angry, but dismissive in a friendly way as well, as if he knows he can't, or shouldn't, direct his bitterness at this man so attentively listening to him.

'My point being . . . look, everything north from that point there is out of bounds, OK. You understand that? It's important. There are overgrown mine shafts and wells everywhere—I've lost cattle that way—and my boys found raw asbestos lying out in the open. See those dongas further down the creek? They're not natural. Towards the Orange it looks like fur in amongst the grass and leaves, and tailings rich with the stuff have washed into the riverbed.'

'You're telling me that whole area is *contaminated*?'

'*Ja*, I don't know what's bad and not so bad, so from here on it's your own risk, not mine. The workers stay south, too, for their own protection.'

'Was this one of Klamm's mines?' asks Harry. His skin suddenly feels sensitive and itchy at the idea of microscopic fibres floating in the air.

'No, I don't know whose it was. But it wasn't one of the big companies— I know that. It must have belonged to one of the tributers.'

'Tributers?'

'Small operators who owned the mineral rights and bought ore by weight from black miners. They in turn transported it to depots where they sold it to the larger companies for milling.'

They start back towards the vehicle, with Harry occasionally grabbing at thorny branches and lichen-covered tree trunks to keep his balance.

'But isn't it dangerous living out here, even south of that contamination?' Harry asks the question to Erasmus's back. 'What if a heavy wind kicks up, or it filters down into the borehole water, what then?'

Willie does not turn around as he answers. 'Could be dangerous, but it's still pretty far from the farmhouse. Maybe . . . I don't know. I'm a simple man with few means, and so are the people working for me. What choice do we have? All the money I have is tied up in livestock and old farm equipment. Where do I go without it all?'

'Do you mind if I ask a personal question?'

'*Ja*, sure.'

'Your wife and daughter, what . . . ?' Harry leaves his question open-ended.

'Happens when I *kak* off? Fuck knows.' Erasmus laughs: it is meant to be dismissive, perhaps even slightly embarrassed, but the titter is almost hysterical. 'Fuck knows.'

EIGHT

A Soldier's Instincts Rekindled

1

8.02 a.m., 29 May 2004, Marydale

'Meyer, what have you got there?' called a voice in Tswana.

'A bent nail,' replied the white cop in the same language. He had gun-metal grey eyes, a silvery blond crew cut, and a pencil moustache. Like many farm children in the Northern Cape, he had grown up learning the language of his father's workers. 'Looks new—there's no rust on it.'

He was now squatting by the side of a long, straight stretch of the N10, where he had found the nail partially hidden in the sand. At the roadblock further up the incline to the south, a truck's horn bellowed impatiently. A three-hundred-metre section of thoroughfare had been completely sealed off, and the alternative routes between the towns of Marydale and Grobler-shoop were long and sandy detours no one seemed willing to drive. There was also no space on either side of the road to allow vehicles to pass, and so traffic was steadily building up in both directions, causing one of the few traffic jams the region ever saw in the course of a year.

'So what?' said the approaching African. He was short, clean-shaven, and had light brown skin. Both men were uniformed police officers, Meyer an inspector, Leo Diseko a captain and the local station commander. 'There are nails scattered on every road from here to Durban.'

'Hear me out.' Meyer was studying the road closely. 'Look at this, see these abrasions? They look fresh, like something recently scraped across it.'

'No, let me see.'

Hunching over, Leo tracked a series of faint white marks on the gravelly tarmac extending all the way to the other side of the road. In the sand immediately adjoining was a long deep print snaking into the grass and weeds.

'Here's another one.' Meyer held up the bent nail triumphantly. 'They're obviously using a homemade chain caltrop.'

'What are you talking about?'

'Buy a thick chain, weave wire through the links, and pack it as tight as you can with nails so that they stand out in all directions. That's how all four tyres always get punctured.' He had switched to using Afrikaans in his excitement. 'What's this?' He picked up a tattered bit of beige hessian lying on the grass. 'This hasn't been out here too long, either.' Meyer's eyes were flicking over the grass, the sandy verge, back to the other side of the road. He hastened across to look for more tracks.

'Are you kidding me, Freddy? Every single cash-car passing through the area is kept on high alert. They'd see a chain lying across the road a mile away.'

'Come here, look at this.'

As Diseko approached, from down the road came an urgent whistle, but he waved his hand dismissively. 'Jesus, we've got officers from four different towns here, all of them suddenly pretending they're the FBI. I'd have a laugh about it, but there's the dead to think about. Freddy, what the hell you looking at now? There isn't anything here.'

'There is.' Meyer was pointing at some marks in the soft sand three metres away from the road. 'See those two dents—they were probably made by elbows. Someone was lying here on his stomach, maybe camouflaged under some sacking. From a distance you wouldn't be able to see him unless you knew what you were looking out for.' He pointed at a patch of flattened grass further back. 'Something heavy lay here—a coil of chain? The person who lay here wasn't very long, maybe your height, and he must've been waiting for the best time to haul the chain across the road. He'd want to shave the timing as close as possible, so the driver wouldn't have time to hit his brakes. And look at the lie of the land—there's nowhere a driver can veer aside to. You hit one of those drainage ditches at any speed, you're likely to go flying through your windshield, even if you're wearing a seatbelt. No, you time it right, there'd be no stopping the car from going over a bunch of nails. Even with armoured tyres, the instant blow-out of four wheels at once would catch any driver off guard, given the speeds at which they race through these parts. And most likely they've been driving even faster since an alert went out that cash-cars were being targeted.'

Diseko was staring at Meyer. 'How can you tell all that? Were you raised by bushmen, or something? Your mama a Khoi?'

Meyer pulled a packet of Pall Malls from the pocket of his blue windbreaker and lit himself a cigarette. Stretching his back he said, 'I shot my first impala when I was five, and my first leopard at twelve. I remember the day we were tracking it: the dogs got so shit scared when they spotted it, they turned on each other rather than advance further. My dad had some trackers living on his farm, and I learnt most of what I know from them. They were Bastars, though—I've never met a Bushman.'

He was not telling the whole truth to his black commander, for he had worked extensively with San hunters during the border war, while serving in the Special Forces Rekkies. For eight years he had tracked SWAPO insurgents across the endless expanse of bush located on the border between Namibia and Angola, his squad sometimes not halting their forced march for days just to close the distance between them and an enemy. It had not mattered to their commander whether they had to shit and piss themselves on the march, or prop up their eyelids with camel thorns to stay awake, orders were orders and that was that. Such was life in the long-term war nationalist whites fought against communist blacks, though Meyer personally had no fundamental problems with any black man or communist. He saw no reason to elaborate on those days now.

Diseko was still trying to make sense of what he had just been told when someone shouted for his attention. He raised his hand to indicate that he had heard, then turned back to Meyer. 'You sure about this chain business?'

'As sure as I can be.' His expression unreadable, Meyer regarded the other police officers over his commander's shoulder. A handful of them were picking over the wreckage of the armoured car lying on its roof in the middle of the road. He could see their approach to this crime scene was inspired more by casual curiosity than by any systematic collection of evidence. Bank documents, empty strongboxes and thousands of glittering loose coins were strewn over a very wide area. The bodies of four victims had been laid side by side on the road surface, and were covered with blankets. One of them had died from the impact of the crash, the other three had been shot subsequently.

'Should we get someone to take photographs of this?' Diseko was still studying the flattened areas Meyer had pointed out.

'Jaap's already taken his camera back home,' said Meyer. 'This is just wasting my time.'

'Really? And what better things have you got to do?'

'Simon Gallows is still missing.'

'*Ag* hell, Freddy, if he didn't go home to his wife last night, that doesn't mean the worst has happened.'

'He's not like that, and you know it.' Meyer settled hard eyes on Diseko. 'If he was going to sleep over somewhere else, he would have phoned her. He's never been late in returning the cruiser, either. The last I heard of him, he told me he was going to check out something in Leopold Ridge. I reckon he'd figured out something to do with this business here.'

Diseko switched back to speaking Tswana. 'So you think he knew someone was going to mount this robbery today?'

'He couldn't stop talking about these heists, like it was the only thing on his mind. Even Elsa, his wife, says so.'

Diseko took Meyer by the shoulder and began guiding him back towards the wreckage. 'OK, so maybe he *is* missing. You're right, he has never done that before, so you better look for him later. Right now I need you to concentrate on this, and help me make our little station look good to the bosses. Loodts tells me the banks and mining offices have just about had it. They started putting serious money up as rewards for information, and they're financing heavily guarded convoys for their cash-cars. It seems some Serious Crimes specialists will be flying out from Johannesburg on Thursday, so help is on its way. Help and a lot of attention, which means we need to look sharp.'

'Leo, you realize this is an inside job. Information about routes and timetables is being leaked to the perpetrators, and that means it's either coming from the security company itself or any of the police stations in the area, which are alerted in advance to cash-car movements.'

Diseko halted abruptly and turned Meyer so as to face away from the other officers. 'I know. You've told me all this before, and I told *you* to keep it to yourself until the big boys get here. You're probably right, Freddy, but, you know what, you and I are too small to deal with stuff like this. Look at me . . . look at yourself. We wear *uniforms.* We're not plain clothes New York detectives. You and I are in charge of a little town with nearly more churches than it has residents. It's our job to roust the drunkards who end up making a nuisance of themselves on Saturday night. We trap speeding tourists, lock up men that beat their wives, and wives that stab their husbands. That's all, Freddy, so we'll play our part by waiting for the big boys to get here on Thursday.'

Meyer shook his head. 'I can't wait that long. This whole district's been running around with its head up its own backside, trying to figure out how to deal with this mess. No one even bothered to take photos at the first two crashes. They just fucking cleared the road as quick as they could, to keep the traffic flowing. We'll be waiting three months for ballistics reports from Pretoria on the Groblershoop heist, and I bet you, no one's really going to know what the reports mean when they *do* arrive. Simon clearly made some connection, and I need to find out what it was. I can't wait until Serious Crimes get here, Leo. I need to find him before it's too late.'

The two men just stared at each other for a moment.

'Freddy,' Diseko began in a measured tone, 'you be patient. You might have killed your first leopard at the age of twelve, but whoever is doing this is smart and dangerous. OK, you go find Simon, but if it looks like there'll be any trouble, you call in the rest of us. Promise me that, Freddy.'

Meyer gave him a curt nod.

'Good.' Diseko balled a fist and bounced it against his lips. Finally he expelled a loud sigh. 'You got a lead on that McGuire consignment yet?'

'No. I've gone around to all the steel wholesalers who we know have bought black-market stuff in the past, and most of the others too, both in Marydale and Prieska. No one knows anything, and they say they don't have any steel on the premises that isn't theirs, either. That doesn't mean much, though. They could have stuff hidden in their backyards at home, but I can't go check on that. You know why?'

'Why?'

'Because I've already spent my petrol budget chasing down this one lead, and I don't have any money of my own to buy more.'

'Jesus Freddy, will you relax? What do you want me to do, give you all the station's budget? I'd love to, but we don't *have* any—bugger all. Think Thursday, Freddy, *Thurs*day.'

'Leo! Freddy!' Loodts was waving to them. 'Come have a look at this. They've changed the way they operate. These doors weren't cut open like the others; they used explosives.'

The armoured side door had been blown apart along one neat seam, exposing purple-singed metal.

'I wonder, why the change?' murmured Diseko.

'They're learning how to save themselves time,' said Meyer quietly. 'It also means they've brought someone on board who knows about linear cutting charges, and how to place them correctly.'

For the second time, Diseko turned surprised eyes on him. 'Where's all this coming from? You not telling me something, Freddy? You sound just like some big detective from the city. Come on, you can tell us: what's your secret?'

'Get me a full tank of petrol, Leo,' he replied. 'I'm going to look for Simon.'

Heading back towards a patrol car parked on the shoulder, Meyer stopped to pick up two circled .38 shells from the spot where one security guard had been shot twice in the back of the head, execution style. One of the men shot dead at the truck stop outside Marydale a few days before had also been killed with two bullets from a .38, and both those shells revealed a hammer indentation that seemed a bit cockeyed, as if the hammer itself was slightly bent. The same was true for the shell he was examining now. He then turned the second one around, and found the hammer mark was positioned exactly where he remembered the others had been. He glanced back towards the other cops lounging around the wreckage, and decided in that instant not to say anything about his new discovery. This would be his hunt—his alone.

2

3.25 p.m., 29 May 2004, Marydale

The low wall in front of which Meyer came to a stop was made of concrete and decorated in repetitive wagon-wheel designs. Two plastercast dwarves stood just inside the creaky little gate, staring up at the post box with merry round faces. A tricycle lay on its side on the yellowing lawn.

Where other houses on Wemmer Street either had no garden, or just a bare sand lot, or a scraggly overgrown thicket, Elsa and Simon Gallows had tended their patch with love and care. There was a beautifully cut puzzle bush in one corner, freshly planted pansies in flowerboxes, a bougainvillea climbing over the porch that was lush with red blossoms in the spring. On the raised concrete *stoep*, pots of every size held ferns, succulents and cacti. Two cockatiels chirruped to each other from separate cages.

The screen door was already opening as Meyer mounted the front steps.

'Freddy, have you found him yet?' A petite woman with shoulder-length hair stood holding it open, a cardigan clutched around her shoulders. She looked like she had been up all night, and tears were already welling up again. 'Where's my husband?'

'Hello, Elsa.' Meyer's voice had compassion in it, but he did not move to touch her. 'Let's go inside.'

The woman busied herself with making coffee in the kitchen as he questioned her.

'Did he tell you where he was going?' asked Meyer. 'Please, think back hard.'

'No, I already told you so.'

'I mean the night before. Did he give you a clue where he was going?'

'No, he didn't.'

'I want you to tell me exactly what was on his mind. I need to know what direction Simon was taking in here.' He tapped his head.

'I don't know,' she repeated as she gathered up cups and spoons. 'He couldn't seem to leave these heists alone, and most of it didn't make any sense to me. I didn't understand a word of what he was saying either, as Simon talks so very fast when he gets excited. He always wanted to become a city detective, move us somewhere like Kimberley or Johannesburg. He's such a dreamer. You know that better than most.'

Meyer nodded as he lit himself a cigarette. 'Did he say anything to you about those trucks that were hijacked?'

Elsa stopped clattering about the kitchen and turned to face him with a look of intense concentration. 'He kept saying he thought it strange that the first heist happened just a few weeks after that truck driver and the prostitute were killed outside Prieska.'

Meyer nodded. 'He told me the same.' What he did not admit to her was that, up until his friend's disappearance, he had only been listening with half an ear. Simon Gallows could talk both ears off an elephant, possessing a fast and high-pitched voice that always seemed to be revving at maximum revolutions.

'I think he thought the two incidents must have something to do with each other,' Elsa went on. 'I don't know. People around here are stealing things all the time, even trucks, but when was it that they started shooting the drivers?'

'Round about that first heist.' Meyer began to pace around the kitchen restlessly.

Elsa clutched a striped dishtowel to her mouth. 'What is it, Freddy?'

'Can I see his workroom?'

'Yes, of course,' she said. 'Down the hallway on the left. I'll finish up making the coffee. You do what you need to.'

It was a compact room with a high, pressed ceiling, and featured a crowded desk, a small bookshelf crammed with second-hand American true-crime books, a floor littered with the debris of a man not quite willing to grow up—exercise weights, rolled-up posters of sports cars, a framed *Huisgenoot* pull-out poster of the 1995 Rugby World Cup winning team.

The weights took him back to the first day he met Simon Gallows. For nearly an hour, Meyer had been working the punching bag around back at the police station, when this fresh unknown face appeared, wearing a silly amateur boxing cap. The newcomer had watched Meyer for about ten minutes before he finally asked if he could try.

Meyer had stopped and replied, 'Me or the bag?'

Gallows smiled mischievously. 'If you're up for it old man, then you.'

It was the first time anyone had been so brazen as to challenge Meyer at the station. Normally he was treated as a loner. He smiled, put up his gloves, and said, 'You're going to regret this, *boetie.*'

The youngster continued grinning, 'I probably will.'

Gallows had landed the first punch—his only one.

On a shelf above the man's desk were old photographs of family and older comrades from his army days; there were also athletics medals, miniature cars, a rusty old horseshoe. An A4 pad on the cluttered desk was covered in calculations. Three routes traversing the Northern Cape region had been boxed: the R357, R386, R384.

Meyer switched on the desk light and frowned. He remembered that three separate attacks had occurred on those three routes on the same day. The handwritten calculations on the page made absolutely no sense to him—he had never been good with numbers—but at the foot of the pad was a crudely drawn map of the region immediately around Leopold Ridge, with the three points of attack marked in blue ballpoint. A triangle and several doodles were drawn over an area that might have encompassed Bernard Klamm's old farmstead. The phone number for the town's police station appeared at the top of this map, circled a few times in the same ballpoint.

The door behind him creaked open wider. 'Find anything?'

Meyer grunted. 'Don't know yet.'

'You still want some coffee?' Elsa spoke softly.

'Mhm.' Meyer looked up at her. 'Where's the little one, Clarissa?'

'Over at a friend's house.' Elsa's hands abruptly rose to her face. 'Freddy . . . what the fuck am I going to do if he's dead?'

'We don't know that, Elsa.' He tore the page off the pad and folded it before sliding it into his pocket. 'Simon's a smart guy. He'll be all right, you'll see.'

Of course, Freddy Meyer knew he was lying. Simon Gallows, who had invited him to be his best man three years ago, who went weekend fishing with him at Boegoeberg Dam, and who had never ever been late in coming home to his new wife and young daughter, was dead. The certainty with which he knew this was now burning an angry hole in his heart, and the longer he held Elsa Gallows's gaze, the surer he became that she could tell he was lying.

3

11.58 p.m., 31 May 2004, Marydale

There were no streetlights in the Marydale township, but he already knew which was Prince Bakwena's place. He had been there before. The day Prince came out of jail Meyer was there to welcome him back and warn him what would happen if he ever tried to sell stolen blasting caps to shady entrepreneurs again. The man had kept a low profile for years since, but now Sergeant Gallows was missing, and someone was using explosives to slice open cash-cars. The coincidence was far too great for Meyer to ignore.

He doused the headlights of his beat-up '74 Chevy and grabbed a torch. Dogs all round were howling and barking at his arrival, though he could see none of them. There was a faint tang of garbage floating over the heavy stench of coal, though the air was freezing cold. He pulled a .45 from a shoulder holster and approached the door to a shack which was leaning heavily to one side. Without bothering to knock, he put a round through the door bolt. The gunshot was deafening in the sleepy silence.

Dogs, poultry, goats, people reacted alike—howling and baying and screaming and scrambling for cover.

A woman grunted in pain as the door he kicked in slammed against her. A second kick sent it flying wide open.

In Tswana, Meyer screamed, 'Out! Everyone fucking *out*.'

Switching on his torch he barged in as a girl in her late teens pushed past him. He yanked back the curtain behind which Prince slept, and there, on a shabby mattress, was his target blinking like a mole against the sudden light. A woman Meyer could not recall was sitting up next to him, clutching a blanket to her bare breasts.

'I said, get the *fuck* out!' he bellowed, veins in his forehead distending to accentuate the dark madness in his eyes.

'Is that you, Meyer?' exclaimed the middle-aged man in alarm. 'What is this about?'

The cop grabbed the slowly reacting woman by the neck and hurled her towards the exit. Some of the blankets went with her as she was lifted clear off the mattress. Getting caught in the curtain, she stumbled into a rickety shelf. Crockery and cutlery clattered, over the loose plank flooring.

'What do—?'

Meyer raised his weapon and fired four times, strobes of light accompanying the ear-splitting explosions. Prince screamed, and went on screaming as the last round punctured the wall behind him. The amount of cordite released in the cramped space was like releasing a canister of teargas.

'Shut up,' growled Meyer. 'Or you get the next one in the face.'

Prince raised his hands and turned his face away from the powerful torchlight. His lips trembled desperately as he tried to suppress his sobbing.

'You selling caps again?'

'What? No! No, Jesus, Meyer, I'm *not*.'

'Give me a straight answer. I know you're selling explosives again.'

'Where did you hear that, man? I don't even work for the mine any more. Where am I supposed to get caps from?'

Meyer lunged out with his foot as if to kick him. The man screamed in terror and tried to back further away.

'Who's selling the stuff, then?'

'I don't—'

'Don't fucking lie to me, Prince!' interrupted Meyer.

'I swear! I swear, I don't know. I carry boxes all day at Konnie's Mean Machines, in town. Phone them, and they'll tell you. What do I know about caps these days?'

Meyer could hear the panicking women screaming for help outside, neighbours gathering and asking urgent questions. There was anger out there, and fear.

Squatting by the mattress's edge, Meyer ejected the used clip from the gun, and replaced it with a fresh one.

'Tell you what, Prince, I'm sure you still see some of your old buddies from time to time. I want you to come back to me with answers in just one week's time. I want to know who's been buying and who's been selling. If I don't hear from you within a week, I'm going to come after you, and everyone you know. I mean everyone.'

Meyer stuck the tip of his pistol under the man's chin, and forced his face up so their eyes could meet. 'You understand me?'

As he left the shack, he kept the gun ready by his side. He stared around at every figure he could make out watching him from the dark doorways of flimsy houses. The hush that fell over Prince's neighbours when they saw him announced a fear that lingered long after the dust of his departure had settled.

NINE

Do you hear the children weeping, O my brothers,
Ere the sorrow comes with years?
Elizabeth Barrett Browning

1

4.16 p.m., 8 June 2004, *Oranje Genot* Farm

The untended lawn at the rear of the farmhouse is a narrow strip long invaded by wild grasses, paper thorns, and crumbly termite mounds. Glancing back up at the small window of his bedroom to get his bearings, Harry
steps out into the dry veldt. It does not take him long to find the spot
where someone has trampled down the brittle grass and dropped the
end of a roll-up cigarette. He picks up the butt and sees it is the typical
smoke of a blue-collar African worker, containing Boxer tobacco rolled in
newspaper.

He has been hearing some interesting things about this farm over these
last two days, most notably from the small supermarket owner in Leopold
Ridge and the district librarian in Prieska. The shop owner cackled with
laughter when Harry told him where he was staying, inquiring whether he
had seen Klamm's creature yet.

'What creature's that?' Harry had asked.

The old wrinkled man had dug into his ear and twirled his pinky
around vigorously, until Harry thought he must be cranking up his brain
before he could speak again. 'You don't know? A man called Bernard
Klamm was the actual owner of that place—Willie, he's just a tenant.
Klamm's daughter disappeared one night years ago, and she was never seen
again. They arrested his right-hand man on the farm, but it was the devil
that got her, some say—collecting his dues, they claim.'

'And what sins did Klamm commit?' asked Harry.

'All kinds,' came the cryptic reply. 'That's why no one will work for
Willie except those foreigners. You speak to anyone from these parts,
they're likely to tell you a version of this same story.' The man touched his

nose and winked at Harry. 'You just make sure you're indoors before darkness falls. Whatever that thing is, we've even seen it here in town. It's killed a few dogs, and a babe or two has disappeared. I'm a cautious man myself, so when I hear such things I just stay indoors with my bible handy. You do the same and stay indoors, mister.'

A customer had called the old codger over before Harry could ask him any more, leaving him to wonder whether the shopkeeper had been serious or whether he was playing the stranger for a fool. Was this, he mused, the kind of thing they tell every tourist to wind them up?

'The devil?' the female librarian had reacted in surprise when he mentioned the story to her. She was clutching a pile of books to her chest, and craned to see Harry clearly in the sombre light of Prieska's library. 'I don't know anything about the devil. No, but my sister, she lives out that way, and she believes Bernard Klamm's daughter haunts the place. This deranged black man raped and killed her in the kitchen, or was it her bedroom? I can't remember.

'She's seen the girl, you know, my sister has. About four years ago, they were driving back from the diamond festival in Kimberley late one night, and there was this fine mist floating slowly over the road. But there was no fog and no clouds that night, it being as dry and cold as any normal April. Yet here was this white cloud hovering about. And she swears—that's my sister—that, the second before they drove through it, the mist turned into a surprised-looking girl holding up her hands as if to ward off their car. A young girl, she was, no older than fourteen. The interior of the car went icy cold as they passed straight through it.'

'But I thought Claudette Klamm disappeared when she was nineteen?' This was one fact Harry was certain of.

The librarian shrugged. 'Fourteen, nineteen, what does it matter when you're dead? The ghost looked fourteen when it passed through the windscreen.' The woman then walked off in an apparent huff, as if Harry had tried to insult her intelligence by questioning her account of Claudette's disappearance.

And so the anecdotes continued, every rumour containing only one similar thread: the people he spoke to were all of the opinion that Claudette was dead, one way or another.

Harry now contemplates the giant red orb of the setting sun, which has steadily been turning the African bush into a canvas of flaming orange hues. Long shadows from distant hills stretch out over this sanguine landscape, like the silhouettes of actors concealed behind a screen. A pair of hornbills rudely break the crisp silence, squawking noisily from an elegant quiver tree, whose bright yellow flowers have begun to bloom early.

Why would someone be standing out here at night in the dead of winter, watching the house inhabited by this destitute family? Watching, or perhaps, waiting? It seems unlikely to Harry that it was just one of Willie's workers, because they knew he might shoot them if he spotted something in the darkness. Harry has already seen enough to know that the man is skittish, what with the shotgun constantly kept at the ready in his sitting room. All three family members have a strange preoccupation with checking and re-checking the locks of that first door along in the hallway, and they are forever peeking out the window. It is not just Martha that does so, he now realizes.

The north-facing side of the house is unremarkable, the architecture more like some old settler building than Cape Dutch. The windows there are small, the two-storey whitewashed wall stark and undecorated except for layers of peeling and discolouring paint. Where the kitchen extends from the building Harry notes a couple of dilapidated doors, reached by steps leading downward, through which loads of coal must once have been deposited into a cellar; the same cellar, Harry muses, in which the devil apparently hides. The wind changes direction abruptly, and both hornbills take flight with loud cries. Seconds later, Harry detects what may have sent them off: a faint stench floating through the air. The unmistakable miasma of death arises from near the spot where they were roosting. Dropping the cigarette end he is holding, Harry heads in the direction of the odour, and spots a deep hole in the ground, flies buzzing over it, and two dung beetles scampering around its rim. It is the diameter of a wine barrel, and is partially covered by knots of dry grass, except where a clear spot has been scuffed out on one side. There, some small bunches of wilted flowers lie in the dust, their stems carefully wrapped in foil and tissue.

'Harry!' Martha is standing by one corner of the house, wiping her hands on an off-white apron. 'What are you doing out there? Come inside and sit with me.' Without waiting for him to reply, she returns to the kitchen, the door whacking closed behind her.

The glare of electric light surprises Harry as he opens the kitchen door. Martha is now standing at the stove, and offers him an embarrassed smile over her shoulder.

'We'll switch it off when he wakes up. Willie's so conscientious about money these days, because he doesn't know how much longer he'll be able to take care of us.'

After their climb to the top of the *koppie* two days ago, Willie Erasmus had confined himself to his bed, feeling too weak to do much else than eat, sleep and watch television.

'You gave me a fright, staying outside there so long. That hole you saw—the place is full of them. You need to watch out for them. I don't think we've even found them all.'

He takes a seat at the kitchen table. 'What are they, anyway?'

'This place is old, and people have been sinking wells and boreholes ever since it was first built. Most of the wells are dry now, though, and Willie uses that one to dump our dead animals—to stop the spread of disease. I don't want him burning corpses anywhere near us.'

'Is that how you got rid of—what was your dog's name, Marcy?'

'The labrador, yes. We lost a Boer bull, too.'

'Mama,' Zelda calls from the living room, 'come here.'

'What is it?' yells her mother. 'You can come here if you want something.'

Harry intervenes. 'Can I ask what happened to the dogs?'

The pot Martha has been handling clangs loudly down on the stove, slopping water everywhere.

'Here, let me get that.' Harry jumps up and reaches for a kitchen towel to mop up the spill.

'Thank you,' says the woman, and Harry catches her glancing at the ceiling. 'I . . . I'm not supposed to be talking about it. Willie doesn't like us mentioning it.'

'Mama!'

'What?' Martha yells.

There is no answer.

Harry decides to approach her with what has actually been bothering him. 'I think someone is creeping around the house at night.'

There is a sharp intake of breath. 'Why do you say that?'

'The night I arrived I thought I saw someone standing outside my window, so I decided to go and have a look if I could find some trace of them. There was a cigarette butt lying in some trampled grass, not far from the quiver tree out there.'

'You sure?' Martha turns back to the stove.

Harry takes a seat again. 'Pretty sure, yes.'

'Could have been one of Willie's security guards.' She glances apprehensively up at the ceiling again. 'They struggle understanding their instructions sometimes, and although he won't admit it, my husband's Portuguese isn't the best.'

'Martha, what do you know of Claudette Klamm's disappearance?'

The woman's shoulders slump and a loud sigh escapes her. When she finally does answer, her back is still turned to him. 'Please, Harry, we don't want any trouble with Ms Campbell—not now with Willie so ill. I don't know what people have been saying about us, but don't think we're mad.'

'Mama-mama-mama-mama.'

Harry looks over his shoulder towards the door.

'*Magtig meisie!* If you want something you can come to your mother. I'm busy here.'

'Is she always like that? Calling you, just for the sake of calling?'

Martha turns around. 'She wants me to run after her, as if I don't have anything better to do. But I won't, I *won't* do it.'

'I haven't heard anyone suggest you're mad, Martha, and I'm not looking for trouble, either. I'm just trying to figure out what happened to Claudette Klamm all those years ago.'

'You really want to know?'

'Yes.'

'Her father killed her.' She tucks her hands behind her back. 'He buried her alive in the cellar, cemented her up behind a false wall no one can find. But she won't stay dead. She won't rest, because she is so evil. She's after my little girl now, and I can't do anything about it. I can't believe I'm living in this place where it all started, but I don't have any choice. This house, the town, everything; it's all wrong. Everything is just *wrong.*'

'Hang on, slow down.' Harry holds a hand up. 'What do you mean she's after your daughter?'

'Haven't you noticed Zelda's arms?'

'Yes, but—'

'Some days she comes in the form of a young girl, Zelda says; other days it's something with claws that traps her, cuts her. I never know when next it's going to happen. She knows when Zelda is alone and upset; she starts whispering things to my little girl. It started for her last year. I first thought it was her schoolteacher hurting her like that, but they told me to take my daughter out of school because she was upsetting the other kids. I still don't understand why *my* girl was the one that had to go. Claudette does it to others, too; even when *I* was at school, it was happening to other children. Claudette Klamm is Leopold Ridge's dirty secret, not just this house's.'

'And what does Willie think of all this?'

'He just denies it!' Alarmed at the volume of her own voice, Martha

Erasmus claps a hand over her mouth, listens hard, then hurries over to the kitchen table, her voice dropping to a near whisper. 'Even when it's happening right under his nose, he refuses to believe it.'

'Have you tried moving away from here?' asks Harry.

'Oh, yes.' She pulls a chair up to sit close to Harry. 'I left school and moved to Koegas. That's where I first met Willie, when he was still working at the asbestos mine. After we got married, somehow we ended up right back where I started. I thought that would be impossible, and I've asked God to explain it to me, like so many other things. But *here* I am.' She indicates the kitchen with open hands, as if a simple gesture of disbelief can transport her somewhere else. 'All I want now is to take my husband to Kimberley—they have a proper hospital there—and I want my daughter to go back to school again.' She smiles bitterly. 'But it's Leopold Ridge that's sucked me back in. It's true. Not many people born here move on to live somewhere else. We are stuck here like seeds sown on barren soil.'

'How can you be sure Mr Klamm killed his own daughter?'

'Doesn't everyone know that?'

A piercing scream suddenly forces its way into the kitchen. As Harry jumps up, Martha is already charging towards the connecting door.

Zelda is crouching on her knees in the living room, crying and screaming for her mother, one hand outstretched as if to ward off a blow. Her terrified eyes are transfixed on a spot near the sofa.

'Make her *stop*, Mama!' cries the girl in Afrikaans. 'Leave me *alone*!'

'Where? *Where?*' Martha's eyes strafe across the room as all colour drains from her face. Seeing nothing, she hurries to her daughter's side, drops to her knees and hugs the panicked child to her bosom. Zelda instantly grabs her mother's elbow and buries her face in the sleeve.

'Is she gone, Zelda?' A fit of sobbing breaks up Martha's voice. 'Oh God, please get *rid* of her.'

Harry eyes the room, his skin growing colder, the hair on his nape rising despite the absence of any perceptible threat. The television is tuned to a children's channel, cartoon characters screaming and howling in the background as loud explosions go off.

'I'm sorry.' Martha cuddles her daughter. 'I should have come straight away when you called, babe. I *know* I should have come. Forgive me. Please, God, forgive me.'

The girl does not answer her; instead, one hand creeps around Martha's back as Zelda forces herself deeper into the folds of her mother's clothes.

Feeling useless and unwanted, Harry goes over and touches Zelda on the head. She instantly flinches at the contact, and Harry quickly withdraws his hand. 'Is there anything I can do? Can I get her some water?'

'No.' Martha rises, and picks up the crying child. 'Just . . . can you get the stove?'

'Sure.'

'Thank you.' Martha hurries from the room.

Moments later a door upstairs slams shut, leaving Harry alone in the silence of the house and wondering exactly what just transpired.

2

8.02 p.m., 8 June 2004, Leopold Ridge

'Jeanie?' A single fluorescent light bathes the front of the Superette store in dirty white light. The night is cold enough to make Harry's teeth chatter and, as far as he can see, he is the only person still outside. 'It's Dad. How are you?'

'Dad?' His daughter's voice becomes instantly excited. 'Why haven't you *called*? We went to the zoo today, and we looked through this thingy where you try to see what an eagle sees from up in the sky, but I couldn't see anything. Oh, and Nan bought me an ice-cream. It was so cold, it hurt my head.'

Harry laughs, happy to hear his daughter's singsong twittering. 'I tried to call a few times, but it looks like you and Nan are very busy ladies.'

'We are. Sam's mom came to pick me up, and I stayed with her yesterday and the other yesterday, I mean the day before. She took us shopping, and she let us try on perfume, and after that, we went to watch *A Shark's Tale.*' She goes on about the film for a full five minutes. Harry closes his eyes and soaks up every single word, a smile playing over his face as he walks up and down the length of the telephone cord to keep himself warm. Then, finally, she asks, 'When you coming back, Dad?'

'I don't know, honey. Maybe the weekend. Is that OK?'

'*Oh, da-had!*'

'I'm sorry, pumpkin, but I gotta do this work first. Hey, you wanna hear about the farm?'

'*Ja*, OK,' she says, somewhat listlessly. In the background, Harry hears his mother correct Jeanie, 'It's yes, not *ja.*'

He briefly tells his daughter about the farm and the people he has met,

136

but all she has to say as he finishes is, 'It doesn't sound like a place Mommy would want you to be at. She says you should be here, with me.'

'I don't want to stay here a second longer than I have to, angel.'

Jeanie sighs. 'I miss you, Dad.'

Harry briefly stops pacing. 'I miss you, too.'

'But I *really* miss you.' His daughter sounds close to tears.

And suddenly he knows she is not only talking about him being away, but about the two of them and how they have drifted apart.

'It won't be long, pumpkin, I promise you that.' He musters the softest tone he can. 'And when I get back I'll make it up to you. We'll go away for the weekend—just the two of us.'

'But Mommy wants you back here *now.*'

It is the second conversation they have had in the recent past in which Jeanie insists on referring to Amy as if she were present. Harry has a sudden vision of Zelda lying prostrate on the sitting-room floor, stretching out one hand, but he quickly forces it out of his mind.

'I'll be back Thursday, my angel. I promise.'

3

9.18 p.m., 8 June 2004, *Oranje Genot* Farm

His drive back to the farm from Leopold Ridge belongs to ghosts. There are no lights along the scraped dirt road; the world trapped in the nimbus of his headlights remains his only grasp on reality. Inside the car there seems only the constant sound of the roaring engine and the heater.

His mind wanders this way and that, led astray by will-o'-the-wisps of his own creation. Is this the same road, he wonders, on which the librarian's sister encountered Claudette Klamm's phantom? Was it really her ghost that haunted Zelda, or was it something else that plagued the girl? He wonders whether there is some connection between the bizarre photographs Bernard Klamm had been collecting and the strange malady afflicting the children of Leopold Ridge.

Claudette does it to others, he can hear Martha Erasmus saying. *Even when I was at school, it was happening to the other children.*

Memories of Amy surface and fade in ebbs and flows of nostalgia. Four years after her death he is still drifting, directionless, at times barely able to put one foot ahead of the other.

'Will you wait for me when you die?' she asked once. 'I mean, if you had to die first, would you wait for me before going to heaven?'

They had been sitting naked under a crumpled blanket one morning, drinking hot chocolate and hidden safe away from a cold, wet world that was nothing to them at that moment but a pale filtered glow through the curtains. They sat facing each other, and Amy had wrapped her legs tightly around his lower back.

'I don't know if they'd let me in.'

She pinched his waist. 'Can't you ever give me a straight answer?'

Harry had shrugged. 'Heaven can't be much without you there.'

She had kissed him passionately then, and said, 'I know. I feel the same.'

The afterglow of this memory shoots past two phantom figures standing by the side of the road: a woman and her son hoping to catch a ride from him. The hitchhikers appeared in his life as suddenly as they disappeared, leaving nothing more behind than the mystery of where they came from, where they were heading, and an unexpected deep-seated concern for their well-being. Are the young mother with the blue eyes and her son all right at this moment? he wonders.

'Where have you been this late at night?' Willie Erasmus is sitting on his large island-like couch, looking both inhuman yet as vulnerable as only a human being can, with the life-sustaining pipes feeding into his nose from underneath a white tablecloth.

Harry closes the door behind him. 'I thought I'd go out and give my daughter a call. I haven't spoken to her since I left home on Saturday.'

The farmer grunts noncommittally and turns back to the television.

'How is Zelda?' Harry unzips his heavy jacket. 'She doing all right?'

'She's asleep. Her mother is still fussing over her like she always does when the girl strips her *moer.*'

'You reckon Zelda is just throwing a tantrum?'

Willie Erasmus's eyes stay fixed on the television. 'What else? She was learning some really bad habits at school and I, for one, was glad they told me she had to go. It saved us some money and got her away from those other kids.'

There is a muffled crash from somewhere beyond the door into the hallway.

'Everything all right upstairs, you reckon?' asks Harry.

Willie Erasmus tears the respirator from his nose and grabs the shotgun resting by the side of the sofa. 'That didn't come from upstairs.'

As Willie and Harry go rushing out into the hallway, they find Martha is already at the head of the staircase, staring down at them with terrified eyes.

'It came from the cellar.' Her tiny gold cross is pressed to her lips.

For a second all three listen intently, waiting for the sound to repeat, but the CB radio squawking from the open study door is all they hear.

'Quick.' Harry makes a move. 'Let's go round back. Got any torches?'

A look of alarm passes from Willie to his wife. '*Ja*,' he says hesitantly. 'In the kitchen.'

'What are we waiting for, then?' Harry asks.

'Don't go,' interjects Martha. 'I mean, I don't want Willie going outside. He's not well. Stay here, both of you.'

Her husband straightens up and chambers a cartridge. 'I'm not too ill to look after my family. Not yet.'

They rush outside through the back door, two blazing torches groping around in the darkness. To the right, one of the degenerated cellar doors is lying flat on the ground, as if ripped off. Harry steps down into the cellar and shines his torch into each corner. The flimsy wisps of old spider webs hang from joints and corners, and cover old paint cans and rotten shelving. The last step of the staircase, leading down from inside the house, is broken and sagging. Coal and dust is spread across the floor, while to the right of the staircase a foundation wall bisects the area, hiding a large part of the cellar from view.

'Look.' Harry shines his torch on the floor where a fresh set of footprints lead in and out of the cellar through the fine coal dust. 'Whoever was in here has already left.'

'Let's check here,' whispers Willie, indicating the half-concealed space to one side. He looks like he is trying to hide behind his shotgun, his shoulders slumped forward, and the weapon tucked under one arm.

Rounding the partition wall, Harry realizes that the cellar is much larger than he first thought, extending under most of the length of the house. His beam of light picks up a mound of freshly turned soil with crumbling bricks tossed carelessly to one side.

'What do you think?' asks Willie, moving to stand behind him. 'What's going on here?'

Harry surveys the excavation. 'I don't know, but I can tell you this isn't the work of any ghost—especially not a dead girl.'

TEN

Siyabiza igazi wetho
Blood calls for revenge
Zulu proverb

1

8.17 a.m., 1 October 1958, Koegas

The explosion had rolled through the hills like thunder, for a moment obliterating the *clack-clack-da-clack* sounds of hammering. Obed Ditlholelo was eleven years old when he heard the mighty blast. He looked up briefly, registering the sound of men hard at work far up in the hills. His father would be amongst those miners.

The sun reflected blindingly off the rudimentary metal buildings of the small mining operation. It strained his eyes, and the ubiquitous flies were a constant irritation. As the last echo tumbled along the valley, Obed smiled and returned to work, separating with deft hands matted clumps of short-fibred asbestos from the longer, better quality strands. Later in the day, his callused fingers would be stinging as if being pierced by thousands of paper thorns.

Along with about another twenty children, both girls and boys, Obed sat out in the blaze of the springtime sun, filling large sacks with the precious mineral, their mothers had expertly separated from the ironstone ore using short hammers. The women were sitting nearby on woven mats laid out over concrete slabs. A few even worked with sleeping babies strapped on their backs. Obed worked quickly and efficiently, stuffing the cottony *doeksteen* tightly into the hessian provided. The energetic youngster liked helping his family process the furry mineral which a smart-looking white man paid for by weight at the end of each day, either with a few shillings, or credit notes for use in his general supply stores. There was no bigger treat for Obed than accompanying his father to the shop at the end of each week to purchase *mielie*-meal and salt with the handwritten chits distributed by that stern-looking Mr Klamm.

The supply shop contained everything Obed hoped to have one day: his own pick, jumper drill, shiny five-pound hammer—maybe even a bridle for his own donkey. There was lots of beer and stronger spirits too, but his father stuck to the traditional sour beer. Their weekly supplies were expensive, *very* expensive, and his father often came away grumbling angrily about the mysterious weekly increases in prices when their wages continued to drop.

Obed did not talk much to the other children as he worked, concentrating instead on packing the hessian sacks as fast and as fully as he could. In another five years, he could sign up as a miner with Mr Klamm, and join the other men early every morning, when it was still dark, on their trek up to the hills with the donkeys to dig in the adits for rich deposits of asbestos. He dreamt of the day that he might uncover a particularly good vein of longer fibres. That would bring in more money, and maybe he might even bring home the occasional bit of meat to supplement their one daily meal, then even buy a goat or two for the family, if Mr Klamm would permit grazing on his land. That would certainly bring smiles to his parents' tired faces.

In a way he was glad when his aunt fell sick with the cough, for it meant he was brought in to help with the cobbing, and thus given a chance to show how hard he could work. They would now see how willing he was to become a man and take on the responsibilities of a miner. He would soon make up for the money lost by his aunt's disability, and the additional wages would help care for her until her inevitable death, because, as everyone knew, once that constant dry cough started, there was no getting better.

But Obed knew something was seriously wrong when, an hour later, a shirtless man from his father's work team came charging through the undergrowth, yelling incomprehensibly. No one came running down from the mines without good reason, and it always indicated injury or death. The man headed straight for Obed's mother, to speak with her in private, but soon everyone else was crowding closer. The earlier blast had collapsed a section of shaft roof, so that several miners were trapped, at least two were dead, and Obed's father had been badly injured.

The miner's two sons instantly jumped up, and Obed's older brother Ishmael headed for the rocky track leading up into the hills, while the younger boy followed the miner heading for the prefab office.

'José,' shouted the man, reaching the door, 'we need the cart, quick.'

Obed peered inside to see the young Mozambiquean's reaction. José

Eduardo Cauto got up from behind the desk. He was tall and handsome, with a deep scar running just above one corner of his mouth. He scared Obed because he had the ear of the big boss; also he knew how to read and write, and could speak languages Obed had never even heard spoken before. His father, who did not like this young man, said his position was unusual, because it was normally an older coloured or a white who acted as the boss's right-hand man.

'What do you need a cart for?' Cauto asked in fluent Tswana.

When the miner told his foreman what had happened, Cauto shook his head. 'Getting the cart out won't help. It will never get up that hill.'

'But José, we need to get him to a hospital.'

The concern in the man's voice carried nothing of the terror and outright panic Obed himself was feeling. The boy knew very little of the adult world of mining injuries or deaths, but he realized that getting his father to a hospital, however far away, was now crucial. Listening to the two men arguing, he grew certain in his young and impressionable mind that just by invoking the hospital's name often enough, he could somehow summon its healing powers to save his father.

'Are we going to the hospital?' he burst into the debate. 'We must take father to the hospital. I'll get the cart, yes?'

Cauto gave the miner a strange look, then glanced at Obed. 'We'll see.'

An hour later, they saw a thin line of miners approaching slowly down the treacherous hill, their donkeys laden with heavy bundles that were clearly not sacks of ore. Obed and his younger sister raced up the slope to meet the column, finding the bundles were two white-dusted corpses, while Obed's father was carried in a makeshift stretcher hooked up behind another of the pack animals. One of his legs had been badly crushed and was bleeding profusely, despite the dirty torn shirt material which had been applied as bandages and crude tourniquets. His father was barely conscious.

'Father,' yelled Obed. 'We are taking you to the hospital. I'm getting the cart ready. You hear, father? Hospital. *Hos*-pital.'

It seemed to the boy that their sad procession could not move fast enough, but when he implored the adults to speed up their descent, they only glanced at him in hopeless sympathy. Confused and scared by their grim faces, Obed clutched his father's limp hand as he ran alongside the litter, thinking, *hospital, hospital, hospital.*

In the camp there was no dressing station, so Obed had to cushion the unused cart with old sacking before his father was placed on it and then removed to the shelter of a zinc-covered lean-to, away from the excited crowd of women and children. Obed's mother wept as she carefully tore away her husband's blood-soaked trousers to reach the mangled leg. She surveyed the exposed damage, unsure where to start in cleaning up the raw expanse of wounded flesh. Only Obed stayed to help her, as the others were now helping with the corpses, or had hurried off up the hillside to find their own loved ones, while some even returned to their work at Cauto's insistence.

Once the wound was relatively clean, Obed's mother rested her head briefly on his father's sweating bare chest. The zinc roof could afford them little protection from the sun's blistering heat, and the air was alive with swarms of buzzing flies attracted to the fresh blood. Obed desperately flailed at the relentless insects, as he listened to his father beg pitifully for something to drink. His mother scooped some water from a bucket with a tin mug, and gently dripped the cooling liquid over his lips, all the time stroking her husband's forehead and whispering to him comfortingly. There was little else they could do for him, except wait for the trucks which arrived regularly every afternoon to cart away the already cobbed mineral. They hoped one of the drivers would agree to take the wounded man with them to Prieska, and the nearest clinic there—a two-hour drive at the best of times.

The injured miner lost consciousness some time later. His lips had taken on a strange hue and he kept complaining about the cold, despite the day's heat. Obed's mother begged her son to call her should his father come to; until then, she would return to her work, hammering out the asbestos that she would be paid for by weight.

Three lorries arrived around four o'clock that afternoon, *Baas* Klamm driving ahead of them in a baby-blue Vanguard, all curves and chrome. By then two more bodies had been carried down from the hill, and finally the rest of the miners had returned in dejected mood. Ishmael, looking tired and covered in fine white dust, had silently approached his unconscious father and held one slack hand. It was as if he was saying goodbye to him, though surely there was no reason for this. After all, thought Obed, there was the clinic waiting in Prieska, and if they could not do anything there for the wounded man, then the hospital in Kimberley surely would manage. Three hundred kilometres was not that far to travel, was it? In Obed's young mind this remote distance had no real meaning; all he could think of was the two geographical points: where his father was now and where he should be. The impossibly rough roads and inevitably slow movement of vehicles in between had no real significance for him.

Obed's father regained consciousness as he was being loaded on top of a load of asbestos bails, and he asked for his wife and told her to look after his boys. He was even lucid enough to wave to them feebly.

'What the hell are you people doing, loading that man on the truck?' Klamm had come over, shoving his way through the crowd, Cauto following close on his heels, looking mean. The boss's face was a furious red, as he pointed at Obed's father with his pipe. 'Who gave you people permission?'

The coloured driver of the truck took a step back, and turned querying eyes on the man who had arrived first down the hill.

'But, *baas*,' pleaded the miner, 'he needs the doctor really soon.'

'You're wasting valuable time,' growled Klamm. 'Nothing's going to save that man, and I'm not paying for a round trip to the clinic and then the graveyard. Get him down from there.'

'Baas, I'll make it,' cried Obed's father from his stretcher. 'You watch me, I'll be back at work end of the week. I promise. Just let them take me. Please, *baas*.'

There was a desperate tone in his father's voice that brought tears to Obed's eyes. A shocked hush spread through the crowd as his mother fell down on her knees in front of her employer. 'I beg you, before God, *baas*, let them take my husband to the clinic.' Obed instinctively followed her example, throwing himself down in front of Mr Klamm, and grabbing hold of one polished shoe. He began chanting those magical English words, 'Hospital, hospital, hospital.'

Klamm pulled his foot away. 'Get up, both of you.' He glowered down at Obed and his mother, the gathered workers, and the truckers shifting their feet uneasily in the sand. 'You people have cost me a whole day's production. Did it take all of you to save this one man? I think not, so get back to work, all of you. And you'll stay here until after dark, otherwise you can forget about getting paid for the rest of the week.' With his pipe stem, he gestured to the driver. 'What are you waiting for? I said get that man down. He's good as dead already.'

'But I'm not, *baas*.' Obed's father's voice was shrill, and tears welled up in his eyes. 'It's just my leg that's not so good. I'm OK, *baas*, really.'

A cruel smile spread itself over Klamm's face. 'Well, then, if you're OK, there's no point in taking you to Prieska, is there?' He stuffed his pipe back in his mouth, turned on his heel, and strode back towards the office.

Obed's father died in agony two days later, a last rattle escaping his feverish throat just after nightfall. His fellow miners and family had not removed him from the mine site, for fear of causing him more pain during his last hours. By firelight they wrapped his body in the blankets he lay in, blessing his passage to the netherworld and bewailing his departure, while cursing the white man they held responsible for his untimely death.

2

1.09 p.m., 1 October 1963, Douglas

Five years later, Obed sat in the mess hut of another tributer camp, located south-west of Douglas, deep in the Asbestos Mountains but close to the muddy expanse of the Orange River. Water was more readily available here, the vegetation greener and the air a bit cooler than at the mine where his father had been mortally injured. There were more insects, too, so apart from the inevitable flies, swarms of gnats and mosquitoes were a constant plague. There seemed to be scorpions nesting under every rock and, at night, bats chirruped endlessly around the camp, feeding on the bugs attracted to the lights. Obed was still getting used to the constant drone of the new mechanized tumblers and crude crushing mills that rumbled all day and night a little way further down the valley.

From where he now sat, he could see the same Mr Klamm gesturing with his inevitable pipe at a rotating drum which sifted gravel and sand from the loads of ironstone ore brought into the camp on cocopans. As usual, José Cauto was nodding deferentially to whatever the white man was saying.

The mess hut itself was little more than a tent-like structure, of rough hewn poles lashed together to provide support for its sheeted corrugated-iron walls. A large groundsheet strung between the trees provided some further shelter against the elements. That same morning, as Obed had walked past the cooking area, he had noticed the bloody sack containing meat, which lay on a bench outside in the heat, crawling with insects, while waiting for the cooking fires to be stoked. Real meat too: not just the sinew and tendons or chicken legs they were usually fed, but beef. There was only one reason for it being here: an inspection by the Department of Native Affairs had been conducted the day before, and this was the miners' reward for keeping their mouths shut about the worst of their conditions. Mr Klamm was indeed a cunning operator.

The sixteen-year-old youth surveyed the other miners sitting on crude wooden benches or tree stumps under the shade of the groundsheet. They were all drinking beer or whisky, because there was not much else they could do here when they were not down some hole in the hillside. Drinking, gambling and *patla-patla* with the women of the camp quickly became a boring routine, which nevertheless alleviated the constant despair they mostly felt. The emaciated form of a young woman passed by him, the girl's smile revealing a toothless mouth. She was married to one of the miners with whom Obed frequently played craps, and she worked in the mess kitchen. But when her man was up in the hills, hacking away at ironstone with his blunt tools, she was busy hustling all over the camp for extra money. She was one among many women there, but still pretty enough not to be relegated to scavenging for fibres in the tailings further down from the mill. Klamm hired only a certain number of people to work the ore; the rest had to be creative in order to survive, whether it meant scavenging, tending small patches of crops, herding a handful of goats, cooking for the miners, or turning tricks.

'She likes you, boy,' observed a man in his thirties sitting nearby. As he grinned, his mouth showed all the signs of scurvy, and the roots of his hair had the orange tinge that indicated long-term malnutrition.

'No she doesn't. She just wants my money.'

'How long you been here?'

'Two months now,' Obed replied.

His mother had disappeared one night a year after his father died. She gathered her few belongings and walked out the door, never to be seen again, leaving Ishmael to fend for Obed and their younger sister. For a while Obed had been angry with his mother for abandoning them; his father would never have done so, he was convinced.

It was Klamm who told him he could begin earning his own wages at fourteen, which stopped him brooding further about the betrayal of his mother. He threw himself at his work eagerly, keen to realize his childhood dreams for the good of his remaining family. When Ishmael fell sick like his aunt had done, and another tributer operating further down the valley offered him a few pennies more in wages, Obed took the chance to get away from Klamm. But a few months later the new *baas*, Neethling, disappeared with twelve weeks' wages unpaid. When Obed returned to Klamm's old site, ready to grovel to the man, he found it, too, abandoned, and it took him a month to track down his old boss near Douglas, by which time he was dishevelled and half-starved.

'You're back,' Klamm had said with a sneer, while Obed hung his head in a suitably submissive fashion, and fumbled nervously with his hat, though feeling nothing but hate for this man. It was an extreme humiliation to beg Klamm, whom he had come to see as his father's murderer, for a new lease of life, not just for himself, but his dependent brother and sister.

'Yes, *baas*. If *baas* would be so very much kind to give Obed a second chance, *baas*, I'll make sure *baas* doesn't regret it. *Baas mos* knows Obed doesn't drink; and this one works hard, *baas. Assamblief.*'

He shuffled uncomfortably under Klamm's burning gaze, not quite sure what he would do if the white man refused him. He had not eaten for three days now, and was not sure whether he would even be able to make it as far as the next mining camp.

'Suit yourself,' Klamm had replied cryptically.

Unsure if he had been hired or not, Obed reported at the administration block the next day. Cauto had been there, as before, and treated him as if he had never left.

Another two months of working there, two months of watching Klamm strut around the camp in his smart suits, never getting himself dirty, never finding anything good to say about the unfortunate people making him so rich, and Obed savoured the anger steadily gestating inside him, till soon he was looking for ways to get back at his employer.

'Ah,' the older miner interrupted his dark thoughts, 'I see, you're an idealist who still sends his money home, instead of blowing it on whores and gambling. But stick around for a while and you'll find things change. Home fades from the memory quickly out here.'

Obed looked down at the nutritious sorghum beer in front of him, and reflected how his father had never bought anything stronger from Klamm's store. He wanted to look after his two siblings the way his father had watched over all three of them, and told himself he would never betray his sister the way his mother had. Two days' journey from here, she was still tending his brother Ishmael, so Obed was the only one of them left generating money. But it was not enough—not enough by far.

The man addressing him must have noticed some inner turmoil surface in his eyes, because he cackled suddenly with laughter. 'This life, it gets us all in the end. You won't be the first or the last to discover that, my boy.'

Later in the evening, Obed was shooting craps with his companions on a flattened cardboard box when he felt a firm hand descend on his shoulder. As he looked up from his winning roll, instantly the other miners tried to sweep his money from the board. But Obed realized his mistake and moved fast to recover his cash before it all disappeared.

'Come with me,' said Cauto. 'The boss wants to speak with you.'

Obed felt a frisson of shock shoot up his spine. What could this be about?

He rose slowly from where he was squatting, and reflexively hauled on the frayed straw hat he always wore during the daytime. The other gamblers smiled jeeringly, for everyone knew none of them was ever called in unless he was about to be fired.

Cauto led the way through the lush foliage towards the manager's office, built upwind from the noisy machinery and the stench of human ablution. Over to one side a handful of cooking fires burnt amongst lean-tos and hastily erected reed huts. Some miners had their wives and daughters with them and could afford to cook their own evening meal.

'You like it here?' Cauto asked him without looking back, his tone uninterested.

Obed shrugged, and kept his voice neutral. 'I make enough money to survive.'

'You have a younger sister, don't you?'

'And my brother, Ishmael, yes.'

'Oh, he's still alive?'

'Yes,' Obed replied briefly.

They had reached a rectangular building constructed predominantly of sheet metal. It was approached by its own narrow access path, which forked off from the main track circling the base of the mountain, and connecting the various tributers' operations to the GGeM railhead about ten kilometres away.

A gleaming red Chevy Impala was parked in front of the lighted doorway, and the sound of soft jazz wafted out of the office and into the night.

Cauto turned around and gestured over his shoulder with a thumb. 'Inside.'

Hesitantly, Obed sidled past the Mozambiquean and, as he started approaching the desk where Mr Klamm was entering figures into a ledger, the white man looked up at his employee with raised eyebrows. 'Obed, come right in.'

Obed entered, dutifully removing his straw hat in the presence of his employer. A clock was ticking loudly in the room, while movement could be heard from behind a closed door over to the right. Mr Klamm closed his fountain pen with a firm click, stood up and came around the desk. He wore his shirtsleeves rolled, and grey braces held up his khaki trousers. For once, his collar buttons were both undone.

'Hello, boy. Tell me, your two months here: how have they been?'

'Very good, *baas*.' Obed nodded vigorously. 'I wouldn't have it any other way.'

'That's good, but the inspector was here yesterday, as you know, and he seemed very happy with us. Except he was informed, just before he arrived in the camp, that the mill had been specially slowed down and wetted so that the dust levels didn't measure too high. I wonder who might have told him this?'

'I don't know, *baas*.' Obed made sure to meet the white man's probing eyes.

'Somebody also told him that I let my blacks do their own blasting, which is in contravention of the Mines Acts. Do you know anything about this, either?'

'No, *baas*, no.' Obed shook his head vigorously.

A sinister smile passed over Klamm's hardened features. 'That's settled then. I'm glad it wasn't you, because I want to offer you a chance to learn more about blasting . . . that's if you want to. Are you up for it?'

Obed glanced cautiously back at Cauto standing guard outside. 'I don't know, *baas*. I don't want to get into any trouble.'

'Oh, come now. Which of my men have got into trouble with the authorities?'

It was a surprising offer, and lucrative, especially for someone so young. Obed looked again over his shoulder at José standing outside. Was Klamm offering him a chance to follow in the Mozambiquean's footsteps? Though it was blatantly illegal for any black to learn the craft, it would certainly secure him a much higher status amongst the other men of the mine, and better pay. He could not be sure, but it seemed to his young mind that the offer could also put him some ways closer to gaining an advantage over this murderer of his father.

'It sounds good, *baas*.'

Perhaps the boss knew something Obed didn't, or perhaps it was the reassurance in knowing which way his workers would react when he dangled something before them, but Mr Klamm rubbed his hands together with a knowing expression.

'I thought you might agree.' Klamm grabbed his employee's shoulders with both hands and eyed him squarely, digging his fingers into the youth's muscles. 'José there will begin training you tomorrow. We'll be hunting out new veins over the next few weeks, and need a few more competent men to handle the teams.' He kept on crushing the thin muscles of Obed's shoulders, but the boy refused to flinch or show any sign of pain. 'But know this,' continued Klamm, 'if I *ever* hear anything about someone talking to the Native Affairs, Health, or Mines inspectors again, you and I will have a talk eye to eye. Do you understand me?'

Obed nodded. He was tearing at the straw hat clutched in his hands in an attempt to control his emotions.

The adjoining door opened. 'Papa.' A girl about his age with jet-black hair stepped into the room. She had alarm in her voice, and a straight razor in one hand.

Obed glanced back at Cauto, wondering whether he should now leave because of the girl's presence, or whether he should stay until properly dismissed by his employer. What he noticed next caught him by surprise, for the Mozambiquean was looking at Klamm's daughter with obvious affection in his eyes, a gentle smile creasing the prominent scar above his mouth.

'What is it, Claudette?' Mr Klamm hastily stepped between his two workers and his daughter.

'I think I heard it again, outside. Scratching at the window. It wanted to get at—'

'Ssh-sh-sh.' Her father put a finger against her lips. 'What did I tell you? Don't ever speak of it. Let's get you to bed.'

Cauto clapped a hand on Obed's shoulder. 'Let's go.'

That night at Cauto's insistence Obed drank seriously for the first time. It seemed to the young miner he had escaped some kind of trap, so he was glad to humour the Mozambiquean foreman. His fears and worries were steadily washed away by the warming shots of brandy. They laughed together, while the girl with no teeth came and sat on his lap, her arms around his shoulders, her malnourished husband, sitting in one corner and eyeing them jealously, rendered compliant by the promise of money. Obed's sister and brother were now far away, out of sight and out of mind. All that mattered was the elation in his heart, the new camaraderie he felt amongst these other men and women of the camp. He could have lost his job, or disappeared in the bush with fractured ribs and a broken skull after his recent attempt to rat Klamm out—it had happened to others before—but not to him, and not tonight. This evening he had come out on top, when others had disappeared. The white devil had spared him.

3

'Let me in! I want to see Klamm!'

The security guard mercilessly shoved Obed away from the building's entrance. Unable to keep his balance with his one wooden crutch, the drunken man stumbled backwards and fell to the pavement.

'I told you before,' yelled the guard in Tswana. 'There has never been anyone called Klamm working at this office. Now go home, Obed. Sleep it off, and stop embarrassing yourself.'

Obed, however, could not let the matter lie. He picked up his crutch and swung it wildly at the security man's legs. The other sidestepped the blow easily, and glanced back at his partner, who was just coming out of the lobby of Griqua Geological and Minerals' office building.

'Where's your son, old man?' The second security guard's tone was less accommodating.

Obed struggled up, refusing the first security guard's attempted help. One leg was crooked and shorter than the other, the result of an accident involving a runaway cocopan, which had ended his career in mining for ever. 'I'm going to see that dog again before I die, you'll see.'

The fifty-seven-year-old miner was a mere shadow of the able-bodied man he once used to be. His grey beard was wild and thick; leaves and twigs were stuck in his matted hair. Though he still possessed most of his teeth, they were now yellow and brown stumps. His clothes were grimy rags, his torn shirt revealing a chest that was almost skeletal. He smelt of cheap hanepoort wine, vomit, and a life of suffering.

Losing his patience, the second guard drew his baton and moved threateningly towards Obed, who instantly shrank away from him.

'Get lost! If I see you anywhere near here again, you're going to get it. And for fuck's sake, get this into your crazy old head: there *isn't* a Klamm working here.'

A sudden shout from across the street attracted their attention, as a stocky seventeen-year-old came sprinting towards them. He was dressed in a red T-shirt and jeans cut off at the knees, and he was barefoot.

'Father!'

'Didn't I tell you to keep him away from here?' The first security guard reproached the boy.

'I'm sorry,' the youth replied, grabbing one of his father's arms. 'He's not right in his head. Just don't hurt him.'

The second security guard sheathed his weapon and turned back towards the lobby, from which bemused faces stared out through the front window. The building was of unattractive, crumbling red-brown brick. Above dirty windows some faded words were printed on a dusty cream sign attached to the upper part of the façade.

'Not right in my head?' grumbled the old man. 'I can still box your ears, boy.'

Obed's son glanced apologetically at the remaining security guard as he coaxed his mumbling father away.

The guard sighed and fumbled in his pocket. 'Here, take this,' he called after them. 'Get yourself something to eat. For the old man, too; just don't buy him any drink.'

Norman's eyes lit up and a glistening smile spread over his entire face. '*Ke a leboga*, Sam.'

'And don't let him come back here this way. They're losing patience with him.'

The boy nodded, tugging urgently at his father's arm.

Nightfall and they were sitting in the cramped confines of their shack, just father and son, because the woman whom Obed had finally married, and who had produced his only child, had left him the same way his own mother had left him so many years ago. A radio was playing in a neighbouring shanty. At times, like when he missed the sound of his own radio, he enjoyed the close proximity of the other ramshackle buildings, built almost on top of each other. Their close proximity provided him comfort whenever he felt lonely. Obed had sold most of his possessions to get money for drink, except the bed he reluctantly shared with a son who refused to leave his side and go find work.

'Tell me about her again, *madoda*.' Norman was eyeing him by the light of a single candle, one hand still greasy from the fish and chips Sam's handout had bought them.

Wrapped up in a blanket against the cold, Obed sniffed at his untouched food and pushed the nauseating piece of fish away. He could not remember when he last had an appetite for solids.

'She's a bitch who is going to burn for ever in hell,' he sneered.

'No, *madoda*, you loved her once. There must've been something you liked about her.'

'I fucked her good and proper, then she ran off like the treacherous dog she was.'

'Don't talk like that. Tell me how you both met by the water pump.'

Obed began vigorously picking his nose. 'Why don't you shut up?'

There was a knock at the steel door. Obed leered at it, as if not quite comprehending that someone could still call at his home. His son, however, did not seem at all surprised.

'Who is it?' he grunted.

'*Dumela*,' answered a deep voice. 'My name is Sheik. Can I come in?'

Norman quickly crumpled up the remnants of his food in its newspaper wrapping, grabbed his father's too, and put it all out of the way on a makeshift counter. He wiped his hands hastily on his jeans before opening the door.

'Sheik,' he said, 'come in. This is my father.'

A large figure stooped to enter the low-ceilinged shanty. The old man did not budge from his seat to greet the stranger, an expression of contemptuous recollection still evident on his weatherbeaten face.

'*Madoda*,' said the newcomer by way of greeting.

'Norman,' said the old man, 'take your friend and go elsewhere. This is not the place for you to meet people.'

'He has come to see *you*, father.'

'Oh?' Obed shifted his eyes to peer at his son through the near darkness. 'Do you know him, then?'

'Yes, I do.'

'Well then,' Obed glanced at the stranger, 'if he wants to talk with me, he had better have something ready to wet my tongue.'

As Norman scowled, Kheswa laughed abruptly. 'I have indeed, old man. You have quite a reputation.'

The boy's disturbed eyes traced the passage of a bottle of Richelieu brandy from his acquaintance to his father's outstretched hand.

'Can I sit?' asked Kheswa. Already the old man was unscrewing the bottle cap.

'Yes,' he replied, now delighted. 'Norman, get the man a stool.'

His knees nearly touching his chest, the visitor sat down on the seat the boy relinquished for him. He watched the old man take two large slugs from the brandy bottle, then smack his lips in pleasure. For the first time, Obed turned welcoming eyes on his visitor.

'Tastes good, doesn't it?' The stranger pulled his black beanie off to reveal a bald head.

'You've hit the nail on the head, my friend. What did you say your name was?'

Kheswa repeated it to him. Norman meanwhile sat down on the floor, crossed his arms over his knees, and waited expectantly.

'What can an old cripple do in return for such kindness, Sheik?'

The visitor chuckled, his eyes gleaming in the candlelight. 'Oh, it was nothing much, nothing at all.'

'Ha!' Obed allowed the bottle to disappear beneath the folds of the blanket he had wrapped around him. 'No one visits old Obed now unless they are owed money. I don't remember your face, so I don't think I owe you anything. I don't have a daughter you might want to marry, and my son comes and goes as he pleases. What, then, is it that you want from me?'

'I've heard you were a miner once.'

Obed began to cackle quietly, and the other two could smell the alcohol on his breath. 'So was just about everyone in this town. These days we just sit around, though, waiting for money to grow on trees and for Christ's second coming.'

'I also heard you know something about explosives.'

Obed shot up suddenly. 'Who told you that?'

The stranger did not look at the boy on the floor, although Norman could not resist glancing furtively at Sheik.

Kheswa shrugged. 'You hear things around town. It seems you were once taught how to use blasting caps and dynamite, at a time when the rest of us did not have such a liberty.'

'It was a trick, a trick to shut me up, to make me docile.'

Sheik glanced at Norman, a puzzled expression on his face. 'What do you mean?'

A hand snaked out from underneath Obed's blanket and stabbed the air between them. 'And Satan stood atop the mountain and said, "Jesus, we are playing poker, you and I. Let's wager the world; let's wager your soul." I used to be good at poker in those camps; I even gambled my lungs. I always won, I was always ahead, but for the one man who collected on me every time. That was the devil himself.'

Norman shifted uncomfortably on the floor and looked up again at Kheswa. The stranger, however, ignored the boy's apologetic glance. *Ja? And who was this man?*

Obed's gaze turned to the candle flame, its orange light reflecting in the black orbs of his eyes. 'Klamm.' The word came out as a hateful growl.

'I've heard that name before.' The stranger nodded. 'Isn't that farm called *Oranje Genot* his?'

The older man's eyes narrowed suspiciously. 'How do you know that? What else do you know about Klamm? What are you doing here?'

'Relax.' Kheswa smiled and brought both hands up in a gesture of acquiescence. 'Like I said, you hear things around town.'

'People talk far too much,' grumbled Obed, running his tongue over rotten teeth.

'Whatever you may have against Klamm is your own business,' said Sheik. He reached for his back pocket and brought out a second bottle of brandy. 'What I want to know now is how much you remember about explosives.'

This time the bottle Kheswa held up was not snatched away immediately. Instead the stranger put it on the little table between them, like a promise. Obed's eyes flicked over to his son. In a chastened tone he said, 'I know enough.'

'That old head of yours isn't too messed up yet?' Kheswa's expression turned serious.

'My head's fine,' spat Obed. 'Now why are you asking me all this?'

'I have certain needs, and I think you can help me with them. I'll pay you, of course.' The stranger glanced at Norman. 'Provided you can keep your mouth shut.'

Obed turned to his son. 'What have you done here?' he whispered.

'He hasn't done anything,' Kheswa laughed abruptly. 'He's a good boy, concerned about the health of his father and where his next meal will come from. The question is: will you help him eat, too?'

The half-full bottle of brandy snuck out from beneath Obed's blanket, and was met by his second probing hand, which hastily unscrewed the cap. The glass mouth of it reached up and kissed his lips long and hard. Suddenly this was not another Tswana man sitting opposite him any more, but the devil in one of his many guises.

'Ah.' Obed wiped at his mouth. 'We're playing poker again, are we?'

A sly smile pulled up the corners of Kheswa's mouth. 'You could say that.'

'Then tell me what the rules are.'

And so Sheik told Obed what he wanted done. He explained to him what the explosives were for, and what components he could procure for Obed. It turned out the old man still retained a lot more sense than it previously seemed. He spoke with an air of professional pride, as if he was conversing with a miner from an earlier age, when asbestos still paid for the food in their stomachs and it still represented an alternative to working on the gold and diamond fields, far away from home.

An hour or so later, Obed struck a deal with the devil for a second time. But this time he stated his own conditions.

His eyes glowed disconcertingly as he leaned forward. 'Yes, I can do that; I can do it all for you, and I can teach you how to place the charges, too. For that I want the money we've discussed, but I want you to do one other thing for me.'

Kheswa also leaned forward, mirroring his co-conspirator. 'And what is that, *madoda?*'

'I want you to find the white devil, find Bernard Klamm. Can you do that for me?'

The stranger hesitated a few seconds, then nodded. 'I will try my best.'

'Good. Because he and I, we have one final hand to play before I die.'

ELEVEN

A Beer with a Stone-Cold Bastard

1

1.51 p.m., 9 June 2004, Upington

A call to the Leopold Ridge police station sends Harry on a two-hour drive to Upington, to find a retired police officer mentioned in Campbell's documents. It is the kind of place that seems to have sprung up miraculously in the arid Karoo for no apparent reason, but the town is an important outpost en route to Namibia, the Richtersveld National Park and Namaqualand, and thus popular with truckers or tourists on safari. It is just a narrow strip of concrete and greenery clinging to the bank of the Orange River, utterly dependent on local irrigation works for its survival. Large enough to boast two hotels, it also has an airstrip, but not much else to keep visitors there longer than a day or two.

On Schroder Street, near the Protea Oasis Lodge, Harry finds Naas Lambert sitting on the whitewashed porch of a converted prospecting house, absentmindedly stroking the ugly pug curled up in his lap. Lambert had been the police officer called out to *Oranje Genot* farm on 3 August 1965, after Klamm first reported his daughter missing.

'Bernard Klamm's dead?' He hands Harry a cold beer from a cooler bag sitting next to the porch table, then cracks one open for himself. 'Murdered, you say?'

'That's right,' replies Harry in the best Afrikaans he can muster. He knows how men like Naas Lambert easily clam shut if a stranger does not address them in their mother tongue first. These are a breed of wilful and stubborn Afrikaners, tough as nails and hammered deep into their wooden ways. 'His widow seems to think that it might have been Bernard Klamm that killed his own daughter, not the suspect José Cauto. I'm up here to try to find out what really happened.'

Lambert is a man in his mid-fifties, over six feet two, with hands like dinner plates. His hair is white, his skin sunburnt red, and his eyes appear so wide open they look manic, although his slow, lumbering movements are anything but. The retired cop studies Harry carefully as he taps tobacco ash from his pipe into a brass ashtray in the shape of the old South African Police Force's emblem. 'That was a long time ago. I'm retired now, and not inclined to talk about such things with a stranger.'

'I totally understand that,' says Harry, 'but Mr Klamm's widow is desperate to find out what happened to their daughter, once and for all.'

'The woman should let sleeping dogs lie. The pair of them were part of the reason why no one knows what happened to their daughter.'

'Miss Campbell—that's what Mr Klamm's widow calls herself these days—she says the same about the cops operating around here.'

Lambert sits back, pulls a box of cigarettes from his pocket, and lights himself one. 'That's right,' he nods, 'blame it on the cops. It's always our fault. People in power want society to look a certain way, so they tell us to shape it for them. They grow tired of that look, or they have second thoughts about it, then the first thing they blame is the police force, never themselves. The people in this country are forever moaning about the way the police do things; even in the days of the National Party they were constantly complaining. But you know what? We got ourselves results back then. Things might not have been all performed above board, but you didn't see then the chaos that reigns now. We got it right because we knew the rules needed occasional bending. We knew who had to disappear, who needed to go to jail and, sometimes more importantly, who had to be kept out of jail. Now, mister, I don't know who you are, and what exactly you want with me, but I did my job that day and I have no regrets about it. I got my orders and I followed them to the T. You can show yourself out now.'

'Mr Lambert, I'm not going to beat around the bush with you. From what I know, you and Klamm, and whoever else was in on it, put a man behind bars for life without a fair trial. I don't know how you pulled off a rape and murder conviction without a body or even the evidence of a witness, and I don't particularly care to go into that with you. Right now, my job is to find out what happened to this girl, nothing else.'

'I don't know anything about her. I never even met her. All I know is that this kaffir had something going with Bernard's daughter. The old man found out, there was a clash, and the daughter was missing from home in the morning. That's all I know.'

'But wasn't the farm thoroughly searched for her body? Or didn't she maybe escape during the night?'

Lambert leans forward and points his cigarette at Harry. 'Mr Mason, my job was to ensure Cauto went to jail. That's the way Klamm wanted it, and that's the way certain high-up people asked me to make it look. Because of the way things were being arranged we couldn't just let any officer in on the job. Like I said, sometimes things were done underhanded, so no, I didn't search the house or the farm personally, but a report was filed nonetheless, which stated that we had brought in dogs and that the whole place was combed with a toothbrush. I know none of the cars was missing, so I can't tell you how Claudette Klamm might have gotten away, if she ever left the farm at all.'

Someone walks by the house just then and greets the ex-cop sitting on the porch. The intrusion startles the dog, which immediately leaps off its master's lap and begins barking insanely, its eyes bulging from their sockets. When Lambert has finally got the creature under control, he spends a few moments patiently putting out his cigarette, then lighting a fresh one. He keeps shaking his head as he does this, and for this reason Harry waits silently until he continues.

'If you ask me, Klamm could easily have gotten rid of his own daughter the way it's rumoured he did. That kaffir was bloody pulp when I got there, and in no shape to stand. I didn't even need to work the bastard over to get a confession; I could just poke him in all the worst places with a finger. In any case, Bernard had probably had the whole night to kill his daughter and get rid of her body. That farm is a few thousand hectares big; she could be buried anywhere. Chances are that the man's wife herself knows better than anyone else what really happened that night—including Cauto.'

Refusing to make eye contact with Harry, he squints along the street at a convoy of white safari Land Rovers arriving at the Oasis Lodge. A plume of white smoke escapes his lips. 'I'll tell you now, mister, if it had been my own daughter fucking some black who lived at the bottom of my garden, I would've shot and buried the both of them. And I wouldn't have bothered calling in the police to help clean up my mess, either.'

'Where was Cauto sent after his conviction?' asks Harry.

'Can't recall,' says the man.

'Do you know if he's still alive?'

'I distanced myself from that whole business a long time ago.'

Thinking of the excavation he and Willie discovered in the cellar, Harry asks, 'Could it be that Bernard Klamm buried his daughter in the basement of the farmhouse? What I mean is, did you go down and look there at any point, or see anything?'

'Wasn't my business,' replies Lambert.

Harry sighs in frustration, then he thinks of something else to ask the retired cop. 'During your time in Leopold Ridge, did you ever hear the name Freddy Meyer?'

Lambert turns one wide eye on Harry. '*Ja*, he was a rookie constable over in Prieska about twenty years back. I used to watch their guys play rugby against some of our men, every first Saturday of the month. He was their captain.' The man suddenly laughs at the memory. 'That boy sure knew how to tackle.'

'Do you know where he is now, or what's happened to him?'

'Last I saw of him was in '92 or '93. Came here asking me the same questions you just did, and I told him the same thing. That's the last I've ever seen of him.'

Not able to get any more information out of the resistant ex-cop, Harry decides to head back to Prieska. Driving south on the 32, Harry reflects on his conversation with Lambert, and realizes the ex-cop's story does not stray much from what Henrietta Campbell told Harry a week ago, except for this visit by Freddy Meyer. Their stories certainly do suggest Bernard Klamm killing his daughter and disposing of her body, especially since the jersey she had last worn has since turned up in her father's safe, covered in blood. But, in Harry's mind, a number of important questions remain. Why would Klamm contact a Prieska police officer back in the nineties to re-examine the night of Claudette Klamm's disappearance, after he had worked so hard to cover up her murder? And where is the body now? In the cellar? Burnt up in whatever is left of Cauto's shed, or somewhere else? As long as there is no body, Harry cannot rule out the possibility that she may have simply fled.

The puzzle of those photo albums in Klamm's house has also been weighing on his mind. The man obviously had some sort of obsession with adolescent girls, and took a particular interest in photographing the marks of the abuse they suffered. Initially it seemed to Harry this was a case of a sadistic paedophile who had at first regularly abused his daughter, then killed her after she reached adulthood. It could then be that he followed up her abuse with that practised on other children—either committing it himself, or acquiring photographs taken by others in some paedophile ring he belonged to. But then Harry has encountered Zelda, who exhibits the ferity and many of the same lesions as the adolescents appearing in Klamm's photographs.

The thought of all those children being photographed in desolate scenes such as only the Northern Cape can offer, propels Harry towards the Prieska library once more. At the helpdesk, the ever-stern Mrs Prinsloo throws his first theory into even greater disarray.

'You're looking for newspaper articles on child abuse and *molestation?*' She clutches at her chest in horror. 'What for?'

Harry explains to her that he wants to compare the histories of any such cases in the area with an investigation he is working on.

'And what investigation would that be?' She is still staring at him warily. 'Are you a policeman?'

Harry smiles. 'I'm still very curious about that girl who disappeared here, Claudette Klamm.'

Mrs Prinsloo sighs and pushes her round spectacles further up her nose. 'Mister, you're not going to find anything related to those girls here in our newspapers.'

'Oh?' Harry replies. 'Which girls are we talking about?'

'The ones possessed by Claudette Klamm.' The librarian glances around to check if anyone is listening to them. 'There are these girls, mostly teenagers from Leopold Ridge, that hurt themselves for no reason one can think of. Some claim it's her spirit that compels them to do so, and it certainly started with her—Claudette Klamm, that is. You won't find any mention in the papers because it's some local madness that just isn't news to us any more. There was even a journalist from the *Huisgenoot* up here a few years back to research the story. At that time, it started the women gossiping all over again; you know, whose girl had been thrown out of school, when and why . . . but it's all got rather stale these days.' She frowns and holds up a finger thoughtfully. 'Now, I wonder whatever happened to the article that young man was intending to write? I kept looking out for it week after week, but . . .' She shrugs. 'Anyway, I think Mr Klamm himself comes back every so often to take photographs of these children. But what he does with those pictures, no one knows.'

Harry does not mention to her that the elderly man was murdered two weeks ago. Instead, his mind turns back to the moment he and Martha had heard Zelda screaming, and they found her on her knees in the living room, begging her mother to save her from some invisible force. 'How do people know these girls actually wound themselves? Some of them seem a bit young to be suffering from sufficient depression or anger to actually do it to themselves, don't you think?'

'Folks have had the best part of forty years to figure that out, Mr Mason.

Mothers, teachers, principals, priests, even psychologists from Kimberley have commented on it. Of course, it doesn't mean anyone has so far been able to *change* things—it just goes on and on. Some claim it's precisely this continuing occurrence over years, across age groups and race, that conclusively proves it's the devil at work. Anyway, that's Claudette Klamm's dark secret for you.'

Their conversation leads Harry to the conclusion that, if it is genuinely self-mutilation these children are exhibiting signs of, and Claudette Klamm was the first example, she might have ultimately committed suicide somewhere there on the farm, especially after her father had almost beaten her lover to death.

2

5.49 a.m., 10 June 2004, *Oranje Genot* Farm

Harry wakes to shrill screams. He sits up in alarm, the terrible sound sending his heart racing, gooseflesh instantly breaking out all over him. For a moment he believes he is in a dark muddy hollow, raindrops pattering on leaves all around, recalling his boyhood. But no, this is something else. Zelda again?

A sigh of relief escapes his parted lips when he finally recognizes the noise as guinea fowl. Just guinea fowl greeting the rising sun. Getting up, he opens the curtains. To his left a pinkish blaze scorches the horizon, silhouetting a lonely acacia tree, while below him a flock of the wild fowl are scratching about the ragged lawn. The house itself remains deathly quiet.

As he dresses, Harry mulls over his activities during these last few days. Though the pace has been easy, nothing at all like the pressures of police work, he is getting frustrated with his lack of progress. Try as he may, he cannot seem to cut through the legend of the girl who was killed on this farm, and get at the marrow of truth.

A little while later he is strolling towards the solitary acacia tree not far from the farmhouse. As the frosted grass crunches loudly underfoot, the fresh cup of coffee he made himself and the smell of dewy earth and grass momentarily vaporize these macabre reflections. His mind is left empty and tranquil as he watches the dawn steadily bathing the whitewashed farmhouse in its growing light.

Over to his left, his eye catches an area where the surrounding bush is not growing so densely, near a copse of shrubs bordering the bottom of the garden. On approaching it, he spots the now overgrown charred ruin of some small rectangular structure, and realizes this is most likely where José Cauto's living quarters once stood. But before he can investigate closer, he hears a diesel engine approach along the sandy road. A police pickup appears, a man with a silvery crew cut and pencil moustache at the wheel. Jogging over to the cattle gate, Harry unhooks the elaborate mechanism securing it and lets the police inspector through.

3

7.20 a.m., 10 June 2004, *Oranje Genot* Farm

'*Môre*.' The officer halts the vehicle next to him. 'Willie Erasmus?' His tone is gruff, his deadpan eyes gunmetal mirrors.

'No. I'm Harry Mason, a guest for just another day or so.' He allows his eyes to flicker over the man's chest where his name badge should be, but a blue jacket covers it. 'Willie's probably still in bed; he's not doing too well.'

'Really?' There is no concern or surprise in the man's disaffected tone. 'What's wrong with him?'

'Maybe you'll want to go speak with him or his wife about that. You could park over there, behind the Land Rover.'

Meyer nods guardedly and drives further in. By the time he is getting out of the car, Erasmus is at the front door, pulling on a well-worn black windbreaker. He throws a sober glance in Harry's direction before turning back into the house.

Seated in the kitchen, Harry's ears perk up when the man sitting opposite him introduces himself as Inspector Meyer from the Marydale police station. Erasmus clanks a coffeepot onto the stove, before settling down in his usual chair at the head of the table. His health seems to have taken a turn for the worse, pink blotches melding with the dark bags under his eyes, his skin a waxen colour that reminds Harry of the clay that forensic anthropologists use to reconstruct the faces of people long dead.

'Mr Erasmus,' begins Meyer in Afrikaans. 'You know a sergeant Simon Gallows?'

Erasmus's eyes widen slightly. 'Aah . . . no, never met him. Why?'

'You sure?'

'Yes, I'm sure.' His eyes flick towards Harry. 'What's this about?'

Meyer shifts forward in his chair, and steeples his hands. 'I'm sure you know about the hijackings that have been occurring recently in this part of the province.'

'You mean the cash-in-transit heists?'

'*Ja*, those. But there have been more. Trucks with valuable goods have also gone missing, presumably disappearing over the Namibian border, maybe even to Botswana.'

'Sure, I've seen something about it on TV.' Erasmus shifts in his chair, thereby throwing a shoulder in Meyer's direction and freeing up his legs from underneath the table, before crossing them.

'You know anything else about these incidents?'

The farmer's eyes try to creep towards Harry once more, but Meyer's sharp tone jolts him back. 'Answer the question.'

'No, I really don't.'

Erasmus has begun to blink rapidly in response to the policeman's aggression. Meyer then turns an evaluating gaze on Harry, as if he suspects the guest of influencing Erasmus's answers. His face is like a pit bull's, thinks Harry, and he realizes what the next question is going to be before the cop utters it. After all, he used the same intimidating tactics when he himself was in the service. 'So why was Gallows on his way to see you when he disappeared two weeks ago?'

'I don't know anything about a policeman being on his way to see me. I can promise you that. Just ask him.' Erasmus nods in Harry's direction. 'I've been in bed ill most of the time.'

'That right?' Meyer asks Erasmus, not bothering to look at the other man drawn into the questioning. He slowly grips one hand into a fist and places it carefully on the table. 'You *damn* sure about that?'

'Uh-huh.' Erasmus nods vigorously. 'Don't get many visitors out here, and I would've remembered if a police officer came by.'

Meyer turns his attention on Harry. 'And you? You know anything about Sergeant Gallows?'

'No. I only got here five days ago. I haven't had a chance to meet anyone much in Leopold Ridge and Prieska.'

'And what's your business here?'

'I'm looking into the disappearance of Claudette Klamm, which happened thirty-nine years ago.' Harry watches the officer's expression carefully, but absolutely nothing stirs in it. 'For a certain Miss Campbell,' he adds, 'Bernard Klamm's estranged wife. He was murdered in Johannesburg on the twenty-fifth of May.'

The pit bull studies him a moment. 'You a cop?'

'Was.'

'Uh, where?'

'I worked Murder and Robbery a few years, up in Jo'burg.'

'Uh?'

Harry nods. 'That's right.'

The kettle behind Meyer begins to whistle and clatter. Just then Martha gets out of bed upstairs, and floorboards creak as her heavy feet start clunking about.

Erasmus jumps up to tend the boiling water. 'That's my wife, and I wish she didn't sound like stampeding wildebeest, but what can I do? Coffee, Inspector? I've only got Frisco.'

'Two sugars, no milk.' Meyer unbuttons a shirt pocket. 'I want you two to look at this photo. You might not know him by name, but you might've seen him around.' He slides the photograph over the table in Erasmus's direction. The man picks the photograph up, but barely studies it, as his eyes start fluttering like a goldfish's gills.

'No.' He hands the image over to Harry. 'Definitely never saw the man.'

'He was last spotted driving a Toyota Hilux pickup,' says Meyer, 'a police-issue vehicle like the one parked outside. He stopped briefly at Leopold police station, where he spoke to Sergeant Kheswa before heading out this way. That was around nine in the morning of the twenty-eighth of May.'

If the invalid had not been so pale already, Meyer might have noticed Erasmus blanch on hearing the Sergeant's name.

Simon Gallows's image looks preppy for a small-town cop: blond hair, brown friendly eyes, a big smile; the kind of man who marries early, goes to church every Sunday, and loves his kids. Harry hands the photograph back with a shake of his head. 'Haven't seen him either.'

Martha's voice then calls to Willie Erasmus from the living room and the man excuses himself, leaving Harry and Inspector Meyer alone in the kitchen.

'So what's with these hijackings?' asks Harry.

Meyer is gazing towards the door, listening to the hurried whispers between Erasmus and his wife. His ears are almost waggling as he tries to better pick up what is being said. Any thought of replying to Harry seems momentarily rejected. When the hushed tones cease, he responds abruptly. 'They haven't taken much money in their heists, yet, way out here they haven't been taking the highest risks, either. The routes followed are poorly policed and those cash-cars travel pretty much on their own over vast distances. But they're professional jobs.'

'What do you mean by professional jobs?'

An annoyed frown crosses the cop's face. He looks back at Harry over his shoulder. 'Murder and Robbery, you say?'

Harry nods. 'Quit four years ago.'

'Why?' Meyer spits the question out as if the thought of anyone ever quitting the SAPS revolts him.

'It was a personal decision.'

'Right.'

Harry hastens to add, 'I have a daughter I wanted to spend more time with. She . . . lost her mother around that time, too.'

'Sorry to hear that, mister. You a PI now, or what?'

'I'm looking into this one case for Miss Campbell.' Harry shrugs. 'After that I might go back to carpentry, or do something else; I'll see.'

'In that case,' Meyer makes a clicking sound with his tongue, 'I'm sure you won't mind if I keep the MO of our hijackers to myself for the moment. It's police business, after all.'

'Sure.' Harry takes a sip of his coffee. 'Mind if I ask you about the work you did for Bernard Klamm?'

This time there is surprise in the policeman's expression. 'Oh,' he says, 'you know about that?'

'The officers investigating Bernard Klamm's murder found your name and number in a safe, along with a photo album from his daughter Claudette's childhood. There was also a woollen jersey caked with blood.'

Some argument has started up in the living room between Willie Erasmus and his wife: low, urgent words passing between them at a frantic pace. Meyer continues doing his best to listen in.

'Ja, so?' he says reluctantly.

'Most people around here—and that includes his wife now living in the city—believe Bernard Klamm killed his own daughter and nailed José Cauto with the rap. It seems Claudette was wearing a white jersey the night she disappeared. If it's the same, I'd like to know what that jersey was doing in Bernard Klamm's safe after all these years, also if you know whether it was his daughter's, and whatever you had to do with the case.'

Meyer turns to observe Harry face to face over the table, the argument in the sitting room forgotten. 'It was some private work I did for Mr Klamm. I promised him confidentiality, and that's what he still gets.'

'Come on, Inspector. Klamm's dead, and his widow's desperate to know what happened to their kid. Can't you sympathize with that? Don't you have kids of your own?'

'No.'

Not to be stonewalled Harry shifts gears. 'This Sergeant Gallows, he's been missing . . . what, two weeks? He's been gone all this time, and you're still chasing after him, not leaving the matter alone. Did you guys work together? Did you do stuff together over the weekend? I'm sure he's married, so what's his wife thinking? Claudette Klamm's been missing thirty-nine years and her mother still hasn't gotten over it. Like Gallows's wife, her mother deserves to know what happened to her.'

Meyer makes another clicking sound with his tongue. 'Klamm didn't kill his daughter.'

'How do you know that?'

'How do I know?' repeats Meyer, a smile crossing his lips for the first time. 'Who the hell contracts a police officer as a private investigator to look into the disappearance of his daughter if he already murdered her? Besides, he called me after receiving a parcel through the post with that white jersey in it. It *is* his daughter's by the way; he positively identified it.'

'Was there any particular heat on him at that stage? Did he maybe send it to himself to help throw the cops off his scent?'

'No, no one was investigating him at that time. And as far as I can tell he certainly didn't send the parcel to himself, either. What happened was that a wrong delivery finally found its way to his doorstep. You know how the post sometimes arrives a few days late? This parcel arrived two *years* late. It was dated 4 April 1990, and was delivered to GGeM offices in Prieska. Klamm had stopped working for them by 1983, and so the parcel disappeared into some musty backroom for two years, because no one could be bothered to track him down. A clued-up clerk rediscovered it during some spring-cleaning, and forwarded it to Klamm's last known address in Johannesburg. When he finally received it he nearly shat his pants. There was no note, just the jersey, and it had been posted at Prieska's post office—that's all we could tell from the packaging. If you know about José Cauto, I suppose you also know the kind of mess Klamm created in getting rid of the man that was screwing his daughter.'

'What did he do between receiving the parcel and first approaching you?' asks Harry.

'He sat tight, wondering whether his daughter was alive or whether he was about to be blackmailed for engineering the wrongful conviction of José Cauto. But nothing followed. He first approached me the year after he received the parcel, with a mandate to find out what exactly happened to his daughter. Klamm had thought he could overlook her disappearance, that he would get over it at some point, but when that jersey arrived, man, I can tell you now, things he kept pent up for years broke loose from under the bed, and came spilling out at night.'

'It couldn't have been his conscience,' says Harry, 'otherwise he would've helped free Cauto from jail.' Harry gets up and begins pacing around the kitchen, one hand in his pocket and toying with his car keys. 'He doesn't strike me as the repentant type.'

Meyer takes out a packet of Pall Malls and lights one with a Zippo. He drags deeply on the cigarette, his eyes tracking Harry across the room as though through crosshairs. 'Klamm still felt justified sending Cauto up, so a bloody jersey wasn't going to change that, but a daughter is a daughter, and I think he missed her more than he cared to admit to anyone.'

'José Cauto has been serving a life sentence for something he obviously did *not* do.' Harry stops dead, stares at Meyer. 'Surely you should be doing something about it? You had firm evidence that he could not have killed her. Why didn't you have the investigation reopened?'

Meyer folds his hands as if in prayer, and holds Harry's eyes through parallel lines of smoke meandering towards the ceiling. 'That's not the way I work, and Klamm knew this.'

'Why you?' It is getting to Harry that these people—Lambert, Klamm, Meyer, even Campbell—show such indifference towards Cauto, who was guilty, as far as Harry can see, only of a liaison with a white girl. Segregation laws of 1960s apartheid or not, it seems preposterous that Cauto should go on rotting in prison despite a lack of evidence backing the original conviction, and the subsequent evidence in the form of Claudette's jersey appearing after he went to jail. 'Why did Klamm come to you in particular? Is it because you operate like Lambert?'

Meyer breaks eye contact and taps cigarette ash into his empty coffee mug. 'I once did some private work for some friends of his in the diamond business. My ability to work discreetly mattered here. I don't allow my private work to interfere with police business, and I don't mix my responsibilities as a police officer with what I learn in confidence. That might offend you, but it's the way I work. Klamm knew he could trust me with his dirty secret. He didn't even want me speaking to his ex-wife because he didn't want to stir up hope where there wasn't necessarily any to be found.'

Harry grabs the back of his chair and nods, disappointment and reproach written all over his face. 'So . . . what's your opinion on what really happened?'

Martha's voice shrills out in the living room, then drops with a silencing hiss. Both men turn to look in the direction of the door. After Meyer realizes again he cannot distinguish what is being said, he continues.

'I reckon four people were present at this house on the night in question. One is dead, like you've just told me; one is serving a life sentence; Klamm's wife is in Johannesburg; and the daughter has disappeared.' Meyer ticks them off on his hand and presents Harry with four fingers. 'There were workers on the farm too, of course, most of whom had previously served in Klamm's mines, but they were generally scared shitless of Klamm. I did go up to Leeuwkop prison to talk with Cauto back in '89, but he refused to see me. I came up with two theories: one, there was another, unknown party involved; two, it was Klamm's wife who killed her. Your presence here discredits my second theory, much in the same way as mine discredits your suspicion about Klamm.'

Harry is still trying to get to grips with how Meyer could live with himself knowing an innocent man is rotting in prison, when the cop stubs out his cigarette and nods back in the direction of the door. 'What are they going on about out there?'

'That depends.' Harry follows his gaze. 'Do you want to hear the story about Claudette Klamm possessing other children, or the one about the devil living down in the cellar?'

'Oh, that.' Meyer chuckles and folds his hands behind his head. 'You know, after I told Klamm there was no way I could figure out what exactly happened to his daughter without employing an expensive investigative team, he seemed to go a bit screwy on me. I heard he began coming back up here and photographing other kids with the same symptoms his daughter exhibited— of what he actually believed to be demonic attacks. To him the fifth, unidentified party was some kind of devil. I met him once again, shortly after I moved to Marydale, and he wasn't the same. It was difficult to tell exactly what about him had changed. I could merely say he'd become more intense, though I reckon he always was a very intense man. But now he was spewing a lot of religious mumbo-jumbo, and was dead-set on proving to his estranged wife that he hadn't killed their daughter. So, I guess, if that meant blaming it on some supernatural force, then that was what he aimed to do.'

'What kind of symptoms are we talking about here, shown by the daughter?' asks Harry.

'She complained of being watched all the time, of hearing a voice. She frequently woke screaming at night because of some invisible force pressing down on her. Her father claimed to have seen bite marks all over her body, cuts and bruises. Sounds like she was one fucked-up child to me,' adds Meyer.

A voice is raised. 'I'm *not* going to ask him, and that's final!' Whereupon Erasmus bursts into the kitchen, breathing in shallow gasps.

Meyer looks up at him. 'Ask what?'

'*Ag man!* My wife wants me to get police protection, because of the break-ins we've had here.'

'Break-ins?' asks Meyer.

'We had an unwelcome visitor one night.' Harry sits down again. 'Someone was trying to dig up the cellar.'

'There's nothing of any worth down there, so what do I care?' Erasmus flops into his own chair, his nervousness around the cop momentarily forgotten in the aftermath of his lengthy argument with his wife. 'Look, are we finished with this Sergeant Gallows you asked about?'

'No.' Meyer's expression hardens. 'We're not finished with Gallows, not by a long shot.'

4

8.31 a.m., 10 June 2004, Prieska

'The photo albums are a dead end, Jakes,' Harry informs his friend when he gets him on the phone. Harry is standing at a Prieska post office external payphone, with a row of Nama *swerwers* sitting on a nearby wall, juggling their hopes of ever finding work with their impatience for the imminent opening of the Solly Kramer bottle store, situated two doors further down. 'They won't point you to your killer, I don't think.'

'Why do you say that?' The detective sounds tired and resigned, but not overly surprised.

'I've just had a talk here with an Inspector Meyer, who confirmed what a librarian told me yesterday. It seems Bernard Klamm returned to Leopold Ridge every so often to photograph various girls who showed similar symptoms to the affliction his daughter was apparently suffering from. I don't know if it's down to some kind of mass hysteria shared by the adolescent females in the community, or maybe some superstitious pandemic dreamt up by the locals, but I don't think Klamm himself was responsible for the abuse shown in the photos. The Erasmus girl displays some of the same injuries, and I witnessed her suffering some severe fit herself. No one else was present in the room, but she was clearly frightened out of her wits.'

'You sure you didn't see anything else in there?' asks Jacob.

'Of course.'

'Could *she* see anything?'

'I think she was certainly pretending to.'

'You shouldn't so easily dismiss the spirit world, Harry.'

Not prepared to engage his friend now in a debate on a subject they have vehemently disagreed upon in the past, Harry tries to redirect the conversation. 'What progress have *you* made?'

Jacob grunts in disapproval of his friend's blatant manoeuvre. 'I've been decoding Klamm's notes and cross-references, and it seems to me he has been matching the attacks on the various girls with supernatural entities recorded from around the world, which are known to attack specifically women. I think he was trying to prove that there was a link between all these girls and one single creature which was regularly victimizing them. I find this strange because Miss Campbell told me her husband did not believe in the supernatural.'

'And Cauto?' presses Harry.

'Tudhope is looking into that,' replies Jacob.

'Let him try Leeuwkop prison in Kimberley for starters.'

'How's your own case going?' asks Jacob. 'You still know how to set about an investigation?'

Harry sneers at the taunt, then proceeds to update Jacob. 'I still don't have a bead on anyone specific that may have been involved in the daughter's kidnapping or murder. My talk with Meyer pretty much rules out Klamm himself, while Campbell recruiting me rules her out, too, and the arrival of the jersey rules out Cauto unless he had an outside accomplice, which I very much doubt. It also rules out a suicide. This thing looks like it's going to hang. My only alternative suggestions are that she left town in a hurry, that someone is lying very convincingly, or that someone else completely was involved. All I know for sure is that I'm heading home for the weekend, and then I'm going to grill Campbell over an open fire.'

Replacing the receiver, Harry eyes the library that stands next door on Stewart Street. Harry left the farm shortly after Meyer ended a heated interrogation of Erasmus that got him nowhere. As Erasmus grew increasingly irritated with his repetitive questions, Meyer had merely smiled and insisted that they drive down to the farm workers' settlement, which made Erasmus even more agitated—most likely, assumed Harry, because many would not possess the proper work permits if this police officer decided to check. Not wanting to become part of that particular skirmish, Harry had grabbed his jacket and hurriedly left the house. But now his curiosity about the possible link that Meyer has discovered between Erasmus and the missing Simon Gallows and the hijackings gets the better of Harry, and he makes a beeline for the neighbouring depository of public information.

'Mister Mason.' Mrs Prinsloo shakes her head. 'Why don't you rather step outside and enjoy the library's lovely garden? You know we've got South Africa's first ever cattle gate standing there—designed in 1926, it was. That's the kind of history you should be enjoying here in Prieska, not the gloomy stuff you keep coming in here to enquire about.'

'I'd like to see those news clippings I'm after first,' he says. 'Then I'll go see your gate, I promise.'

'You'd better not miss it,' the lady warns him. Harry can see she is being playful, though her face remains dour. 'I don't want people thinking we live in fear here like all those folks in Johannesburg. My sister's daughter tells me everyone there wears panic buttons around their necks, and they have to go jogging with clubs in their fists. What a life *that* must be, I tell you.'

The library occupies only a cramped single-storey rectangle building. In the gloom of its interior, dust forms a kaleidoscope of particles dancing endlessly in musty air that smells a thousand years old. Small windows set high in the walls, up near the ceiling, allow for a degree of natural illumination, while fluorescent tubes flicker at a level of power that does not necessitate them being replaced from the piteous annual budget, but gives readers a headache instead. The ugly green industrial-standard carpet is lifting free from the floor in places. Periodic coughs and sneezes can be heard from along the aisles of books, although Harry has not yet spotted a soul other than Mrs Prinsloo herself. As far as sick buildings go, this place is terminally ill.

In front of him, the newspaper articles spread out on an oversized reading desk date back several months. He does remember reading about a handful of armed robberies and heists in the area in the national newspapers, but it turns out that the regional newspapers have been carrying a lot of additional information on hijackings across the entire Northern Cape, some occurring as far south as De Aar, and a few even near the Namibian border post at Nakop. Incidents are recorded of truckers sleeping in their haulers at night, by the roadsides or in remote truck stops, being roughly awoken with guns pressed to their heads by unknown assailants. Others have been found shot dead with no clue to what became of the cargo they were transporting. Though such crimes are not altogether new in the area, there has been a sharp increase of incidents since December 2003. In amongst all the photographs and news items of violence, stolen goods and cash thefts, Harry finds a photograph of Inspector Simon Gallows proudly holding up his three-year-old daughter for the camera.

'Hello,' says a soft, deep, female voice behind him. Harry looks up and round from the detailed notes he is scribbling on a sheet of white A4. He finds a woman with eyes like drops of blue Arctic ice peering down at him, her mouth twisted to one side as if unsure of what to say next. The winter garments he gave her are now bundled in her hands.

'Oh, hi.' He gets up hastily. 'It's you . . . from the roadside, the other day.'

She rises up on the balls of her feet like a little girl who has been paid a compliment, and the smile that suddenly warms up her face reveals one front tooth slightly overlapping the other. 'Yes,' she says in Afrikaans. 'I recognized your car parked outside, and went home to fetch these for you. I'm glad I caught you.' She holds the bundle of clothes out to him.

He takes them hesitantly, impressed by this complete transformation. A few days ago she was a grimy, unwashed creature with a broken thong on one foot and only a thin summer dress to protect her against the cold. He remembers thinking she might be beautiful if ever she got cleaned up. Though now dressed simply in light-blue fleece pullover, a tight pair of jeans with sparkling embroidery around the pockets and flat white shoes with laces, she looks fresh as flowers.

'You didn't have to return them,' he says, scratching his head nervously. 'Wow, I . . . you look *good*.'

She smiles and blushes deep crimson. 'I *wanted* to return them because they're yours. And, anyway, they're too big for us.'

'I'm glad you've fallen on your feet again.' Harry begins to fidget with the ballpoint still in his hand. 'You looked . . . I don't know . . . I've been wondering what happened to you and Gabriel.'

The hitchhiker nods. 'We're staying with my mother for the time being, as I didn't know where else to go. So, *ja*, thanks again, mister. *Shooh*, it sounds like I'm just thanking you all the time.'

'It's all right. Just don't go on calling me mister. It's Harry.'

'Oh, my name is Salome, Salome Arendse.' She sticks her hand out.

'Salome.' Harry tastes the name on his tongue. 'That's a nice name; I've heard it before in a song.'

'Really? There's a song with my name in it?'

'Yeah.' Something about this young woman again reminds him of his wife. Whether it is her proud yet playful demeanour or the way her lips curve up into dimples when she smiles, he does not know, but it attracts him to her in a way he has not felt in years. 'It's something by the band U2. You know them?'

'No,' she shakes her head, her hands still interlocked in front of her. 'Never heard of them.'

'Oh,' says Harry. He looks away, a sudden sense of guilt jolting through his mind, as a voice says, *No, you can't compare Amy with her. You must never do that.*

He fiddles amongst his notes, listening to the twin waves of guilt and attraction crashing together inside him.

'They're this Irish band,' he blurts finally, with a sense of release. 'Really good, they are. I'm sure you'd recognize some of their songs if you heard them.'

The woman nods encouragingly, as though she is expecting still more information.

His ears are ringing with an unexpected rush of blood and excitement. 'Would you . . .' he begins. *Would you what?* He grabs the backrest of the chair as if for support. Before that reproachful voice in his head can seal his lips and kill his words, he forces them out. 'Is there perhaps somewhere we can go have coffee?'

It is a silly question, and he knows it. His car is parked just outside a fast food diner, as she would have noticed.

'Yes.' Salome nods encouragingly. 'There's the Wimpy just down the street.'

5

11.24 a.m., 10 June 2004, Prieska

Harry stirs his coffee with nervous concentration. It seems to him, glancing over Salome's shoulder, that the two waitresses are staring in their direction as they talk in hushed tones. The air conditioner inside the fast food diner makes his nose tingle with ionized air.

'So where's your boy now?' he finally asks.

'My mother's looking after him.' Salome gently blows onto her coffee, elbows resting on the white formica tabletop. 'Just while I'm out trying to find work.'

'Yeah? What sort of work are you looking for?'

'Don't know.' Salome gives a little shrug. 'I could be a secretary, I guess, but I haven't really done enough that'll look good on an application. I had . . .' She purses her lips. 'It's just difficult to find anything, especially out here.'

Harry nods reassuringly. 'That's good. I'm glad you're out looking. Most people give up so easily. You don't seem like the type that would.'

'No?' Salome smiles that same smile he is finding so irresistible. 'I don't know . . . these last three weeks I've been thinking some real bad things— you know, about just giving up. Three weeks ago I thought I had everything I needed to survive—a husband with a steady job, a fair enough house. Even if I wasn't very happy, I thought I'd be all right because I was standing on my own two feet, relying on my husband and not my parents. But then the carpet got yanked out from under me.' Her expression wilts like a cut daisy left out in the sun.

'No,' Harry agrees, 'life never seems to happen the way you think it will. That much I've learnt. So you have a husband?'

'Not any more. The son of a bitch . . . sorry, no. He left me. Recently.'

'Is that how you ended up hitchhiking from Kimberley?'

'Ja.' Salome sets her coffee mug down and hastily brushes at her dampening eyes. 'It all just went to hell. Just like that. Out of nowhere. That's not quite right: I could've seen it coming, yet I chose to ignore the signs. But you know what you do when you fall down? You get up because there's not much else you can do. You try again and again and again, because that's how God designed us to be. Sometimes I think that hope and the instinct to survive are the same thing.'

'We don't need to talk about it, if it upsets you.'

'No, it's all right. I'm sorry. *I* brought it up. Really, I'm sorry. It's not your problem.'

'Don't worry.' Harry smiles. 'We all go through a rough patch every now and again.'

Salome grunts a strong affirmation to this and looks away. Harry watches her staring out the window in silence, obviously battling to regain control over freshly stirred emotions. It occurs to him that this woman who has been dumped by her husband is thinking along very similar lines as he did when Amy died. One gets up after such a blow, because that is what one does; one moves forward because there is no moving backwards. Life drags a person inexorably towards death, no matter what he or she tries to do. This is a familiar litany for Harry.

'Do you want to tell me what happened?' he asks tentatively.

Salome laughs nervously. 'You mean you want to hear about it?'

He shrugs with an open smile. 'I've got the whole afternoon, and it looks like you could do with someone to talk to.'

'If you're up for it?' Her voice has a playful warning to it, letting him know his suggestion may prove to be to his detriment. When he reassures her that he is, she sits up. 'I married what is considered a successful man, for these parts. He had his own trucking company, transporting goods all over the Cape provinces, Botswana, Namibia. I thought I could settle down and be the little domestic woman men want us to be. Of course, I didn't know he was off gambling in Kimberley when he told me he was away on business trips, and he didn't tell me about all the cheap women he was screwing around with when he supposedly stayed late at the office. All that came out later.

'The entire town knew before I did that my husband was bankrupt. My *mother* was the first to tell me. When I confronted him about it there was an argument. He beat the living hell out of me, with my child howling in the other bedroom. He then stormed out of the house, leaving me to bleed all over the kitchen floor. That's how Gabriel found me when he finally plucked up the courage to come out of his room.

'Two months later Hannes was back, apologizing for what he'd done to me. It took him an afternoon to convince me that I shouldn't have provoked him just when he was doing his best to get us back on track. So I ended up apologizing to him. What else could I do? I didn't have any money—not even my own bank account—and I was already selling bits of our furniture to feed Gabriel. I had *nothing* without my husband. So I took him back, on his promise that he was coming into some money soon, and that our fortunes were going to turn. I didn't realize the only reason he came back to me was because the floozy he had shacked up with tossed him out.'

'It didn't end there, did it?'

Salome shakes her head. 'I suppose it never does. It's funny, when you stand on the outside looking in, you always think, "No, that won't ever happen to me," but when it does, all these emotions, they swamp the way you think, and before you know it, you're ducking out of people's way because the questions they ask you are the questions you can't answer, even to yourself.'

'So how did you end up in Kimberley?'

'A time came when Hannes suddenly became particularly sweet towards me. Till then, it was always these ups and downs, from love to hate, one minute to the next, but all of a sudden he was pampering me like when we first started dating. He was talking about us going on a holiday to Durban, just the three of us. It was going to be the first time we ever went away as a family, can you believe? So he made plans, booked us flight tickets from Upington to Durban, *nogal*. I wasn't stupid—something was going on—but he was being very secretive, so what could I do? He became very insistent that we go, and got annoyed with me when I worried about the cost, so I let it be. A day before we were meant to leave, he said some important business had come up which he needed to attend to, that Gabriel and I should go on ahead, and he would catch up.'

Harry sits forward resting crossed arms on the table. 'But he never did?'

Salome shakes her head, her eyes peering at the bottom of her empty coffee mug. They stay there when she finally speaks again. 'I phoned my mother when he didn't turn up when he said he would, because I just knew he had done something horrible. She went over to our house in Breytenbach Street, and found he'd cleared out everything. *Everything.*

'It took us a week of begging by the sides of roads to get as far as Kimberley, a week of fishing for food in garbage dumpsters behind roadside restaurants. I had to sell off what little we took down to the coast to survive, because my mother didn't have any money to send me for return tickets.' Salome wipes away the tears rolling down her cheeks. 'That week I learnt about the heartlessness of people, but then you came along.'

'Jesus,' exclaims Harry. 'So where's he now, do you know?' One of the waitresses, wearing glittering plastic clips in her hair, comes over to refill their coffee cups.

Salome shakes her head; it is a motion of resolve, a rejection of his question rather than a negative answer. 'I don't want to know, and I don't care. I'm not chasing after him for anything, and I don't want to ever see him again.' She pushed her coffee cup firmly away as if it was her husband himself. 'Anyway, what are you doing here in Prieska?'

'I'm actually based on a farm close to Leopold Ridge. I'm looking into an old missing persons' case.'

'An *old* one?' she asks, clasping one wrist with her other hand. 'I suppose you mean Claudette Klamm's disappearance? Are you a reporter or a cop?'

Harry smiles as he nods. 'Why is it you all know what I'm talking about before I even mention her name?'

'Her father is the only man rich enough around here to keep sending people to ask questions. That in itself is enough to cause a stir in every bar and hair salon from here to Cape Town.'

'And yet everyone thinks it's her father who killed her?'

'Yes.' Salome laughs. 'That's true. But different people tell different stories, and it also depends on who's doing the listening. I think every thread of rumour becomes part of a thick coil of rope which binds the people around here together, and begins to have a life of its own.'

'So what's the strand you yourself braid into that rope?'

She shakes her head. 'I don't much care about the whole thing. It was all such a long time ago, and folks should just give it a rest. But if I'm forced to give an opinion, then I say she escaped from that farm, from that awful mother and father of hers, and now lives somewhere nice like Cape Town, or the Hibiscus Coast. Maybe she's even in Mozambique, where that man she was messing with came from. She's happy, married to someone decent, with two kids, a boy and a girl, but . . .' She shrugs. 'That's just another version to tell.'

Harry shifts in his chair with a chuckle. 'I wish I could have you explain all that to her mother.'

His mobile cuts off Salome's reply with its melodic chimes. Harry checks the caller identification, but does not recognize it. Excusing himself, he answers.

'Harry?' says a high, brittle voice. 'It's Ma-artha. Can . . . can you go back to the farm a-a-and lo-ho-ck up the hou . . . house.' She breaks down in tears.

'Martha?' Harry jumps up and heads for the street, where there is no one to listen in and no music. 'What's happened? Tell me.'

'Willie just collapsed.'

'Where are you now?'

'The h-h-hospital. In Prieska.'

'And Meyer? Where's Meyer?'

'He left . . . a-about an hour ago.' She manages to bring her tears under control. 'It's him . . . it's because of him. He u-upset Willie badly.' More tears disrupt their dialogue. In the background Harry hears an intercom chime.

'And Zelda?'

'She's here, with me.'

'I'll go there immediately,' says Harry, not knowing an intruder is already inside the house.

6

1.02 p.m., 10 June 2004, *Oranje Genot* Farm

The moment he steps into the living room he notices the twelve-gauge shotgun is gone from its customary place leaning against the sofa.

'Wait.' Harry grabs Salome's arm behind him.

'What's wrong?' she whispers.

He has invited her to accompany him to the farmhouse, intending to drive her home after running this errand for Martha Erasmus.

'What is it?' urges Salome, her arm hanging slack in his hand.

Harry touches a finger to his mouth and cocks his ear to listen. The television, however, drowns out any more muted sounds he might hear. Out of force of habit Harry draws his pistol.

Salome hisses, 'What are you doing? She just asked you to lock up here.'

He could tell her to go straight back to the safety of the car, but he cannot be sure there is not more than one intruder. He turns to glance through the window at the scrubby patch of garden, and the even wilder bush beyond it.

Decision time.

'*Shsh.*' He looks her square in the eye, glad to see apprehensiveness rather than outright panic. 'There might be someone in the house, or out in the yard. Just stick close behind me.'

Harry leads the way through the eating area and nudges open the kitchen door. The room is empty.

There's a sudden loud thump and a crash from beyond the second connecting kitchen door, leading to the central hallway.

'*Wat de vok was dit!*' swears Salome.

Harry feels his hackles rise; his grip on the gun tightens. Salome follows close behind as he moves quickly towards the hallway door. He opens it a crack. Nothing else, except a dull thud from beyond the door that is kept bolted and locked.

'Fuck,' exclaims Harry. 'Not again.'

'Is that the cellar?' Salome's face pales, despite her earlier scepticism about the rumours that circulate in the district. 'Isn't that where she's supposed to be buried?'

A loud grunt reaches them, then a spill of bricks.

'That's no ghost.' Salome's frown makes her look impossibly cute to Harry, despite the tense situation. 'What's going on down there?'

'Look,' whispers Harry, 'you head upstairs. I'll deal with this.'

'Why? Can't we just go—'

Their hands touch by accident and Harry grabs hold. 'Salome, listen to me. Whoever it is might have taken a shotgun from the living room. Just go upstairs now. Please.'

Her grasp tightens. 'Be careful,' she says and heads for the staircase.

Harry tests the kitchen outside door, but finds it locked. Outside the front door he moves around the right side of the building. To his left are the barn and car garage. The corner leading to the back of the house comes up, and he peeks around it past the kitchen door. Both the coal chute doors have been opened and thrown aside. The sound of someone huffing and puffing as he shovels earth and stones is now much clearer. Harry approaches carefully, his back against the outside wall, the semi-automatic poised by his ear. A spade strikes stone, then bites deep into soil. The sound sends an involuntary shudder up Harry's spine as he remembers a murder occurring in his childhood.

At the gaping cellar door, he takes a few quick steps down into the basement, but sees nothing more than a light beam playing across the far right-hand wall, its source hidden by a stone foundation wall that cuts the cellar into two smaller rectangles. He steps over the threshold, forgetting the fragments of old coal still scattered across the cellar floor. There is a loud crunch underfoot. The digging instantly stops.

Harry winces.

Hastily he ducks to the left, deeper into the gloom. Pressing up against the lowest of three rotting shelves filled with grimy paint cans, he waits. A silence follows, both intruders listening for each other in the shadows. The dusty air smells of mould, while the flimsy remnants of old spider webs, hanging from joists above him, brush against his face. To one side are the wooden steps that lead up into the house. Hard coal is still heaped nearby, and a long wooden ladder has been stored away on hooks hanging from the roof.

'Who's down here?' asks Harry, at last.

He receives no reply.

'I'm armed and ready to fucking shoot, so answer me.' He repeats the threat in Afrikaans.

'Who are you?' asks an African voice, speaking in English. The question sounds self-assured, even taunting.

Realizing this cannot be one of the Portuguese-speaking farm hands Willie Erasmus employs, he calls out, 'Harry Mason. If you have the shotgun drop it, and come out real slow where I can see you.'

'I'm busy,' is the gruff reply.

Harry trains his gun over to the wall, at the height of a man's eyes. 'You're trespassing.'

'With good reason,' comes the quick response.

Though the man's English is very good, Harry cannot place the foreign accent.

'I'm not fucking around here, and I don't care what your justifications are. You can explain all you want, once I can see your hands.'

A spade clangs to the ground, followed by the unmistakable sound of a shotgun round being chambered.

'It doesn't have to be this way,' calls Harry.

'I'm not surrendering to you, or anyone else. I've done enough of that. All I want is to be left in peace.'

'To do what? Dig your way to China?'

The first discharge blows the two shelves immediately above Harry's head to smithereens. Brick fragments and wood splinters spray everywhere, almost blinding him; heavy paint cans hit him on the neck and shoulders as he stumbles aside. A second blast bites a sizeable chunk out of the wooden crossbeam just above his head, destroying a hook holding the ladder in place. Harry barely has time to roll on his stomach before it tumbles down on top of him.

He is still trying to push the ladder away when a heavy boot strikes him in the small of his back, forcing him back to the floor. As the same boot comes down again, this time grinding the hand still clasping the automatic, the mouth of the shotgun is simultaneously pressed against the nape of Harry's neck. He cries out in pain and lets go of his weapon.

'What are you doing here, Harry Mason?'

'Jesus!' Harry cries. 'Get *off* me, you heavy fuck.'

He twists his head and briefly catches sight of his assailant. The man is tall, and in his sixties, with a barrel chest and fists like cinderblocks. His greying hair has receded, but the large scar just above his mouth remains the same. Before Harry can react to the surprise of seeing José Cauto towering over him, his attacker hefts a can of Dulux lacquer-paint from the remaining shelf, and brings it down on Harry's head. He blacks out in a spray of colour.

7

1.57 p.m., 10 June 2004, *Oranje Genot* Farm

'Harry.' Something warm and wet brushes over his face. 'Wake up, for God's sake, wake *up.*' The woman's voice is filled with tenderness and concern.

He opens his eyes and only then realizes his head is lying in Salome's lap, and she is looking anxiously down at him. With a groan he tries to move, but the back of his head feels like a white-hot ice pick is buried in it.

'Jesus, that hurts.'

As she helps him into a sitting position, he reaches back to feel a lemon-sized swelling.

'What happened?' Salome wipes more coal and dust from his face. 'All I saw was this large man running off into the veldt.' She points up the short flight of stairs but his eyes are still too sensitive to peer directly into the bright light outside. 'That was lying just outside.'

Harry glances towards where she is pointing. Willie Erasmus's automatic shotgun is lying in the black coal dust.

'Did you handle it?' he asks.

Salome shrugs. 'He must've dropped it, and I picked it up. Shouldn't I have?'

'We might lose some fingerprints because of that.' Harry frowns. 'Did you see what he looks like?'

'No,' she replies, 'I only saw the back of him.'

He still cannot quite believe that it was José Cauto himself, but the scar above the man's mouth makes him unmistakable, despite his age. What was he doing here?

'I need to get to a phone, *now.*'

'No,' says Salome in the firm voice of a mother. 'I think you should sit down a minute. You've taken a hard knock.'

Harry struggles up. 'You don't understand. That man is the principal suspect in a murder case.'

'Whoever he is, he's gone now. You should rest a bit; you look awful.'

Harry staggers towards the door. 'I need to call the police.'

'There's a phone in the hou—'

'Doesn't work,' he cuts in.

'The radio?'

Harry turns around to stare at Salome. 'The CB? Yeah, that's it. Thanks.'

It takes fifteen minutes before anyone in Leopold Ridge answers Harry's emergency callout, by which time the pain like an ice-pick buried in the back of his head has transformed into a cacophony of jackhammers drilling into his synapses. The sergeant who directed him here the night of his arrival answers the call, and Harry is promptly told in a jovially apologetic tone that it will be impossible to send out a patrol car.

'What the *fuck* do you mean by that?' he shouts into the handset. The man's apparent foolishness has gotten too much for him to handle.

'Hey!' Kheswa's good humour shatters like surface ice. 'You don't talk to me like that, *né*. I am the police. You think because you white you can talk to me like that? Where's Willie? Why's he not telling me about this?'

'He's in the goddamned hospital, that's why. I've got a murder suspect trespassing on the farm who's just attempted to kill me with a stolen shotgun, and you're telling me you can't send someone out? That's got nothing to do with race, Kheswa, and you bloody well know it.' Harry glances at Salome standing in the doorway of the study, but her eyes are rooted to the floor.

'*Ja.*' Kheswa's voice grows angrier. 'And I'm telling you there's no one here. Later this afternoon maybe; tomorrow even, but not now. You can come in and make a statement, if you—'

'You know what, Kheswa? Fucking *forget* it!'

Harry throws the microphone into one corner. 'Bloody hell! I can't believe that arsehole.'

'What now?' asks Salome, her voice carrying a reassuring weight.

'I'm going to burn down the bloody police station, that's what.' Harry begins pacing up and down the room, grumbling to himself. Salome crosses her arms and leans her head against the doorframe. 'How the hell am I supposed to catch the bastard now? Tell me that?' he asks, without expecting her to answer.

'Is that what you're actually here to do? To catch that man who ran off?'

Harry stops to look at her. 'No,' he replies, 'I suppose not. Although I'd like to talk with Cauto, that's for sure.'

'Who is he?'

'He's the one Claudette Klamm had something going with.'

'You mean he's still alive?'

'Looks like it.' Harry nods. 'And he's still built strong enough at sixty to bring a house down.'

The way Salome smiles at Harry makes him feel as if she has just reached out and touched his cheek. 'You should be glad nothing worse happened.'

Cauto had been within five metres of him with a shotgun. At that range, and with that spread, even the worst shot in the world should have plugged at least a few pellets in Harry. The man could also have easily sprayed the contents of his skull all over the floor after he had pinned him to the ground, but Cauto never pulled the trigger. Harry closes his eyes and takes a deep breath to steady his frayed nerves.

'I don't know,' he mumbles, almost to himself.

'What was he doing down there, anyway?' asks Salome.

Harry opens his eyes. 'He's been digging the place up, either when he knew the Erasmuses were in bed, or when they were away from home.'

'What for?'

'Your guess is as good as mine. Whatever it is, he wants it badly. Besides trespassing and breaking and entering, I'll bet Cauto was the one that killed the family dogs a few weeks back.'

'Do you think . . . could it be that he's looking for Claudette Klamm's body?'

'And risk getting shot for it?' Harry raises his eyebrows. 'I don't know. Whoa, I'm sorry I dragged you into this.'

'No, it's fine,' says Salome, though her smile is strained and her face now pale. 'It's been more interesting than going around looking for work.'

'*No*,' replies Harry in an insistent tone. He comes to stand near her, but does not touch her shoulders. 'It's not fine. I promised you a quiet cup of coffee, and you almost end up with a dead man on your hands.'

Salome laughs. 'That's OK. It was just like being in a movie. Besides, it's a reminder that whatever I've been through, no one stuck a shotgun in my face, and no one's beaten me over the head for a while.'

'Are you taking pleasure in my pain?' Harry raises a mischievous eyebrow.

The young woman shrugs as she laughs. 'Maybe.'

Harry grins back at her, then looks at his watch. 'Can you give me half an hour? I still have to drive back to Jo'burg today, and I need to get my gear together. If you'll wait a bit, I'll drop you off.'

Salome's cheerful expression falls like dead autumn leaves. 'You're going back to Johannesburg?'

'Yeah, I've got a daughter of my own, and she's waiting for me.' A twinge of regret passes through him when he sees her expression cloud over. 'But I'll be back.'

For a second it looks like she is about to ask him something else, but she only turns to glance down the hallway. 'Shouldn't we be worried about that man coming back?'

'I don't think so.' Harry looks out the window. 'He could've easily killed me, but he didn't. He has some other purpose, and we don't fit into the equation. He'll wait now until we're gone.'

8

3.12 p.m., 10 June 2004, Prieska

'Is there a chance you might want to go for dinner Monday?'

It just came out. The sentence slipped past Harry's lips when he thought he desperately wanted to keep it in. Salome had just got out of the car, and then leaned back in through the open window to say a final thanks.

'That depends.' Her expression grew strained. 'Are you married?'

'I was married.' Harry's face sobered. 'I lost my wife four years ago.'

'Oh, sorry to hear that.' Salome winced and glanced over her shoulder at her mother's front door. 'I don't know,' she said, after she turned back to look at him expectantly. 'I mean . . .' She trailed off.

Though the words felt like they were stuck to his tongue, and could not possibly escape, they rolled out more easily than he thought possible. 'Come on. I think it'll be fun.'

Her face brightened when she saw him smile. '*Ja*, OK,' she said. 'Why not?'

'You sure?' Harry asked, feeling himself blush.

She nodded. 'Seven, Monday night. Now get going before that woman phones you again.' With that she gave him a wink and was off.

By the time he pulls into the small parking lot of the Dr C. Sleggs Memorial Hospital, he discovers Martha Erasmus has left three messages on his mobile phone, lined up after two from Tobias Rees. He ignores them all.

In the pneumoconiosis wing, Martha spots him walking towards her and rises from the crude wooden bench set against one wall. Her face is red and puffy with tears, the tissue clasped in her left hand now a crinkled mush. The perpetual rash on her throat has been aggravated further by her constant fiddling with her gold necklace and cross.

'How bad is it?' asks Harry.

'I don't know if he's going to make it, I honestly don't. The doctors aren't very hopeful. Oh God, Harry, he's been driving himself too hard, worrying himself sick about this and that, never talking to his daughter or me any more. It's been hell for him; this disease has changed him so much. You know, he used to cuddle Zelda all the time but when he found out about the mesothelioma, he just . . . he went into hiding somewhere deep inside himself. He's kept all his hurt pent up. Then this morning, that policeman . . . I don't know what happened, but Willie . . . he just collapsed, he just *fell* down on the kitchen floor as he walked back in.' The woman blows her nose as she shakes her head. 'I've sent him over the edge—I know it was me. I should've been firmer with him, I shouldn't have let him go on the way he was. He's been driving himself too hard.'

Tears begin to twinkle afresh in her eyes. Harry reaches out and hugs the big woman uncomfortably. Behind her, down an ill-lit corridor, he sees Zelda's silhouette hovering on the threshold of a ward, like a ghost waiting to be invited in.

'Martha, listen to me. Have you got somewhere else to stay other than out at the farm?'

'What?' sniffed the woman. 'Why?'

'I saw the man who has been breaking into your house. His name's José Cauto. I want you to stay somewhere else until he can be caught. It's too dangerous out there for you and Zelda, right now.'

Her face grows both terrified and confused at the same time. 'It's Cauto that's been haunting the house?'

'He's for real, Martha. Flesh and blood, like the rest of us.'

'But what's he doing in *our* house?'

'That's what I want to find out, but I need to get back to Jo'burg for the weekend first.'

'You're *leaving*?' She grabs his forearm.

'I've got to. My daughter's waiting for me. Besides, I want to get the investigating officer in a murder case down there to apply pressure on these idiots in Leopold Ridge.'

'But—'

'No "buts", Martha, this guy's dangerous.'

'But it's our home.'

Just then a man wearing a green Castrol baseball cap swaggers into the waiting room, his arms burnt a reddish-brown under their covering of black hair, the glint of his brown eyes half concealed beneath thick eyebrows and wrinkled skin. He smells of stale cigarette smoke.

'Everything all right here?' he asks in Afrikaans, resting his hands on his narrow hips.

Martha Erasmus nods, then introduces her husband's cousin, Jacoe.

'That's settled then?' says Harry. 'You're not going back there until the police have searched that farm from top to bottom.' Harry nods towards the ward Zelda is hovering outside. 'Is he conscious?'

'He's sleeping.' Martha allows herself to be hugged round one shoulder by her in-law. 'I'll take you to him, if you like.'

Willie Erasmus is the only white man in the ward, his bed the middle of three on the left-hand side. Electronic beeps, human wheezes and coughs, punctuate the silence in the small ward, while the watery smell of cancer hangs heavily in the air. On approaching the sick farmer, Harry can see how much worse he has gotten. His face is an ashen grey, so that the pinkish splotches on his skin have paled significantly, while the perpetual rings under his eyes have darkened. A respiratory mask clouded with condensation covers his nose and mouth. The patient's breathing is staccato, his skeletal chest rising and falling in jittery movements. The dying man's rheumy eyes open abruptly.

Harry tries to smile reassuringly, but somehow this feels contrived. 'How are you, Willie?'

At first it seems the sick man is unable or unwilling to respond, but then a hesitant nod acknowledges his presence. Jacoe steps up to the bed and grabs hold of his brother's hand while Martha moves to brush lank hair from her husband's face, and then plant a kiss on his sweaty forehead. She calls over her daughter, who has up until now continued hanging back by the ward's entrance. Zelda's face is lowered, as if the gravity of the situation weighs down on her as heavily as it does on the adults.

Eyeing the man's pallid skin, Harry decides not to ask him any questions for now. 'I'm heading back to Jo'burg for the weekend,' he explains, 'but I'll see you again Monday.' He lays a hand on Willie's shoulder. 'Then we'll talk things through, see what your options may be.' Not wanting Martha to grasp the full implication of his words, Harry makes sure of holding Willie's full attention, before raising his eyebrows ever so slightly to let the man know he wants an honest talk with him about Meyer's visit. After a few moments, the sick man nods faintly, closing and opening his eyes for emphasis. Harry pats his shoulder, hoping they have genuinely understood each other. 'You hang in there, and I'll see what I can do for you.'

Returning to the reception area, he turns around to glance back in the direction of the ward. He is wondering what exactly he could possibly do for a farmer whose life is fast leaking away, who is being pursued by a pit bull policeman for some unwise decision he might or might not have made, and who will soon be nothing more than a trace of sadness in the memory of a poor and voiceless family. He realizes with surprise that Zelda has followed him, her face now looking unusually animated. Even now, with her father on his last legs, she stands on her own.

'Come here,' he calls to the girl, bending towards her. To his surprise she comes over to him without hesitation.

'How old are you, Zelda?' he asks in Afrikaans, as he puts an arm around her skinny shoulder.

'Almost eleven,' she replies gravely.

'Wow! You're really brave for a girl that young, you know that?'

'Is Papa going to be all right?' she asks.

'You keep your fingers crossed for him, and he might just come out of this OK. You understand?'

The girl nods.

'Good girl. Your papa really needs you, you know, even if he doesn't show it. Us old men, we get scared sometimes too, and that's when we sometimes forget about others. Here,'—Harry fishes around in his pocket—'give these keys to your mother.'

The little girl smells earthy and wild. Without explanation, he suddenly feels a kinship with her, seeing something of his own trapped boyhood reflected in that mirror-like obsidian gaze of hers. He tucks a couple of strands of her black hair behind her ears. 'I'm sure your dad will come right.'

Zelda nods, her eyes already wandering back towards the ward.

'One more thing.' Taking a fifty rand note from his wallet, Harry hands it to her. 'Give this to your mother as well.' Then a smile spreads over his face as he thinks of Rees's and Campbell's promises of covering his expenditures.

'Actually, take it all. I'll be back on Monday, so look after your mother. She needs you as much as your dad.'

The reclusive child nods again, then shyly thanks him in Afrikaans. He watches her scamper barefoot back to the ward, clutching his gift of money like a bouquet of flowers.

TWELVE

The Vice Health Director Who Smells of Toffee

1

9.17 a.m., 11 June 2004, Johannesburg

'You want to hear about Mr Bernard Klamm?' asks the woman sitting opposite Jacob.

The office on the fourth floor of the drab sandstone Centre for South African Occupational Health building is small and cramped. Jacob's impression of Dr Elizabeth Reynolds with her aquiline nose and curly, black hair is that she must be of Greek descent. The vice director sits back in a chair that creaks in loud protest. An implacable smell of toffee permeates the room.

'Yes. Specifically in the years between 1965 and 1983, when he worked for GGeM.'

'GGeM,' echoes the woman rhetorically. 'That's before my time. I take it you're interested in the asbestos industry?'

'Two weeks ago, Mr Klamm was murdered by an unknown assailant. The nature of this attack suggests an act of revenge. There are a number of leads, one being the company he worked for before his retirement. I contacted GGeM's London offices, but was then referred back to their recently dissolved South African subsidiaries. The company is less than willing to deal with me, and since they're based in London, I can do little about it. I'm sure you know how it is, Dr Reynolds, when no one seems willing to give you clear information. It's very frustrating, so here I am. I understand the CSAOH had considerable funding from GGeM at the time Klamm worked for them?'

'Yes, it's a storm cloud still hanging over this institution, and it won't subside any time soon, I'm afraid.'

The light in the room is yellow, giving everything a hue of old parchment.

'What was Klamm's role in the time he dealt with you as a representative of GGeM?' asks Jacob.

'My predecessors had nothing good to say about that man, ever. Mr Klamm was appointed as some sort of medical adviser to GGeM in 1965. What qualifications he had to lead the health and safety division of such a large company, I don't know. What I *do* know is that he had his fingers in just about every pie that directly or indirectly affected the asbestos industry, from the sixties right up to the late eighties. He was a draconian meddler as far as our pneumoconiosis researchers were concerned.'

Jacob pulls out a notebook and pen. 'Yes?'

'It seems to me his role was not so much that of a medical adviser, but that his purpose might have been to obfuscate the early results of South African asbestos research, and stem the tide of international objection to the mining practices regarding the mineral.

'In the early fifties a doctor named Van Copenhagen at West End hospital in Kimberley started documenting unusual cases of tuberculosis amongst mostly black and coloured miners in the Northern Cape. He eventually got in touch with two of our pathologists, Drs Bucke and Shaeffer, and the three of them eventually demonstrated a link between mesothelioma and asbestos exposure—*any* asbestos exposure. They had case studies of kids who had slept on used hessian sacks developing cancer, golfers who played on turf surfaced with old tailings, dry cleaners emptying out miners' pockets, you name it.

'In 1959 the CSAOH got together with the Department of Mines, the Department of Health, the CSIR and the four major asbestos producers, including GGeM. If Van Copenhagen, Bucke and Shaeffer were right, we had to assume that we had an epidemic on our hands, and so needed to move fast. The industry in question asserted it knew nothing about the incidence of lung disease, and feigned concern. The research team that was formed was called the Unit for the Study and Prevention of Pneumoconiosis—or USPP—and was funded almost entirely by the asbestos industry itself. Executives and board members from the funding companies and various asbestos interest groups picked one man to supervise this survey: Bernard Klamm, a recently appointed executive with GGeM. How he managed to get himself appointed to this post became clear only later.'

'Wait a minute,' says Jacob. He shifts forward in his seat to put his notebook on the doctor's desk. 'Are you saying a team was put together to investigate the working conditions of miners and other people living in the asbestos-mining towns, with every aspect of the research being run through one man: Bernard Klamm?'

'That's exactly what I'm saying,' says the doctor. She pushes her glasses back up her nose. 'And why not? The team needed a project co-ordinator and, more importantly, direct access to the companies' workers. They needed what few medical files and records of miners had been kept, and the cash the industry was willing to inject, because the apartheid government certainly wasn't going to pay for it. The funding was not necessarily suspect, nor was the intention of the interest groups to appoint someone to this unit sinister.'

'But—'

The doctor smiles as she holds a hand up. 'Yes, I know what you're thinking. In hindsight it is always easier to pass judgement, isn't it? It all started out well. The companies were compliant, offering a great deal of support: financial, logistical, plain old helpful advice about the industry. The pilot study moved ahead fast, and thousands of residents in Prieska, Koegas and their surrounds were examined. But when Shaeffer and Bucke wanted to release some of their initial findings, their own directors, as well as the companies funding the USPP stonewalled them. They were instructed to have everything cleared with Klamm first.

'Shaeffer was furious when he heard that some executive with no background in medicine was wielding that much power. Klamm had successfully convinced the departments of Mines and Health, the CSIR and the CSAOH that the information was of a highly sensitive sort, and could destroy the Northern Cape's economy. After all, it was a multi-million dollar industry.'

Jacob looks up from his notes. 'He suppressed the entire survey?'

Reynolds rummages in her handbag, resting on the floor behind her desk, and produces some bottled water. She takes a quick sip. 'He didn't so much suppress it as reject the findings outright. Here was a man possessing some of the most astounding medical proof against asbestos mining at that time, yet he argued it wasn't enough. It provided the strongest proof that mesothelioma was directly related to even minimal exposure to asbestos, but he demanded there be one hundred per cent certainty before he would jeopardize the industry. Now, every pathologist will tell you there is nothing like *perfect* proof, purely because some people's bodies are more resilient than others, and also various environmental factors can never be completely excluded. Klamm got his way, though, in the end.'

'How?'

Reynolds shrugs. 'The apartheid government was not overly concerned with what was happening to coloured and black miners, and it wanted its position as the world's largest producer of crocidolite, or blue asbestos, protected at all costs. The people in the region were dirt poor; they had no unions like the gold miners in Johannesburg, no money, no voice. They were nothing and nobody in the eyes of their employers, and their government.'

'So what happened to that report?'

'It was basically rewritten, played down, and banned from the media for fear of inciting both mutiny on the mines and panic in the thousands of South African households into which asbestos had been introduced. The information was swept under the carpet until world sanctions against apartheid, and the toxic mineral itself, forced these companies and the government to finally accept that the days of asbestos were over.'

'When was that?'

'About twenty years later.'

'You mean asbestos-related disease remained hidden for all of twenty years, because this report was tampered with?'

'No. People knew about asbestosis well before fifty-nine. It was disseminating the evidence of mesothelioma and environmental exposure that suffered a setback.'

Jacob scratches his head in consternation. Suddenly he understands what animosity everyone had against Klamm. If his involvement in this kind of cover-up became widely known, there could be literally thousands of suspects for his murder, and then some. Anyone who had lost family and friends to these terrible diseases might have good reason for killing the man out of revenge.

Reynolds interrupts Jacob's thoughts. 'Mr Bernard Klamm was concerned not so much with promulgating health and safety in the industry but with manipulating public opinion on asbestos mining. He became the Goebbels of the asbestos industry, if you will.'

'How bad was this epidemic?' asks Jacob.

'*Is*. New cases are still on the rise.' The doctor holds his gaze a few moments then sighs. 'In my opinion, it's the worst environmental disaster this country has ever seen, more so because we have no record of its true extent because many important documents have been destroyed by government officials and industry leaders. We hardly have the money to compensate victims, let alone reclaim old mine sites, and no strong lobby and charity groups exist to raise that much-needed cash. Most of the miners worked for tributers who didn't give a toot about mining regulations. In England, with their occupational health and safety standards, it took workers in contaminated factories about eight years to develop asbestosis, but out there in the Northern Cape, people who didn't even work directly in a mine or mill were contracting the disease. Asbestos dust settled everywhere; it coated everything, from growing fruits to porches, to the mosquito nets over people's beds.'

'Who exactly knew about Klamm's involvement in whitewashing this study?'

'Before 1998 I would say very few. It was handled secretively, and only top-level people in the industry would read the eventual report. But, after recent litigation in Britain and America, who knows what secrets might have leaked out?'

'What about the doctors involved?'

'You mean, could they have got angry enough to kill him?' Reynolds allows herself a chuckle. 'The irony is Klamm outlived most of them. Bucke and Shaeffer are dead, Van Copenhagen is retired. Another doctor, Siefert, refused to take part in the survey, declaring it was unethical for the asbestos companies to fund it. He moved to Europe some time in the early seventies. Then there is Doctor Jeffrey Rosen, a young pneumoconiosis specialist who replaced Siefert and did some wonderful work strengthening the link between crocidolite and mesothelioma. He wasn't involved with the USPP survey in its early stages, but he certainly came into personal contact with Klamm. At the height of his career he quit abruptly and went overseas, saying the political climate surrounding the mineral in this country was too much for him. No one was surprised to see him leave.'

Something about the last sentence's intonation hints to Jacob that there is more to come.

'Where did he go?'

'First he went to the States, then England. I think he might be back in this country, though.'

'And no one was surprised to see him go?'

Reynolds shrugs. 'There were a lot more opportunities for asbestos researchers in Britain and the United States. Shortly after leaving South Africa and finally publishing his findings in international journals, he was acknowledged for his contributions at conferences held in New York, Sydney and Llandough in Wales. He snapped up a short tenure at Stanford University, then a prominent position as a medical researcher in Barking, England.'

'And you think he might be back here now?'

'A colleague of mine recently ran into him on Nelson Mandela Square.'

'What was his relationship with Klamm like?'

'At first it was affable, but Rosen grew frustrated with Klamm's power, as did everyone else. Like Bucke, he then took his knowledge overseas, where he became a respected and recognized member of the scientific community, and wasn't going to be treated as an imbecile by corporate executives waging a political war. When asbestos-related litigation broke out in America, he was in the thick of things, giving expert evidence about the link between crocidolite and mesothelioma. Klamm was also embroiled in that furore, representing his cronies. I can't tell you much about the details of their relationship, as I didn't know either of them personally.'

Jacob finishes off his notes with a resounding full stop and thoughtfully closes the notebook. 'Neither do I, but I'll be finding that out.'

2

11.22 a.m., 11 June 2004, Johannesburg

For once Jacob's desk is an untidy mess of amorphous papers and reports, photographs, albums and books retrieved from Bernard Klamm's house. Looking at this stuff, he realizes his work space currently expresses exactly how he feels about this case. Up until yesterday he had been following up two strong angles: tracking down José Cauto and unravelling the macabre puzzle of Klamm's photo albums and library, in the hope of identifying other suspects. So far, the shorthand notes and references jotted in the numerous books and articles have kept him up into the early hours of the morning, with only modest breakthroughs; locating Cauto has also proven difficult. This morning, thanks to Tudhope and Dr Reynolds, another bucket of worms has been opened. Not only can he now add Tobias Rees to the list of suspects, but also virtually every surviving victim of asbestos-related diseases who might, or might not have, known about Klamm's role in this industrial disaster cover-up.

Switching on his reading lamp, Jacob pulls down the topmost album from the shelf and turns to the image he has been puzzling over most, it being the only one in the many volumes depicting two adults as well as a child. The photograph shows a shirtless Nama male, with a concerned expression on his face, seated in a hanging chair outside on a porch. Next to him is seated a woman whose nose and cheeks have been ruined by years of alcoholism. Between them sits a girl similar enough in appearance to the adults to suggest that they must be her parents. One of the man's arms is thrown lovingly over the girl's shoulder, whilst the woman rests one hand on her knee, levelling a look of silent appeal at the photographer through the smoke twirling up from her cigarette. On the girl's forearms and cheeks are the familiar scars he has seen elsewhere. Jacob only noticed the photographer's own image reflected in the window behind the three subjects on his third careful study of the photograph. It seems to be Bernard Klamm, one outstretched hand indicating for the family to remain still, the other pressing a remote shutter release.

What was the man trying to prove with this secretive documentary? And was this obsessive crusade of documentation what eventually cost him his life?

His phone rings, and it is Harry. 'I'm back in town for the weekend,' he says. 'Have you found out any more about José Cauto?'

'No,' replies Jacob. 'Tudhope is still waiting for information from correctional services. Why do you ask?'

'The bastard took a shot at me yesterday. He's there in Leopold Ridge right now, digging up Klamm's old house, looking for God knows what.'

'You're kidding me.'

Harry hastily fills him in on the details of the last twenty-four hours. 'I suggest if you want to catch this guy, you get out there yourself because the bloody yokel cops clearly couldn't give a shit about tracking this guy down.'

'You were right about Rees.' Jacob spots Tudhope swaggering towards him, his face bulging with excitement. 'There are a number of clues that *could* link him to Klamm's death.'

'I bloody *knew* it. Meet you in half an hour?' suggests Harry. 'At Joey's?'

Jacob smiles. 'Like old times.'

'Tell me I'm not the world's *kiefest* detective,' says Tudhope, the minute the receiver leaves Jacob's ear. 'Check *this* out, bru.' He tosses a large folder onto Jacob's desk.

'Let me guess,' says Jacob. 'José Cauto was released from prison.'

The deflated look of surprise on Tudhope's face is priceless.

3

11.58 a.m., 11 June 2004, Johannesburg

Joey's, near the Carlton Tower, actually belongs to Miguel, a first-generation Portuguese immigrant who fled Mozambique after FRELIMO took control of the country thirty years ago. With his big droopy ears, long, slightly bent nose and dirty apron, he looks every bit the takeaway chef he is. In the twenty years he has owned the joint, he has seen his exclusively white customers turn into mostly black ones, and he has served them all with the same zest.

Harry is sitting in a corner of the cramped café, drinking a Coke and talking to Miguel himself, when Jacob steps in from the street.

'Ah,' cries the proprietor, holding up his hands in a gesture of welcome. 'The other side of the coin. It's been a long time.'

Jacob grins and allows the balding man to pat both his cheeks. They exchange a few words together, before Miguel hurries around the counter to personally prepare their regular order.

Harry laughs as Jacob sits down. 'You'd think he has an à la carte menu.'

'You seen Jeanie yet?' asks Jacob.

The night before, when he arrived close to midnight, things seemed fine, his daughter racing out of bed to greet him in the cold. But then at the kitchen table this morning, when he was feeling the effects of getting thumped over the head with a full can of paint and then driving twelve hours straight afterwards, he did not immediately reply to something his daughter said.

'Hm?' he said. 'Did you say something?'

Jeanie crossed her arms. 'No.'

'You sure?'

'I never say anything,' she replied. To her grandmother she added, 'I told you.'

The upset evident in her words cut Harry in a deep place where guilt had left unhealed scar tissue over many years; however, it was the sudden realization that her demeanour so closely resembled Zelda's that truly shocked him.

'What am I supposed to do, Jakes?' asks Harry. 'Whatever I do, or don't do, seems to upset her these days.'

Jacob raises his eyebrows. 'You're asking me for *my* advice?'

Harry peers around the takeaway, clearly uncomfortable with the subject. 'I need a bloody cigarette.'

'Harry, you can't deny that your head is more often somewhere else than not. You have this uninterested look about you that doesn't do a daughter well when she depends on you to be her friend, her mom, in a way, as well as her father. Just acknowledge her presence more. Really *be* there when you're with her.'

' "Really *be* there when you're with her?" Jesus, Jacob. What the hell does that mean?'

Jacob shakes his head. 'If you don't know what I'm talking about, you need to think harder about it. No one can do that for you.'

Two plates arrive laden with Russian sausages, vinegar-soaked *slap* chips and Sauerkraut. Miguel begs his two customers to smell their food first and tell him what they think.

'I've got new distributor. Very Good. Grain-fed beef from Louis Trichardt. Here you only eat the best.'

After the proprietor is gone, Jacob first fills in Harry on what he learned from Dr Reynolds, then goes on to Rees. 'He had a very successful career, first as an architect, then as a property developer in partnership with a man called Carsten Groenewald. At first that was a good move, since the returns on real estate have gone through the roof over the last ten years.'

Harry drowns his chips in ketchup. 'But?'

'Well, somewhere along the line their company, Green Future Holdings, started leaking money heavily. To plug the deficit, they began cutting corners in the design of many of their projects. They bribed building inspectors to authorize licences and pass non-existent safety tests. The first large collapse occurred in 2002—I don't know if you remember that mall in Pretoria. Four were killed because of cutting costs by thinning the cement-to-sand ratios. More claims followed as a number of townhouse complexes, all of them constructed by companies linked to Green Future Holdings, began showing structural instability. In December last year, one of the urban renewal projects in Braamfontein began showing cracks along structurally crucial walls. The building was evacuated, pending further investigations by the fire department and civil engineers. In short, Rees and Groenewald's company is now facing a dozen lawsuits, and he personally may be facing bankruptcy, if not jail.'

'How the hell did you dig all that up?' asks Harry. 'Especially with that dim-witted sidekick of yours.'

'Hey.' Jacob grins as he points at one eye. 'Just because I'm black doesn't mean I don't get rings under my eyes from lack of sleep.'

'But surely Klamm's estate isn't enough to cover the kind of litigation Rees is facing.'

Jacob hurriedly scoops some chips into his mouth. 'This is where it gets very interesting. Klamm's estate, on the surface, doesn't seem to total more than five million, not enough to save Rees and his company from a bill that could total tens of millions. However, the farm *Oranje Genot* is the critical issue. I've been speaking to people in the mining industry, and that region is not just about a now defunct asbestos industry; there are diamonds out there—other minerals, too.'

Three young African men enter the shop and approach the counter behind Jacob. As he furtively surveys the shop, one catches Harry's eye. Apart from the former partners sitting in a corner, there is an aged woman occupying a central table, pensively chewing on a single chip, while a black couple in business suits joke with each other over soft drinks.

'We're talking mineral rights and land speculation, aren't we?' asks Harry.

'Yes, which means the farm could be worth millions more than it might seem. Rees's potential motive therefore depends on how much of a gambler he is.'

When they first met, Rees had mentioned Campbell holding off surveyors until Harry's investigation finishes. Now he wonders whether these surveyors he was talking about were real-estate agents or geologists. 'I think his company's history spells out clearly how much gambling he has already been involved in. I can see where you're heading regarding the motive. Does he have an alibi for the twenty-fifth of May?'

'I haven't asked him yet, mostly because I don't believe Rees possesses the physical strength to attack Klamm the way he was treated.'

'Someone else might have done it for him. Besides, if you say Klamm refused Campbell a divorce, yet kept hounding her from time to time to sell the farm, it may have been a sufficient motive for Rees to react violently. My point is, go question him, let him know we're onto him, and see what his reaction is.'

Jacob winked. 'We?'

'I meant you.'

Jacob chuckles. 'I thought I'd go over there later today. Do you want to come along?'

Harry leans forward and begins to fidget with a napkin. 'I'd love to, but wouldn't that wanker you've got attached to your side object?'

'Tudhope's all right, Harry—at least since Niehaus gave him a written warning. Take a look at what he found.' Jacob nods in the direction of a file he brought along. 'There's more information in there on José Cauto and Klamm than I've managed to come up with myself.'

Harry wipes his hands and opens it. 'Where did he get this stuff?'

'Magistrates' court in Kimberley.'

Harry pages through the amassed documents. 'You got authorization to go to Leopold Ridge yet?'

'I'll have it by the end of the day. I just hope the prosecutors will have an arrest warrant ready, too. My only worry is that Cauto will have gone into hiding after trying to gun you down.'

'Are you kidding me?' asks Harry. 'The guy has practically been mining under the house while people slept. I bet you he'll lie low for a bit, keep an eye open for the police, and when he sees none coming, I'm sure he'll just go on digging until he finds whatever he's looking for.'

Jacob smiles abruptly. 'Didn't I tell you you'd enjoy yourself with this stuff?'

Voices behind him grow urgent as the three new arrivals crowd the counter in a tight half-circle.

'What's that supposed to mean?' Harry peers at his friend over the file.

Jacob laughs. 'I don't think you'll be going back to carpentry soon, will you?'

A firearm is suddenly discharged, its impact amplified by the narrow takeaway shop. Harry glances up in time to see a look of surprise appear on Miguel's face, before he sinks down behind his beloved counter.

One of the robbers leans over the counter and fires twice more. Another pulls at the till, but it has been bolted to the aluminium tabletop. The third, in a luminescent green shirt, whirls around, eyes glazing with fear, a switchblade in one hand. He screams something incomprehensible.

A hand grabs the front of Harry's shirt, and Jacob yanks him off his chair and down to the floor.

'You all right?' whispers Jacob.

Realizing how he had frozen, Harry replies, 'Yeah.'

'Carrying?'

In response Harry draws his pistol and nods.

Jacob draws his own firearm. Rolling onto his back, he is in time to sight the lone gunman charging down the aisle towards them. The detective fires twice, both slugs plugging the moving robber in the shoulder and sending him crashing through a line of empty tables.

Harry scrambles up to spot the thief with the knife lunge for the older woman, who is struggling to get away from him. Harry curses at not having a clear shot.

'Out of the way!' he yells and, storming forward, manages to yank her roughly out of the knifeman's reach.

'*Poyisa!*' shouts Jacob in Zulu. 'Drop the knife!'

The till robber dives for his partner's weapon on the floor. Jacob fires two rounds that hit nothing but a wooden table. At the same time Harry's opponent slashes out at him, but misses. Before Harry has time to bring up his gun, the man quickly reverses his thrust to cut at him in a backhanded arc. Harry dodges, steps in, swinging the butt of his pistol into the man's face. There is a loud, satisfying crack as he connects with the thief's nose. Without pausing, he brings his knee up into the man's groin.

'No!' someone shouts. Later Harry will not be able to tell whether it was the second robber or Jacob who called out.

A shot rings out. Too late, Harry throws himself aside, only to see the till thief fall dead near his partner, a .38 round having pierced his temple.

'Jesus!' yells one of the suits. 'Shot himself, Jesus!'

Harry gets up and kicks the knifeman's weapon clear. Jacob is already clambering over the counter while shouting for the wounded shopkeeper's backroom assistant to call for an ambulance. He turns briefly. 'You OK, Harry?'

Harry is panting hard and takes a second to nod. 'Yeah.' Abruptly his stricken face turns into a harlequin's grinning mask. 'Shit, yeah! I'm all right.'

Jacob rises from the fallen proprietor's side, and wipes his forehead with one arm. 'Like old times, hey?'

'Yeah.' Harry surveys the damage. 'Just like old times.'

4

2.41 p.m., 11 June 2004, Johannesburg

By the time the adrenalin has worn off, statements have been taken at Jacob's office, and old friends have greeted Harry as if he had never left the police force. But a second bout of the shakes overtakes him as he is driving home. More violent than the first, it forces him to pull off the road.

Twice. Shot at twice in two days; two times more than should happen after his firm promise to Amy and Jeanie.

What the fuck are you doing, Mason?

He stares back at the frightened man visible in his rear-view mirror, and sees there a barely recognizable face.

Just like old times.

Is this how it was? Because it certainly does not feel that way. Harry wipes his face with both hands and tries unsuccessfully to slow his breathing. His world has been turning inside out: first the steady downward spiral of his fortunes, then the poisonous degradation of his formerly loving relationship with Jeanie, and now this investigation work he swore he would never touch again. But . . .

What then?

Well, what exactly are you doing with Salome? Fixing a bloody date, Mason?

He shakes his head as if physically trying to dislodge his anxiety, and steady his scrambled thoughts. Harry gazes down at his shaking hands and thinks of heading back to his mother's house and the daughter he seems to be letting down at every turn, no matter what he does. He finds he suddenly cannot face either of them, especially Jeanie.

What did Jacob say: really *be* there when you are with her? How can he, when his mind is being steadily shredded by this life gone pear-shaped. The loneliness is crushing, and any attempt for him to end it is met with tides of guilt and painful memories. His mother is right: he has clammed up after Amy's death, hidden himself in his garage with only dead wood for company, and confined his lively daughter to the empty spaces of a building that could barely be called a home.

He turns on the ignition, throws a u-turn, and roars away in the direction of his own house—away from his waiting daughter.

Four hours later, sitting in his kitchen, he is fighting a pounding migraine. The lightbulb throws a greenish hue over the file resting on the kitchen table; a new bottle of Night Watch stands next to a large mug of coffee. His mobile lies in one corner of the room where he threw it when it suddenly rang. There is no sound in the house other than Harry's steady breathing, and the metallic clicks and clacks as he reassembles the pistol he has dismantled.

What kind of a cop freezes during a robbery?

A well-used rag is stained with lubricant, its tangy smell enveloping him in cloying folds. As he works, thoughts of Amy and Jeanie try to crowd into his mind, but the ritual of cleaning and oiling creates a barrier. He needs room to breathe, to find his centre again.

Just like old times? Sure, Jacob.

Harry smiles bitterly and takes a deep drag from a Lucky Strike, the rough tobacco smoke welcome in his lungs after a four-year absence.

Is he merely a cop pretending to be a carpenter, he wonders, or a carpenter pretending to be a cop? The issue has been plaguing him for a long time, but it was only after the attack at Joey's that it came climbing out from underneath the bed to show itself in all its glory. The truth is that he has sedated himself with empty promises to his daughter and dead wife; he has been lying to himself all these years to appease the memory of Amy, to appease his feelings of guilt over her death. She always wanted him to do something other than police work, and so, when she died, he did just that. He did it for her, for Jeanie, but it has gone against everything he basically is. He has denied himself for Amy and Jeanie, and in so doing, has become a creature no one recognizes any more.

He refills his tumbler to the halfway mark and knocks it back. The whisky's bite stuns him, makes his eyes water.

Like old times? he hears a shaken voice saying. *Get a bloody grip.*

He slams the pistol's magazine home, pulls the slide, and aims at the dinner plates displayed on the shelves opposite. But before he can pull the trigger a vision of Amy slips into his head.

'Fuck!' He pushes the weapon across the table and jumps up, the chair clattering loudly to the floor.

Standing in the dark and shivering from cold, despite the cheap whisky still coursing through his veins, Harry is contemplating the low black fence surrounding West Park Cemetery. The gates to the graveyard were closed two hours ago, but here he is now, wondering when last he felt this drunk. Casting his eyes left and right along the street, Harry quickly scales the fence and drops into this sanctuary for the dead.

The moon sits high in the sky, bathing the landscape in colours of soft blue. Harry lumbers through the silence, finding it difficult to get his bearings in the darkness. Firelight flickering in a nearby clump of trees brings him to a stop. He tries to focus on it, wondering whether it belongs to a freezing security guard or a group of derelicts, but the shadows dancing before his eyes unnerve him, and so he continues. Finally he finds

Amy's grave next to a strange gravestone with the image of its dead incumbent's beloved German shepherd carved on it.

'Hi,' he says aloud in the darkness. 'I was missing you, and just wanted to see how you're doing.' Harry's voice cracks as he laughs at these ludicrous words. 'Guess I've come to haunt *you* for a change, huh?'

The carnations he brought the previous Saturday have already wilted, so he throws them out, spilling their stale water over the black marble of Amy's grave. Taking out his handkerchief he begins to wipe its surface clean of accumulated dust, treating it with a sensuality usually reserved for a living body.

'Jeanie's getting moodier all the time, and I don't know what to do about it. Well, maybe I do, but I don't know how to get started.' He realizes tears have begun to trickle down his face. 'You were always better at that than I was: getting me started. You knew when I needed prodding and when I needed to be left in peace. Fuck, Ames, you knew me better than I do myself.'

Harry sits back on his haunches and silently watches the flickering fire in the distance, phantom silhouettes occasionally moving in front of it. When his unblinking eyes finally begin to ache, Harry cups his hands before his mouth and blows warm air on them. Then he abruptly laughs. 'My brains were spilling over with things I needed to tell you, but here I am, and nothing's coming out. Still the same old thing, isn't it? I guess what I really need to say is . . . I've got to do this, Ames. I've got to change the way things are going. I know I made promises, but . . . I'm no good at pretending; I've got to move on.'

He waits as if for an answer, but the only sound he hears is some faraway geese kicking up a racket. He sighs, stands up, and closes his eyes. He then listens in a desperate attempt for some sign, a voice to tell him he is absolved. For a moment he imagines hearing Amy whisper to him, even feeling her lips on his neck: but that is all it is, he tells himself, an illusion. His eyes flicker open with an incredible sense of dejection. Where Jeanie seems comfortable clinging to the idea that her mother is still with her, Harry cannot quite bring himself to believe it. Not when the world is so cold and all he feels is a growing black pit in his chest, steadily devouring his precious memories.

Steeling himself, he speaks up. 'I'm sorry, but this is the only way I see myself pulling out of this slump.'

Walking back the way he came, over the dry grass between the graves, a lump like lead is still trapped in his throat. On reaching the black palisade fence, there is a sudden gust of gentle wind which sends a shiver down his spine. Harry turns around and stares back into the cemetery. Without a sound or a sign, a sudden sense of relief washes over him. It occurs to him that if he cannot believe in Jeanie's illusions, he can at least have faith that Amy will have wanted the best for her family. With that insight, he nods gratefully into the darkness, and begins to scale the barrier back into the world of the living.

THIRTEEN

Love ceases to be a pleasure when it ceases to be a secret
Aphra Behn

1

7.11 p.m., 2 December 1957, Carltonville

The warning came too late.

Something sharp flashed in the dull orange light. José turned, ducked, but it was too late. The knife punctured his cheek and drove into his gum, dislodging a tooth. The world went red for a moment; he was not aware if he screamed or not. José stumbled backward into someone who pushed him right back towards his opponent. People were jeering, whistling, chanting; hands were clapping. A least the crowd was having fun.

His sight returned.

José was in the courtyard running between two long rows of white-washed buildings: prefab constructions housing hundreds of miners, each room identical, each room overcrowded and filled with fleas and disease. There was a circle around him, men clapping and stomping their feet, cheering on the Zulu who had taken offence at this adolescent immigrant who had come to the Rand in search of making his fortune.

Blood was gushing into his mouth, and down his chin. He pulled the dislodged tooth loose with his tongue, spat it out. The light was fading, dusk settling over the land. It was hot though; the air smelled of cooking *mielie pap*, and sweaty miners back from a day's work in the gold shafts underground.

His attacker stood on the far side of the circle, taunting him, knife held out in front of his body.

'Come on, Joe,' he laughed. 'Show me what you're made of there in Mozambique.'

The man was well built, ten years older than him and comfortable with his body—clearly a veteran of fights here in the hostels.

José lurched, blinking dizziness from his eyes. If he faltered now, they would be on him like a pack of wild dogs.

'Haah!' His opponent gasped with approval when he picked up on José's resolve to see this through. He tossed the blade from one hand to the other in keen anticipation.

'Wa-hu! Wa-hu!' The cheering around them turned into a synchronized chant, as the others realized a proper showdown was approaching. A man with a rolled cigarette in his mouth and a bowler hat began taking bets.

José tore his hemp shirt off, wrapped it around his forearm, spat out more blood. He had already seen enough of such fights to know what was coming next.

His opponent suddenly rushed him, moving low, leading with the blade. José scrambled to one side, deflecting the weapon just in time with his wrapped arm. The eye above his wounded cheek was tearing up, blurring his vision. He stumbled backwards until rough hands thrust him into the circle again. Fearful sweat was already glistening all over his body, which was much darker than that of his Nguni counterparts.

From the cheers he figured his attacker was called Mbube, 'The Lion', here on the goldfields. The man was parading for his fans, an expression of mock astonishment on his face that José had survived the first round.

Briefly José thought of pleading, of trying to reason with the miners, but there was a bloodlust brewing that knew no logic, only continuing violence. This unrest had started once the layoffs began. The black foreigners were always the first to be blamed for the job losses, the white controlling bosses safely hidden away from reprisal in their towering offices miles away, barricading themselves behind pass laws and armed police lines in their whites-only cities.

This time Mbube advanced more slowly, half-crouching, the knife held loosely, level with his stomach. José mimicked the man's stance, and they began circling each other like two scorpions locked in a courtship dance.

'Phuthuma, Mbube, hurry!' shouted someone over the chanting. Someone else laughed shrilly in a high voice as a companion cracked a joke.

Circling each other, they drew ever closer towards the centre of the ring, as if drawn together by violent centrifugal forces. Soon they could almost reach out and touch each other, see clearly the dilated pupils, flared nostrils, beads of sweat on each other's upper lip. Muscles were coiled up like springs, the circle around them shrinking and expanding, breathing heavily with anticipation.

Mbube never expected José to make the first move. The Mozambiquean pounced, swinging his protected arm in a deflecting arc. Instantly Mbube jabbed at the incoming limb, but he had not anticipated José's right arm simultaneously swinging in a full circle straight for his head, fist balled to form a hammer. Mbube twisted in reaction and tried to bring his knife up in time to meet this overhead strike, but not fast enough, and it glanced off his head, struck his shoulder.

The crowd roared and surged forward as Mbube staggered back to regain some equilibrium. José pressed his advantage, kicked out to connect with his attacker's thigh. Mbube lost his balance this time, fell to the dusty ground. José followed with three rapid stomps aimed at the grounded man, but he managed to roll clear. Up he came again, slashing wildly for José's legs.

The violent dance broke up. Back they went to circling each other, the superior smile on Mbube's face now missing. The crowd was whooping, some of the miners leaping into the air, demanding blood. After dark, here in these courtyards, they made their own laws and complex rituals. Here they vented their frustrations on various scapegoats singled out from the pack, sometimes for committing serious transgressions, often for the most pointless of reasons.

Mbube howled as he charged, scything a giant cross into the air in front of him. José stumbled back, feinted right, moved left, and managed to deliver a heavy blow to his attacker's ribs before he could reverse the blade in a backward arc, which missed.

José was beginning to feel dizzy from his bleeding wound. He would have to end this quickly if he was to survive both the Lion and the crowd. It occurred to José that the knifeman worked only with his weapon; it was the focus of his entire attack. If José could disarm him, it just might be enough to bring their fight to an end.

Mbube caught him by surprise, with a lightning-fast onslaught, and this time the blade cut a deep furrow into José's left side. He screamed in pain but somehow managed to stay focused, then quickly retaliated, swinging a high right hook that connected solidly with the knifeman's temple. For a moment Mbube's eyes rolled. It was all José needed.

Clamping the man's knife arm against his own bloody side, he stepped in and followed through with his right elbow straight into Mbube's face. Lips burst like ripe plums. Then as his opponent swayed, José heaved, with a loud groan, swinging the dazed man in a tight circle. Mbube went flying, parting the crowd before him, and hitting the ground face first.

If he had stopped there, José might have registered the expectation in the crowd's eyes, their predatory instincts lighting up at the sight of one of their own falling, but he did not pull back there. Instead he pounced, blinded by panic and pain and the primal rage of a wounded animal. He seized the fallen man's head and began pounding it into the ground, swearing and taunting the so-called Lion. José hammered and hammered his rival's skull into the compacted soil, till the earth began to show a dent, but still he did not stop there.

When the anger and panic finally ebbed, and he realized to his horror it was another man's crumpled head he held in his gory hands, he looked up to see the faces of the howling miners were now frozen in shock and disgust. Although he could see the lips of frightened men moving, he could hear nothing but a high-pitched ringing in his ears. José shuddered and swallowed iron-tasting blood, as the crowd began to disperse.

They left him alone that night, as he tried to stem his bleeding and collect his few belongings. He barely made it to the company dressing station, where old Dr Grobbelaar offered him whisky from his private store and tended to his wounds. The man stitched carefully with clean instruments, where other white doctors, treating a black miner in the middle of the night, might have been happy with a cruder effort. Three days later José stumbled out of the building, still weak from the loss of blood, but vowing two things to himself: one, he would never speak to anyone of what happened to his face, and two, he would never work on a goldfield again.

2

3.04 p.m., 15 January 1965, Douglas

'Why does Papa allow you near me, but no other black man, I wonder. He would have anyone else whipped if they came this close.'

They were right at the brink of the Orange River, with Claudette standing in front of José, staring down at him wilfully. He regarded her from where he was sitting with his back against a fissured weeping willow. She was certainly growing up to be a fine woman, he thought. Her long black hair glistened in the afternoon sunlight, her pupils black as coal, the whites of her eyes like alabaster. Claudette's bottle-green summer dress discreetly covered her shoulders and fell down to her knees, but she had removed her shoes to reveal pale and delicate feet.

'José, why?' Her tone was lilting, if slightly admonishing, which should have irritated him but did not.

He shrugged and threw aside the ring of plaited grass he had been weaving. 'Perhaps he trusts me more than anyone else. We've known each other long enough, and I'd say I'm like a son to him.'

'You, my brother?' She laughed. 'Or perhaps it's because it's only you I allow near me in this dreadful camp. After all, Papa cannot spare a single minute to be with the dutiful daughter who has travelled all this way just to be with him.'

He got up and stared into the distance, where he could see a pack of baboons crossing a hillside. Though she often teased and taunted him this way, he loved listening to Claudette. He loved the unusual slowness with which she pronounced her words. To him, she seemed like a leopard languishing in the shady branches of a tree.

'A girl like you should not be walking about on a mining site.'

'And what kind of a girl am I?' asked Claudette.

'You're white and educated.' He wanted to add that he considered her fit to be the wife of a king, but feared that would overstep a boundary between them.

Claudette smiled, her lips twisting to one side. 'I'm a lonely and desperate girl, that's all I am. Not true, José?'

'But your father loves you.'

'My father only loves his work and the money it brings him.' She brushed a hand at the green sheaves of some nearby reeds. 'No, it's only because he is so oblivious to me that he allows a black man like you to accompany me.'

'Your father trusts me because he and I have been through a lot together, and you don't find many dependable employees on mines.' He began walking back towards a cluster of huts constructed from empty asbestos bags that had been filled with mud. He soon stopped when she did not follow.

'You're too young to be trusted, José.' The girl gave him a smile caught somewhere between arrogance and sadness. 'You're *young*, like me.'

'Don't be silly, Miss Klamm,' he said.

Claudette laughed. '*Miss* Klamm? When last did you call me that? These days you only call me that when you're feeling anxious. Am I making you nervous, José?'

She moved closer, her chin turned up to the young man towering over her. He could not bring himself to meet her eyes. 'Your father will start missing us if we don't get back soon.'

'Then let him miss me for once.' Her eyebrows furrowed as her expression turned petulant. 'What do I care?'

Later on he would berate himself for his stupidity, and ponder exactly why he allowed himself such a slip, but at that moment he reached out to her instinctively. 'Don't speak like that,' he said. 'He *does* love you.'

The girl danced away, allowing only one of his fingers to brush hers. 'José, you are *so* silly. I'm nothing more than a spoilt brat, and you, nothing more than a black boy working himself to death on my father's mine. Who are you to even try to touch me?'

'I . . . I'm sorry,' he stammered.

'You better be,' she smiled mischievously.

Vexed by her arrogance, he retaliated. 'What are you doing here, anyway? Where is your mother and why aren't you at home with her?'

'Most likely she's drowning herself in another bottle of gin with the mayor's wife somewhere in town.' Claudette slinked closer. 'And I'm not at home because I'd much rather be here.' She stopped very close to him and peered up into his eyes. Just as it seemed she was about to mouth *with you*, she said instead, 'With Papa.'

'But you should all be together. Why would a family live apart if you don't need to be?'

'I don't know!' She rose on her toes, till her nose might have touched his lips had he not pulled back. 'I'm past caring, and anyway it's got nothing to do with me. I'll do what I want, *when* I want; I don't need him or my mother to hold my hand any more.'

José stepped back to contemplate her quietly. 'It's not right for someone your age to talk like that.'

'Like what?' Claudette moved after him. 'Talk like what, José? Do I sound too bold for your liking? Am I being too disrespectful for your polite sensibilities?'

'I don't understand how you can be so indifferent to them.'

Abruptly she turned away from him, shaking her head. 'You know so much about me already, dear boy, but I know so little about you. Where did you get that scar, for instance, and how did you learn to speak English so well? What did your family do back home that you're so cultured? You never answer me about that, but I go on asking anyway. What I wonder about most often, though, is how to make you understand that, despite you being so poor and working so hard on this mine, you still must have enjoyed more of life when you were younger than I ever will.'

'And I ask myself why your life must always seem such a tragedy in your eyes. Your father provides everything you could hope for, and he really does love you, whatever you might think.'

'Oh, stop it, José.' Claudette crossed her arms in mock irritation. 'Just because my papa has been your saviour, that doesn't mean he is the angel you make him seem to be. You're never going to understand what it's like having him as a father.'

'I work closely with him almost every day, so what could I be missing?'

'That's my point, dear boy. It's you he spends most of his time with, not my mother or me.'

Claudette turned to lead the way back to the camp, along the well-worn footpath used by the handful of women who washed the camp's clothing and fetched water.

'What is it that haunts you?' he called after her. 'What is it that comes after you?'

She turned back, but not completely. 'It is something that is not indifferent to me, which will have me rather than reject me. It is something that's always with me.' She peered at him over her right shoulder. 'Can you understand that?'

'I overheard your mother talking to your father about what happened, and I realize you're not here out of your own free will,' he said. 'I know about the spirit that attacked you.'

Claudette allowed a lopsided smile as she waited for the Mozambiquean to catch up with her. José came up close enough to feel her breath on his chest, knowing that if they got spotted now, her father would have him bound to a tree in the centre of camp, then flay the skin from his back with a whip.

'Maybe it's evil,' she said in a voice only slightly louder than a whisper. 'But when it breaks windows and furniture, my father comes to me. When it hurls me across rooms and my head smacks against walls, I am comforted by the look of horror and confusion on his face, because he is, finally, looking at me. When it rips my sides as I sleep and I scream in fear and pain, both my parents—'

'Stop it!' José grabbed her shoulders and shook her. 'It isn't right that you invite these things. You can't make a deal with these spirits just to get what you want from your father and mother.'

The black orbs of her eyes glittered as she smirked. 'But, José, I'm only tempting *you*, and you are tempting me in return. Perhaps you too can play a part in this spirit's game?'

'Never,' he replied immediately.

Claudette sighed. 'Come on, before my father catches us and breaks your legs.'

3

11.54 p.m., 3 August 1965, *Oranje Genot* Farm

Curled up now on his cot, her naked sleeping form still entranced him. In the soft candlelight, light amid shadows slowly waxing and waning, her lithe body seemed to undulate like a snake's. The stained white sheet was clamped tight between her knees, her head resting on his only pillow. Claudette's back was turned to him, her long black hair sprayed out over shoulder blades that were like two arrowheads directing his wandering gaze down the valley of her spine towards the perfectly rounded mounds of her buttocks. The air was heavy with a musky scent that, within the confining walls, created the impression of being in a fragile womb that sheltered them both from the world outside.

On another occasion he might have enjoyed just leaning there against his doorframe and admiring this young woman whom he had loved for years, and who had finally come to him. But tonight he was overwhelmed by the sadness and trepidation that had been steadily building up inside him ever since their first kiss under the yellow pom-pom blooms of an acacia tree. This woman curled up in his bed was the daughter of his boss, his business partner, his friend, and José knew he had overstepped a line he would never again be able to re-cross. He was not normally a superstitious man, but he somehow felt this transgression of his had put him at odds with fate and with God.

Gazing down at her sleeping form he knew that the real source of his apprehensiveness was not only the trust he had violated; it arose from doubt, too. Did Claudette love him as much as he loved her? Or did she love him only because he showed such wholehearted devotion to her? As she played her suggestive games with him, he often wondered if she was not just using him for some other purpose, which she kept firmly hidden away in that strange mind of hers.

There was a knock at his door.

'José,' came a secretive voice. 'It's Bernard. Wake up.'

His heart hit his throat. Claudette instantly jerked awake and nearly screamed as she sat up in the bed, clasping a blanket to her naked bosom.

Forcing his heart back down into his chest, José feigned sleepiness. 'Bernard, what time is it?'

'Open up.' The boss's voice sounded muddled but urgent. *'Quickly.'*

José watched Claudette roll down over the other side of the cot with a blanket to conceal herself.

'Just a second.' José pulled on a pair of faded jeans. He could not allow Bernard into the single room, since the fresh scent of sex hanging in the air would certainly betray them.

When he opened the door, he found Klamm looking haggard and reeking of gin. His greying hair was dishevelled, he wore no tie, his mouth was tightly drawn, and his eyes seemed out of focus. José squeezed out through the slit in the doorway, closing the door behind him before Klamm could invite himself in.

'What is it?' he urged.

They stood in darkness, the night cool but still warm enough for José not to freeze without his shirt. His bare feet curled away from the sharp stones on the ground. Over Klamm's shoulder, he could see the man's wife framed in the glowing orange doorway of their farmhouse, watching them expectantly from a distance. From the way her hands were set firmly on her hips, he guessed they had just had another row.

'Claudette has gone missing again.' Klamm's speech was slurred. 'Have you seen her?'

'No, I haven't. Is she not with that friend of hers—the one with the irritating poodle?'

Bernard began pacing, quartz and sand crunching under his shoes. 'Hanlie says she hasn't seen Claudette since Sunday.'

José waited for more information.

'Damn!' Klamm shook a fist at no one in particular. 'What is that child of mine up to now?'

'Perhaps it was someone—'

'She is lying to me, just to irk me, as she always does. What is it with that brat? When will this end? What have I done to deserve a little shit like that? Jesus *Christ*! A son would never have behaved like this.'

José took Klamm gently by his shoulder and led him back towards the main house, hoping that Claudette had not overheard her father. 'I'm sure she is fine, Bernard. There must have just been a mistake.'

'A *mistake?*' Klamm stopped abruptly. 'That plotting little hussy has never missed an opportunity to irritate me. She's probably out whoring around the bars, looking to get herself filled by every goddamned redneck in Prieska right now. I raised that child to become a decent member of society, and this is all the spoilt little cunt ever does for me—cause trouble.' Klamm stared back towards the farmhouse, the trouble he was alluding to obviously framed in the doorway.

'Don't speak of your daughter that way.' José lowered his voice. 'You're angry and you've had too much to drink. Go to bed and sleep it off, boss. I'm sure Claudette will get back soon.'

'It's bloody well true!' A loud belch punctuated this exclamation.

'Calm down, Bernard.'

'Don't you get stroppy with me, José. I may confide in you, but by God, you raise your voice, and I'll . . . I—I'm sorry, José, I didn't . . .'

The front door slammed shut, the orange glow and silhouetted figure snuffed out, as if the last warmth from the house had been extinguished.

Klamm moaned softly. 'You know, José, she always hated the mines, even though they fed us. Now that I've negotiated this farm and the house in Johannesburg, a much better situation, all of it, it still isn't good enough for her. What more do they both want from me? Jesus, I'm starting to wish I had stayed out there on the mines. At least that way I could ignore the old bag's constant nagging.'

He stumbled, and it was only then that José realized just how drunk the older man was.

'The only person that's ever been grateful to me is you. Tell me, José, what is it you have that no one else shows?'

'I don't think I'm so much different from other people. But you gave me a chance when others didn't, and for that I'm grateful.'

'Ha!' Klamm reached out and steadied himself against a lichen-covered tree trunk. 'I only took you in because you were the only bloody kaffir that could speak English and behave like a civilized human being.' He leered back at the farmhouse, holding onto the tree for dear life. 'That child of mine has brought nothing but misery into my house. She has turned out to be a slow poison to us, José. I love my wife as I love none other, but she really thinks I have something to do with that little bitch's craziness. Claudette— what a handful! There was a time she was this old man's sweetheart. She came into my life like a little living piece of heaven, all wrapped up in white, and I doted on her. I can tell you, she was an angel. She deserved everything I could possibly offer her, until all this humbug started.'

'But you told me it stopped,' said José.

A twig snapped in the undergrowth behind and both men turned to look. There was a momentary crunching of dry leaves, then abrupt silence. Alarmed, José stared into the brush, sure he could see Claudette frozen there while sneaking away.

'Stopped?' Klamm turned to stare at José, one eye drooping closed. 'Yes, yes, I suppose it has. But with Claudette that only means something else is afoot.'

'Not necessarily.' José was beginning to feel the cold and hugged his naked torso.

'Wait a minute. Why are *you* defending her? Are you defending my daughter against me?' Klamm burped and made a cutting motion in the air between them. 'I know her better than anyone else—and she's up to something, I can tell you that. She has discovered her antics have no more effect on me, and now she is willing to try going one step further.'

'She may have just changed.'

'Bollocks!' Klamm let go of the tree and righted himself tentatively. 'I've had enough, José. You know what has happened in my household, the strain that little harlot has put us under. I'll sort her out good and proper.'

'What do you mean?' José felt ice crystallize in his blood.

Klamm seemed to taste the words first on his tongue, as if chewing over the decision to utter them. Then, 'She should have been a boy. A son would never have done this to his old man, *never*. Even if he hated me as much as she does, he would have pointed a gun at me instead, and I would've told him to just pull the trigger.' Klamm aimed at an imaginary target and pulled an imaginary trigger. 'But *her* . . .'

José was stumped, doubtful whether he correctly understood Klamm's insinuation. It took everything he had not to assault the drunkard, who was now trying to focus his eyes on José's chest. 'Boss, you go home and sleep. Let your wife talk to her when she gets back.'

'*Boss?* What is it? José, have you got something to say to me? Have I not told you that you don't ever call me that any more, my friend? The two of us, you and I . . . we . . .' He burped into the back of his hand.

José did not wait to hear what else he had to say. Turning on his heel, he strode back the short distance to his own shed nestled in the copse of trees. He cast an eye sideways towards where he thought he saw a figure standing, but could discern nothing in the darkness. He hoped that Claudette had slipped away, though he had no idea how she managed to sneak out of his hut undetected.

'José!' Klamm called after him. 'You and me, we're survivors!'

José kept walking, his arms crossed over his chest, fists firmly clenched in his armpits.

Claudette was sitting on his cot when he entered, fully dressed in her pink cotton dress and favourite white cardigan. She put her hand on his thigh as he sat down next to her, but he did not reach out to her as he normally would.

'I thought you had snuck out.'

'Don't be silly,' she whispered, then she kissed him on the cheek. 'There's only one door, and it was facing directly your way.'

'Your father is looking for you. You've really upset him.'

'Tell me everything he said.' She shifted on the bed to face him. 'I want you to tell me how he wanted a son, not a daughter.'

'If you know what he told me out there, then why do you want to hear it again?' he asked.

'Just tell me.' She tightened her grip on his thigh. 'He sounded really angry. How angry was he exactly? Was he disappointed?'

José turned to peer at her suspiciously, and found Claudette's gaze laden with some emotion that made him shudder. Her eyes were glassy, as if she was in a faraway place, and her voice contained a dreamy quality. Nothing of the terror she had shown earlier remained.

'No,' he said, 'I don't think I will.'

Claudette withdrew her hand and frowned. 'Why not?'

'Why is it you come to me, Claudette?'

'Because you love me and . . . I love you.' Her hesitation made him flinch.

'No, José, don't look away.' She reached out and took hold of his face in both hands, forcing him to look at her. 'I *do* love you.'

He closed his eyes. 'You love me only as long as you can use me in some game you are playing with your father.'

'Poor puppy.' Claudette stroked his cheek. 'You didn't know this? I think you've known all along that this day would come, and yet you've done nothing to extricate yourself from me.'

José moved suddenly, seizing both her wrists. 'It's because I can't *help* myself. This is the one thing I can't keep locked up, in which I cannot depend upon myself.'

'Ow! Let go! You're *hurting* me.'

'Who *are* you?' José shoved her back onto the cot, and stood up. 'You behave much too old for your age. You seem to know too much of the world's misery already.'

Claudette followed him up, brushing the folds from her dress. 'When you're alone you tend to hear voices, and you think about the things they say. You learn about the world when you find you can look deep enough inside yourself. My heart and this world, I've learnt, are both places floating in a sea of darkness. But don't you worry, babe. All that should matter to you is that I'm with you now. Come on, I need to go now, before Mama calls the police.'

She had already pulled the bolt of the door back when his hand found hers. 'Claudette, he is a good man, in his own way. I'm sure he loves you, even if it doesn't seem that way. When will you forgive him and let this end?'

Claudette glanced at him over her shoulder and smiled with genuine sorrow. 'If I had any control left over it, I would have it end the day Papa will be satisfied with having a daughter. But I am not in control of anything any more, so it is not for me to let this end.'

José pulled her towards him. 'And what about me . . . us? We can't just keep sneaking around like this. I don't want it this way.'

Claudette rested her head against his chest. 'You've got what you've always wanted: me. How long you get to keep me I can't tell, but that's a risk you are taking for yourself. You know what we're doing now will never be accepted by my parents, or anybody else, and yet you enjoy me as much as you can, whenever you can. That, too, has nothing to do with me. All I know is that I'm the only one who hasn't yet found what she really wants.'

'Claudette, how . . . ?' José shook his head. He searched those obsidian eyes of hers for the answer to the real question he wanted to ask: *What is going on in that head of yours?* He knew full well she did not belong to him, but that he instead belonged to some design of hers. He should leave her, he kept telling himself—leave and never look back.

'Shshsh.' She kissed him on the mouth. 'I really have to go now.'

With those words she covered his face in soft kisses, and stepped out into the darkness.

4

1.44 a.m., 3 August 1965, *Oranje Genot* Farm

Thunderous knocking at the door to his shed.

'José, open up!' Claudette's voice was hysterical. 'Open up for God's sake!'

In the distance he heard Bernard Klamm roaring angrily. José jumped up to unbolt the door. It burst open and his lover threw herself into his arms.

'I've told them, José,' she panted breathlessly. 'I told him about *every-thing*.' She slammed the door shut behind her.

'What?'

As the first shot rang out, a bullet whizzed through the brush growing adjacent to his shed.

The shock was like someone had doused him with a bucket of ice water. Just two hours earlier it had seemed he might know happiness a while longer. Now the desperation in her tearful eyes told him everything was over.

Another gunshot rang out, this time hitting the shed. It punctured the wall up near the ceiling.

'He's coming for us, José. He's going to *kill* you.'

'You did *what*?' is all he managed to expel.

'Please, do something, *any*thing.' Terrified, she looked back over her shoulder at the door.

'Claudette, come out here!' There was the sound nearby of another car-tridge being chambered in Klamm's .308. 'Get away from that son of a bitch. I'll teach that bloody kaffir about having his way with my daughter.'

'He didn't rape me!' she yelled shrilly. 'I told you, he loves me!'

'Rubbish, you little bitch! What do you know of love?'

'More than you'll ever know!' she howled.

This time another bullet ripping through the wall shattered José's portable radio. The terrified pair threw themselves down on the narrow stretch of floor between cot and wall, expecting more gunfire instantly.

'Damn you, Cauto. Come out and face me. Face the father of the little girl you've dishonoured.'

'I'm not a little girl, Papa,' shrieked his daughter defiantly. 'I'm a *woman*, now.'

José clamped a hand over her mouth, so that any further provocation died in muffled murmurs against his fingers. She struggled to fight him off, but he held her down firmly. He became aware of another strange sound outside, and it took José a few moments to realize that it was Mrs Klamm wailing somewhere close by. He got up to open the door a crack, hazarding a glance out into the night. Klamm was standing right in the middle of the path leading to his shed, and the rifle was aimed straight at the door.

'I can see you, you bloody kaffir! Get out here right now, or I torch that shed with the two of you still inside.'

Claudette whimpered behind him, and José glanced back at her. 'What have you done?' he whispered.

'I'm sorry, José.' There seemed now to be only panic and fear in her voice; all the previous rebelliousness and guile had evaporated. 'I'm *so* sorry.'

He stooped to kiss her briefly on a mouth that was salty with tears. 'Stay here.'

Taking a deep breath, José then stepped out, closing the door behind him slowly and firmly.

Klamm let out a sardonic laugh. 'There you are. You proud of yourself, then?'

In a voice far steadier than he felt, José began, 'Bernard—'

'Shut up! Not a fucking word out of you. Only someone that respects me gets to call me that, and you . . . you're the worst piece of shit I've ever come across.'

'Claudette—'

The rifle's discharge was a blinding flash in the night. José flinched. When he opened his eyes again, Henrietta's wailing had climbed several notches in volume. He looked down, half-expecting to find a gaping hole in his stomach. There was nothing different.

Klamm immediately loaded another cartridge with a quick jerk of the bolt. His teeth were bared, his eyes narrowed, eyebrows dancing like white flames. 'I . . . cannot express myself.' He shook his head, swallowed hard. 'All those times that girl insisted on coming to visit at the mine, all those walks, alone. I trusted you. How . . . could you?'

The Mozambiquean forced himself to straighten up. 'I love your daughter.'

'You're nothing but a filthy fucking kaffir sniffing out tail. The arrogance! The fucking *ar-ro-gance*! What did I think, ever trusting you?'

José sucked on his bottom lip. 'And she loves me.'

'That is not true.' It was Henrietta Klamm speaking now as she stomped further along the pathway towards the two men. Her make-up was smeared, her hands clenched at her side, the grey jacket and skirt badly crumpled. 'You're an abomination, Cauto, nothing but a devil who has taken advantage of a confused and vulnerable child.'

The door behind José creaked open and Claudette peered out.

Klamm nodded roughly to her. 'Into the house. *Now.*'

'You should've paid more attention to her, Bernard.' José turned to look deeply into the young woman's eyes as he said this. 'Maybe then she'd never have wanted to come out there to the mines, and instead would have found love elsewhere, amongst the white men in your sports clubs.' A bitter smile dimpled his scar. 'And then it would have been someone more suitable than me.'

José never noticed Klamm reverse the grip on his gun, step forward, and swing the stock of his rifle at his employee's head. It connected with a loud crack.

5

6.03 a.m., 4 August 1965, *Oranje Genot* Farm

Something constricting was clenched around his throat as he was yanked into consciousness again, gagging, choking. José found difficulty opening his swollen eyes when he felt himself being lifted from the wet grass.

'What have you done with her?' demanded a giant police officer in Afrikaans. His eyes were wide and manic-looking, his hands crushing José's larynx.

Bernard Klamm stood there beside the cop, looking drained and exhausted. His knuckles were heavily bruised and swollen.

'Where the hell is my daughter, you bastard? What have you done with her?' Despite the aggression in his tone, he sounded as tired as he looked.

Dangling from the cop's vice-like grip, José gagged and struggled for air, unable to speak. He could not even shake his head in denial.

'Naas,' rasped Klamm, 'let him breathe.'

Dropped once more to the ground, José lay frantically gulping in air. As he fought to remain conscious, his memories of the night before began to return. His face felt barely recognizable, and the fingers of one hand refused to move. Even his lungs struggled to draw in air because of cracked ribs chafing against delicate tissues.

'I . . .' José shook his head violently. '. . . What are you talking about?'

Klamm sighed impatiently. 'We can do this the easy way or the hard way,' he snarled, 'and believe me, if it's the latter, this is going to be a long, hard day for you. I threw her down into the cellar last night, and now she's gone. I tied you up, but this morning I find you untied and sprawled out here on my lawn. So I'll ask you again, where is she?'

José looked up at Lambert, the heavyset police constable looming over him with his hands on his hips, and realized he could say nothing that would rescue him from his predicament.

José felt panic bordering on hysteria. 'You're going to send me to jail for something I didn't do,' he managed to gasp. 'You killed her yourself.' These last words came out as barely more than a sob.

'That's enough of that, boy.' Lambert booted the prone figure in the stomach. He turned to Klamm. 'What do you want me to do with him?'

Staring into the distance, Klamm pondered carefully, then he leaned over Cauto. 'You took advantage of my daughter and brought shame on my wife and myself. Now my Claudette is gone and, you know what, your suffering is just starting. Do whatever you want with him, Naas. Just make sure nothing of it comes back this way.'

'No worries,' said the sergeant. 'We have a proper way of dealing with kaffirs that don't know their place. I'll have the truth out of him by the end of the day. I guarantee it.'

As the pickup van carrying him in the back rolled away, José managed to sit up just long enough to see the familiar acacia tree behind the smouldering remains of his hut. It was under the same tree that he and Claudette had ventured their first kiss. The yellow blooms were now gone, though, and so too was the young white girl who had allowed him to love her.

FOURTEEN

The Day After Whisky, Smokes and a Night by the Grave

1

8.34 a.m., 12 June 2004, Johannesburg

The violent appeals of his mobile tear Harry loose from his dreams. Sleep clogging his eyes, he moans and fumbles around, knocking loose pages of José Cauto's forced confession and court testimony off the table. The green and white kitchen curtains barely cut out the dawn light that strains his eyes.

'Mm-yeah.'

'Mr Mason?' It is Tobias Rees. 'I leave messages on your phone and you don't call me back. Is that how a private investigator normally operates?'

A half-full mug of cold coffee stands next to what remains of the bottle of Night Watch. Harry takes a sip of whisky to wash the cotton wool from his mouth.

'Morning to you, too, Rees. Is there anything urgent enough to discuss this early on a Saturday morning?'

'We've been waiting anxiously for some feedback from you. Henrietta is turning into a nervous wreck day by day, the longer this business drags on.'

'Are you sure it's not you that's the anxious one?' Harry yawns, and gets up to switch on the kettle.

'What's that supposed to mean?'

For a moment Harry considers confronting Rees with the details he learned of the architect's financial troubles at Green Future Holdings, but common sense nevertheless burns through his clouding headache. By letting slip such information, he could jeopardize Jacob's investigation.

'Nothing at all. I haven't got back to you properly because the farm's phone line has been down and the mobile network doesn't work out there.'

'So what have you got for us, then?'

'Not much about what happened to Claudette herself, but I can pretty confidently say Bernard Klamm did not kill his daughter.' Harry goes on to tell Rees about the bloodied jersey recently discovered at Bernard Klamm's house, which the man apparently received twenty-five years after the girl's disappearance, and then reports his discussion with Meyer, who had tried to pick up the trail of Claudette's disappearance back in 1993.

'Henrietta never said anything to me about this jersey,' says Rees doubtfully. 'Are you sure it's genuine?'

'That's because Miss Campbell didn't know about it. Meyer told me Klamm didn't want to get her hopes up without something more concrete, so he kept it secret, especially after nothing further came of it. Instead, it seems he was becoming increasingly obsessed with the notion some supernatural entity killed his daughter. You know anything about that obsession?'

There is a sigh from Rees. 'Perhaps it's best you discuss that with Henrietta. It's a sensitive issue for her. Well, anything else?'

'Nothing concrete, and I warned you a cold case like this could become expensive in the long run.'

'We contracted you for a week and that period expires today. Unless you have a better strategy than relating ghost stories to us, I suggest you come report back to Henrietta and let's get this over with promptly.'

Harry's eyes fall on the cover-story photograph in a newspaper lying on the counter next to the fridge. It depicts a cash-car lying on its roof, much of the canopy torn from the body of the vehicle after a high-speed crash near Grobblershoop. Four bodies, with grey blankets thrown over them, are lined up along the tarmac road. He remembers buying the copy the day Jacob contacted him with Miss Campbell's details, and recalls that there had been something bugging him about these recent heists the day Salome interrupted his researches at the library.

'Mr Mason, are you still there?'

Harry yawns into the receiver. 'You want to hear what *my* ideal situation would be?'

'OK, what is it?'

'I might suggest we have the case reopened, and José Cauto's role in Claudette Klamm's disappearance re-exam—'

'That's absolutely out of the question.'

'Why? Are you hiding something? I mean, *besides* Miss Campbell's complicity in sending a man to jail without proper trial.'

'No, certainly not.'

'Then hear me out.' Harry stirs milk into his fresh coffee and sits down at the table. 'Firstly, I want to talk to Cauto. He has been released from jail and I have a good idea where to find him. Secondly, we need to take a DNA sample from Miss Campbell and compare it with the blood found on that jersey. If it really is Claudette's blood, we'll be closer to proof that she was murdered, and even if it's not, we will still be getting closer to someone who might know more about her disappearance.'

'What do you mean? Of course she was killed.'

Harry lights a cigarette without a moment's thought of the four years he had been clean before last night. 'Not necessarily. Until we find a body, we must assume she could have left that farm of her own accord.'

'But the jersey—'

'For all we know Claudette might've posted it herself. Even some stranger she hooked up with at a later stage might have sent it, who knows? We can't be sure at this stage, and I'm keeping the options open.'

'It sounds—'

'Just hear me out, Mr Rees. My ideal strategy would be to bring in forensic technicians and examine that farm thoroughly, at least certain areas of it. The police might undertake that if the case is reopened, though I doubt whether they have the resources or inclination to do it. So our only option would be a private forensic investigation of two places in particular: the cellar, where people suggest Klamm buried his daughter, and the burnt-out hut where Cauto used to live. We might still find human remains after all this time, and if we don't, we will at least be able to close that chapter with a measure of certainty.'

Rees suddenly laughs. 'I would never have thought you'd be such an opportunist.'

Harry exhales smoke with a hiss. 'Meaning?'

'You know exactly what I'm talking about. It sounds to me we've recruited a first-class freeloader.'

'Coming from you, Rees, that's a classic. Just remember, Miss Campbell hired me, not you, and judging from the way she objected to your interference last time we spoke, I'm sure she'll be delighted to hear about you rejecting my proposals without discussing them with her first. Now, if you don't mind, I've got a weekend planned with my eight-year-old daughter, and I'm not going to sour my mood with your crap before the day's even started.'

Harry hangs up the phone and reaches for the old newspaper he noticed a moment ago. Folding it, he heads upstairs for a quick shower and a fresh change of clothes, feeling as though clouds have parted to allow the sunshine through at last.

By the end of the weekend he has still not read the newspaper, but has spent more money than he can afford on treats and spoils for Jeanie. Even though Campbell's cheque will not be in the bank for some time yet, Harry considers those pizzas, videos and other presents well worth it, and it makes him feel lighter than he has done in years. Father and daughter have reconnected on a level that has less to do with communication and more with a primal intuition of love and affection. As he packs for a second trip to Leopold Ridge, he recalls his last visit to Amy's grave, and considers how cemeteries are perhaps as much to do with the living learning about forgiveness and the ephemeral nature of happiness, as they are about simply remembrance of the dead.

2

11.52 a.m., 12 June 2004, Johannesburg

The address at which Doctor Jeffrey Rosen resides is in the predominantly Jewish neighbourhood of Norwood. The Houghton golf course's high fence flickers past them on the right as they drive up Grant Avenue, while on their left towering whitewashed walls rear up behind the bare liquidambar trees.

'Jesus, did he bitch when I tried to set up this meeting for a Saturday,' says Tudhope. He is drumming his hands on the dashboard in rhythm to some song stuck in his head. 'So I said to him, "Fuck you, we're the police, and what we say goes." Bru, you should've heard him.'

'How are you managing with Klamm's documents?' Jacob has given Tudhope a sizeable chunk of the papers found in the deceased's bureau to work through, while he continues to focus on the numerous photo albums, collected articles and books.

Tudhope stops his finger drumming. '*Ag*, you did that on purpose, didn't you? I mess up with the prosecutors once, and you heap up, like, a billion pages for me to get through—most of them from lawyers.'

'Lawyers?'

'*Ja*, old Klammie babe was involved in a whole bunch of asbestos lawsuits, most of them happening in America. He was often getting called as a witness for both sides in compensation cases. GGeM features in them, but a whole bunch of pro-asbestos lobby groups too. I don't understand fuck all about it, but I'm looking carefully through them.'

'Good, Ben; you're doing well. Keep at it.'

It takes a second for the compliment to sink in. 'Shit, what can I say? Thanks, bru. So Niehaus is sending you after Cauto on Monday?'

'That's right.'

'And Harry's going with you?' Tudhope says this almost like a petulant child.

'He has his own business to deal with up there, but yes, Harry should be able to help me hurry things along a bit. Here, I think this is it.' He pulls into a driveway lined with lavender.

Dr Rosen's constantly moving eyes remind Jacob of a plover on its guard for predators. In his early sixties, he is stockily built with a small, aquiline nose, a high forehead and shiny bald head. His immaculate white shirt, black chinos and loafers look like they were bought at Bloomingdale's or Selfridges. The two detectives have been received in a baroquely over-decorated living room, its floor containing unpacked boxes standing in corners.

'My apologies.' Rosen speaks in an anxious, nasal voice. 'I arrived back in the country two months ago and, as you can see, I'm still looking for a house of my own. The temporary inconvenience irritates my orderly sister no end.' Rosen rearranges the neat square of his handkerchief on his knee. 'So? I mean, what can I do for you?'

'Dr Rosen, are you aware that a former USPP colleague of yours, Mr Bernard Klamm, has been murdered?' asks Jacob.

The man nods. 'I never really considered him a colleague, and he certainly never was part of the USPP team. But I know about his death.'

'Then you worked *for* him at one stage?' asks Jacob.

The man grunts in agreement. 'Indirectly. The asbestos advisory group which he headed up pretty much had control of the USPP's funding.'

'Can you describe your relationship with him?'

A nervous titter escapes Rosen. 'I'd be lying to you if I claimed it was all wine and roses.'

Jacob raises his eyebrows.

'The man was unethical in his dealings,' Rosen continues. 'The moment the results of our research began to look like they might negatively affect the industry, he pulled the plug on the entire project, without concern for our reputations.'

'How did he do this?'

'Simply put, he and the men backing him offered us the means to conduct detailed research into mesothelioma and other asbestos-related diseases here in South Africa by volunteering sensitive company files and, in turn, securing from our superiors the right to review our research before it was made public.' Rosen brushes a hand over his head, and Jacob notices a large sweat stain under his armpit. 'Our sample was tiny, but already we had uncovered an epidemic on a scale no one could imagine. To give you some idea: the Wittenoom mine in Australia produced two per cent of the world's blue asbestos or crocidolite. An estimated two thousand people will eventually lose their lives because of the mine's activities. The Northern Cape produced ninety-seven per cent of blue asbestos in the world—I'm sure you can reach your own conclusions.

'Klamm suppressed our findings and accused us of inadequate planning and manipulating observations. At one stage he brought in Dr Sutcliffe, GGeM's leading medical officer, from London, for whom I had, up to that point, the greatest of respect. Do you know what *he* did? He rejected all but two of our seventy diagnosed mesothelioma cases in the two days he spent visiting those contaminated areas.' Rosen holds up two fingers of one hand. '*Two* days it took them to refute the evidence we had collected over a period of months.'

'I suppose this upset you,' says Jacob.

'*Upset* me? I was forced to leave the country—as was Dr Bucke, my colleague at the time. We just couldn't continue with our work in such a negative climate. It was a humiliating and embarrassing experience, to have spent the first ten years of my career building up a reputation as a research specialist, only to be later threatened by the same institutions that once supported me. They threatened me with disciplinary action if I decided to reveal the truth about the USPP survey. I was told I was threatening the entire country's economic structure, and that I'd be a traitor to the nation's ideals if my opinions ever saw the light of day. That was a time when Klamm seemed to have the entire industry's support. They all pandered to a line of thinking he virtually invented: if one hundred per cent proof of a disease's causes could not be shown, then it was no proof at all. I mean . . . ?' Rosen holds out his hands in silent exasperation. 'I heard this same line the world over, but nowhere in the international community was the refrain louder than here.'

The handkerchief on Rosen's knee is turning into an origami masterpiece. He makes to get up, but then seems to decide against it, flopping back down into his seat again. Jacob and Tudhope exchange glances at his strange behaviour.

'Dr Rosen.' Jacob pulls out his notebook. 'I must ask where you were on Tuesday night, the twenty-fifth of May.'

'Why are you asking that? What I've told you everyone knows and can confirm.' Rosen's eyes dart from one detective to the other. 'Surely you can't make a suspect of me because of what I've just said. All this happened thirty years ago.'

Jacob glances again in Tudhope's direction. 'I'm sure you haven't kept a grudge that long, Dr Rosen; that would be unreasonable for me to assume. After all, he was just a very difficult man to work with. No, I understand that, but could you still please tell me of your whereabouts on that night?' His tone is convivial, uninflected with cynicism.

'I don't have a proper alibi, if that's what you're asking.'

'Oh?'

Rosen's voice flattens out, slows down. 'I'm a sixty-two-year-old man who has just arrived back in this country. My sister was out while I sat at home watching television.' He titters again. 'I don't even know if my driver's licence is still valid; I just haven't been back here long enough to deal with such details.'

'What movie was on television that night?' asks Tudhope.

'What kind of question is that?' retaliates Rosen with visible alarm.

'What were you watching? A movie, the news, or one of those National Geographic documentaries?' Tudhope glances at Jacob for support. 'You say you were watching television, so what was on?'

'I . . . don't remember.'

'You don't remember?' Jacob echoes.

'No, I don't. It's been three weeks. Can you bloody remember what you watched three weeks ago?'

'OK. When was the last time you saw Mr Klamm?' Jacob presses him.

Rosen shows some relief at this question. 'It was Baltimore, 1981, at a conference where the worldwide banning of amphiboles was being discussed. We didn't really talk, just exchanged greetings.'

'Amphiboles?' asks Tudhope.

'Blue and brown asbestos, both of which were intensively mined in South Africa.'

'And you didn't meet again after that?'

'No, never.'

Just then Jacob's mobile rings. He answers it, more to let Rosen hang than anything else. It is Harry Mason, enquiring when they should go see Rees and Campbell, whom they had forgotten about after Friday's failed robbery at Joey's. Rosen looks like he is about to tear his handkerchief in two. Glancing up at Tudhope as he finishes the call, Jacob sees his partner signalling to him that they should leave.

'Dr Rosen.' Jacob rises. 'Thank you for your time. We'll be in touch.'

'Wait a minute.' Rosen holds up a finger. 'There's something I could help you with.'

'And that is?' asks Tudhope.

'I . . . well, working with Klamm I heard that there was an incident in his life a few years back. His daughter disappeared and this man, one of his workers, was convicted of killing her.'

'That's interesting, Dr Rosen,' replies Jacob. 'Do you know who this man was?'

'I don't know, but you could easily find out. I know Klamm was divorced, so maybe you can track down his ex-wife for information. She might have a photograph or something.'

Tudhope looks over at Jacob with exaggerated seriousness. 'We could do that.'

'Yes,' says Jacob, 'we'll look into that. Thank you, Dr Rosen.'

The moment their car doors slam shut, Tudhope lets out a guffaw and claps his hands. 'Is that guy for real?'

Smiling, Jacob agrees. 'He was strange, that one.'

'Bru, not even a fifteen-year-old heroin junkie with the shakes gets *that* nervous. The guy's a *poes*, man.'

'It could be that he is just the nervous type.'

'That's why I wanted us to leave. Drive a short way down here, then let me out. I've got an idea.'

It does not take more than fifteen minutes before Tudhope is back in the car with a smile big enough to cut his head in half.

'I was right, Jakes. That fucker is lying. He's been driving around the whole of last week in a chromed blue Rav4. The old lady living next door says she's been wondering who he is. Fucking smart-ass intellectual types; they're like lawyers, but worse.'

Jacob laughs. 'Yes, but lawyers at least know how to disguise their feelings.'

FIFTEEN

A Doctor Makes a Devilish Pact

1

3.12 p.m., 6 March 1966, Prieska

'I really don't know what to say.' Dr Walter Sutcliffe held up the last of the seventy X-rays to the fluorescent light, his glasses perched precariously on the tip of his nose. The man was in his fifties, his bottom lip permanently turned down in what suggested contempt.

'It's incredible, isn't it?' enthused Dr Jeffrey Rosen. Though still in his early twenties, the younger man was almost completely bald. He glanced quickly at his colleague, Dr Shaeffer, and then at Mr Klamm, before stepping closer to Sutcliffe. 'All the symptoms are noted in the reports: persistent coughs, weight loss, anorexia, vomiting, lassitude. From some of these patients we have to draw off three or four pints of fluid a day to keep their chests sufficiently mobile to allow them to breathe. These clouds you see on the X-rays indicate tumours of the pleurae. Combined with the large amount of asbestos we found in these patients' sputum, and the crackles in their lungs, it seems unnecessary for us to request full biopsies on all of them. It's quite clearly mesothelioma we're dealing with here.'

'I know what meso is, Dr Rosen,' said Sutcliffe, tossing the last X-ray on top of the piles, 'and this isn't it. All of these, except perhaps for those twelve I've placed separately, are something else—almost certainly asbestosis aggravated by years of smoking.'

'That can't be!' exclaimed Dr Shaeffer, shocked.

'Oh, don't sound so surprised.' Sutcliffe laughed. 'It's not the first time a misdiagnosis of this kind has occurred. This disease is notoriously difficult to isolate, and you certainly have limited resources out here.'

Rosen had turned pale. 'But these are surely textbook cases, Dr Sutcliffe?'

'I think not. I wrote the textbooks. Our research undertaken at Barking in the UK took months to confirm through biopsies. I have no idea how you lot can put so much reliance solely on the evidence of X-rays.'

'I did confirm a number of these very cases through biopsies.' Shaeffer's tired face had suddenly gone red. 'And with autopsies performed in Johannesburg. Asbestosis is a formation of excessive scar tissue in the lungs deriving from inhaled particles. These X-rays show tumours, not scars.'

With a sudden swivel of the hips, Sutcliffe turned to face Klamm, who had remained silent all the while the doctors had been examining the X-rays. 'And what do you think?'

Klamm shrugged and smiled unpleasantly. 'You're the specialist in mesothelioma, not me.'

'I don't understand.' Shaeffer rubbed his forehead. 'How can you suggest that we've misdiagnosed?'

'This is *not* mesothelioma,' reiterated Sutcliffe. He clasped his hands behind his back and marched a short way through the door leading into a ward filled with the research unit's patients. He eyed the black nurses administering to the terminally ill patients in the ward for non-white patients. Sniffing loudly then pushing his glasses further up his nose, he turned around and spoke loudly for all there to hear. 'Filthy, this place, absolutely filthy. I cannot believe that in this day and age these blacks still suffer from significant vitamin deficiencies, and worse.'

'Those miners,' replied Shaeffer, gesturing towards the ward, 'now have scurvy because they were forced to survive on a single meal a day provided by your company. How could one scoop of maize porridge and a few fatty bones a day be expected to keep them alive?'

Rosen's gaze flitted between his seniors. 'Dr Sutcliffe, the symptoms—'

'We all of us here know those symptoms can mean a hundred different things.' Sutcliffe stepped back into the office. 'Jeff, it's preposterous to suggest that mesothelioma is manifesting on such a scale. Seventy cases in as small a sample as yours? That's absolute rubbish. The mines up here are filthy and the environment is polluted, yes, but nowhere near as dangerous as you suggest.'

'If you could just come out to West End,' Rosen pleaded, 'where Dr Van Copenhagen has better facilities, and where most of the patients are—'

'Who is this Van Copenhagen? I've never heard of him. Is this some hick practitioner who thinks he knows more about this disease than qualified thoracic experts? No, my good fellows, I don't have the time to visit yet another hospital to investigate false claims. I suggest instead you revise your methodology and stop concentrating on local communities for your samples. A proper study should be conducted in a laboratory, under experimental conditions. I will agree with you that the ten men here on this ward have the disease, and they should be studied and treated in a proper pneumoconiosis unit, such as exists in Johannesburg. Those last two X-rays indicated also need to have biopsies taken, but under no circumstances have all these other patients got mesothelioma.' He swept his hand over the stack of X-rays he had refuted.

Dr Shaeffer wiped at the sweat building on his top lip. 'But you've seen the working conditions of these miners, the women, even the children, and it is entirely possible.'

'Yes, I've seen the conditions, and I will certainly recommend that the tailings should be kept damp and covered with grass, and that the dust exhausts at the mill be improved. The local managers should also do their best to curb the smoking habits of these natives.'

'Is that all?' Shaeffer blurted. 'That mill right in the centre of town needs to be relocated, if not *closed,* and the workers should be properly informed of the dangers they face in this industry.'

'Hang on there.' Klamm stepped forward, holding up a warning finger. 'There's no need to alarm the workers unnecessarily. They can't fully understand what we're talking about here, and it'll just cause a panic and hinder us from recruiting new labour at a time when the industry is thriving. We're not saying you people are entirely wrong, just that you're heading too far in the wrong direction. Let's keep things in perspective.'

Shaeffer held Klamm's gaze for a second, then stormed from the room. 'I cannot fucking believe this,' he yelled back.

Sutcliffe raised his voice sufficiently for the departing Shaeffer to hear. 'Doctors, I assure you that in time your work will unfortunately be discredited. In an environmental study of this magnitude, your methodology lacks the necessary controls to ensure the validity of your data. Like I said, send these ten patients to Johannesburg, at GGeM's cost, where they can be properly examined and cared for.' This last instruction he directed at Rosen.

'But if they are terminally ill patients, we should really send them to West End instead,' said Rosen timidly. 'Doesn't it make sense sending them to Kimberley? It is closer, and Dr Van Copenhagen has set up a decent care unit there. Johannesburg is five hundred kilometres away, and the flight there would cause them severe discomfort and pain.'

'I said nothing about a flight. These patients will travel by train. As I've said before, what happens at West End does not concern GGeM or myself.'

'Are you crazy, Sutcliffe?' All eyes turned to Shaeffer, who had returned and was leaning heavily against the doorframe. 'These people have families living at subsistence level. How can you so casually break them up? They don't have the money to travel to Johannesburg to visit them. Think about that, man!'

Sutcliffe turned a cold eye on Shaeffer, before calmly pulling off his glasses and beginning to polish them with a clean handkerchief. 'Dr Shaeffer, I see no problem with giving these men the best possible care my company can offer.'

'That's bullshit,' cried Shaeffer. 'You want to know what I think you're up to?'

'Please, don't let me stop you.'

'You're simply removing these poor sods from a situation of potential conflict. If this community finds out what is really going on, you'll lose your workers and you'll have your fucking mills torched. You don't care about their health at all; you want to diffuse the unease that's been on the rise ever since people figured out by themselves that asbestos is dangerous.'

'That's enough, Shaeffer!' Klamm yanked the doctor back into the office, closing the door behind him. 'I thought you were a bloody professional, not some hotheaded shop steward. What do you care about these kaffirs, anyhow? One dies, ten of them are willing to take his place, every one of them boozing as hard as the one before, and fucking everything that moves. Christ, they clog up every hospital from here to Kimberley because they don't even know how to wash themselves. Their dying has nothing to do with mining—never has been, never will be. If they understood personal hygiene they wouldn't be so vulnerable to lung disease. You know it. I know it. Now, if you can't toe the line, GGeM will be forced to bring its own doctors here to the Northern Cape, and you know what that means, don't you? Every GP in this district will soon be run out of business, thanks to you. You're also forcing me to discuss your position at the CSAOH.'

Shaeffer drew himself up straight and combed back his shiny brown hair. 'Is that a threat?'

'You think I can't control a pissy little doctor like you? This is a matter of national security and stability.'

'Bernard, I am fast beginning to believe you were right,' interjects Sutcliffe. 'The money we put into this little lark might have been better spent building shithouses out in the desert.' Sutcliffe prodded the stack of X-rays with an extended index finger, as if it were a dead rodent. 'This here is a sad farce of science.'

Throughout the altercation, Rosen had stood crumpling and smoothing out a neatly typed report. His eyes darted from one speaker to the other. He knew there was no question about the diagnosis, but to add his voice to such dissent was . . .

Say something, he urged himself.

Shaeffer caught his eye, and there was something imploring in his expression.

Bloody well say something! But his mind felt as limp as his arms, his legs.

Abruptly, his colleague opened the door, slipped out, and slammed it behind him, so hard that Rosen jumped. Before he knew it, Shaeffer was gone.

Klamm came over to him with a calm expression on his face, all traces of his anger gone. A hand with long fingers was clapped on the doctor's shoulder. 'It's a pity, Rosen. I thought the lot of you were a bit cleverer than this.'

Rosen wished he could think of something biting to say in retaliation, but he was not used to this kind of conflict. The words refused to come to him: he was a scientist, not a politician. Besides, he could not help but think that if he said something out of turn now, his research would be taken away from him.

As things turned out, it was to be taken from him anyway.

2

9.24 p.m., 4 September 1981, Baltimore

'Ah, Dr Rosen, I'm so glad you decided to come up. Enter, please.'

Klamm held the door open, a bemused smile crinkling his wrinkled yellow skin. He was still in the sober grey suit which he had worn all day at the conference, although he had at least taken his tie off. A lit pipe was clasped in his right hand.

Rosen hovered on the doorstep, casting a nervous eye back down the plush corridor. There was no one else to be seen at this time of night, although he could hear the clatter of dishes somewhere near the service lift. His first step was hesitant, the third and fourth more hurried, propelling him into Klamm's room before anyone could see him.

Klamm closed the door behind him, turned around and stuck out his hand, palm facing downwards. 'How long has it been? Fourteen years?'

His grip was as steely as Rosen remembered it, though his expression had somehow softened or, better yet, saddened. 'Fifteen, actually.'

'Sit.' Klamm gestured towards a pair of wicker chairs with embroidered green cushions. 'Drink?'

'No, thank you.' Rosen took a seat, but did not allow himself to get too comfortable. He began scratching the cuticle of one thumb with the nail of the other. In the intervening years he had grown more nervous than ever.

With the pipe hanging from his mouth, a periodic *pip-pip* sound as he sucked on it, Klamm took his time in pouring himself a drink. Then he positioned himself in the second wicker chair so that it faced Rosen more directly.

'You've come far since I last saw you, Rosen. Read about you all the time these days. Are you still at Stanford?'

'No, I am consulting privately at the moment.'

Klamm nodded and laid aside his pipe, which had now gone out. 'I notice you're embroiled in a little tussle between Harper Asbestos Ltd, down in Texas, and the unions.'

'Something like that.' Rosen's eyes roamed around the hotel room. The walls were a pastel combination of orange and cream, a brass chandelier hanging from the ceiling, and three gold-framed watercolour landscapes adorning the walls. The bottle-green curtains, printed with gaudy scenes of a hunt in brown and gold, were drawn shut. On a little counter lay Klamm's tie and an out-of-place photograph of an adolescent girl with black hair, smiling at the camera.

'My daughter,' explained Klamm, following Rosen's gaze. 'I took that picture in front of one of my stores up near Prieska.' He got up, fetched the photo and brought it back. 'You have any kids, Rosen?'

'A son.'

'How old?'

'Fifteen.'

'Does he live with you?'

'I'm going through a divorce right now. My wife's won custody.'

'Sorry to hear that.' He placed the photo of Claudette on the circular glass-topped table between them. 'My own wife left me for a younger man, an architect, and my girl's been missing since before I met you.'

Rosen, for the first time, met Klamm's eyes directly. He shifted uncomfortably in his chair at receiving this personal information. It was the first time Klamm had ever confided in him, and it seemed utterly without context since they were supposed to be professional opponents. 'That's terrible.'

The other man shook his head, looked back at the photo of his daughter. 'This business we're in, you and I, it's burning us up slowly, until all that'll be left is the asbestos itself. We're flimsy things compared to the stuff I've been mining and you've been demonizing. You know what the Native Americans call it?'

Rosen shook his head.

'Salamander Cotton. Apt name, don't you think?'

Hesitating, the doctor nodded. It certainly did look and feel like rough cotton, and it was immune to heat like the mythical salamander.

Klamm's eyes strayed again towards the photograph. 'Sometimes I wish I could be like that: soft and indestructible at the same time. As it is, years of working with the stuff have hardened me. I've been burnt many times and yet survived, but still there's one person I wish I could've stayed soft for.' Klamm trailed off and stared into space. Suddenly he raised his glass, the look of loss in his face now burnt up and gone. 'A toast to my dear Claudette.' He tossed half his cognac back with a loud gulp. 'Anyway, I guess I owe you an apology, Dr Rosen.'

Klamm's surprise words splashed over the doctor like ice-cold water. 'Sorry?'

'Oh come, you don't need to drag it out of me. I'm sorry we shut down your survey in Prieska. I realize now that you boys might've easily proven the link between blue asbestos and mesothelioma twenty years before everyone else did.'

Rubbing at his face, the doctor stood up. The room suddenly felt cloying and he took a few hesitant steps. He wanted to lose his temper but, at the same time, wanted to turn back to re-confirm what he had just heard. As the impact of the man's words sank in, disturbing the silt of unpleasant memories, a wave of anger jolted him into response.

'Is *that* it? Is that *all* it's going to be? A little gentlemanly chat over a brandy in a hotel room?' Rosen wiped a hand over the mouth that had begun to stutter regularly over the last year. 'You fucking destroyed my career back home; you *threatened* me, *f-forced* me to leave the country. You put me into a p-position where my wife would no longer l-l-live with me.'

'Sit down, Jeff. Don't get so uptight, will you?' Klamm gestured him back towards the other chair. 'I understand things were tough for you, but it was an extraordinarily sensitive subject at the time. Besides, the move served you well, didn't it? You got your tenure at Stanford and the worldwide recognition you always wanted, not just some piddling nod in South Africa.'

'I can't believe you're saying this.'

'I'm telling you now, *you* were right and *we* were wrong.' Klamm set his glass down on the table and relit his pipe. 'Surely that admission's worth something to you?'

Rosen shook his head in disbelief as he began to pace around the room. 'What is it you want from me?'

Klamm coughed in surprise. '*Want* from you?'

'Ever s-s-since you came over and greeted me this m-morning, I've been watching you, wondering what it is you w-want. You were there circulating with the same people you always do, lobbying for p-policies in favour of your employers. You haven't changed your position on asbestos, so why come to m-me now and offer this . . . apology? I'm not in your camp, and never will be. You and I both know this conference will lead to the eventual banning of amphiboles throughout the developed world, and I'll see to that as best I can.'

His opponent lowered the tips of all five fingers of one hand to the rim of his brandy glass. They stayed there, steepled, as Klamm maintained the cool silence which Rosen had come to associate with the man's patronizing and aggressive attitude. 'Jeff, come,' he said finally, pointing to the other chair with his pipe. 'Please.'

'No,' said Rosen. 'I think I will be on my way.'

The seated man sighed. Though he did not actually go as far as rolling his eyes, Rosen suspected the twitch in Klamm's white eyebrows meant something similar. 'I don't want anything from you. I would like to offer you something.'

Rosen again began picking at the skin on one thumbnail. 'Offer me something?'

'GGeM is very much concerned about what amphiboles could do to our employees and to the consumers of our goods, now that proof of a firm link with mesothelioma is mounting. We'd like to offer you access to the records of our blue and brown asbestos mines in the Transvaal and Cape. In short, we want you to make sure the evidence is indubitable.'

'Indubitable?' The doctor narrowed his eyes in suspicion. 'I'm not going through all that again. Last time you spoke of irrefutable proof, you then refused to accept the evidence—evidence that the world has now sanctioned and which has brought all the stakeholders to this point where the production of asbestos has to be stopped.'

'You got me there.' Klamm smiled, again brandishing his pipe. 'I was always the one that demanded one hundred per cent proof from you. Just get as close to irrefutability as you can, then. I'm still offering you access to our records and a retainer to boot.'

'A retainer?' Rosen sidled back to his chair and sat down on its very edge.

Klamm nodded through a cloud of smoke. 'Nine thousand dollars a month. You get to complete a lifetime's research on amphiboles, maybe become the world's leading specialist, if you will, while we pay you. And we won't interfere with your work, not this time. This I guarantee you.'

'How long?'

'As long as you want.'

'What's that supposed to mean?'

Klamm shrugged. 'Exactly what it means.'

The doctor shook his head. 'Then I'm going now.'

'Why?'

'You forget I worked for you once before. I can't trust you when you say something that vague.'

There was loud laughter as Klamm drained the remainder of his cognac. 'All right, I confess, I'm not being altogether altruistic. We are jettisoning our blue and brown asbestos operations. Played right, hiring you and then selling off our rapidly devaluing mines means very good business.'

It took Rosen a full minute to understand what the other man was implying. 'You mean you'll wait until one of your competitors buys up all your amphibole mines, then you drop the bombshell of my research to hasten up the banning of blue and brown asbestos. You want them instead to end up with useless assets?'

'Clever.' Klamm winked as he got up. 'Cleverer than I once thought you were. Wait here a moment.'

He disappeared into the adjoining bedroom of the suite. Momentarily there was the sound of a drawer opening and closing. Rosen closed his eyes and tried to stop his mind from spinning out of control. He could not help but think that entering another agreement with this man would mean professional suicide, yet unlimited access to GGeM's files would secure him the environmental information he so direly needed to complete his research. Medical and attendance records of the miners, their wives and children; uncorrupted dust counts in mills and mines . . .

He became aware of someone standing in front of him. Opening his eyes he saw a wad of cash dangled in front of his nose. 'Here,' said Klamm. 'What I've just told you is strategically vital and I have to ask you to keep it to yourself. The money here is your first month's pay.'

'I can't—' Rosen took a deep breath. 'I can't accept it.'

'Sure you can. There's nothing unethical in taking it; we're hiring you as a legitimate researcher who will hopefully pin the tail on amphiboles, once and for all.'

Rosen pulled at his nose. 'You keep talking about amphiboles. What about *white* asbestos? Not enough research has been done on chrysotile, so what happens if that part of your mining and manufacturing also comes under scrutiny?'

'Jeff,' sighed Klamm, 'what is your area of speciality?'

Rosen looks up at the white-haired man towering over him. 'Asbestos-related disease.'

'Wrong. *Amphibole*-related diseases.'

'But—'

'Jeff, this furore over mesothelioma is going to be over sooner rather than later, because only amphiboles are responsible for mesothelioma.'

'That's not been proven,' interjected Rosen. 'It's only that the research so far has been concentrated on amphiboles.'

Klamm held up one hand. 'You just told me you're going through a messy divorce and that you've got a son to consider, whom you might want to send to medical school, for all I know.' Klamm shook the money, which rustled like dry leaves. 'All that takes money, and I know you academic types don't get paid all that much. This cash is clean, and it's a safe bet on the future.'

Rosen tried to turn his face away from the proffered dollars, but somehow they seemed to follow him around. Meekly, he said, 'But what if people find out?'

'Your precious reputation is safe,' Klamm pointed a finger at him, 'so let's wrap this up and get on with the job. From my point of view I'm only hitting my competitors hard, and the two countries that produce most of this planet's amphiboles.'

'South Africa and Russia,' whispered Rosen.

'Not exactly proving the most angelic of governments, are they?'

Rosen stood up and diverted his eyes. Limply he held out his hand for the money. 'I'll expect the relevant files within the week. And this is going towards my boy's education, nothing else.'

There followed another of Klamm's hateful, calculated pauses. 'Of course it is.'

SIXTEEN

A Policeman's Body Is Found

1

10.23 a.m., 14 June 2004, Leopold Ridge

Two blue and white police pickups are parked in front of the gutted club-house on the outskirts of the old mining town. From a distance, a number of children watch three police officers spill out of one ruined side building, their noses turned up in disgust, their faces grim. The mother of the two small brothers who discovered the policeman's two-week-old corpse is clutching them to her legs and stroking their heads and making soothing sounds, while her husband asks the officers if he too can take a quick look. They let him past after some haggling, despite the risk to disturbing the evidence or destroying vital clues.

Sergeant Kheswa separates himself from the busy onlookers trampling and contaminating the crime scene, and lumbers towards his vehicle. Outwardly he looks calm, though his mind is ticking through departure plans which began the day Simon Gallows appeared in Leopold Ridge. That nosy Mason character clamouring for an intensive search of the farm and the newly formed investigative team now based in Kimberley, which arrived there this week from Johannesburg to help crack the hijackings, are just further omens that the time has come for him to take off, leaving nothing but the dead and some dust behind him.

Fifteen minutes later he is seated at his desk in the empty offices of the Leopold Ridge police station. 'Jabu,' he says, after his partner picks up his mobile, 'they've found the body.'

The other man laughs dryly. 'I was beginning to think no one ever would.'

'Meet me at the mine in an hour?' With a pencil Kheswa is gouging thick black lines into the notebook page in front of him. 'It's time to move on.'

'Make it two hours. I'm on my way back from Ariamsvlei. Another week around here and I'd have said we kill that customs official I've been talking about. He's a pain in the arse and his price keeps going up.'

'That doesn't matter any more. We just leave the last haul where it is—we can do without it.'

'*Without* it? That's forty grand you're talking about.'

'You can't use forty gees if you're sitting in jail, so don't argue with me. We move on today, before they corner us.'

There is a momentary silence. 'What about Erasmus and that money we paid him?'

'Just forget the money. I'll drive out to Prieska in the next half an hour; it'll be easier for me to walk into that hospital and do what needs to be done. See you some time towards one o'clock.'

'The boy and his old man?'

'Pick them up on your way to the mine.' Kheswa finally snaps the pencil tip on his notepad. 'It's a pretty good place for people to disappear.'

2

10.26 a.m., 14 June 2004, Prieska

'Zelda, why don't you come when I call you?' Martha pushes open the door.

Her niece's room, temporarily given to Zelda while Willie is in hospital, has been whitewashed with a layer of paint thin enough to show the greyness of concrete walls beneath. The room is bare except for the shabby yellow curtains, a pile of dirty laundry in one corner, a bare light bulb hanging from a knotted wire, and, of course, the single bed with its often-mended orange and brown coverlet. Martha's daughter lies curled up on it, clothed in a simple black dress, with her back to the door.

'It's already after ten, Zelda. Time to get up. What is it with you?'

On entering the room Martha notices simultaneously a sketch lying on the floor and the silent sobs sending spasms through her daughter's body.

'What's this?' she asks, stooping to pick up the drawing. Two halves of a broken pencil roll off it.

She studies the crude stickmen depicted, some drawn with overemphasized features, others merely scratched in indistinct strokes. Her face reddens as she gradually makes sense of the picture. In the foreground are two figures, both female, one short and unhappy, the other taller and much bigger, her face jagged with rage, her sticklike hands resting on her oversized dress. The larger figure's eyes extend beyond the frame of the face, its gaze focused intently on the smaller figure. In the background a man is lying in a box under a small hill, a grave obviously, both eyes little crosses, and also the farmhouse, their home, where a girl with long black hair is framed by the exaggerated cellar entrance at its rear. Hers is the only figure lacking feet and her pupilless eyes are turned on the dead figure lying under the mound.

'This is *horrible*!' Martha raises the cross dangling from the necklace around her neck and bites on it. 'Why did you draw this, Zelda? Answer me!'

Her daughter says nothing, her continuing whimpers of pain her only reply.

'What are you doing there, girl?'

Stepping forward, Martha grabs her daughter by the shoulder and tries to roll her over. It is only then that she notices the blood smeared across the backs of Zelda's hands, over her forearms and wrists. A piece of broken glass is held between two fingers.

Martha screams.

3

11.31 a.m., 14 June 2004, Marydale

Meyer drops the receiver back into its cradle as he stands in his best friend's living room. The curtains are drawn closed, blocking out the view of a garden once beautiful but now scattered with dead leaves. The room seems dark and stale, despite the clear day outside.

'Who was that on the phone?' Elsa Gallows's voice has steadily degenerated from the sprightly tone that her husband once loved to a world-weary whisper. She is standing in the doorway, dressed in thick layers of clothing despite the cloying heat inside the house.

Himself looking pale and haggard in the twilight, but not as wraithlike as the woman behind him, Meyer turns around to face her. With a leaden voice he answers her. 'It was Leo.'

'And?'

'I'm afraid it's not good, Elsa.' He bites his lip, unsure of how to express himself properly. 'They found his body this morning in Leopold Ridge.'

Elsa Gallows collapses to the floor, her mouth open but no sound escaping it.

Walking over to the wife of his dead friend, Meyer sinks to one knee next to her. Only when he touches Elsa's thin shoulders does a long, desperate wail escape her. Extremely uncomfortable being this close to the woman, Meyer sighs with a shiver. 'Elsa, I have to go. There's a man I must go see about some answers.'

4

11.36 a.m., 14 June 2004, Prieska

'I don't *believe* it!' Harry sits up straight in the passenger seat. 'I can't believe I missed it before.' He had finally turned his attention back to the notes he collected in the Prieska library, and compared them with the newspaper article he has been meaning to read since Saturday. What he has finally gathered from these two sources sends wheels turning fast in his head, as he rapidly calculates distances, times and locations.

Jacob peers over at the clutter of paper on his friend's lap and all over the dashboard. 'Have you figured out why Meyer was at the farm?' During the last two hours of the long drive from Johannesburg to the farm, Harry has been managing to keep him awake with an account of the cash-car heists occurring in the Leopold Ridge area, speculating out loud as he tried to figure out what Willie Erasmus might have to do with these hijackings.

'I think so. It was always the three attacks occurring on the same day that bugged me about these heists. If you assume these hijackers hitting the cash-cars and the transport trucks are the same group, and you look at this map here—a cash transport on the R357, a Bonanza supermarket truck on the R386, a construction vehicle transporting a bulldozer here on the R384—the attacks form a rough triangle. There's only one way they could've reached these three targets on such different routes: they would have had to cross *Oranje Genot* land at some point. They would never have been able to hit those transports where they did by using the national roads only.'

Jacob frowns. 'But it could be two very different groups involved, or one large syndicate that split the jobs up.'

'I know that but, judging from the newspaper articles, there weren't any cash-car heists before this sudden rise in hijackings, so I think it has to be the same group that's diversifying. I don't think there'd be enough loot from these various attacks to satisfy the members of a large group, though, so that means it must be a smallish gang involved.'

'The timing necessary for what you're suggesting means someone has a great deal of prior knowledge about the movements of—'

'Yes,' interrupts Harry, 'someone is either monitoring the security-scrambled radio broadcasts or has access to sensitive information some other way.'

Jacob begins to decelerate the white police Almera as they reach the outskirts of Prieska. 'A person who works for the security company itself?'

'Could be.' Harry shrugs and refolds the newspaper.

They pull into the same garage in Prieska where Harry stopped little more than a week before to unload Salome and her son. As he gets out, stretching and yawning, he glances towards the corner around which the two hitchhikers disappeared that night, half expecting to see her standing there, but nothing other than a mountain of perilously stacked tyres presents itself to his view. Did he really arrange to meet her tonight for dinner? And what will Jacob have to say if he tells him about it? Harry wonders.

'I've just about had it with that stretch of road,' he says in an effort to distract himself from his anxiety. 'Three times in little over a week is too much for this old body.'

'But, now, do you think Willie Erasmus even knows a gang used his farm as a central point to commit the three robberies?' asks Jacob as he too gets out. He looks considerably fresher than Harry after their ten-hour drive.

'I'm positive.' Harry nods. 'He looked just like a guppy floundering out of water when Meyer turned up the heat on him. And it was so obvious how he was constantly trying to keep tabs on me while I was in the area.'

Jacob leans on the roof of the Almera and fixes his friend with a serious gaze. 'Harry, do you want to know what I think?'

'What's that?'

'I'm glad to be working with you again, even if it's just for this trip, OK?'

Inquisitive, Harry turns to face his friend. 'Sure, it's been good for me, too.'

'And I also think it's good that you're getting yourself so involved; I haven't seen you this interested in anything since you left the police service.'

Mirroring Jacob's stance, Harry asks, 'What's this about? Just say what you want to say.'

Jacob regards his sensitive friend for a second, knowing well his intended approach may start an argument.

'You're here to find out about Claudette Klamm,' he finally says, 'not to go after hijackers, Harry. You're not a police officer any more, so bear that in mind.'

'What?' Harry makes the indignant face of the falsely accused. 'I know *that*. Of course I know that. I'm just saying I want to talk with the guy today. I promised Willie I'd go over to the hospital and hear him out.'

Jacob raises his hands in submission. 'I'm not saying you can't care about Erasmus, just that you should consider sticking to your original assignment. Pass on anything you know and leave it at that.'

'To whom? These small-town cops don't know their arses from the backs of their hands.'

'This Meyer guy sounds pretty sharp.'

'He's a bag of skin packed with enough C4 to flatten a city. There's no way I'm feeding Erasmus to him unless I'm certain he's guilty of something really heavy.'

Jacob lets his arms slip off the roof, irritation registering on his face for the first time. 'I must say, Harry, I didn't drive right through the night to wait about in a hospital reception while you talk to Willie Erasmus. I've come here to track down Cauto, and you're here to ask him a few questions too—no more than that. Anyway, I want to get out to that farm as quickly as possible. You said you've warned the man's wife to stay clear of the place; isn't that enough for now?'

'All right, all right! I just thought since we're in Prieska we could drop by there. I'll visit the hospital later.'

'Are you sure?'

Harry regards his friend with visible agitation. 'Am I sure? Yes, now that you've squeezed it out of me, I'm sure.'

5

11.47 a.m., 14 June 2004, Prieska

Kheswa knows the hospital in Prieska well enough, mostly because of having to deal with the tourists who have mangled themselves after falling asleep at the wheel on their drive back from the Namaqualand blooms during September, and the locals who get skunk drunk over weekends and lay into each other in bars that seem to exist solely to stoke up old hatreds and fire up new ones.

Not for the first time does Kheswa feel exhilaration over the way he can walk into almost any building in this backwater province without attracting undue attention, and with nothing but this police uniform needed to camouflage his true nature. How easy it was for him to pass the police exams and then be offered a service pistol and a badge to instil fear in the ignorant—like this nurse passing him now, with her watch pinned so neatly to her lapel.

Bad boys, bad boys . . . the refrain calms his nerves, while setting off a familiar excitement at what he is about to do. There is no one in sight as he advances over the squeaky linoleum, and the air seems to thicken in anticipation around him. *This Bad Boy is coming for you.*

Sudden cackling breaks out from the tearoom down a side corridor, where a few nurses are clustered around a kettle, abandoning their station. Without wasting time, Kheswa ducks into the ward he seeks. A quick glance around the room reveals there are neither nurses nor visitors, though the ward is filled to its last bed with men in various stages of dying. A stench hangs in the air, as of something that drowned several weeks ago, forcing even Khewsa to wrinkle up his nose. Two emaciated patients glance his way, to whom he merely nods. Asleep in a bed over on the left, Willie Erasmus looks wraith-like, wrapped in white blankets. His eyes are closed, and a translucent green oxygen mask is cupped over both mouth and nose.

What are you gonna do when I've come for you?

Hardly missing a beat, Kheswa draws the stiff lime-green curtains round the bed, without waking up the patient. Finding Willie's hand lying under the sheet, he squeezes it gently. The man responds with a feeble squeeze in return, perhaps thinking it is his wife and child come to see him. His head shifts slightly and eyes flutter open.

Kheswa smiles. 'Hello, Willie.'

The patient's pupils dilate, eyes flicking wide open, but no sound escapes him.

Khewsa has to stifle a self-satisfied laugh at the terrified reaction. 'Can't even scream? Lungs too rotten?' he whispers, with a glance over one shoulder.

When a soft moan finally does escape Willie's lips, it is little more than an explosion of vapour that opaques the clear plastic of the oxygen mask. Kheswa reaches over and pulls it up quickly onto Willie's forehead, then abruptly forces his palm against Erasmus's mouth, while clamping his fingers over the man's nose. Erasmus's eyes bulge, feeble hands batting loosely at his attacker's forearm, but there is nothing that will allow him the strength to save himself.

Laying his free hand on the man's thin chest, Kheswa presses down further, bringing almost all of the weakened resistance to a stop. Legs kicking out become entangled in blankets; the drip is torn from the farmer's hand, but still he goes on trying to fend off the police sergeant.

'Shshsh.' Kheswa closes his eyes and smiles as the last of Erasmus's breath erupts against his palm. 'Yours was a life no longer worth living anyway,' he adds in Tswana.

As he straightens up he sees a flashing red light above his victim's head. Emergency monitors must by this time be screaming all over the empty nurse's station but, listening carefully, he surmises the man's death has gone unnoticed by the tearoom gossips. Wiping his hands on the sheet covering the cooling body, Kheswa escapes through a gap in the curtain, ignoring the vacant stares of the two patients that saw him enter.

6

11.49 a.m., 14 June 2004, Johannesburg

Ben Tudhope rolls to a stop in the empty street, diagonally across from the driveway lined with its cultivated bushes of lavender growing in neat little rows. He gets out, checks the roadway to the left and right, then hurries across the street.

Since Dr Rosen's neighbour mentioned that she saw him out driving a car when he supposedly had not yet renewed his driver's licence, Tudhope has narrowed his search to documents taken from Klamm's study that refer directly to the doctor. So far it seems to him that Rosen has clocked up two lies. Correspondence from Klamm's drawers has shown that Rosen and the victim communicated long after Baltimore, which was where Rosen said he last met with the murder victim in 1981. Tudhope will be the first to admit that he does not understand much of the content of these letters concerning amphiboles and dust counts and crackles in the lungs, but he is sure of one thing: Rosen is trying to cover up a close relationship between himself and Klamm.

One other lead he has left pursuing for far too long. While Jacob concentrated on unravelling the questions regarding Cauto's past and the significance of the photo albums, he should instead have been focusing his attention on the petrol can found at the murder scene. Contacting an auto-parts dealer with the serial number of the petrol can, Tudhope urged them to concentrate their search on a product designed for a Toyota Rav4. The tired-sounding woman in the customer services department took down the description and various numbers he had found on the container, replying with a loud *clack* of chewing gum bursting and a weary promise to call him back.

Peering through the trellised gate, Tudhope sees all he needs to know for now: the Toyota Rav4 that Rosen's neighbour claims he is occasionally using is still parked in front of the garage.

Back in his unmarked police cruiser, Tudhope settles in for a long wait by popping a cold beer, turning up the volume on radio Highveld, and opening yet another of Klamm's files to rest on the steering wheel.

7

11.53 a.m., 14 June 2004, Prieska

The now familiar creak of the green Jetta's opening door announces Jabu's arrival to Norman, who is sitting in the kitchen corner of his father's shack. Somewhat surprised by this visit, the boy glances at his father's sleeping form behind the partitioning curtain, where he is snoring loudly on the new mattress he bought himself two days ago, before promptly drinking himself into oblivion on it.

The shack looks considerably improved since that night when Sheik Kheswa first stepped into it: a new radio sits on one kitchen shelf, a TV has been illegally wired into the transformer just outside their home, and a new Cadac gas stove stands in one corner with a greasy new pan still resting on top of it. Norman's clothes have also seen some improvement: the sneakers on his feet are new, while a heavy windbreaker is draped around his shoulders. His enthusiastic mood, though, has cooled somewhat along with winter's arrival. This kitchen stool is where he now spends most of his days, staring into empty space, as an occasional frown or the widening of his eyes express the emotions that twist agitated days into sleepless nights.

A fist hammering on the door startles him, despite Norman realizing its inevitability.

'*Hola*,' the man cries with humourless bravado. 'It's Jabu, open up.'

The muscles in Norman's stomach clench painfully, a reaction intensifying in the boy as the days spent raiding truck stops and waiting by the sides of roads, or lying in wait by roadsides camouflaged by dirty old hessian sacks, have gradually turned into months.

He gets up from his stool and grabs the .22 lying on one shelf, next to a tin of snuff. Not ever wanting to appear ill-prepared, Norman has opened the door to Kheswa and Jabu fully armed ever since they entrusted him with the pistol. The flood of sunlight momentarily blinds him as he swings back the creaky door.

'Jabu, what are you doing here? I thought we were meeting on Monday next week.'

'Is the old man in?' Jabu's hand snakes around the doorframe as he peers into the gloom.

'He's sleeping. Why?'

'Wake him. We've got work for him. I'll wait for you in the car.'

There is something changed about Jabu's face, thinks Norman. It is looking rather strained, despite his natural sullenness, and he has never before said he will wait out in the car. The boy mulls this over but cannot come up with an answer, so he turns to rouse his father from his familiar fug of alcohol.

8

12.16 p.m., 14 June 2004, *Oranje Genot* Farm

As Harry tests the front door, Jacob gazes down the sloping lawn towards the rusty corpses of machinery lying in the overgrown grass. The sky above is baby-blue, the sun uncomfortably warm whenever the cool south-easterly breeze drops. Listening to the windy silence punctuated by the occasional melancholic call of a cuckoo in the surrounding bush, Jacob is reminded of an ancestral burial ground he once visited in his native Kwazulu Natal, a place frozen in time and teeming with whispers.

'The place is still locked.' Harry steps back to peer up at a first-floor window. 'At least it looks like Cauto is done raiding the house itself. Let's go round back where our friend's been excavating. You got the torch?'

Jacob holds it up as Harry brushes past him.

Whatever they are expecting as they round the corner, nothing could prepare them for what they see there.

'Jesus!' exclaims Harry.

'*Haua!*' Jacob rests his hands on his hips and surveys the damage. 'One man did this in just three days?'

Bricks that once formed the cellar's floor lie strewn in a half-moon around the wide-open entrance, while knee-high mounds of soil have been heaped to one side.

'Like I said,' mutters Harry, 'the man is on a mission.'

Inside the cellar the air is dank with the rich, loamy smell of freshly turned earth. In places holes have been dug up to a metre deep.

Harry squats to scoop up some earth with one hand. 'You think he found anything down here?'

'No, I don't think so,' replies Jacob. 'Look over here.'

He is inspecting the edge of the partition wall behind which Cauto was hiding when Harry first discovered him. It has crumbled where someone has repeatedly smashed against it with the stock of a spade, revealing fresh stone underneath. In the dirt lie two halves of the broken tool.

'I reckon Cauto must've lost his temper,' says Jacob.

'He wasn't the only one excavating; he had help. Shine there.'

Jacob turns his torch beam in the direction of Harry's pointing finger. Close together, a second and third spade have been spitted into the earth near the far wall.

'Three people,' suggests Harry.

Jacob nods. 'I wonder if Cauto has anything to do with these heists you were telling me about. There's a lot you can learn in prison in thirty-nine years.'

When Harry does not reply, Jacob shines the beam of light in his direction.

A dawning idea is written on his friend's face. 'I think I might know where he is.'

'Where?'

'Come on.' Harry is already heading for the door.

'Where are we going?' asks Jacob, hurrying after him.

'The workers employed on this farm might be helping him,' Harry says over his shoulder as he leads the way back to the car. 'He might not be an Angolan, but he certainly speaks Portuguese. I know a couple of people we could ask.'

9

12.28 p.m., 14 June 2004, *Oranje Genot* Farm

Kheswa has taken his usual route out into the Asbestos foothills, which extend deep into the northern section of the *Oranje Genot* property from the east. Inching along a track that branches off the dust road leading to Niekerkshoop, a hamlet as desolate as Leopold Ridge and even further away from the tarred N10 national road, he glances back at the fine dust the car has kicked up in red swirls. Only heavy vehicles could crush the sand and gravel into that kind of powder—trucks like the ones he and Jabu have been bringing through this north-western gate during these past few months.

Ahead of him the veldt opens up to reveal a flat expanse like a saltpan glittering in the sun. To the south, the parallel ruts of a dirt road run through the high, dry grass, eventually leading back towards the farmhouse itself. To the right, broken heaps of blackened stone glisten blue with some substance Kheswa has never seen before. The empty husk of a small yellow-brick building stands in the shadow of a rubble-littered hill, its glassless windows staring at him imploringly, its doorway looking like a broken nose. Parked close to it, under a massive brown military camouflage tarpaulin, is a truck piled high with a hijacked shipment of steel beams that Kheswa and Jabu will no longer have time to shift.

He parks the police pickup he has been using all this while and gets out. For a moment Kheswa listens to the eerie sound of the wind blowing over the terrain, but he cannot abide it too long, for to his keen ears the comparative silence makes him think he is missing out on some vital knowledge, like a deaf man just about to be hit by a train from behind. Out here he has learned to crave the constant buzz of the townships, where over the years he has developed a feel for any fluctuations in the constant din, enabling him to instantly discern when something unusual is about to happen.

Looking at his watch, Kheswa wonders with some annoyance where his partner is, feeling sure that the nurses will by now have discovered Willie Erasmus's body hidden behind the ward curtain. It is also possible that the other patients will already have given the police a sufficiently accurate description of him for an APB to be circulating. Whatever the outcome, he took the time necessary to change out of his uniform and pack the few belongings he kept in Leopold Ridge before coming out here to the hideout.

In the sparse shade afforded by the damaged building, Kheswa kicks a foot back against the wall and settles his back comfortably against it. Unfurling his flick-knife he pulls a strip of *biltong* from one pocket and begins carving off slices, which he brings to his mouth on the blade. If he has to wait, he will wait—but not for too long.

10

12.46 p.m., 14 June 2004, *Oranje Genot* Farm

'The devil dances out there,' remarks Obed to no one in particular, from the passenger seat in the front of the Jetta. 'This is his place, and we shouldn't be here.'

Norman thought he heard his father gasp the moment they turned into the property from the dust road leading to Leopold Ridge, but could not be sure of his reason for doing so.

'Why have you brought us here?' The old man turns his gaze on Jabu.

'Shut up, old man.' They are the first words Jabu has spoken to either of them since setting off from Prieska, his face having remained set like a block of rough-hewn stone during the entire trip. 'We're fetching something that's up in the hills. Sheik is waiting for us there.'

'In the hills?' Norman notices his father shiver. 'We used to mine up there . . . all along this belt.' Obed grabs the handle in the ceiling to steady himself as a nasty bump rocks them from side to side. Jabu is certainly driving as though he is in a hurry. Obed continues. 'You shouldn't have brought us to this farm. Bad things have happened on this land—it's cursed, didn't you know?'

Awed, Norman shifts forward to grab his father's headrest. '*Madoda*, is this the old devil's land? Is it, really?'

'Bernard Klamm is dead,' says Jabu, 'Sheik told you that last week.'

Obed shakes his head. In a whisper, he adds, 'He's out there, come back to this cursed place of his. I can hear him dancing and laughing.'

Jabu turns to glare at Obed. 'Can't you keep quiet for just one second, old man? You don't talk, is that understood?'

Norman sits back in his seat, dismayed by Jabu's rancid temper. He has been watching the man closely ever since they got into the car in Prieska. Periodically, he would catch Jabu glancing at his two passengers with a strained expression rather than the open contempt Norman has gotten used to.

'Jabu.' Obed chuckles. 'You can get angry with me all you want. I don't have anything left to fear, least of all you and Sheik. Those hills in the distance, I've known them all my life, and I've lost everything that ever mattered to me to the cotton I pulled from the holes we dug into them. No, my friend, you can't threaten me any further. We let loose things much worse than your threats up in those mountains, and they won't go to rest any more. Yes.' He licks his cracked lips. 'Those hills up there, and any land in their shadows are places where the devil dances.'

'You're mad, old man.' Jabu wipes at the sweat beading on his upper lip. 'There's nothing up there but dust and grass and empty tracks.'

A fork in the road appears and Jabu suddenly slams on the breaks. A cloud of dust like a red djinni catches up with them and envelops the car.

'What?' asks Obed. 'You don't even know where we're going in such a hurry?'

Ignoring the snipe, Jabu stares along the left-hand track, then looks at the clock on the dashboard, next at his own watch.

'Norman, you got your gun?' Jabu asks into the mirror.

'*Ja.*' The boy pulls it out of his waistband and brandishes it for him to see.

'What is this?' asks Obed.

Jabu shifts in his seat and pulls out a pistol. 'Good. Keep it in your lap. We might need it.'

As abruptly as he stopped Jabu shifts into first and roars down the right-hand track, which has clearly seen more use than the alternative route. It is not long before a two-storey farmhouse appears through the vegetation over on their right. It is built on a slight rise, overlooking a large camel thorn tree at the bottom of a grassy incline. After a moment, the road loops back to the right, and they shoot through an open gate to park in front of a garage standing to the left of the farmhouse. Jabu is out of the car the moment it comes to a stop.

'Now you listen to me.' He turns to Norman before hastening around the back of the vehicle. 'We're going in there now. If anything moves, shoot it. I want to be out of here in five minutes. Sheik is waiting for us.'

'What are we looking for?' asks Norman.

'Don't you worry about that. Just keep your eyes open while I search the house.'

At the front door, Jabu first tests the lock then throws a shoulder to the wood. There is not even a creak from the solid oak. Stepping back, he aims his pistol at the locks and fires three times. The wood splinters and the locking mechanism resounds. Two kicks and the door flies open to slam against the inside wall.

Quickly Jabu skips in, trying to point his gun in all directions at once. Norman follows him, more cautious, breathing in short, hyperventilated gasps. The .22 clutched in his hands is far too close to his body to be used effectively. Norman watches Jabu race on into a hallway and up stairs to the left, in search of occupants. He swallows hard as he studies the kitchen door, through which he knows Jabu would want him to go investigate. The energy is fast sapping out of his limbs, rooting him to the spot, when a sudden noise behind Norman startles him. He turns, almost about to fire, but it is only his father hobbling toward the house on his single crutch.

The spell of fear broken, Norman propels himself forward into the hall-way, past a bolted door, hoping that his father did not notice how he was momentarily frozen into inactivity.

11

12.49 p.m., 14 June 2004, *Oranje Genot* Farm

It takes the two friends a little more than half an hour to negotiate the badly eroded track to the chicken enclosures in the low-slung Nissan Almera, with an over-cautious Jacob at the wheel. Harry indicates for him to park where Willie Erasmus had halted the Land Rover a week before.

'If the police department forces me to pay up for a new sump and ex-haust, I'm sending you the bill, Harry,' mutters Jacob through gritted teeth. 'If I had known the accesses were this bad, I'd have booked one of the cruisers.'

'Will you relax? They won't be sending you a bloody bill.' Harry pulls a cigarette lighter from his pocket and begins to twirl it through his fingers.

'You smoking again?' asks Jacob.

Harry glances at him. 'Maybe.'

A face pops up from the high grass clustered round the base of the tall thorn tree where the guards have made their camp. One of the men whis-tles and waves them over. Stripped down to his trousers in the afternoon heat, he is busy cleaning filth off the shells of a few chicken eggs waiting next to a pot of boiling water standing on an open fire. Harry and Jacob go over and greet the man, who nods enthusiastically at them in response.

The introductions quickly falter, though, both sides stumbling over half-spoken words and hesitant sentences.

Harry pockets his lighter and points at the worker. Counting two on his fingers and raising his shoulders, he asks, 'Where's the other guy?'

The man lowers the last of the four eggs into the boiling water then makes a walking motion with two fingers of his own.

'On patrol?' suggests Jacob.

'Yes,' comes the answer.

'Where to?'

'Yes,' replies the man with absolute certainty. He stands upright and dusts his hands.

Harry looks at his colleague in frustration.

Stepping forward, Jacob enquires in Tswana: 'José Cauto, have you heard of him?'

The man's confused and embarrassed smile rapidly gives way to guardedness.

'Where is he?' interjects Harry. 'We need to talk to him.'

Jacob shrugs and opens his hands in a pleading gesture. 'Cauto, where?'

The man lowers his eyes and shakes his head.

'Bullshit!' exclaims Harry. 'Stop acting dumb and tell us where he is. *Poyisa*, understand me? That's us. We're looking for him because of a murder.'

Harry surveys the area around them, as if half expecting to see Cauto standing out in the open. He sees a reservoir further down the slight embankment leading to the dried-up riverbed, its windmill creaking lazily; two enclosures for the chickens, with cobweb-covered feeders and old sacking stacked high to one side of them; an outhouse around which insects are flitting in a blur; a small temporary sleeping hut for the two guards, its wooden door standing slightly ajar and the new corrugated-iron roof reflecting the sunlight.

Having followed Harry's gaze, Jacob heads towards this last structure. 'I'm going to check the hut.'

'Hi. No there.' The security guard makes a move to grab Jacob by the shoulder but is too late.

Harry steps between them and holds up his hand. 'You hiding something there, mate?' Over his shoulder he yells, 'There were three spades down in the cellar, and this guy, his partner and Cauto make three.'

'José Cauto!' calls out Jacob, still a few metres away from the windowless cabin. 'This is Detective Inspector Tshabalala. Please come out if you're in the hut. Keep your hands where I can see them.'

There is no reply except some loud creaking as the hut's roof ticks in the heat.

'You all right there?' calls Harry, keeping his eye on the Angolan. He casts his eyes about for the shotgun that was evident when he first visited Willie Erasmus, but now has to assume it is with the other guard. 'Where's your gun?' he asks the Angolan, remembering these two were also equipped with pistols.

The man stares silently and uncomprehendingly at him through the steam rising from his pot.

Harry pulls his weapon and points at it. 'Your *gun*, where is it? I know you have one because I saw you carrying it last time, so where the hell is it?'

The security guard takes a step backwards, his wariness transforming into open anxiety. His hands come up.

'Stand where you are.' Harry wants to take a look over his shoulder but feels he cannot risk it. 'Jacob! Talk to me.'

There is a loud crash from the hut, followed by a dull thump. Harry glances back on instinct.

At that moment the guard kicks the pot of boiling water off the fire in his direction, and Harry swears as he ducks away from it. When he again focuses on the guard, the man is already streaking through the underbrush, zigzagging this way and that, so as to make it difficult for Harry to draw a bead. He decides to let the man go, turning instead towards the hut.

Out of the door emerges Jacob with their suspect, except that Cauto is half concealed behind the now disarmed policeman, who has one arm twisted behind him at an impossible angle. Cauto has a thick forearm tightly wrapped around Jacob's neck, the tip of a curved bowie knife positioned right behind his ear. Though Cauto has to be almost thirty years Jacob's senior, the man's massive size dwarfs the wiry policeman.

12

12.54 p.m., 14 June 2004, *Oranje Genot* Farm

Freddy Meyer might have driven straight up to the farmhouse had he not first noticed the African standing hunched in the doorway. As it was, he brought his Chevy to an immediate stop and, observing through the dusty vegetation lining the dirt track, he silently watched the old man hobble round towards the back of the house, leaving the front door wide open.

The insides of Meyer's cheeks are raw from where he has been chewing on them. He still cannot believe it: his friend and colleague Simon dead, murdered in cold blood and dumped in an abandoned shower stall. Willie Erasmus has turned out to be his strongest lead, and he intended returning to the farmer sooner rather than later to force some answers out of him, but now there seem to be an unknown number of strangers in his house.

Meyer closes his eyes and probes the inside of his mouth with the tip of his tongue, relishing the sharp pain that blankets the memories threatening to overcome him. When he opens his eyes and realizes nothing new seems to have happened down there at the farmhouse, he reaches over to the passenger seat and picks up his Glock .45, a sleek matt-black weapon as ugly as it is solid and efficient. The way he now sees it, there is only one hard and fast way of getting sure-fire answers about the fate of his friend. Whether it will be Willie Erasmus or one of his accomplices down there in the house supplying the truth, he does not care, so long as he learns soon who Simon Gallows's killer is.

He pulls back the slide on his weapon, opens his door carefully, and slips out as silently as a snake gliding through the grass.

It is by chance that Jabu looks out of the first-floor window of Willie Erasmus's bedroom and spots the glinting windows of a car parked up at the bend of the road shortly before the farmhouse's cattle gate.

'What the fuck?' he murmurs in disbelief.

Glancing at his watch, he sees there are only a few more minutes left before Kheswa gets murderous about the delay. Hastening to the other window he checks the front garden in all directions, seeing nothing out of the ordinary.

'Norman! Obed!' he shouts. 'Can you see that car? When did it arrive?'

There is no answer from the floor below.

'Norman!' he calls again, starting for the staircase with a mixture of annoyance and fear pounding in his chest.

'What is this?' Obed asks himself, as he rounds the corner of the farmhouse to discover the broken cellar doors discarded under a swathe of loose bricks and mounds of excavated soil.

It has been decades now since he lived on Klamm's property. When the boss closed his mine up in these hills to the east of here, he took on many of his former miners as farmhands, Obed included. It had seemed a welcome change of lifestyle, with adequate housing built for them over to the south of the property, and not involving so much hard physical labour as hauling rock all day seven days a week; though there had been less money for gambling and more time to ponder his miserable destiny over beer and spirits.

His prematurely ageing heart begins to race as he approaches the dark maw of the basement. Obed had only been up as far as the house a handful of times before Klamm packed up and moved to Johannesburg permanently, leaving his workers to beg the new tenant for their jobs. Of course, he knows what eventually happened between *Baas* Klamm and José Cauto—everyone knew how Claudette Klamm had come between the two. It was glorious to see the two former allies facing each other in a white man's court with hatred burning in their eyes, where before it had always been the two of them conniving together to exercise their hateful control over their workers, and deciding the fates of innocent men like Obed's father. The reversal of fortunes there had been something to talk about in the local shebeens for years afterwards.

Further entering the gloom, Obed leans on his crutch to survey the recent damage done to the cellar floor. The rumours about Klamm's daughter—how she was buried here, that it was her ghost which was haunting the people of Leopold Ridge, that her father himself killed her—bring a smile to Obed's face. The white devil's bluff was called on that occasion, he recalls, and Klamm was shown to be nothing more than a man possessing the same vulnerabilities as any other.

Norman Ditlholelo has decided to impress Jabu by helping to find something of value, in reaction to the infectious hurry the man has been projecting, and so he is trashing the study, tearing the CB radio from its place, and upending loose shelves and drawers on the floor. When he happens to step on a spot where the floorboards do not creak but ring hollow, he feels a thrill of excitement shoot up his spine.

Norman falls down on his knees, lays aside his weapon, and tugs a corner of the patterned carpet aside. But before he can investigate further he hears a heavy tread at the door. Expecting Jabu, he looks up, his face gleaming with the excitement of a secret discovered.

'Norman!' comes Jabu's muffled shout from upstairs.

The figure that appears at the door is not Jabu—not even a black man.

A heavy gun is aimed at Norman's forehead, two gunmetal grey eyes glaring at him over the sights.

'Get up,' orders the man in Tswana.

The mouth of the barrel seems to grow wider and wider the longer Norman stares at it.

'I said, get up.' The man's voice is charged with a world of violence. 'Slowly.'

It can happen in situations occurring too fast for thought, or too unfamiliar to our everyday experiences, that instincts kick in which we cannot explain and which override all forms of rationality. People then react extraordinarily, like soldiers rushing back into battle to save the lives of their companions or mothers leaping into raging seas to rescue their children, but really they are only adopting one of two very predictable reactions: either choosing to stand or choosing to flee. Despite his terror, Norman's right hand reaches for his pistol.

'Don't.' The warning shake of the man's head is half hidden over the barrel.

'Norman, where are you, you little shit?' Feet start clattering down the staircase at the far end of the hallway. The sound of them breaks through the moment's inertia.

The boy lunges for his weapon, but Meyer is faster on the trigger. A single bullet hits the youth in the forehead: the neat coin-sized hole rupturing his ebony skin there, nothing like the mess exploding out the back of his head.

Swivelling from the waist, Meyer then brings his weapon to bear in the direction of the stairs, just a second before another intruder collides with the wall opposite the staircase in his hurried descent. Faster than Meyer would have expected, the man brings up his weapon and fires. The first slug hits Meyer in his side, throwing his own shot wild. A second nicks his head just above the ear. The cop dives to his right, into the study, impacting with the teenager's prone body, and rolls up with his Glock aimed at the doorway. He waits, waits, and waits. He does not dare check his wounds for fear of losing control of the situation.

Running feet, a door slams loudly. Outside he hears someone yelling in blind panic. Meyer slumps back with a sigh of relief. Touching the wound at one side of his head he finds that blood is already oozing over his ear and down to his collar. He pulls his blue-striped shirt up to survey the damage done to his abdomen. The bullet wound looks close enough to his liver to pose a serious problem.

'Fuck,' he grunts. The pain, till now dulled by shock, is already beginning to register as his mind applies itself to decisions.

A car engine roars to life outside, urging Freddy Meyer to struggle upright.

13

1.10 p.m., 14 June 2004, *Oranje Genot* Farm

'Jesus,' murmurs Harry helplessly as he brings up his pistol to take careful aim at Cauto. 'Let go of him.'

'No one's taking me back to a prison.' The deep scar above the ex-convict's mouth contorts his angry features. 'I'm done with serving time.'

'Harry.' Jacob gags. 'Aim that thing *higher.*'

Instantly the captive is jerked around roughly. 'Quiet!' snarls Cauto.

'Come on, Cauto, put down the knife. We just want to talk, that's all. No one said anything about prison.'

'I don't believe you! That's the only reason why you'd come looking for me.'

'Cauto . . .' Harry hesitates, his mind spinning with something convincing to say. 'We know you didn't kill that girl Claudette. Come on, we're on your side.'

'I'm not talking to you—or to anyone else.'

The Mozambiquean keeps steadily shuffling towards the Almera, careful to keep Jacob between himself and the gun with which Harry tracks his every move.

'How are you going to drive out of here holding on to a hostage?' asks Harry. 'Tell me that. Just calm down and we'll both lay down our weapons, what do you say?'

'I'm not laying down anything. Where are the fucking car keys?'

By the way Jacob is slumping, Harry guesses his friend is close to passing out from the asphyxiating pressure on his throat. 'I don't have them—he does.'

'José!' A figure emerges from the dense undergrowth behind Cauto. '*Noa facas isso!*'

A few things happen in that same second, splitting it into fractions of events. José Cauto whirls around violently, dragging Jacob with him to face this new threat. But when he realizes it is only the other guard, holding the shotgun by its stock while his other hand is raised in a pacifying gesture, he frantically turns back towards Harry. But Harry gets off a shot before the ex-convict can shield himself again. There is a soft splat as the single round strikes the Mozambiquean's bicep. The two men's eyes lock for a moment, surprise passing between them—Cauto at being hit, Harry at the accuracy of his shot—then Jacob spills free of the wounded arm holding him and staggers away.

The new arrival's face stiffens with shock and, dropping the shotgun, he quickly brings his hands up. 'Please, *baas*, please,' he shakes his head. 'No shoota, please.'

The pistol again fixes on Cauto. 'Drop that fucking knife, you shit!'

But the blade is already tumbling to the ground, the arm that held it no longer controlled by its ravaged muscles. Cauto reaches up to stem the blood welling out of the wound, all thoughts of Harry and Jacob erased by his pain.

Something gives inside Harry just then, like an overstretched high-tensile cable finally snapping. The world fades into a monochrome red as he drops his gun and charges at Cauto with his bare hands.

'Harry!' Jacob calls out weakly. 'Stop!' The warning is, however, too distant to filter through the raw emotions boiling up as though in a pressure cooker deep inside the man. Harry's first punch winds Cauto, a second wild swing connecting firmly with his jaw. The Mozambiquean starts crumpling into a heap as Harry is abruptly knocked aside by a tackle around the waist.

'Harry!' The ex-cop's shoulders are grabbed and pushed into the dirt. 'Get a hold of yourself, man. *Hei Wena!*'

Rolling over in the dust, Harry blinks to clear his vision and sees Jacob getting up, wiping away sand stuck to his face. 'What were you doing, hey? Pull yourself together.'

Trying to bring the world back into focus, Harry shakes his head. Immediately he looks for Cauto, realizing he has been left with the knife and Harry's pistol lying nearby.

'No you *don't*.' Jacob quickly moves to block another onslaught from Harry.

'I'm OK, all right.' Harry holds up his hands in submission. 'I'm OK now, just . . . let's just get the asshole cuffed before he goes for my gun.'

Jacob glances over his shoulder at the man lying curled up into a tight ball, fighting for breath. 'That man, he is not going anywhere. Not now.'

The security guard steps forward hesitantly, gabbling in Portuguese. He has picked up the shotgun again, but is holding it loosely by its barrel.

Having satisfied himself that Harry has found his equilibrium again, Jacob heads back towards Cauto, kicking the knife far out of reach. 'José Eduardo Cauto, you are under arrest for the murder of Bernard Klamm, for assaulting a police officer, for breaking and entering, and assault with the intent to cause grievous bodily harm.' While reading the rest of the man's rights, Jacob starts pulling his arms behind his back to be handcuffed, but desists when Cauto screams in agony.

'Looks to me like your friends here were ready to help you dig for treasure, but not to cover your arse,' says Harry to Cauto, as he sweeps his gun up from where it lies in the dirt. 'How does it feel to end up alone in the ditch again, this time of your own doing?'

'Fuck you!' yells Cauto. 'You don't know anything about it. Thirty-nine years in jail, for what? For *what*!' The man balls a bloodied fist and looks set to attack again, till Jacob shakes the cuffs at him.

'I tried to understand, mate. I really did,' says Harry. 'I even pitied you, until you tried to blow my brains out.'

'I don't want your pity; I want justice. It was Klamm killed his daughter, not me. All I've been doing here is trying to find Claudette's body and give her a proper burial. She deserves that, at the very least.' The Mozambiquean struggles to his feet, then adds, 'And if I really wanted to kill you, you wouldn't be here now.'

'Did you kill Klamm?' asks Harry straightforwardly.

The man swears at him in a language he does not understand, though the intent is clear.

'Where were you Tuesday the twenty-fifth of May?'

Jacob cocks his head suddenly. 'What's that sound?'

Harry stops to listen too. 'I don't know.'

'Sounds like cars coming this way.'

In the distance are car engines sounding as if they are about to blow gaskets. A heavy crack-thump is closely followed by another, as a green car is briefly glimpsed through the foliage, closely pursued by a blue one. Three gunshots ring out in quick succession, the echo of them bouncing up and down the shallow valley.

The two friends look at each other briefly then leap into action. Harry hustles the wounded Cauto into the back seat at gunpoint, while Jacob leaps for the hut and the gun he lost during Cauto's ambush. Moments later an arc of golden yellow is thrown up as they swing the Almera back the way they came, leaving the confused security guard standing in the cloud of their departure.

14

1.12 p.m., 14 June 2004, *Oranje Genot* Farm

The uneven shuffling of his feet sounds clamorous in the sudden silence. Obed drops his crutch when he spots a fresh spray of blood at shoulder height along the left wall. The hallway is still hazy with stinging cordite.

'Norman?' he asks in a weak voice that cracks with desperate hope.

He heard the exchange of gunfire inside the house while he was still outside. As he rounded the house, he was in time to see Jabu reversing his vehicle wildly, its spinning wheels blowing sand all over the forecourt, then shoot out the gate without a backward glance. Obed realized his boy was not in the car. By the time he got back to the front door, a second car, hidden by foliage, was starting its engine. Gears ground violently as it was ratcheted into reverse. It, too, then gunned up the track at breakneck speed, in close pursuit of the green Jetta.

At the moment before stepping into the study, Obed does not think of all the rejection he has heaped on his child, the lifetime's bitterness he frequently vented on the boy, the times he flat-out ignored the son who was growing up hungry both for food and his father's attentions. That regret will come later, when wave upon wave of contradictory emotions will lash against the shores of his eroded mind. Sensing what must lie beyond the threshold, Obed Ditlholelo, with lips and hands quivering, his leathery features twisted into the epitome of a final defeat, steps into the room. There, in a glistening pool of blood, lies his only son, legs twisted under his body at a weird angle, one hand resting motionless in the lap of his new jeans, the other thrown over his shattered head. His Colt .22 is lying close by.

15

1.20 p.m., 14 June 2004, *Oranje Genot* **Farm**

Sheik Kheswa is busy loading his belongings into the police pickup as well as Jabulani Mahlangu's, having grown weary of waiting for his wayward partner to show up. He is about to start up the vehicle when he hears the faint high-pitched whine of a car engine in the distance. Stepping out, he leans against the door, listening more carefully. There are two vehicles, he decides, one's engine smaller than the other, and both revving well into the red. Curious, he slams closed his own car's door and heads over towards the centre of the sandy flat, this formerly silent landscape resounding with unnatural noise.

It takes another three minutes before Jabu's green Jetta comes streaking up the incline, slipping and sliding from side to side as the loose sand under its wheels disperses in all directions. As Kheswa watches the driver approach with alarming speed, he hears Jabu leaning heavily on the car horn and sees a hand flailing a gun out of the window. Kheswa draws his own service Vector and retracts the slide, a look of confusion flitting across his face. He starts forward, then comes to a stop, undecided what to do next.

The second car has now appeared, not far behind the Jetta, gleaming blue in the sunlight and bouncing around madly on its worn-out shocks. It swerves slightly, a split-second before a series of gunshots crackle over the angry roar of car engines. Kheswa watches helplessly as Jabu's car suddenly jerks hard to the left, then gets over-corrected to the right, as its driver loses control over his speeding vehicle. Arcing around broadside, the Jetta emulates a cumbersome whale in the soft sand, slowly lifting off two wheels and tipping towards Kheswa as it digs up huge clouds of dust. Just as it seems about to roll over completely, the car comes to a halt and falls back on all four wheels. Instantly Kheswa rushes forward, letting loose a hail of gunfire at the pursuing blue car.

'Jabu, get out!' he shouts. 'We'll take the pickup.'

He stops, dropping to one knee to take better aim, and fires again. A white welt appears across the middle of the oncoming vehicle's windshield. The Chevy's driver immediately adjusts his trajectory, pointing his vehicle at Kheswa without the slightest change in the sound of the engine.

'Jabu!' Kheswa scrambles up and heads over to one side in a frantic attempt to get Jabu's car between himself and the approaching Chevrolet.

He barely manages to reach it. As he ducks behind the vehicle, the blue car clips the boot of the stationary Jetta hard enough to shift it a few feet, knocking Kheswa off-balance. He comes up in a crouch against the car's passenger door and takes a shot at the rear of the passing blue vehicle, now heading straight for the pickup and the camouflaged truck parked beyond it.

The door just to his right clicks open and Jabu falls out with a groan. A high-calibre round has punctured the rear window and gone straight through the back of the driver's seat to embed itself deep in his partner's back.

Kheswa leans over him. 'Jabu, can you move?'

The man glances up at him, a glad but vacant smile spreading over his face. '*Ja, ai* problem.'

'Let's go, then.'

As Kheswa hauls his wounded partner to his feet, the other car skids to a halt. The driver's door cracks open and a white man with short-cropped blond hair struggles out, his striped shirt awash with blood down his right side. Dropping to the ground, he comes up on his elbows and fires heavy rounds which hammer into the Jetta's bodywork all around them. Jabu whimpers as they both scramble for safety around the front of the car, to put as much chassis as possible between themselves and the gunman.

'Shit!' bellows Kheswa. 'Who is this guy?' He comes up over the bonnet to return fire, but his aim is not nearly as good as his opponent's.

A .45 round punches right through two opposing doors, to exit near Jabu's head with a loud *clonk* a mere second before another bullet hits the radial of one of the front wheels.

'Sheik, *do* something!' Jabu shrieks in a girlish voice, trying to make himself as small as possible.

'What the fuck do you want me to do?' yells Kheswa, ramming a second clip into his gun.

'Who is that coming now?' gasps his partner, gesturing south. Sweat is now pouring down his face.

Kheswa catches sight of a white car with two occupants speeding towards them, a cloud of beige dust roiling out behind it.

'Get up!' he growls.

'I can't, Sheik,' Jabu's voice cracks. 'It hurts—and I'm cold.'

Two more bullets punch through the bodywork, only to clatter around inside the engine block. Throwing a glance back over the bonnet at their opponent, Kheswa is surprised to see the man is advancing slowly, one hand training the gun, the other clutching at his blood-soaked side. The man's jaw is resolutely clenched and his eyes burn with a fire Kheswa has rarely encountered in his life of preying on the poor and the weak. For the first time ever, he feels impotent and unsure of his place in the pecking order of humanity. A grotesque feeling of wanting to piss himself invades his crotch, rather than the usual triumphant hard-on.

Abruptly he grabs Jabu by the neck and hauls him upright. 'Bad Boys, Jabu—remember the fucking Bad Boys. We don't give up.' He shakes his partner violently. 'We don't *ever* give up, you fucking hear me?'

Jabu's reply sounds less than convinced. '*Ja*, Sheik, Bad Boys.'

'That's Meyer!' exclaims Harry, as he briefly peers back over his shoulder to see what is going on in front of them, while still aiming his gun at Cauto sprawled in the back seat. 'Jesus, how many rounds has he taken?'

Ahead of them, two figures are heading up the rubble-strewn hill behind a derelict mine. The blood-soaked Meyer is plodding after them, about equidistant between his prey and the Almera, but losing pace fast.

Cauto sits glaring at Harry, seeming unconcerned with the occurrences outside.

'We've got to help Meyer,' says Harry.

'We have a suspect in the back seat, Harry,' replies Jacob, slowing down the vehicle. 'We can't just leave him here.'

'Let's cuff him.' Harry nods at Cauto. 'I don't care about his wounded arm; he was bloody well threatening to slit your throat. Why are you always so goddamned soft on bastards like him?'

Jacob keeps quiet, though he can think of an answer.

Suddenly, Meyer stumbles to his knees and pitches forward, face first, onto ground that is rockier with quartz fragments and broken ore as he gets closer to the sudden rise of the hill. The moment Jacob skids the vehicle to a halt next to him, Harry is out of the car and pursuing the two men scrambling up the hill a hundred yards away. He shouts 'Cuff him' over his shoulder. Jacob pulls a pair of handcuffs from the door compartment, and climbs out of their vehicle.

'Get out, Cauto,' he orders in Tswana.

The ex-convict stares back at him defiantly from the rear seat, and Jacob can see how he is shivering and sweating, since the shock of the gunshot has worn off. 'Come on, get out! I don't have time for this.'

Cauto reaches for the door and steps out reluctantly. Blood has stained the seat of the car, as well as his shirt. Jacob throws the cuffs towards him to put on.

Jacob licks his lips nervously as he watches Harry race after the two armed men who have obviously already tried to kill the fallen policeman. If they are indeed the hardened hijackers Meyer has been pursuing, his friend Mason could end up in a deep mess by trying to take them on by himself.

'What are you going to do now?' asks Cauto, understanding the gist of Jacob's dilemma.

Jacob has a sudden idea. Leaning through the driver's window he pulls the car keys from the ignition and holds them up towards Cauto. 'See these? I'm keeping them. I'll leave the cuffs off, but for that you help me. Understand?'

Cauto leans heavily against the side of the car and nods wearily.

Jacob drops to his knees and gently rolls Meyer over, eventually finding a head wound just above the ear, under sweat-matted hair, dirt and drying blood. The gunshot to his abdomen looks particularly severe, and blood has already soaked his pants all the way down to one knee. 'God bless,' he mutters. His eyes turn to find Harry already heading up a narrow footpath in pursuit of the two fugitives. Harry is still out of range of their pistols, though the gunmen have already spotted him. Quickly, Jacob feels for a pulse and, after finding something weak and erratic, presses down on the wound to Meyer's gut.

'Come here,' he orders Cauto. 'I want you to press down here as hard as you can.'

Cauto moves over and reaches out with one hand. 'Is he going to make it?'

'I don't know. You just keep the pressure on there.'

Unbelievably, Meyer's eyes flutter open and manage to focus on Jacob. 'Who are you?' he whispers in fluent Tswana.

'Detective Inspector Jacob Tshabalala,' he replies. 'I'm with Murder and Robbery in Jo'burg.'

'Hah,' is all Meyer manages, before closing his eyes again.

Two gunshots echo down the hill, jerking Jacob's eyes up just in time to catch Harry scrambling for cover behind a middle-sized boulder with bushes clustered around it. Further up, one of the fleeing men is now lying on his side, struggling to take aim, while the other is successfully pinning Harry down with gunfire.

Jacob turns to Cauto, trying to fix him with a hard expression, which comes off just looking anxious. 'I need you to do this for me. Just keep the pressure applied there,' he repeats.

'Yes, I'll do that.' Cauto returns his gaze with an empty expression. He raises his eyebrows, turning a wandering gaze over the empty landscape. 'Where could I go anyway?'

A sound like a string of firecrackers going off pulls Jacob's gaze back up the hillside. Harry is trying to make himself as small as possible behind the boulder, while the two gunmen have again begun to inch further up the broken path winding up the incline. Picking up Meyer's Glock and then drawing his own gun, Jacob surveys the scene, overly conscious of the many directions in which Cauto could escape, left to his own devices.

'Right.' Jacob swallows hard at his decision. 'Keep your hand pressed just where it is, and I won't forget what you've done for us here later. Is that a deal?'

Cauto nods. 'Sure.'

At that, Jacob leaves his suspect behind and sprints off up the hill in a bid to reach Harry Mason before he gets himself killed.

Harry cringes behind the boulder, closing his eyes tightly as splinters and dust spray all around him from the latest volley of missiles striking his cover. The gun feels slippery in his hands, and he realizes he is hyperventilating, sweat trickling uncomfortably into the corner of one eye. Quickly as the barrage of shots began, it ends, and Harry opens his eyes to see Jacob sprinting across the flat expanse below him. His eyes then flick across to see what his friend has done with Cauto and the unconscious Meyer.

Unbelievably, he spots the wounded police officer back on his feet, leaning heavily on the stout Mozambiquean as he shuffles toward the green Jetta standing nearby, with its driver's door lying open.

'Jacob! What the hell's going on? I thought you were going to handcuff him!' Harry gestures in the direction of the cars, hoping that his friend will hear him. 'I've got things covered here. Turn back, you dumb arse!'

Before he can yell anything further, another volley of gunfire strafes his position, and Harry throws himself flat on the ground. An unintelligible argument then breaks out above him, allowing him the chance to slide his pistol around one side of the boulder and return fire. One shot, two—but the third attempt is an empty *click, click, click*. Automatically Harry reaches for the second clip he would always have carried as a police officer, only to realize he has not been carrying a replacement all this time. Cursing himself, he ducks back behind the rock.

'Jacob!' he shouts. 'Get the fuck over here!'

More bullets come hailing down from higher up.

Jacob is still about a hundred yards away when the gunfire ceases abruptly. Harry watches him drop to one knee and take aim towards his position, as he simultaneously hears Jacob shout a warning and fragments of rubble slide loose nearby. Too late, he sees a shadow fall over him and looks up in time to recognize the heavy bulk of Sheik Kheswa come flying over his cover, smashing into him like a truck full of bricks. The impact sends both men tumbling down the steep incline in a cloud of dust and sliding rock. Seconds later, their forms separate as their momentum slows, Harry skidding free from Kheswa, who has managed to grab hold of a shrub sticking out of the fragmented ore. Harry is still coughing, frantically wiping at his dust-clogged eyes when his attacker's heavy boot connects with his jaw and propels him yet further down the hill.

'Hah!' yells a voice. 'Harry Mason? What *you* doing here?'

Shaking his head to clear the stars from his vision, he catches a quick glimpse of Jacob flitting from cover to meagre cover, heading away from him with his weapon trained on the wounded gunman further up the rough track ahead. A car's engine roars to life, distracting Harry and drawing his gaze towards the vehicles clustered by the ruined mine building. He barely has time to see the driver's door of the Jetta slam shut when he hears Kheswa approaching rapidly behind him. Instinctively he rolls to his left, narrowly missing a kick aimed towards his face. Harry keeps on rolling, his arms wrapped around his head for protection, until he finally manages to escape the reach of the lumbering killer and regain his feet.

'Kheswa?' he gasps. The sergeant unfolds a flick-knife and advances towards him. '*You* were involved with Erasmus?'

'That's right.' Kheswa lunges for Harry with his knife, casually testing the man's reactions. 'Why else do you think I would know exactly where that idiot lives?'

Harry manoeuvres to reach higher ground, finding his footing difficult on the uneven terrain. Now that all the cards are on the table he might have guessed a cop was involved in the heists for which Meyer has been pursuing Willie Erasmus. A policeman would, of course, have been one of the few to know the movements of cash-cars through the district's hinterland; and it certainly would have been easier for a cop to misdirect detectives in any ongoing investigation.

'So it wasn't a coincidence that you trailed me out of Prieska last week? Erasmus must have told you I was coming.'

Kheswa merely nods. Pearls of sweat bead on his forehead.

'Did you threaten his family?' asks Harry. 'Or did you pay him off? What did you promise him?'

Sheik lets out a gruff laugh. 'Everyone has his price, and that Willie's price wasn't too high.'

'You took advantage of a dying and desperate man.'

'We're *all* desperate!'

Kheswa grunts as he lunges fast, purposeful. Harry manages to evade the blade by scrambling backward, but the broken ore he steps on slips out from underfoot and sends him sprawling downhill. There is a triumphant roar from Kheswa, who follows up his attack with a stomp directed at Harry's head. The prone victim just manages to bring up his hands in time to grab hold of the oncoming foot. With a loud grunt, Harry twists the man's leg sideways and heaves Kheswa away from himself. The rotund African lurches awkwardly but manages to regain his balance. However, instead of turning back to face Harry, he turns tail and flees downhill, triggering a small rock slide in his wake. Harry leaps up and races after him over the precarious surface.

Surprisingly deft on his feet, Kheswa gains an early lead on his opponent and is already past the northern side of the ruined building and the truck when Harry finally catches up with him, launching himself into a high tackle around the man's neck. The force of the impact is powerful enough to throw Kheswa forward into the tailings, which still have washes of blue asbestos clinging to them. The pair go down in a confusion of limbs, Harry cracking his shoulder against a rock that sends a laming jolt of pain down his arm. The knife is knocked from Kheswa's grip, but comes to a rest closer to him than to his opponent. They both recover, find their bearings and simultaneously spot the weapon lying between them. For a second they merely eye each other, panting like embattled boxers in the eleventh round. Kheswa is the first to make a move, throwing himself forward to snatch up the blade. Harry, however, charges straight at the rotund African, his lowered shoulder connecting with the man's chest. Kheswa is thrown backward over a thigh-high mound of ore. Immediately Harry is upon him, driving two hard punches into his solar plexus. He is about to deliver a third to the man's face when he hears Jacob yell from behind him.

'Harry, get away from there!'

'Will you give me a break!' growls Harry, falling down on his hands to straddle Kheswa. Something in his colleague's voice makes him turn to regard Jacob, whose face is contorted in horror.

'What?' he yells in annoyance.

'Harry,' Jacob shakes his head, 'that's raw asbestos you're sitting in, isn't it?'

Mason turns back to look at Kheswa gasping for air beneath him. The man's hair and face and clothes are covered in fine needle-like dust. Harry's own hands are covered in the same bluish substance. The sight of the deadly material quite so close to him momentarily numbs his senses in a way that no threat from gun or knife or fist might have done. What eventually propels him into action is not an image of Willie Erasmus on his deathbed, but the unassailable feeling that his body is being invaded and contaminated by millions of hairy spiders crawling over his face, into his mouth, down his throat and into his lungs, their legs prickling him like needles, the way the fibre itself might. Harry leaps back, frantically batting at his hands and forearms. He feels obliged to clear his throat and spit. 'Jesus, this stuff's all over the place!'

Jacob moves forward to kick away the knife from the still prone Kheswa, while patting his belt for his handcuffs. Harry turns on him, his fear and shock quickly turning into anger. 'I thought I told you to cuff that fucking Cauto?'

The detective holsters his weapon and turns to stare at Harry in disbelief. 'I had a choice to make, and I made my own. If you weren't so stupid as to go charging after two armed men on higher ground than you, I would still have a suspect, not this mess.'

'You could still have cuffed him,' grumbles Harry.

'I needed him to look after Meyer!'

Kheswa distracts them from their conflict as he rolls off the mound of tailings and rears himself up on hands and knees. His breath still comes in loudly prolonged wheezes.

'Don't you bloody *move*, Kheswa,' bellows Harry, checking himself again for stray fibres, 'or I'll gut you with your own knife, I swear it.' To Jacob, 'What happened to the other guy?'

'I don't know.' Jacob angles himself so that he can see past the camouflaged truck towards the cars. 'He collapsed up there on the hill, so maybe he's either dead or unconscious. Who is this Kheswa, anyway?'

'Sergeant Sheik Kheswa here is with the Leopold Ridge police station, and is probably the one using access to all the information about cash-car movements throughout the district. This bastard peddled himself off to me as a friendly yokel the first night I arrived here, but it looks like he might have got rid of me as easily as laughing.' He glares over at Kheswa. 'Like you did with Simon Gallows, no doubt.'

'Harry.' Jacob's tone sounds both subdued and surprised at the same time.

Harry walks over towards his friend, keeping a wary eye on Kheswa. 'What?'

'Cauto is gone—'

'I bloody well know that.'

'—with Meyer,' finishes Jacob. He reflexively pulls his mobile from its holster on his hip, to call for backup, but as usual there is no signal.

SEVENTEEN

Revenge proves its own executioner
John Ford

1

10.01 a.m., 16 June 2004, Johannesburg

The Chris van Wyk building in Braamfontein, where the largest Murder and Robbery Unit in South Africa is stationed, looks the same to Harry as the day he left it thinking he would never return there on a job. The glass double doors he then closed behind himself, when he quit after Amy's death, open just as easily as they used to when he now holds them open for Miss Henrietta Campbell and Mr Tobias Rees.

Negotiating their way towards the meeting room where Senior Superintendent Niehaus and Jacob helped set up this meeting for him, Harry glances back at the elderly couple. Both seem stoic, resolved and solemn, wearing similar grey outfits, although Miss Campbell, her eyes darting from person to person they encounter in the corridors, is clutching tightly at Rees's forearm, a crumpled white tissue bulging in her other fist. Harry's growing impression of her had been of a hard personality, until he broke to her the news that her daughter had indeed been killed on the night of her disappearance, when the woman had cracked like abused porcelain and immediately fallen apart on Rees's shoulder.

They find Niehaus standing in the corridor outside the meeting room along with Jacob, casually tossing single peanuts from a bag into his mouth. His suit—several shades darker than those worn by Rees and Campbell—looks slightly too small for him, despite his losing weight since Harry last saw him. As soon as the head of Murder and Robbery notices his old colleague, a sunny smile breaks out over his moustached features.

'Harry, long time no see, *boet*? Your face looks just like it always did.' Niehaus then chuckles to see the fresh bruises and scratches on Harry's face, before he turns to shake hands with Rees and nod at Campbell. 'You two are *bladdy* lucky to have had this *oke* on your case.' To Harry he continues bemusedly, 'You know Molethe keeps badgering me to recruit you into Serious Crimes.'

Harry starts scratching his neck, abashed by the sudden flattery. 'Yeah, well—'

'Let me just tell you,' interjects Niehaus. 'If you ever decide you want to return to the service, you come to me first.'

Jacob steps forward. 'Miss Campbell, Mr Rees, let me take you inside. There are a few things I'd like to make you aware of before we proceed further.'

The couple are bundled into the soundproofed meeting room, which has a transparent Plexiglas wall facing the corridor. Harry watches Jacob seat them at one end of the oval table, where he begins briefing them on what is about to happen.

'They found her remains this morning, where he said they would be,' explains Niehaus quietly in the corridor. 'It's a female skeleton, all right, and the decayed pink fabric still adhering to it fits the description of the dress Claudette Klamm was wearing the night of her disappearance. They're currently running an autopsy in Kimberley, and the results should be ready in two weeks' time. The most important step has been to corroborate the suspect's confession.'

Harry shakes his head in disbelief. 'I took a look down that very well a week ago. Willie Erasmus used to dump his dead animals down it.'

'Him and everyone else that came before him, by the looks of it. The guys that excavated it let us all know in no uncertain terms how *vrot* the air was. My only question is why she was never found in the first place.'

'It seems no one looked properly for Claudette after she disappeared,' replies Harry. 'Just like no one ever really took an interest in her when she was still alive.'

'I wonder how the hell we're going to catch that Cauto, now that you two have flushed him out.'

'There's something wrong with your assumption that Cauto murdered Klamm.' Harry pulls out a box of Lucky Strikes, then thinks better of that, replacing them in his pocket. 'Firstly, how does a man his age, with no income, travel the five hundred kilometres from Kimberley to Johannesburg to locate and then murder Klamm? It's feasible that he did it, sure, but for an aged poor man like him it would have presented an extraordinarily difficult task. And secondly, Cauto drove Meyer away with him to try to save him, even dropping him off at the Sleggs hospital in Prieska. That's not entirely the profile of a cold-blooded killer, is it?'

Niehaus shrugs, then tosses a couple more peanuts into his mouth. 'Cauto didn't have any problem with Meyer, but he had one with Klamm. And if there is one thing about that man which stands out, it's his tenacity. He probably knew where Klamm was intending to move to in Johannesburg even before the incident out on the farm. Besides, Tudhope tells me that Klamm was listed in the telephone directory.'

'Like I said,' says Harry, 'it's all perfectly feasible, but it's still not sitting well with me.'

Niehaus curses under his breath. 'You lot are making this far too complicated. Jacob wants to hit Rees with some questions about his business dealings, Tudhope has gone traipsing off after some doctor, and you don't think it was Cauto who killed Klamm. It was him, *boet*, I'm telling you. Now, why don't you come back to join the service, Harry? You still have a lot of friends here.'

'Whoa!' The ex-detective holds up his hands. 'I'm not making any hasty decisions, and certainly not today.'

'No, seriously,' says Niehaus. 'You think I'm up here myself just to watch you two monkeys set up a confession?'

Harry sighs. 'To tell you the truth, I've been considering it—quite a lot.'

Niehaus grunts approval. 'Make sure you reach the right decision.' A few seconds' silence passes between the two men before Niehaus raises his chin and gestures towards the elderly couple seated at the table. 'What do those two in there know about your investigation?'

At this Harry laughs out loud. 'If they realized the solution to this case practically fell into my lap I'd find myself out of luck and a lot of money. They know only what they need to, and I see no reason for it to be otherwise.'

A high court translator arrives, and greets both Harry and Niehaus before entering the boardroom to be briefed by Jacob.

Harry looks at his watch. 'Where the hell are they?'

Niehaus shakes his head, a knowing smile playing over his features. 'Walk with me; I need to get back to the office.' He heads for the lift. 'This guy Kheswa and his partner have some of the longest criminal records I've ever seen. Since we started processing their fingerprints Monday, a colourful history has been unfolding. There's a trail of unsolved cases spanning at least a decade, stretching right from Prieska to Pretoria. The two of you did a good job there.'

'We had nothing to do with it,' interrupts Harry. 'Freddy Meyer was the one who first caught wind of it.'

'He died last night in intensive care; did you know that? Haemorrhagic shock, or some such cause. The poor *oke* had virtually no blood left in him by the time Cauto dumped him off at the clinic.'

Harry shakes his head in mute sadness at the tangible loss he feels, despite having met the dead man only once. He could have uttered some platitude in return about how senseless the cop's death was, or how Meyer did not deserve to die the way he did, but all that would be ultimately meaningless.

The lift door slides open to reveal three male Africans. One is dressed in a sober black suit, in his early thirties, another is a grim-looking police officer in a blue uniform steering the wheelchair of a third man in his sixties wearing the distinctive green overalls of a prisoner. The last man's wrists are shackled, his shoulders slumped, his expression slack with empty despair.

'I just wish you two had held onto Cauto once you had him, more so because he stole his own case files from the car you two left unattended.' Niehaus shakes his head as he squeezes into the lift past the three men filing out. 'How many times do I have to tell my detectives to leave the bloody dockets in the office? It's set this investigation back—how far, I don't know, but it doesn't look good. Cheers, *boet*. See you soon.'

Harry waves Niehaus goodbye then turns to the three men who are now waiting for him. 'Obed Ditlholelo,' he acknowledges in a stern voice, before nodding to the man's state-appointed lawyer and guard. 'This way, please. Miss Campbell is waiting to hear what you told us yesterday.'

2

12.03 a.m., 3 August 1965, *Oranje Genot* Farm

'But you told me it had stopped, didn't you?' remarked José Cauto.

Wearing nothing but shorts despite the freezing night, the Mozambiquean stood on his own doorstep conversing with Bernard Klamm.

Watching them from nearby, Obed's obsession with Klamm had been growing steadily during the two months he had now lived on his employer's new property, to the extent of making increasingly frequent trips such as this up to the house at night to spy on the man and his family. The white devil of the mines suddenly seemed to him as vulnerable as any man living a routine domesticated life. His word no longer seemed a form of martial law amongst his employees, and in front of his wife and daughter Klamm no longer dared abuse his workers with the previously accustomed impunity. This return to more civilized behaviour made Klamm seem like a bull with its horns sawed off—increasingly a perfect target on which Obed could finally exact revenge for the death of his father and the dissolution of his own family. A ripple of joy had coursed up and down his spine as he began eavesdropping that same night. Such was his excitement that he shifted his position carelessly in the undergrowth, so a twig underfoot snapped sharply.

Obed froze, his elation instantly turning into panic. Instinctively he began backing away, but the crunching of leaves under each hasty footstep eventually brought him to a fearful standstill. Looking up, he was alarmed to find their conversation had stopped, Klamm and Cauto both peering into the darkness in his direction.

'Stopped?' The obviously drunk Klamm turned back to face José. 'Yes, yes, I suppose it has. But with Claudette that only means something else is afoot.'

'Not necessarily,' was all that Obed could hear further, as he retreated out of earshot, much more cautious now about where he placed his feet. Slowly he circled away through a thin copse of trees, heading towards the rear of Cauto's hut. He knew Claudette Klamm was inside, as she had been many times previously, when screwing her father's foreman with a zeal that surprised Obed the first time he watched them through the tiny back window.

'José,' Obed heard Klamm yell out. 'You and me, we're survivors!'

Both survivors and gamblers at the top of your game, thought Obed.

From where he now positioned himself underneath the small window, Obed could hear the door to Cauto's shack squeak open, and Claudette Klamm question her lover urgently about what had been said outside. He looked up at the dull orange gleaming faintly through the glass above him, in an effort to better hear the dialogue, but the two were now speaking in hushed, urgent tones, and Obed's English was not good enough to keep up with the flow. His mind gradually wandered from their conversation; after all, what they had to say to each other was as inconsequential to him as their secret was important to them.

Ever since he discovered the illicit affair, the thought of using it against Klamm had compelled Obed to return every night and eavesdrop in the hope of seeing them together. He had early decided not to inform on them, because the mayhem that would follow certainly would not sufficiently satisfy the suffering he himself had endured at Klamm's hands. To his mind, the white devil's decision that Obed's wounded father should stay in camp and bleed to death was as much an act of murder as slitting his throat or suffocating him with his bare hands. The humiliating powerlessness Obed had felt that awful day in '58 was as fresh in his mind now as it was seven years ago. His mother's desertion of her family, his brother's death, his own subsequent neglect of his younger sister—Obed could all of them relate directly to Klamm's callous tyranny. The white devil had manipulated him for every ounce of his soul, and for this he would eventually pay. To kill Klamm outright was too simple, because he would then leave this life without ever knowing the kind of suffering he had caused the eighteen-year-old. No, Obed had decided tonight would be the night to teach Klamm his lesson by taking from him his only child.

Settling himself closely up against the shack wall, then curling up into a tight ball against the bitter cold, Obed began his wait for the girl's departure, which regularly occurred around four in the morning. Eventually dozing off, he completely missed Claudette sneaking out the door.

When suddenly roused by a hammering on Cauto's door and hysterical pleas, Obed cursed himself and jumped up to peer through the back window. He watched Cauto fling open the door, only to be propelled back inside by his tearful lover.

'I've told them, José.' Claudette Klamm threw herself breathlessly into José's arms. 'I told him about *everything.*'

'What?' blurted Cauto, and slammed the door shut behind her.

Obed's heart shrank as he heard this, feeling his opportunity for vengeance slipping away before his eyes.

Then the first shot rang out, and he doubled back out of harm's way, just in time to spot Klamm swaying drunkenly in the farmhouse security light, erratically aiming for the hut a second time. Wailing unintelligibly, his wife stood in the front doorway, silhouetted by the bright electrical light beyond. A second gunshot rang out, followed shortly by a piercing scream from inside the hut. A blind panic began pulsing in Obed's throat as he watched his plans crumbling away before him. Was the white devil trying to rid himself of his only child? A part of Obed wanted to rush forward and stop these events unfolding, but he knew he was powerless and it was already too late. Instead, he crept towards the farmhouse in an effort to get out of the way of Klamm's drunken line of fire. From behind the camel thorn tree in the garden Obed watched the ongoing dialogue between Klamm and Cauto; his eyes followed Henrietta Klamm as she emerged from her vantage point and charged over to scream at the Mozambiquean from behind her enraged husband.

He clearly heard Cauto's bitter reproach to Klamm. 'You should've paid more attention to her.' Meanwhile Claudette had crept out from his hut. 'Maybe then she'd never have wanted to come out there to the mines, and instead found love elsewhere, amongst the white men in your sports clubs. Then it would have been someone more suitable than me.'

Obed grimaced at the sound of the rifle butt connecting firmly with the side of Cauto's skull. He had never been comfortable around José Cauto, never sure whether to admire him for having risen so far above his station, or to loathe him for associating so intimately with the white devil; but at that moment he had to respect him for his courage.

As the Mozambiquean collapsed unconscious, Claudette threw herself forward and hugged her lover's head to her bosom. Her long black hair concealed her face as she bent over to kiss his, urging him back to consciousness.

'Get yourself *off* of him,' shouted her father, his makeshift club still raised above one shoulder. 'Get off of him now, Claudette, or I swear I'll beat the shit out of you.'

'You can't do this.' Claudette held up a hand as if to ward off any more blows. 'He was your *friend*, and José did nothing wrong, Papa. *I* did it so punish *me*.'

'You just watch me, girl,' Klamm growled as he stepped forward. 'You've been nothing but trouble and pain to this family.'

'*No!*' Henrietta Klamm grabbed her husband's forearm. 'That's enough, Bernard. She's your daughter.' She stepped between her husband and child, one hand still raised warningly in his direction. 'Let me take care of her.'

'Yes, Mama, help me.' The sobbing girl began trying to raise Cauto up from the ground. 'He's heavy; I can't pick him up by myself.'

Mrs Klamm suddenly grabbed her daughter's arms. With two violent tugs she wrenched loose her daughter's hold on the Mozambiquean.

'No!' screamed Claudette. 'Let me go.'

Mrs Klamm shook her daughter hard. 'For once in your bloody life, child, you will listen to your mother.'

'Keep a good hold on her,' Klamm muttered. He prodded Cauto with one shoe before turning back towards the house. 'I'll be back in a moment.'

'What are you doing?' shrilled Claudette at her mother. 'José needs a doctor.'

Mrs Klamm slapped her viciously then, not just once, but again and again, while the girl tried to wrestle free from her. 'You're a child of God,' the mother snarled. 'And what you've done here is an abomination in his eyes. You've ruined yourself, Claudette, but I won't let you live your life in shame, not if I can help it. Your antics end here, tonight.'

Claudette's shoulders slumped as she put her hands up to her face. 'It's going to visit me again; I swear it.'

'Nothing visits you.' The older woman's voice had grown hoarse. 'I won't be made a fool of any more, Claudette. From this day on you *will* obey your father and me.'

With that she grabbed her daughter by the hair and mercilessly pulled her back towards the house, her other hand gripping Claudette's neck tight enough to stretch the skin. Obed watched Klamm return, his face set like stone as he converged with his wife on the narrow footpath under the farmhouse's security light. He carried a large green petrol can and a thick coil of rope in each hand. From the way he was staggering, Obed could see that the man was still very drunk.

Mrs Klamm jerked her daughter to a halt, and rasped to her husband, 'I don't want that man talking about what he's done here around town, Bernard. I couldn't bear it.'

'I'll kill him first,' he said in a grim tone, his eyes fixed angrily on his defiant daughter.

'Rubbish,' snapped Mrs Klamm, as for a moment she had to struggle with Claudette's terrified reaction. 'Just make sure I never see him again. I never understood why you trusted him so much anyway.'

'He's made a whore of my daughter,' snarled Klamm.

'No.' Mrs Klamm tugged cruelly again at Claudette's hair. 'She did that all by herself.'

'What was that?' Klamm abruptly glanced up as a spasm of cramp forced Obed to change position noisily. 'Who's there?' he barked.

The voyeur's eyes widened in terror as the white devil took an uncertain step in his direction. Quickly he ducked back behind the camel thorn tree.

'Help!' screamed Claudette. 'They're going to kill him.'

'Shut up,' he heard Mrs Klamm snarl at her, then she turned to her husband. 'Bernard, stop wasting time and go deal with Cauto.'

'Throw her in the cellar,' said Klamm. 'The little slut's not going back inside our home any time soon.'

Obed at last let out his breath after Mrs Klamm careened past him, hauling her daughter towards the front door of the farmhouse. She even glanced in his direction, but nothing suggested to him that she noticed anything suspicious in the shadows where he was lurking.

After the front door slammed shut behind mother and daughter, Obed stayed exactly where he was, in case Klamm might still be watching the surrounding darkness. Moments later, he cautiously peered around the side of the tree to see the white devil splashing petrol all over the floor of José Cauto's hut before he tipped over one of the paraffin lamps and charged outside. As the hut burst into flames, he watched Klamm truss up the still unconscious form of the Mozambiquean with the rope, then lift his limp body from the dust. For a moment, the white devil stood contemplating the growing flames, as if about to heave Cauto through the blazing doorway. However, instead, he staggered further away, then dropped the man to the ground again. That was when the beating began in earnest.

Obed closed his eyes in anger and revulsion as he fought to control the impulse that threatened to drive him forward to save the helpless foreman from such appalling abuse. But however much he hated Klamm, a deep-seated fear of the man held him back. Whether this stemmed from a lifetime of subservience on the mine fields, he found he could not respond at a moment when he so much wanted to act.

A light winking on in a top-floor window distracted Obed. He looked up to find a curtain pulled back, and Mrs Klamm silently watching her husband venting his rage on the prone body at his feet. When the roof of the blazing hut finally caved in, she swung open the window and called, 'Bernard, come in now. Leave him where he is. If he makes it through the night we'll call the police in the morning.'

Stooped vengefully over his victim, exhausted arms dangling loosely and drunken body swaying, Klamm resembled most of all a primate at that moment. He acknowledged her intervention with a grunt that only Obed could have heard. Then, after checking Cauto's bonds one more time, Klamm turned and trundled back toward the house, rubbing his bruised knuckles. Minutes later, the lit windows of the farmhouse closed their eyes one by one.

Knowing about the exterior cellar door, and the unpadlocked bolt that kept it closed, Obed hastened furtively across the lawn. Skirting the lone pool of light from the security lamp, he stopped at the kitchen door, where he could make out the discarded array of plumbing equipment that Klamm kept carelessly stacked against the wall. Picking up a solid steel pipe, he let his hands run up and down its coarse surface. Though his heart was racing in terror of what he was intending, he focused his thoughts on the memory of his father bleeding in that boiling lean-to. He remembered his mother sobbing desperately as she washed the mangled leg, and Klamm ordering his father to be removed from the truck that would have saved his life.

Clenching his jaws determinedly, Obed rounded the corner of the house between him and his objective, feeling as though he had been taken over by some malevolent spirit. All he was aware of now was the cold steel gripped in both his hands, suppressing the fearful part of him that was screaming not to go through with this.

The double doors kept *clack-clacking* with every thump of Claudette's fists. Her voice pleading through the sturdy wood sounded tired. Obed took a last deep breath and gazed up at the bright spill of stars. It occurred to him that he had learnt she was only a year older than him; this mollify-ing revelation, however, was quickly expelled from his mind by the power of the unknown force animating him. Fingers that were his own, but felt numb and lifeless, reached out to retract the bolt separating him from the instrument of his vengeance. Obed then stepped back to receive her into the dead of night.

Claudette pushed open the flap doors to greet her own death. Obed no-ticed that her face was almost completely in the dark, while the shroud of pink and white dress glowed luminously in the heavenly light. She gasped and paused in her exit when she saw his silhouette looming. Silently, they faced each other, then she uttered a whisper filled with wonder or despair. 'Who are *you?*'

For decades afterward, Obed would imagine it was neither a question motivated by surprise nor an enquiry as to his identity; instead, it sounded almost as if she had known his dark form all along, had grown accustomed to the shadow that was him, and it was only now she finally asked her dop-pelgänger its true nature.

'My name is Obed,' he said harshly in Tswana, 'and your father killed my father.'

He never knew whether she understood the full implications of his words, or whether she only recognized his intentions, but she seemed com-pletely unafraid as she replied with complete resignation, 'Kill me, then. It's what you always wanted.'

3

11.34 a.m., 16 June 2004, Johannesburg

'That is *not* true!' Miss Campbell is out of her seat before anyone has time to react. Her open hand connects viciously with Obed Ditlholelo's tear-moistened face. 'You're a murdering liar,' she sobs. 'My daughter would *never* have said something like that, and I never did *half* the things you describe. You . . . you . . . filthy pig, you. I *loved* my daughter.'

Rees is up on his feet at the same time as the translator and lawyer, to grab hold of the woman's shoulders. 'Henrietta,' he urges, 'please, come sit down and let's hear the man out. You've come this far, so let's have this over and done with.'

Though Obed's hands have come up to deflect any further blows, his head remains hung in shame. 'I'm not the liar,' he murmurs in Afrikaans. 'These things I see with my own eyes, and they stay with me all the long time.'

'If my client continues to be assaulted like this, we are leaving.' The lawyer, who seemed to doze off through much of his client's confession, feigns agitation. 'He came here of his own free will and should be respected for that.'

'Let's just all calm down.' Jacob rises from his chair. 'Miss Campbell, if you have any more questions for Mr Ditlholelo, he has assured us of his full co-operation, otherwise we will move on.'

'Obed.' Harry Mason steps away from the Plexiglas wall against which he has been leaning all this time. 'Exactly *why* are you here? I mean, why did you choose to tell us all this?' They had found the old man still slumped over the body of his son when Harry and Jacob returned to the farmhouse to radio in their capture of Kheswa.

The elderly man wipes tears from eyes still averted and answers again in Afrikaans. 'The white devil, he has taken everything that was important to me. I still don't know why. Even when dead, he take my son. I can't play this game with him any more. I'm telling you, there is no beating him. Now I come to ask forgiveness from the mother of the daughter I kill. I've come to ask her before God because I now know what it is like to lose a child.'

'You won't have *any* forgiveness from me.' The elderly woman thumps the table with her fist. 'Thirty-nine years I've had to live without knowing what happened to my daughter. It was my husband that ordered your father off that truck, and yet you punished *me*. There is no justice in that, none.'

'Henrietta!' Rees urges in a loud voice. Both his hands rest on her quivering shoulders. 'Please, we both knew this would be difficult.'

Harry holds his hand up for silence. 'Obed, how did you find out that Mr Bernard Klamm was dead?'

'This man, Sheik Kheswa, he come to me for my knowledge of the explosives. I trade him my services for finding out where Klamm was. By the time he find out, Klamm was already dead.'

'And what would you have done if you did find him?'

The lawyer interrupted. 'That has no bearing here. I advise my client not to answer that.' He repeats his words to Obed in Tswana.

Harry glances at Jacob. 'Strictly off the record?'

The detective nods. 'If Mr Ditlholelo is willing to answer.'

The manacles around Obed's wrists clatter on the table as he folds his hands. 'I wanted to tell him about what I did.'

'Why?'

'I . . .' Obed begins in Afrikaans, but pauses. Looking to the translator he goes on in Tswana. 'That night I was young. Once the spirit of revenge left me, after I killed her, I suddenly felt very frightened, like the boy I was. I wanted to hide the bad thing I had done, so I dragged her body over to the hole by the quiver tree and threw her in, keeping her jersey as a reminder that it really happened. For many years I told myself that it was enough to know that I had avenged my own father. But really it wasn't, because Klamm had another man convicted of his daughter's murder. I was there, and that one he did not look sad at his loss, or remorseful for what he did to José Cauto.'

'You're *lying*. Losing Claudette drove him to the very brink of madness.' Miss Campbell glances around the room, her expression hovering between confusion and appeal, as though she hopes to find some pity for her estranged husband amongst the assembled faces. 'What you did drove us apart. That man spent the rest of his life trying to prove to me that he hadn't killed her, that he *loved* her. How can you say he wasn't remorseful? He was angry at what happened, and so was I. Anyone can feel anger! Jesus.' She buries her face in a white tissue, and chokes with resignation, 'Who are you to paint Bernard so inhumanely?'

Harry is impressed by Obed's patient pause as the woman fights to regain her composure, even though his squirming hands betray his anxiety. Finally he continues. 'When my wife found that jersey in our home many years later, and accused me of going with another woman, I decided to send it to the mining company where I knew Klamm had been working. It was the only way I could bring myself to show him that she was dead.'

'You're a bloody coward!' hisses Miss Campbell. 'That's what you are.'

Harry sees Obed's lawyer raise a critical eyebrow at this outburst.

Jacob moves around the table to lay an encouraging hand on Obed's shoulder. 'And what did you do for José Cauto that night, Mr Ditlholelo?' His eyes are riveted on Miss Campbell's.

'I crept back to his burning hut to see if he was still alive. He was conscious again, and trying to roll away from his burning house. He was very disoriented. I did not want anyone, even him, to know I had been there, so I untied him quickly and left him to escape on his own.'

Rees rises, his eyes fixed on Jacob. 'I don't care for the way you are looking at my partner, detective.'

Jacob raises his eyebrows and steps away from Obed. From the rigidity of his shoulders, Harry knows his friend is as livid as he was when he first heard the old man's story yesterday. 'Mr Rees, remember I am a black man, and what happened out on that farm sickens me to my very heart. If there wasn't a twenty-year statute of limitation on the crime of having given false evidence in court, I would be arresting Miss Campbell right now.'

'How dare you?' hisses Rees through clenched teeth. 'At this time, too.'

Harry notices Miss Campbell's eyes grow wider as her face blanches. It seems she never considered for a second the possibility that she could be brought to book for her own past behaviour in this affair.

'I am truly sorry for the loss you suffered, Miss Campbell.' Jacob turns back to her. 'But what you did, and so readily kept quiet about while José Cauto rotted in a jail for thirty-nine years, was contemptible.'

'What kind of a cop are you?' One of Rees's fists is balled tightly at his side. 'How can you wave a finger in her face, as she hears about the murder of her daughter? You should be telling us about your efforts to find this foreman Bernard beat up.'

'We still don't know for sure that Cauto is involved,' says Jacob. 'Especially since recent information suggests *you* may have had as good a motive to kill Bernard Klamm.'

The architect almost sways backward at the accusation. Harry is surprised that Jacob should bring up the misfortunes of Green Future Holdings in these current circumstances, which only signals to him that his ex-partner is losing control of his temper. But before he can interject, Obed's lawyer rises to his feet.

'Unless there is anything else you have to discuss with Mr Ditlholelo, I think we should excuse ourselves.'

His eyes travel rapidly from Jacob, to Rees, to Campbell, all of whom are too intent on each other to pay him any attention. Finally he glances at Harry, who nods and says, 'I think we're done here.'

'Will you repeat what you just said, detective?' Rees reaches for a black leather handbag and fishes out his mobile. 'Because I'm sure my lawyer would love to hear it, too.'

Quickly rounding the table, Harry puts a restraining hand on Jacob's shoulder. 'Ho, let's just all relax.'

Rees continues to dial a number.

'Mrs Klamm.' Obed holds up a hand to restrain the police officer who is about to haul him away. '*Missies*, I . . .' He shakes his head and swallows a few times. 'It is now I wish I could bring your daughter back for you. This I wish before God, but—'

'Take him away!' the woman screams. 'I don't want to hear another word, and I don't ever want to see him again.'

Obed's eyes widen at this vehement rebuke, then his shoulders slump and, his head still shaking from side to side in disbelief, he is wheeled out of the room.

'Come, Henrietta.' Rees closes his mobile and holds out a hand to the distraught woman. 'I've had enough of this fracas. Detective, you'll be hearing from my lawyer later today. Mr Mason, thank you for arranging this meeting, although I can't say it has been a pleasure. I always knew that digging up the past would end like this.'

When the elderly couple have gone, the translator close on their heels, the two friends are left staring at each other, Harry's mouth twitching on the brink of a smile.

Finally Jacob slaps his hand on the table. 'I know, I know. Laugh all you want. I just couldn't believe that Campbell woman calling Ditlholelo a coward, after what she had done.'

4

4.51 p.m., 16 June 2004, Johannesburg

'You little shit,' exclaims Tudhope. He holds the document up to the fading sunlight through the windshield, as if this will better confirm its legitimacy. The interior of the unmarked cruiser parked in Norwood looks as though a tornado has blown through a paper factory, and it smells of stale smoke, sweat and sour beer. The detective's face is dark with stubble and lack of sleep. A radiant smile transforms it back to life, though, as Tudhope realizes he has finally found enough evidence to justify a warrant for Rosen's arrest.

Klamm's signature appears clearly at the bottom of an affidavit, which was countersigned by attorneys Duval and Gigliotti in Houston, 16 December 1992. It unequivocally confirms that Dr Jeffrey Rosen received nine thousand dollars a month from GGeM and the Asbestos Trade Initiative during the eighteen months he conducted research at GGeM's amphibole mines, and also for another eight years afterward, when he was no longer in their employ but instead served as an adviser on the boards of various anti-asbestos non-governmental organizations. During this time he continued battling to prove the safety of white asbestos—a mineral ultimately found to be equally carcinogenic as the blue and brown varieties. The letter therefore implied a conflict of interest and, judging from the other papers accompanying the affidavit—Klamm's own documents detailing a lawsuit filed by the residents of Barberton versus the American mining group Marks & Farrell Inc.—it had been used to contest Rosen's reliability, not only in the Barberton case, but in the Houston lawsuit for which it was originally procured.

Tudhope cracks open another can of Castle and toasts his discovery. It seems Klamm had kept this letter as the trump card with which he subsequently devastated Rosen's credibility, and that was most recently effected during the Barberton case in a Nelspruit high court, only two months ago.

'I've got you, bru.' As he glances up the road towards Rosen's residence, he spots the doctor reversing his Rav4 out onto the street.

Spilling beer over himself, Tudhope is out the car and sprinting up the roadway even before Rosen can engage first gear.

5

5.08 p.m., 16 June 2004, Johannesburg

Driving along the long straight of Cedar Road towards Dainfern, Harry watches the low, weakened sun turn the surrounding sky into a mottled stain of orange, red and deep purple. He has arranged with Miss Campbell to meet at her house after her weekly game of bridge, which she refused to cancel despite that morning's trauma. It is on Jacob's behalf that he wants to discuss with the elderly couple the possibility that Cauto might still come after the woman who helped put him behind bars. Although Jacob felt obliged to inform the couple that the docket Cauto stole from the Almera contained, amongst other sensitive information, Campbell's address, the police officer had declined to talk to them directly after a vociferous telephone call was made by Rees's lawyer to Senior Superintendent Niehaus earlier this afternoon.

For the fourth time this Wednesday, Harry is playing the song 'Salome' on the car radio, and ruminating over Monday night, his first date in fifteen years. The evening had started out well enough, after he borrowed the Almera and picked up Salome at her mother's house in Prieska, still feeling badly shaken and sore from the gun battle with Sheik Kheswa and Jabulani Mahlangu that afternoon. She looked attractive and wholesome as she headed towards him down the garden path, wearing a loose-fitting white turtleneck and with her light-brown hair tightly braided.

They chose a quiet restaurant off Loots Boulevard, near the Ria Huysamen Garden. It was flamboyantly named *Chateau de Marlene*, and filled a converted square house with moulded ceilings and a veranda stretching all around the outside. The moment they sat down opposite each other at a softly lit table, Harry started to feel awkward and anxious. He stammered his way through an explanation of how his face had become so bruised and one badly scraped hand managed to knock over his beer.

'Harry, is there something wrong?' Salome asked eventually as his silences during the main course began to stretch out longer and longer. 'You seem very tense this evening.'

Harry felt any confidence deflate as his heart rate quickened. Wiping his mouth with a paper serviette, he sighed. 'No, it's not that. I . . .' He shook his head miserably.

'What?' Salome smiled encouragingly, and rested her chin on folded hands. 'Come on, you can tell me.'

'It's just . . . you remind me so much of someone.'

'I remind you of another woman?' Her tone was playful and teasing, the way Amy's had often been.

He gulped the remainder of his fifth beer that evening. 'Actually, it's my wife you remind me of.'

'Oh.' The smile on Salome's face wavered slightly. 'Is that a good or a bad thing?'

Suddenly becoming aware of the other people around them, Harry hesitates to reply. The pause is enough to wipe the smile off Salome's face.

'Both, I guess,' he admits at last. His fingers are fidgeting incessantly with the beer glass. 'It's been four years since I lost her, and I still think of her every day. Everything I do seems to be influenced by what I think she would say, or how she would react. She still plays such a large part in my life, though I know she's gone and I know I need to move on. That's what would be best for myself and for my daughter, too, but every time I reckon I've taken a step forward, it seems like all I've really done is take a step back. I'm like . . . the moon out there, destined to endlessly orbit her death.'

Salome tries to smile reassuringly, but it's little more than a sad twitch of one corner of her mouth. She reaches over the table to grasp his hand. 'You loved her very much, didn't you?'

He does not look at her when he sighs in acknowledgement.

'Be glad you had your time with her, then. I thought I knew real love when I first met my husband, but it turned out to be nothing more than a cheap imitation of what I see inside you now.'

Harry shook his head vigorously, as if wanting to negate what he had just admitted. 'Look, I'm sor—'

She silenced him, squeezing his hand. 'Don't apologize.'

'But I screwed up. Anyway, I didn't bring you here to complain about my life.'

Her laugh in response was slightly strained, but it broke the ice that had encrusted them. 'Maybe we're both not quite ready to think of dating again, so let's just enjoy a good meal tonight, no strings attached. God knows, I could do with an evening that's a little less serious.'

The evening itself had progressed well after that admission, and later, when he dropped her off at home, he knew that a genuine friendship had been forged.

Now, two days later, Harry stops at Dainfern's boom-gate to speak to the guard with a clipboard in his hand. The man seems ready and willing to wave him straight through, unlike his more punctilious colleague on the previous occasion.

'This is Detective Inspector Jacob Tshabalala's card.' Harry scribbles a licence plate number on the back of the business card and hands it to the olive-uniformed guard. 'If a green Jetta carrying that licence plate tries to get in here, phone this number immediately. It is a stolen car and the driver is wanted by the police.'

'Why are they looking for him?' The guard takes the card and squints at it.

'It's in connection with a murder investigation.'

The sun dips behind the distant hills, the world descending into dusk and the hours of uncertainty. Parking across the street from the architect's house, he notices that the garage door at Number Fifteen is standing wide open, with no one in sight, revealing a black seven-series BMW and a Porsche SUV parked side by side.

Stepping up to the front door, Harry is about to ring the bell when he hears, from inside the house, a muffled bellow, and a shrill response that sounds like Miss Campbell. He immediately draws his pistol and carefully tries the front door handle, but finds it locked. Glancing left and right, he then skirts a flowerbed of pansies and spearmint groundcover to reach the open garage.

6

5.17 p.m., 16 June 2004, Johannesburg

In the nick of time, Tudhope manages to seize the door handle before Rosen can accelerate the car up the street.

'Rosen, stop!' he yells, tugging at the locked door.

Startled, the doctor slams on the brakes. But when he turns to look at the gleeful face grinning back at him through the window, he almost hits the accelerator.

'I'm Detective Tudhope. Open *up*.' The police officer repeatedly bangs against the glass with his open palm.

Rosen reluctantly cranks down the window. 'What the hell are you doing, officer? You scared the life out of me. I assumed you were a hijacker.'

Tudhope steps away from the car and gestures back to the gateway. 'Park the car back in your drive and step out.'

'What's this about?'

'You know exactly what this is about, bru. Don't try playing dumb with me.'

Rosen seems to hesitate for a moment, then puts the car in reverse. Tudhope follows the Toyota SUV until it is parked back in the driveway. The moment the driver door is unlocked, the powerful cop yanks it wide open and hauls Rosen out by the front of his shirt.

'Let me see your driver's licence, fucko.'

'W-what are you doing? I-is that beer I smell on your breath?' Rosen's already nervous tone climbs several notches in pitch, his stutter growing even more pronounced.

Shoving Rosen up against the car's bonnet, Tudhope kicks the doctor's legs apart. 'Just get out that driver's licence you don't have, buddy, and let's see why you've been lying to us.' Despite the detective's pleasure at his own cleverness, somewhere deep inside him a warning begins sounding that he perhaps has consumed a lot more beer than he realizes.

Rosen is fishing out a wallet from the inside pocket of his olive corduroy jacket when a light suddenly goes on over the front door. Onto the veranda steps a tall woman with permed brown hair, wearing a white blouse and jeans, a book in one hand.

'Jeff?' She squints over her reading glasses into the gloom. 'I thought you'd left already. What's going on? Who is this man?'

'N-n-nothing, Belle.' Rosen's face is alarmed as Tudhope grabs his wallet from him. 'Just get on the phone to Barry. T-t-tell him I'm being assaulted by the po-police.'

'What the fuck you talking about, Jeff?' Tudhope looks up from his examination of the wallet, an injured expression on his face. 'I'm just checking that you're carrying the appropriate driving licence, that's all.' He turns to the woman on the porch. 'Everything's fine here. We're just having a chat, Jeff and me, so don't get your panties in a knot.'

The woman gasps at the cop's audacious language, then hurries back into the house. Turning back to the doctor, the detective pins him up against the car with one hand against his throat. 'I thought you said you didn't have a driver's licence. So what's this, then?'

'I—I got it yesterday. My sister drove me to collect it.'

'If you got it only yesterday, that means you've been illegally driving around without it these last two months.'

'H-h-ow do you know that?'

'And you lied to us during a murder investigation. Not too bright for a doctor, are you, pal?'

'I—'

Tudhope grinds a finger into Rosen's chest. 'You *also* told us that you didn't see Klamm again after that conference in Baltimore in 1981. Tell that again, I dare you.'

'OK! I did see him again. So what? That doesn't mean I killed him.'

'You also took bribes from him, which eventually ruined you, isn't that it? Isn't that why you're squatting at your sister's?'

'It wasn't bribery!' Rosen pulls himself free from Tudhope's grasp, and begins to slide around the front of the car towards the house. 'I was being paid by him for highly specialized research.'

'For the first eighteen months, maybe, yes.' Tudhope follows him. 'But what about the nine years after that?'

'Belle!' Rosen's voice is shrill as he shouts for his sister. 'Belle, get Barry over here, quickly.'

'You were deliberately covering up how dangerous you knew white asbestos to be, weren't you?'

'I w-w-wasn't, never.' Rosen looks from side to side, desperate to find a way to escape. 'Please, detective, leave me alone.'

'It was your job for them to lay the blame for mesothelioma solely on the amphiboles, so that those damned companies could go on selling white asbestos for as long as possible.'

'It wasn't my *job*!' Rosen pauses his gradual retreat and tries to summon some dignity. 'My job was to discover the clearest links between asbestos and the cancers they cause, and if that meant entering a deal with one of them to uncover all the information they were hiding, then that's what I had to do.'

'Where do all the asbestos victims out there fit into your dreamy little picture?' Tudhope reaches out and shoves the man towards the garage. 'What about all the people affected by your delays of the banning process? You ever care about them?'

'There was the research to think about, the—'

'Klamm ruined you in court,' interrupts Tudhope. 'That's why you're back in SA, crashing at your sister's. Why did he do that?'

Rosen tries to dodge aside and head for the house, but Tudhope quickly nips between the man and his goal, herding him backwards over the driveway again, and up against the grey brick wall separating one property from the next. The familiar face of the neighbour who first informed on Rosen's driving habits, pops around the gatepost to investigate the commotion.

'Why did he do it?' insists Tudhope.

Rosen stumbles over a lavender shrub bedded against the wall, sliding sideways towards the car again. 'For f-fuck's sakes, detective, just back off and let me answer.'

'*Why?*' yells Tudhope, as if intoxicated with his newfound sense of power.

'I refused him, that's why. OK? I just couldn't go on pretending that white asbestos was any less harmful than the coloured amphiboles,' yells Rosen. This time the provoked doctor stands his ground firmly. 'The world had moved on after the ban of amphiboles. My evidence claiming the relative harmlessness of white asbestos was starting to sound completely ridiculous.'

Tudhope nods enthusiastically, as if this explains everything. 'You refused him, so he went out to sink the credibility he helped you earn, first in Houston in 1992, then in Nelspruit just two months ago. What a bloody coincidence that Bernard Klamm is found dead a few weeks later. You couldn't stand the fact that he sank you a second time, could you? Come on, Rosen, let's stop fucking around here. Confess that you killed Bernard Klamm. Just admit it.'

'I didn't kill him!' His bird-like face now an angry pink, Rosen thrusts a finger boldly in Tudhope's face. 'I h-hated that arsehole because he flouted everything I set out to achieve. But I'm *not* a man who'll k-k-kill over differences of opinion. You f-forget I'm a d-d-doctor.'

'Doesn't matter what business you're in, my *boet*. If you're guilty of murder that's all that counts in the dock.'

'If you think I k-k-killed him because he tried to ruin my career you're wrong.' Rosen catches sight of his eavesdropping neighbour, and forces himself to quieten down. 'Yes, perhaps I did accept m-money when I shouldn't have. I might have defended the use of white asbestos for longer than was prudent, but the relative dangers of chrysotile are still a c-c-contentious issue. So if you're looking to pin a tail on me for that, detective, you may be trying a while longer still.'

Tudhope's mobile phone has begun ringing. Somewhat unnerved by Rosen's newfound defiance, the detective decides to answer the call and thus buy himself a little time to figure out what to do next.

'Ben?' says his partner, Jacob. 'There's a fax here from a Libby at Midas Motor Spares. That petrol can you've been trying to trace? It doesn't belong to any Toyota range. It's a product made specifically for the new Porsche four-by-fours.'

Detective Sergeant Ben Tudhope's face blanches under his facial shadows of sleeplessness, stubble and drunkenness. A hand comes up to scratch one cheek as his mind absorbs the implications of what Jacob has just told him. Up to now he has firmly believed that the petrol can abandoned at Klamm's place by the murderer would be positively identified as belonging to a Toyota Rav4 and, by proxy, to Dr Jeffrey Rosen. He has gone after any clues discovered on his own with blind enthusiasm, convinced he was on the right track and would demonstrate to Jacob Tshabalala and Senior Superintendent Niehaus what he was capable of. As it stands, he has done nothing but chuck his oars and punch a hole in his own boat, while far out at sea.

'Ben, are you there?' asks Jacob. 'Did you hear what I just said?'

'Sure, Jakes.' The cop's voice breaks. 'I heard you.'

At that moment a speeding BMW pulls up behind the Rav4 standing in front of the residence. Both the doctor and Tudhope see a grim face behind the steering wheel as the engine cuts out and the car door opens. Just then Belle rushes out onto the porch, yelling and gesticulating at Tudhope.

'Where exactly are you now?' asks Jacob over the phone.

As Advocate Barry Horst climbs out, Tudhope, with a sense of unreality flooding his damaged boat from all sides, whispers, 'In the biggest load of *kak*.'

7

5.42 p.m., 16 June 2004, Johannesburg

The kitchen door of the Dainfern residence stands wide open, white light cutting a triangle over the four-wheel-drive Porsche.

'I said get out of my house!' Rees bellows from somewhere deep inside the place. His angry tone nevertheless manifests an undercurrent of uncertainty.

Campbell sounds meek and panic-stricken when she finally speaks up. 'José, *please*, I promise you, I had nothing to do with her death. We only heard today, it was a man called Obed Ditlholelo who killed our Claudette.'

She is greeted by a deep, disbelieving laugh that also sounds tired and hollow. 'You expect me to believe this, after you put me away for thirty-nine years? I haven't been a saint during my life, I'll admit it, but at least I've been prepared to bear the weight of my own sins. You lot do nothing but shirk your own responsibilities.'

Moving silently through the kitchen, Harry arrives at the door of the living room. The sliding door facing on the garden is standing open. Grass carried in from outside is scattered over the coarse-weave carpet. On the coffee table in front of the silent television lies José Cauto's missing file, loose pages from it spilled over the glass surface.

'Cauto, you have no right doing this.' Rees's voice originates from the elevated study straight ahead of Harry, the two sides of the panelled sliding door pulled partly ajar.

'No right? No *right?*' There is the sound of something toppling, fragile objects breaking and shattering, a women's yelp. 'Shut up, Rees, and stay put.'

Harry slips through the gap just as Cauto again laughs in derision. The three of them are at the far end of the room. Rees is seated in one of the armchairs near his whisky cabinet, looking dishevelled as though he has been recently manhandled. Miss Campbell sits in a chair against the wall, wearing a birdseye-pattern suit, her make-up smeared with tears. Her handbag is still slung over her one shoulder, as though she has just arrived home. Diagonally between Harry and the seated couple, behind the antique globe that occupies the centre of the room, stands José Cauto. He wears a long-sleeved shirt and crude bandages under one sleeve. In his left hand is clutched a pistol, while his wounded right arm is tucked into the pocket of his jeans. When he glances up in surprise, his face looks sweaty and discoloured.

'Harry Mason,' he says without taking his gun off the elderly couple. 'You're like a fly always hovering around a horse's arse.'

Rees jumps up and points. 'Mason, shoot the murdering cunt!'

'Mr Mason.' Miss Campbell's eyes hover on the edge of blind panic, her lips quivering as if she is dying of cold. 'For goodness' sake, tell him how Ditlholelo killed Claudette—not Bernard or I.'

'Put the gun down, José,' says Harry as calmly as he can muster. 'I know you're very angry, but it doesn't have to end this way.'

'Is that true?' asks Cauto, turning back to stare at the woman. 'And I suppose you're also now going to tell me justice will prevail?' Harry does not know how to reply to this, and so Cauto continues. 'Did Obed really kill her?'

'He did.' Harry keeps his voice neutral, unthreatening. 'We found her body exactly where he said it would be.'

The man seems to wince at hearing Harry's words. He remains silent a few moments, the muzzle of the gun in his hand beginning to shake, his face a feverish riot of conflicting emotions. When Cauto finally speaks again, his voice sounds as broken as he looks. 'Because of what happened to his father? Is that why?'

'That's what he says,' replies Harry, moving cautiously into the room. Despite the gun in the man's hand and his obvious agitation, Cauto seems to Harry more confused and in pain than focused on killing the Campbell woman.

'Mason, I *demand* that you get rid of this man.'

'Shut up, Rees.' Harry keeps his eyes on Cauto, ready for any abrupt change in his mood. Though the intruder has two hostages at gunpoint, Harry feels a greater affinity for him than this manipulative elderly couple. 'Stop aggravating him. Both of you well knew he was rotting in prison for crimes he didn't commit, and yet you did nothing about it. The least you can do is hear him out.'

Cauto glances at Harry, something akin to a smile of gratitude passing over his tired face. Then he again turns his attention to Rees, who, in flustered speechlessness, drops back into his armchair.

Cauto chuckles bitterly. 'That girl was the only reason I held on there for so long, Harry Mason. No one else seemed to care about what had happened to her. It was as if the earth swallowed her up and everyone just accepted it that way. For a long time I felt directly responsible for what happened. I took joy in the pain they inflicted on me, I was happy to be confined in their cages. It was my penance. But I always knew that I would have to be the one to find her and give her a proper burial. For thirty-nine years I knew—in here—that she'd been killed.' Cauto points at his own heart. 'And all the time I thought it was Klamm. Do you have any idea what it is like to lose someone so unnecessarily, Harry Mason? And then not know why you should be punished for it? I tried to find Claudette afterwards, but I couldn't even do that for her.' He shakes his head in resignation. 'Obed? Who would have thought?'

'I'm sorry for what happened.' Campbell sobs aloud.

'*You're* sorry?' roars Cauto with such sudden vehemence that he startles everyone in the room. 'You . . . you sat there in that court in Kimberley and *lied* about me. Day by day you spat *lies* about me, and without shame. The only reason you're apologizing now is because I have this gun pointed at you.'

Campbell shakes her head, her eyes fixed on her lap. 'No, that's not—'

'You sent me off to jail for something I did not do, just because I assaulted your twisted sense of decency. Do you know what it's like to stand and be accused of the rape and murder of the woman you loved? Night after night, Claudette would come to my hut and tell me of your neglect, of how you tried to fashion her into a reflection of her father, without a speck of concern for what she ever wanted. It was you who destroyed your daughter; *you* that brought the madness into her life.' Cauto steps forward and presses the weapon against Campbell's forehead, unbridled hatred suddenly let loose across his fevered expression.

'Cauto,' warns Harry, 'I know she's done you wrong, but you can show yourself better than her. Walk away from this.'

The Mozambiquean stares at the ex-detective. 'Harry Mason, you and this woman have just told me that I hung on there for thirty-nine years for nothing, that I killed for nothing. Walk away? There is nothing I can walk away from.'

'What do you mean by that?' asks Harry. 'Who did you kill?'

'There!' Rees sits forward in his chair, his hands imploring Harry. 'The man's just admitted to being a killer. Shoot him now!'

Cauto sinks down exhausted on his knees in front of Miss Campbell, and lays aside his weapon.

'Who did you kill, Cauto? Did you kill Bernard Klamm?' Harry moves forward, his grip tightening on the pistol. 'For Christ's sake, answer me.'

Gently taking the woman's hands—which she offers him willingly, the moment she understands his gesture—Cauto gazes deep into her tearful eyes. 'You and I, Henrietta, we have lost Claudette together, but it was *you* who drove her away from you. You have suffered for what you did to her, I can see that, but it still leaves what you have done to me.' The elderly woman flinches, tries to pull her hands back, but he holds on. 'Every morning we kaffirs in Block C were forced to strip down completely and shower in freezing water, then to jump up in the air while pulling our buttocks wide open for inspection, to confirm to our masters how primitive we were as well as show that we weren't hiding any weapons up our arses. Would you do that for me, hmm? To show me how sorry you are? Would you go down on your knees in front of men, as I did, open your mouth and receive them, day in and day out, so you could sleep safely until daybreak, in a communal cell filled with murderers? Would you do that until the day you expected to die? Because, even then, you could *never* appreciate exactly what you've done to me.'

Campbell reaches out and tentatively touches Cauto's greying head. 'I'm sorry, José. I'm truly sorry. What more do you want me to say? I can't make it go away. I was angry, I was afraid and confused. The two of you should never have done what you did.'

José swipes her hand off his face, agitated by her lack of genuine understanding and remorse.

'Jesus, will you stop tormenting her, you crazy son of a bitch?' Rees is about to stand up again, but Cauto suddenly turns on him.

'Harry Mason,' he says, 'you wanted to know who I killed.' His voice sounds clearer, more forceful, as though he has come to a decision.

Rees glances uncomfortably at Harry, uncertainty now painting his face whiter than it already was. Then his eyes graze over the gun on the floor, not a metre away from him, to focus on Campbell burying her face in yet another tissue.

An unnerving amorphous realization begins to dawn on Harry. 'Spill it, Cauto,' he whispers.

The Mozambiquean's gaze has tracked Rees's eyes over the gun and up at Campbell. 'There is an African saying: *Behind the whitest smile is the blackest heart.* Bernard certainly had the blackest heart of all, but you, *Baas* Rees, come a close second. Did you think after thirty-nine years in jail I wouldn't have learnt my lesson, that I would just come out and swap one evil master for another?'

'No!' yells Rees, as if the volume of his protest can block Cauto's words from escaping. 'Shut up, you bastard.'

'I didn't bring you your petrol can back,' says Cauto mockingly. 'I thought if you're rich enough to fly down to Kimberley and fetch me back up to Johannesburg, you can afford to buy yourself another one.'

Miss Campbell's breath catches and she frowns. 'What is he saying, Tobias?'

Harry glances from Rees to Cauto and back again, his mind racing to catch up with the Mozambiquean's insinuations.

Cauto gets up to face Harry, his mouth twisted into a forlorn smile. 'You see, Harry Mason, I *did* kill Bernard Klamm. I killed the man who I thought killed my sweet Claudette and then laid all the blame on me. That night he broke fifteen bones in my body, and then his cop added a few more. Thirty-nine years later, this stranger here comes to visit me in jail one day, and tells me that he has as much of a problem with Klamm as I do. I didn't really believe him, but he told me he knew where Klamm lived, and would take me there once I got out. He gave me his own telephone number and we arranged for a meeting.' Cauto glances at Miss Campbell. 'So I killed your husband, and now I've betrayed your new man to you.'

Harry narrows his eyes in disgust as he turns to focus on Rees. 'You sicced Cauto here on to Klamm the moment you saw she couldn't persuade him to sell the farm and give her a decent cut?'

'No! That's not true.'

Abruptly, Rees launches himself down towards the gun. Cauto hears him move, but keeps his eyes fixed on Harry, a slight smile frozen on his face. The pistol is in Rees's hands, as Harry yells something unintelligible and rushes forward. The gunshot sounds deafening within the room's confines. Cauto's eyes open wide in that surprised expression Harry remembers well from when he himself shot at the Mozambiquean. Then the man's eyelids droop, and he stumbles to one side. A spray of blood blossoms just above his heart.

'Tobias!' shrieks Miss Campbell. 'What have you done?'

The architect blinks, almost as surprised by his own action as the others are. Cauto falls to the floor, a loud groan escaping him. Before he has a chance to recover Harry has hurled himself on Rees, wresting the weapon from his grasp and yelling desperately for the hysterical woman to call an ambulance.

EIGHTEEN

An Ice-cream Box of Hope for Four

1

4.11 p.m., 24 June 2004, *Oranje Genot* Farm

Although most of the farmyard looks as it always has, two trucks and a large pickup are parked in the space where Willie Erasmus usually left his Land Rover. They are heavily laden with furniture and farming equipment. A large red and white 'Clint Francis Real Estate' board has been hammered into the ground next to the cattle gate.

Martha Erasmus finally having received word that the farm is about to be auctioned off, has stripped the house bare. Gone is the massive couch on which Zelda would jump up and down when her parents were not around; gone is the television the family watched together every night, surrounded by a nimbus halo of the paraffin lamps her father insisted they use. Only in the kitchen is there any sound, as Zelda's mother is busy checking the last of the drawers before they depart. Zelda stares out the window at her uncle, who is leaning against his truck with a cigarette pinched between thumb and forefinger. They will be staying with him a little while longer, but Zelda does not mind that. Her young cousin's company seems a welcome reprieve after the endless months of entertaining herself out there on the farm, feeling utterly alone after their two dogs were butchered.

Zelda's arm is still bandaged where she injured herself with the broken glass, but the pain has been easing, along with the pain of missing her father. In her other arm she clutches a floppy and somewhat grimy pink doll which her cousin donated to her from her own sparse toy box. Zelda glances back through the door into the hallway that is shaped like a cross, and sees the crucifix in her playroom at the far end has now gone along with everything else. Even the locks securing the cellar door have been removed. She takes a hesitant step in that direction just as the outside kitchen door creaks open, her mother heading out towards the vehicles. Zelda's first footstep on the wooden floor rings hollow, the house now completely empty but for her. A further quick succession of footsteps brings her through into the hallway, the empty walls echoing the sound back eerily. Her feet freezing to the spot, Zelda tightens her grip on the pink doll, her breath coming faster. Now that the locks are gone, she is unsure whether she should be more or less scared of the girl they say once lived down below.

Abruptly she holds her breath, pinches her eyes closed, then shuffles along against the wall before she can chicken out. One metre, two metres, three, down the corridor she goes. Zelda opens her eyes and, careful not to look back, bolts the remaining distance to the study.

The carpet that her father threw over the loose floorboards is gone, but it looks like no one has disturbed the wooden planks. There is a massive dark stain which was not there before, and a faint smell of blood still hangs in the air. Zelda listens for a moment, in case anyone is approaching, then drops to her knees and lays the doll aside. Quickly she prises the boards loose, only to stare into the dark hollow beneath. It seems to lead straight down into the cellar.

'Zelda, where are you?' Her mother calls from outside.

The girl looks up, startled.

Without wasting any time on her habitual fears of this house, she plunges her hand deep into the hollow and fishes around. Spider webs cling to her fingers, dislodged gravel grates over mortar, until finally her hand alights on the white plastic ice-cream box. She pulls it out.

The front door opens. 'Zelda-a-a.' Her mother's voice has a singsong note, where before she would have already lost her temper.

'I'm here, Mama,' calls the girl. 'I've found Papa's box.'

She begins tearing off the plastic lid just as she hears Martha hastening towards the study. 'What box would that be?' asks her mother as she steps into the room.

Zelda holds it up to her mother. Inside are thick wads of rolled-up hundred rand notes, the money with which Sheik Kheswa bought Willie Erasmus's silence.

2

2.32 p.m., 26 June 2004, Johannesburg

Deep in thought, Harry is strolling along the water's edge at the Zoo Lake in Parktown, not five minutes' drive away from the house where Bernard Klamm was murdered. There are patches of green grass still, despite the winter's bite, and Jeanie is splashing water from the duck pond in all directions with a stick, getting herself wet and making a racket, no doubt for the sheer hell of it. He has devoted the last four days almost exclusively to her, and enjoyed every minute of them. At first it had been an uncomfortable experience, like stepping slowly into ice-cold water, but as her reactions warmed to him his own mood began to ease. If only he had known her temperament was that malleable, he might have spent more time fawning over his daughter, and less brooding on what he has lost.

He has a week's holiday planned for them—a trip into the Drakensberg—Henrietta Campbell having paid him his fee and a hefty bonus on top of it. Whether she had done this out of gratitude, embarrassment, shame, or as some kind of danger money she felt obliged to hand over, he could not decide, and he did not enquire either. He figures she has enough on her plate to keep her preoccupied for the rest of her life, without him picking over the details.

As Harry tags along behind Jeanie, flitting from one attraction to another, his mind keeps wandering over the occurrences of the last few days. Cauto died on his way to Johannesburg General after being shot by the architect. It is a pity that his anger ultimately consumed him, and Harry will not soon forget that look of resignation on Cauto's face as he turned away from Rees, as if somehow realizing the architect's purpose. Cauto wanted death at that moment, whether that was purely because his life's meaning had ended, in the truest sense, or whether he wanted to impose some final punishment on Campbell, Harry cannot tell, and will never know. All he can feel sure of is this: that Cauto has, with his death, brought a cycle of revenge in full circle.

Tobias Rees is currently in jail, awaiting trial for the murder of José Cauto, and for aiding and abetting the murder of Bernard Klamm. It seems that he grew tired of waiting for Miss Campbell to wrest a percentage of *Oranje Genot* from his rival, so decided to take matters into his own hands. He had always lived beyond his means, and never allowed prudence a whisper when greed had his full ear. Knowing of one man who might be keen to kill Klamm, Rees had first visited Cauto in jail four months earlier. It was evidence of those visits which have so far proved the resistant architect's undoing. Up until yesterday, Rees's pleas that Cauto was lying fell on uncertain ears. But that was until a detective tracked down one of the wardens at Leeuwkop prison who remembered Rees visiting Cauto, and wondered why a white man would suddenly come to see a black prisoner who has not received another visitor since 1992—when Inspector Freddy Meyer was there.

'Jeanie,' calls Harry, when he sees his daughter struggling out of her new gumboots. 'Don't take those off.'

'But I *want* to,' she moans. 'They make my feet sore.'

'You wanted to wear them,' he reminds her. 'And you put them on this morning, too.'

'But I don't want them now.'

He squats down next to her and sighs. *The power that you have over me*, he thinks. Reaching out, he strokes her curly hair as she pulls at the rubber. 'The grass is wet and it's cold. You'll only get your socks wet.'

'But they're hurting me.'

It seems there had been a turning point in Klamm's life, either gradual or abrupt, perhaps starting when he received Claudette's blood-stained white jersey in the post, or even earlier when the man came to believe that his daughter really *had* been taken by the demon she professed to see on a regular basis after turning fourteen. According to Miss Henrietta Campbell, her estranged husband had collected and documented photographs taken by himself and those he could access from police files kept in Leopold Ridge and the Department of Social Welfare in Kimberley, in an attempt to persuade his wife that he had not killed his own daughter. But he never managed to find conclusive proof of the creature he decided had tortured her, just as he was never satisfied by the proof against asbestos that specialists working for him had accumulated. This was a strange twist of fate that turned against him. Harry wonders whether this man had ever considered that he himself might be the demon in his daughter's life, and how she had steadily turned him against himself.

As for the female victims of all those mutilations, whom Bernard Klamm photographed so zealously, the answer to the mystery seems to lie in psychology, rather than in the supernatural. Even Jacob yielded to the evidence, for once. A number of fundamentalist religious texts his ex-partner salvaged from Klamm's home eventually pointed him in the right direction. It seems Klamm became intent on believing the supernatural spin hardline religious leaders proffered for as yet unexplained psychological phenomena. Self-mutilation and negative attention-seeking behaviour like Zelda's, in the presence of intense emotional stress, has been well documented. But the sudden spread and perpetuation of that same behaviour, amongst individuals sharing certain characteristics, such as age and gender and income level, is still not adequately explained by the men and women in their high ivory towers and whitewashed institution halls. Whether it is for them to judge what exactly it is that terrorizes the human soul when the lights go out, the house falls deathly quiet, and nothing and no one is there for you, is another matter, thinks Harry.

Immensely glad that Jeanie has pulled out of her depression, Harry hoists his gleefully squealing daughter onto his shoulders, then picks up her discarded gumboots with an exaggerated groan. 'You're getting too big for this, little ladybug.'

Jeanie claps her hands over his eyes. 'No, never. Let's go to the tree, Dad. *Run.*'

A few steps forward . . . and a few back; Harry has realized he will be haunted for a long time yet by his wife's death, just as the community around Leopold Ridge will continue to bear the scars of its asbestos history, and will tell the story of the haunted girl who passed on her unhappiness to succeeding teenagers. Cauto was haunted by the love he lost, as Campbell could never forget her own fateful role in the disappearance of her daughter, and as Obed had kept alive a burning vengeance for the death of his father. All these thoughts revolve like a dance in Harry's head: steps forward, steps backward, some twirls and circles coming to an end, some of them destined to be repeated.

Perhaps, he reflects, our ghosts are what really drive us, our ethereal memories that are as solid and undeniable as our living instincts.

BIBLIOGRAPHY

A few insightful books and articles on the very dirty business of asbestos mining, trade and distribution influenced the writing of this book. The following are a selection of materials that kept me up till the early hours of the morning, glued to pages that often seemed more like fiction than the genuine history of absolute greed and corruption in South Africa:

Paul Brodeur, *Outrageous Misconduct: The Asbestos Industry on Trial*, New York: Pantheon Books, 1985.

Barry I. Castleman, *Asbestos: Medical and Legal Aspects*, 4th ed., New Jersey: Aspen Law and Business Books, 1996.

A. Dalton, *Asbestos: Killer Dust*, London: BSSRS Pub. Ltd, 1979.

L. Flynn, *Studded with Diamonds, Paved with Gold: Miners, Mining Companies and Human Rights in South Africa*, London: Bloomsbury, 1992.

A. Hocking, *Kaias and Cocopans: The Story of Mining in South Africa's Northern Cape*, Johannesburg: Hollards, 1983.

Ronald Johnston and Arthur McIvor, *Lethal Work: A History of the Asbestos Tragedy in Scotland*, East Linton: Tuckwell Press, 2000.

Jock McCulloch, *Asbestos Blues: Labour, Capital, Physicians and the State in South Africa*, London: James Curey, 2002.

Geoffrey Tweedale, *Magic Mineral to Killer Dust: Turner & Newall and the Asbestos Hazard*, Oxford: Oxford University Press, 2000.